"It took me about a page and a quarter to completely enter the world Wolfe creates in *The Knight*. Having arrived, I believe I'll spend the rest of my life here." —Steven Brust

"Gene Wolfe is the smartes
today, in genre or out of it.
missed out on something im
people will laugh at you."

"Gene Wolfe not only entert
plexity and trickiness that place him among the most important American writers of our time..." —*The Washington Post*

"Wolfe's new novel—the first half of a massive epic—is a reminder that no one gets called a great writer about being first a great storyteller... this is a compelling, breathtaking achievement." —*Publishers Weekly* (starred review)

"*The Knight* ranks among Wolfe's most enjoyable and accessible books, and it leaves the reader eager for the concluding volume." —*San Francisco Chronicle*

"With *The Knight* and its sequel, *The Wizard*... Wolfe takes his fantasy in a new direction that should appeal to a wider audience... *The Knight* is a success." —*Rocky Mountain News*

"Another triumph from the greatest writer in the English language alive today. *The Knight* is astonishing: deep, involving, humane, and absolutely original." —Michael Swanwick

"*The Knight* is his latest superb novel, non-stop action of a surreal majesty. By the time he's done, knights and wizards will never seem the same." —Kim Stanley Robinson

"*The Knight* by Gene Wolfe will be a portal that invites many new readers to discover his works." —Robin Hobb

"Gene Wolfe has written a fine, carefully crafted novel, filled with mythic adventure and populated by fantastic creatures." —Brian Herbert

"Wolfe's version of Faerie is both allusive and elusive, beautiful and fatally glamorous." —Tad Williams

BY GENE WOLFE FROM TOM DOHERTY ASSOCIATES

THE WIZARD KNIGHT

The Knight
The Wizard

THE BOOK OF THE SHORT SUN

On Blue's Waters
In Green's Jungles
Return to the Whorl

THE BOOK OF THE NEW SUN

Shadow and Claw
(comprising *The Shadow of the Torturer* and
The Claw of the Conciliator)
Sword and Citadel
(comprising *The Sword of the Lictor* and
The Citadel of the Autarch)

THE BOOK OF THE LONG SUN

Litany of the Long Sun
Epiphany of the Long Sun

NOVELS

The Fifth Head of Cerberus
The Devil in a Forest
Peace
Free Live Free
The Urth of the New Sun
Latro in the Mist
(comprising *Soldier of the Mist* and *Soldier of Arete*)
There Are Doors
Castleview
Pandora by Holly Hollander

NOVELLAS

The Death of Doctor Island
Seven American Nights

COLLECTIONS

Endangered Species
Storeys from the Old Hotel
Castle of Days
The Island of Doctor Death and Other Stories and Other Stories
Strange Travelers
Innocents Aboard

THE KNIGHT

BOOK ONE OF
THE WIZARD KNIGHT

GENE
WOLFE

TOR®
fantasy

A TOM DOHERTY ASSOCIATES BOOK
NEW YORK

THE KNIGHT

Edited by David G. Hartwell

A Tor Book
Published by Tom Doherty Associates, LLC
175 Fifth Avenue
New York, NY 10010

www.tor.com

ISBN 0-765-34701-6
EAN 978-0-765-34701-5

First edition: January 2004
First mass market edition: August 2005

Printed in the United States of America

0 9 8 7 6 5 4 3 2 1

Dedicated with the greatest respect
to Yves Meynard, author of
THE BOOK OF KNIGHTS

THE RIDERS

Who treads those level lands of gold,
  The level fields of mist and air,
And rolling mountains manifold
  And towers of twilight over there?
No mortal foot upon them strays,
  No archer in the towers dwells,
But feet too airy for our ways
  Go up and down their hills and dells.
The people out of old romance,
  And people that have never been,
And those that on the border dance
  Between old history and between
Resounding fable, as the king
  Who held his court at Camelot.
There Guinevere is wandering
  And there the knight Sir Lancelot.
And by yon precipice of white,
  As steep as Roncesvalles, and more,
Within an inch of fancy's sight,
  Roland the peerless rides to war.
And just the tip of Quixote's spear,
  The greatest of them all by far,
Is surely visible from here!
  But no: it is the Evening Star.

—LORD DUNSANY

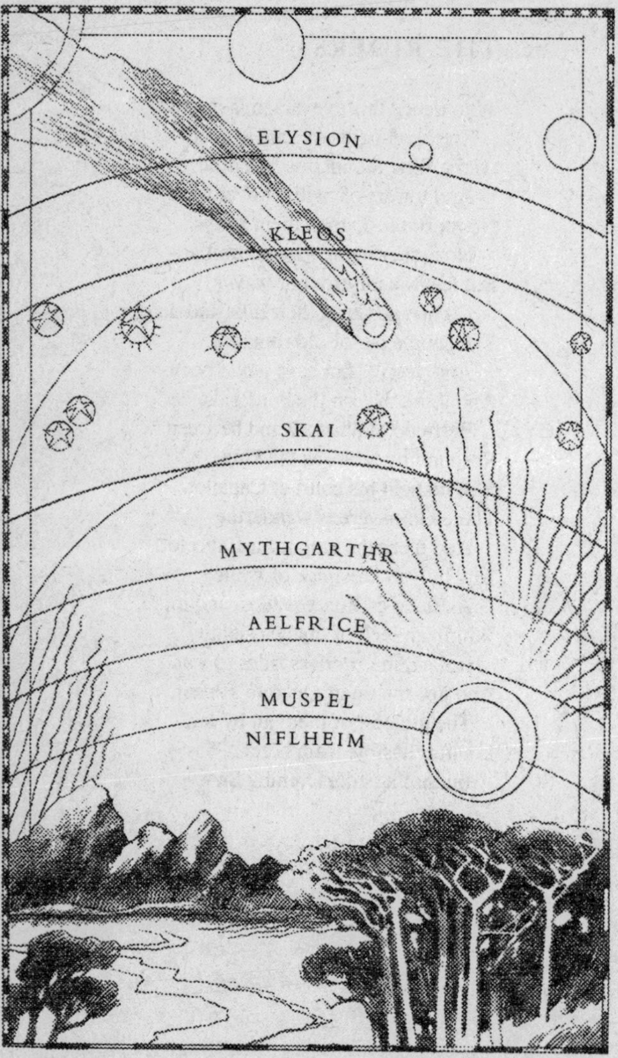
ELYSION
KLEOS
SKAI
MYTHGARTHR
AELFRICE
MUSPEL
NIFLHEIM

Ben, look at this first.

I have been reading through the first part of this letter, and there are an awful lot of names you will not know. So I have listed most of them here. If you come across one and wonder who that is, or where it is, you can look here. You would be wasting your time to read this now. It is just to look the names up in.

If a name is not here, I missed it or I do not know either, or I knew you would know already. Here they are.

ABLE	This is the name I use here. It was also the name of Bold Berthold's brother.
AELF	Fifth-world people. They do not work much, protect trees and so forth, and see certain things differently.
AELFRICE	The fifth world, under Mythgarthr.
AGR	He was Marder's marshal, and I have known worse people.
ALVIT	One of the shield-maidens who ride for the Valfather.
ANGRBORN	The giants who got forced out of Skai. All of them are descended from a famous giantess named Angr, or say they are.
ARNTHOR	The king of Celidon. His picture was on the money. Disiri gave me a message for him.
ATL	One of Thunrolf's servants.

AUD Thunrolf's steward.

BAKI A Fire Aelf girl I met at the Tower of Glas. She and Uri said they were my slaves.

BALDIG One of the peasants who used to live in Griffinsford.

BATTLEMAID Ravd's sword. Swords get names, like ships.

BATTLE WITCH Garvaon's sword.

BEAW One of Garvaon's men-at-arms. He was a good guy too.

BEEL The baron Arnthor sent to Jotunland.

BEN My brother back in America, who I still miss. Did you read this, Ben?

BLACKMANE Ravd's charger.

BLUESTONE CASTLE Indign's castle. Some Osterling pirates wrecked it.

BLUESTONE ISLAND A high, rocky island about a quarter of a mile from the main-land.

BODACHAN Earth Aelf. They are one of the small clans.

BOLD BERTHOLD The peasant from Griffinsford who let me cook my grouse and live with him in his hut. We said we were brothers, and he believed it.

BREGA A peasant woman who lived in Glennidam.

BYMIR The first Angrborn I ever saw.

CASPAR The head warder at Sheerwall Castle.

CELIDON A big country, longer than it is wide, on the west coast of the mainland. Irringsmouth, Forcetti, and Kingsdoom are all towns in Celidon.

COLLINS My old English teacher.

CROL	Beel's herald.
DISIRA	Seaxneat's wife.
DISIRI	The queen of the Moss Aelf.
DOLLOP AND SCALLOP	The inn where we stayed in Forcetti.
DUNS	Uns' older brother.
EAST HALL	Woddet's manor.
EGIL	One of the outlaws.
EGR	One of Beel's upper servants.
ETERNE	The Mother of Swords.
FINEFIELD	Garvaon's manor.
FIRE AELF	The clan Setr took over completely.
FORCETTI	Marder's town, a seaport.
FREE COMPANIES	Outlaw gangs. This was the polite name.
FROST GIANTS	The Angrborn, especially the raiders.
GARSECG	The name Setr was using when I met him.
GARVAON	Beel's best knight.
GAYNOR	Arnthor's wife, the queen of Celidon.
GERDA	The girl Bold Berthold was going to marry.
GERI	The girl you were dating when I lost America.
GILLING	The king of the Angrborn.
GLENNIDAM	The village where Ulfa and Toug were born.
GORN	The innkeeper at the Dollop and Scallop.
GRENGARM	The dragon who had Eterne.
GRIFFIN	The little river running past Griffinsford and into the Irring.
GRIFFINSFORD	A village the Angrborn wiped out.
GYLF	My dog. The Valfather lost him, and I got to keep him until the Valfather wanted him back.
HEIMIR	Gerda's son by Hymir. It made him a Mouse.
HEL	The Overcyn woman in charge of death.

HELA	Gerda's daughter by Hymir, Heimir's sister.
HERMAD	One of Marder's knights.
HOB	One of Caspar's warders.
HORDSVIN	The cook on the *Western Trader.*
HULTA	A woman in Glennidam.
HYMIR	The Angrborn who got Gerda.
HYNDLE	Hymir's Angrborn son.
IDNN	Beel's daughter, pretty small and next to beautiful. Her voice and big dark eyes were what you remembered.
INDIGN	A duke Osterlings killed. Bluestone Castle was his.
IRRING	A big river.
IRRINGS-MOUTH	Indign's town, where the Irring empties into the sea. Osterlings had burned a lot of it.
JER	The head of an outlaw gang.
JOTUNLAND	The Angrborn country, north of the mountains.
KELPIES	Sea Aelf girls.
KERL	The first mate on the *Western Trader.*
KINGSDOOM	The capital of Celidon, a seaport.
KLEOS	The second world, above Skai.
KULILI	The person responsible for the Aelf.
LADY	The Valfather's youngest daughter. No one is supposed to use her name in ordinary talk, so we say the Lady.
LUD	One of Marder's knights.
LUT	The smith who forged Battlemaid.
MAG	Bold Berthold's mother.
MAGNEIS	The charger Marder gave me.
MANI	The big black tomcat who followed Gylf and me.
MARDER	The duke of the northernmost duchy in Celidon.
MICHAEL	A man from Kleos.

MICE	People who are half Angrborn and half human.
MODGUDA	A servingwoman in Sheerwall.
MOONRIDER	Any knight the Lady sends to Mythgarthr.
MORCAINE	A princess. Arnthor and Setr are her brothers.
MORI	A smith in Irringsmouth.
MOSS AELF	Disiri's clan.
MOSS-MAIDENS	Girls of the Moss Aelf.
MOSS-MATRONS	Older women of the Moss Aelf.
MOSSMEN	Men of the Moss Aelf.
MOUNTAIN OF FIRE	A gate to Muspel.
MOUNTAINS OF THE MICE	Same as the Mountains of the North.
MOUNTAINS OF THE NORTH	The mountains between Celidon and Jotunland.
MOUNTAINS OF THE SUN	The mountains between Celidon and Osterland.
MUSPEL	The sixth world, under Aelfrice.
MYTHGARTHR	The fourth world, where Celidon is.
NEEDAM	An island south of Celidon. I have never been there.
NJORS	A sailor on the *Western Trader.*
NUKARA	Uns' mother.
NUR	The second mate on the *Western Trader.*
NYTIR	The knight I beat in the tap of the Dollop and Scallop.
OBR	Svon's father. He was a baron.
OLOF	The baron who took over the Mountain of Fire while Thunrolf and I were in Muspel.

ORG	The ogre I got from Uns.
OSSAR	Disira's baby.
OSTERLAND	The country east of the Mountains of the Sun.
OSTERLINGS	People who eat other people to become more human.
OVERCYNS	The people of Skai—the Valfather's people.
PAPOUNCE	One of Beel's upper servants.
PARKA	A woman from Kleos.
PHOLSUNG	Beel's grandfather. He was King of Celidon.
POUK BADEYE	A sailor I got to help me.
POTASH	He taught Chemistry and Physics.
QUEEN OF THE WOOD	This means Disiri. A lot of people are afraid to say her name because they think she might come. (It never worked for me.)
RAVD	The best knight I ever saw.
REDHALL	Ravd's manor.
RIVER ROAD	The main road inland from Irringsmouth. It runs along the north bank of the Irring.
ROOM OF LOST LOVE	A room that was like another world when you got inside. Sometimes dead people were alive again in there.
ROUND TOWER	The biggest castle at the Mountain of Fire.
SABEL	A dead knight.
SALAMANDERS	The Fire Aelf. Uri and Baki were Salamanders.
SCAUR	A nice fisherman in Irringsmouth.
SCHILDSTARR	One of the most important Angrborn.
SEAXNEAT	A man in Glennidam who traded with the outlaws.
SEAGIRT	Thunrolf's castle.

SETR	A dragon with a human father.
SHEERWALL	Marder's castle.
SHA	A fishwife, but she was nice to me.
SKAI	The third world, above Mythgarthr.
SKJENA	A girl that lived in Griffinsford.
SPARREO	My math teacher. She was pretty nice.
SURT	Hordsvin's helper.
SVON	Ravd's squire.
SWERT	Beel's valet.
SWORD BREAKER	My mace. Sort of like a steel bar.
THIAZI	Gilling's minister.
THOPE	Marder's master-at-arms.
(OLD) TOUG	Ulfa's father.
(YOUNG) TOUG	Ulfa's brother, my age or little older.
TUNG	A master of arms who taught Garvaon.
ULD	A farmer who used to live in Griffinsford.
ULFA	The girl who made clothes for me in Glennidam.
URI	A friend of Baki's. (Sometimes they said sister.)
UNS	A handicapped peasant.
UTGARD	Gilling's castle, also the town around it.
VALFATHER	The king of Skai.
VALI	A man old man Toug got to help him kill me.
VE	Vali's little boy.
VIDARE	One of Marder's knights.
VOLLA	Garvaon's dead wife.
WAR WAY	The main road north from Celidon into Jotunland.
WELAND	The man who forged Eterne. He was from Mythgarthr but he became king of the Fire Aelf.

WESTERN TRADER	The ship I took from Irringsmouth.
WISTAN	Garvaon's squire.
WODDET	The biggest knight at Sheerwall.
WULFKIL	A creek that emptied into the Griffin.
WYT	A sailor on the *Western Trader.*
YENS	A little port between Forcetti and Kingsdoom.
YOND	Woddet's squire.

There they are, Ben. It has been easy for me to name them. What was hard was making you see them. Remember that the Osterlings had long teeth and starved faces, and the Angrborn stunk. Remember that Disiri was a shapechanger, and all her shapes were beautiful.

CHAPTER 1

DEAR BEN

You must have stopped wondering what happened to me a long time ago; I know it has been many years. I have the time to write here, and what looks like a good chance to get what I write to where you are, so I am going to try. If I just told everything on a couple of sheets, you would not believe most of it. Hardly any of it, because there are many things that I have trouble with myself. So what I am going to do instead is tell everything. When I have finished, you still may not believe me; but you will know all that I do. In some ways, that is a lot. In others, practically nothing. When I saw you sitting by our fire—my own brother—there on the battlefield . . . Never mind. I will get to it. Only I think it may be why I am writing now.

Remember the day we drove out to the cabin? Then Geri phoned. You had to go home and did not need a kid around. So we said there was no reason for me to go too, I could stay out there and you would come back the next day.

We said I would fish.

That was it.

Only I did not. It did not seem like it was going to be much fun with you gone, but the air was crisp and the leaves were turning, so I went on a hike. Maybe it was a mistake. I went a long way, but I was not lost. Pretty soon I picked up a stick and hiked with it, but it was crooked and not very strong. I did not like it much and decided I would cut a good one I could keep out at the cabin and use whenever we were there.

I saw a tree that was different from all the others. It was not very big, and it had white bark and shiny leaves. It was a spiny orange tree, Ben, but I had never heard of them. Later Bold Berthold told me a lot. It was too big for me to cut the whole thing, but I found a branch that was almost straight. I cut off that and trimmed it and so forth. That may have been the main thing, my main mistake. They are not like other trees. The Mossmen care more about them.

I had gone off the path when I saw the spiny orange, and when I got to it I saw it was right at the edge of the woods, and past it were the downs. Some hills were pretty steep, but they were beautiful, smooth and covered with long grass. So I hiked out there with my new stick and climbed three or four hills. It was really nice. I found a little spring at the top of a hill. I had a drink, and sat down—I was pretty tired by then—and carved the stick some, making who-knows-what. Just whittling. After a while I lay down and looked at the clouds. Everybody has seen pictures in clouds, but I saw more that afternoon than I ever have before or since—an old man with a beard that the wind changed into a black dragon, a wonderful horse with a horn on its head, and a beautiful lady who smiled down at me.

After that, a flying castle, all spiky like a star because there were towers and turrets coming out of all its sides. I kept telling myself it had to be a cloud, but it did not look like a cloud, Ben. It looked like stone. I got up and chased after it, waiting for the wind to blow it apart, but it never did.

Night came. I could not see the castle any longer, and I knew I had to be a long way from our cabin. I started back across the downs, walking fast; but I got to walking down a slope that had no bottom. Somebody grabbed me in the dark, and somebody else caught my ankle when I slapped that hand away. Right then somebody said, "Who comes to Aelfrice!" I still remember that, and for a long, long time after that, that was all I could remember. That and being grabbed by a lot of people.

I woke up in a cave by the sea, where an old lady with too many teeth sat spinning; and when I had pulled myself together and found my stick, I asked where we were, trying to be as polite as I could. "Can you tell me what place this is, ma'am, and how to get to Griffinsford from here?" For some reason I thought Griffinsford was where we lived, Ben, and I still do not remember the real name. Maybe it really is Griffinsford. They are all mixed up.

The old lady shook her head.

"Do you know how I got here?"

She laughed, and the wind and the sea were in it; she was the spray, and the waves that broke outside her cave. When I talked to her, I was talking to them. That was how I felt. Does it sound crazy? I had been crazy since I was born, and now I was sane and it felt wonderful. The wind and the waves were sitting in that cave with me twisting thread, and nature was not something outside anymore. She was a big part of it, and I was a little part of it, and I had been gone too long. Later Garsecg said the sea had healed me.

I went to the mouth of the cave and waded out until the water came up to my waist; but the only things I could see were cliffs hanging over her cave, deep blue water farther out, gulls, and jagged black rocks like dragons' teeth. The old woman said, "You must wait for the slack of the tide."

I came back, sea-wet to my armpits. "Will it be long?"

"Long enough."

After that I just leaned on my stick and watched her spin, trying to figure out what it was that she was turning into string and why it made the noises it did. Sometimes it seemed like there were faces in it and arms and legs coming out of it.

"You are Able of the High Heart."

That got my attention, and I told her my old name.

Up to then, she had never looked away from her spinning. "What I say aright, do not you smite," she told me.

I said I was sorry.

"Some loss must be, so this I decree: the lower your lady the higher your love." She stopped spinning to smile at me. I knew she meant it to be friendly, but her teeth were terrible and looked as sharp as razors. She said, "There must be a forfeit for insolence, and since that's how it usually is, that one shouldn't do much harm."

That was how I got my name changed.

She went back to spinning, but it looked like she was reading her thread. "You shall sink before you rise, and rise before you sink."

It scared me, and I asked if I could ask her a question.

"It had best be, since you ask one. What do you want to know, Able of the High Heart?"

There was so much I could not get it out. I said, "Who are you?" instead.

"Parka."

"Are you a fortune-teller?"

She smiled again. "Some say so."

"How did I get here?"

She pointed with the distaff, the thing that held the stuff she was spinning, pointing toward the back of the cave, where it was all black.

"I don't remember being there," I told her.

"The recollection has been taken from you."

As soon as she said it, I knew it was right. I could remember certain things. I could remember you and the cabin and the clouds, but all that had been a long time ago, and after it there had been a lot I could not remember at all.

"The Aelf carried you to me."

"Who are the Aelf?" I felt I ought to know.

"Don't you know, Able of the High Heart?"

That was the last thing she said for a long while. I sat down to watch, but sometimes I looked at the back of the cave where she said I had come from. When I looked away from her, she got bigger and bigger, so I knew there was something huge behind me. When I turned and looked back at her again, she was not quite as big as I was.

That was one thing. The other one was that I knew that when I was little I had known all about the Aelf, and it was all mixed up with somebody else, a little girl who had played with me; and there had been big, big trees, and ferns a lot bigger than we were, and clear springs. And moss. Lots of moss. Soft, green moss like velvet.

"They have sent you with the tale of their wrongs," Parka said, "and their worship."

"Worship?" I was not sure what she meant.

"Of you."

That brought back other things—not things, really, but feelings. I said, "I don't like them," and it was the truth.

"Plant one seed," she told me.

For a long time, I waited for her to say something else, waiting because I did not want to ask her questions. She never did, so I said, "Aren't you going to tell me all those things? The wrongs and the rest of it?"

"No."

I let out my breath. I had been afraid of what I might hear. "That's good."

"It is. Some gain there must be, so this I decree: each time you gain your heart's desire, your heart shall reach for something higher."

I had the feeling then that if I asked more questions I was not going to like the answers. The sun stretched out his hands into our cave and blessed us both, or that was the way it seemed; then he sank into the sea, and the sea tried to follow him. Pretty soon the place where I had stood when I had waded out was hardly wet at all. "Is this the slack of the tide?" I asked Parka.

"Wait," she said, and bit her spinning through, wound a piece of it from her bobbin onto her hand, bit it off, and gave it to me, saying, "For your bow."

"I don't have a bow."

She pointed to my stick, Ben, and I saw it was trying to turn into a bow. There was a bend at the middle; except for that it was completely straight, and because I had whittled on the big end, both ends were smaller than the middle.

I thanked her and ran out onto what had turned into a rough beach under the cliff. When I waved good-bye, it seemed like the whole cave was full of white birds, flying and fluttering. She waved back; she looked very small then, like the flame of a candle.

South of the cave I found a steep path to the top of the cliffs. At the top there were ruined walls, and the stump of a tower. The stars were out by the time I got there, and it was cold. I hunted around for a sheltered spot and found one; after that, I climbed what was left of the tower.

The tower had stood on a rocky island connected to the mainland by a spit of sand and rocks so low it was nearly under the water even at low tide. I must have stared at the waves breaking over it in the starlight for five minutes before I felt sure it was there. It was, and I knew I ought to get off the island while I still could, and find a place to sleep on shore.

I knew it, but I did not do it. For one thing, I was tired already. Not hungry and not particularly thirsty, but so tired that all I really wanted was to lie down somewhere. The other was that I was afraid of what I might find on shore, and what might find me.

Besides, I needed to think. There was so much I could not remember, and what I could remember (you, Ben, and the cabin, and the house where we lived, and those pictures you have of Mom and Dad) was a long, long time ago. I wanted to try to remember more, and I wanted to think about what Parka had said and what it might mean.

So I went back to the sheltered place I had found among the blue stones and lay down. I was barefoot, and it seemed to me while I lay there that I should have had hiking boots, and stockings. I could not remember what had become of them. I was wearing a gray wool shirt without buttons and gray wool pants with no pockets, and that did not seem right either. I had a belt, and a little leather pouch hanging from it by its strings; but the only things in it were Parka's bowstring, three hard black seeds, and a little knife with a wooden handle and a wooden scabbard. The knife fit my hand like it belonged there, but I did not remember it at all.

CHAPTER 2

THE RUINED TOWN

The sun woke me. I still remember how warm it felt, and how good it was to be warm like that, and away from the sound of other people's voices and all the work and worry of other people's lives, the things the string kept telling me about; I must have lain in the sun for an hour before I got up.

I was hungry and thirsty when I did. Rainwater caught by a broken fountain tasted wonderful. I drank and drank; and when I straightened up, there was a knight watching me, a tall, big-shouldered man in chain mail. His helm kept me from seeing his face, but there was a black dragon on top of his helm that glared at me, and black dragons on his shield and surcoat. He began to fade as soon as I saw him, and in a couple of seconds the wind blew away what was left. It was a long time before I found out who he was, so I am not going to say anything about that here; but I do want to say something else and it will go here as well as anywhere.

That world is called Mythgarthr. I did not learn it 'til later, but there is no reason you should not know it now. Parka's cave was not completely there, but between Mythgarthr and Aelfrice. Bluestone Island is entirely in Mythgarthr, but before I drank the water I was not. Or to write down the exact truth, I was not securely there. That is why the knight came when he did; he wanted to watch me drinking that water. "Good lord!" I said, but there was no one to hear me.

He had scared me. Not because I thought I might be seeing things, but because I had thought I was alone. I kept looking behind me. It is no bad habit, Ben, but there was nobody there.

On the east side of the island the cliffs were not so steep. I found a few mussels and ate them raw. The sun was overhead when two fishermen came close enough to yell at. I did, and they rowed over. They wanted to know if I would help with the nets if they took me on board; I promised I would, and climbed over the gunwale. "How'd you get out there alone?" the old one wanted to know.

I wanted to know that myself, and how come they talked funny; but I said, "How would anybody get out there?" and they seemed willing to leave it at that. They split their bread and cheese with me, and a fish we cooked over a fire in a box of sand. I did not know, but that was when I started loving the sea.

At sunset, they offered me my choice of the fish we had caught for my help. I told the young one (not a lot older than me) that I would take it and share with his family if his wife would cook it, because I had no place to stay. That was okay, and when our catch had been sold, we carried the best fish and some others that had not sold into a crowded little house maybe twenty steps from the water.

After dinner we told stories, and when it was my turn I said, "I've never seen a ghost, unless what I saw today was one. So I'll tell you about that, even if it won't scare anybody like the ghost in Scaur's story. Because it's all I've got."

Everyone seemed agreeable; I think they had heard each other's stories more than once.

"Yesterday I found myself on a certain rocky island not far from here where there used to be a tower—"

"It was Duke Indign's," said Scaur; and his wife, Sha, "Bluestone Castle."

"I spent the night in the garden," I continued, "because I had something to do there, a seed I had to plant. You see, somebody important had told me to plant a seed, and I hadn't known what she meant until I found seeds in here." I showed them the pouch.

"You chopped down a spiny orange," Sha's grandfather wheezed; he pointed to my bow. "You cut a spiny orange, and you got to plant three seeds, young man. If you don't the Mossmen'll get you."

I said I had not known that.

He spat in the fire. "Folks don't, not now, and that's why there's not hardly no spiny oranges left. Best wood there is. You rub flax oil on it, hear? That'll protect it from the weather."

He held out his hand for my bow, and I passed it to him. He gave it to Scaur. "You break her, son. Break her 'cross your knee."

Scaur tried. He was strong, and bent my bow nearly double; but it did not break.

"See? You can't. Can't be broke." Sha's grandfather cackled as Scaur returned my bow to me. "There's not but one fruit on a spiny orange most times, and not but three seeds in it. You chop down the tree and you got to plant them in three places, else the Mossmen'll come for you."

"Go on, Able," Sha said, "tell us about the ghost."

"This morning I decided to plant the first seed in the garden of Bluestone Castle," I told them. "There was a stone bowl there that held water, and I decided I would plant the seed first and scoop up water for it. When it seemed to me I had watered it enough, I would drink what was left."

They nodded.

"I dug a little hole with my knife, dropped a seed into it, replaced the earth—which was pretty damp already—and carried water for the seed in my hands. When there was standing water in the hole, I drank and drank from the bowl, and when I looked up I saw a knight standing there watching me. I couldn't see his face, but he had a big green shield with a dragon on it."

"That wasn't Duke Indign," Scaur remarked, "his badge was the blue boar."

"Did you speak to him?" Sha wanted to know. "What did he say?"

"I didn't. It happened so fast and I was too surprised. He—he turned into a sort of cloud, then he disappeared altogether."

"Clouds are the breath of the Lady," Sha's grandfather remarked.

I asked who that was, but he only shook his head and looked into the fire.

Sha said, "Don't you know her name can't be spoken?"

In the morning I asked the way to Griffinsford, but Scaur said there was no town of that name thereabout.

"Then what's the name of this one?" I asked.

"Irringsmouth," said Scaur.

"I think there's an Irringsmouth near where I live," I told him. Really I was not sure, but I thought it was something like that. "It's a big city, though. The only really big city I've been to."

"Well, this's the only Irringsmouth around here," Scaur said. A passerby who heard us said, "Griffinsford is on the Griffin," and walked away before I could ask him anything.

"That's a stream that flows into our river," Scaur told me. "Go south 'til you come to the river, and take the River Road and you'll find it."

So I set out with a few bites of salt fish wrapped in a clean cloth, south along the little street behind the wattle house where Scaur and Sha lived, south some more on the big street it led to, and east on the highroad by the river. It went through a gap without a gate in the wrecked city wall, and out into the countryside, through woods of young trees where patches of snow were hanging on in the shadows and square pools of rainwater waited for somebody to come back.

After that, the road wound among hills, where two boys older than I was said they were going to rob me. One had a staff and the other one an arrow ready—at the nock is how we say it here. The nock is the cut for the string. I said they could have anything I had except my bow. As I ought to have expected, they tried to take it. I held on, and got hit with the staff. After that I fought, taking my bow away from them and beating them with it. Maybe I should have been afraid, but I was not. I was angry with them for thinking they could hit me without being hit back. The one with the staff dropped it and ran; and I beat the other until he fell down, then sat on his chest and told him I was going to cut his throat.

He begged for mercy, and when I let him up he ran too, leaving his bow and quiver behind. The bow looked nice, but when I bent it over my knee it snapped. I saved the string, and slung the quiver on my back. That night I scraped away at my own bow until it needed nothing but a bath in flax oil, and put his string on it.

After that I walked with an arrow at the nock myself. I saw rabbits and squirrels, and even deer, more than once; I shot, but all I did was lose a couple of arrows until the last day. That morning, so hungry I was weak, I shot a grouse and went looking for a fire. I had a long search and almost gave up on finding any that day and ate it raw; but as evening came, I saw wisps of smoke above the treetops, white as specters against the sky. When the first stars were out, I found a hut half buried in wild violets. It was of sticks covered with hides; and its door was the skin of a deer. Since I could not knock on that, I coughed; and when coughing brought nobody, I knocked on the sticks of the frame.

"Who's there!" rang out in a way that sounded like the man who said it was ready to fight.

"A fat grouse," I said. A fight was the last thing I wanted.

The hide was drawn back, and a stooped and shaking man with a long beard looked out. His hand trembled; so did his head; but there was no tremor in his voice when he boomed, "Who are you!"

"Just a traveler who'll share his bird for your fire," I said.

"Nothing here to steal," the bearded man said, and held up a cudgel.

"I haven't come to rob you, only to roast my grouse. I shot and plucked it this morning, but I had no fire to cook it and I'm starved."

"Come in then." He stepped out of the doorway. "You can cook it if you'll save a piece for me."

"I'll give you more than that," I told him; and I was as good as my word: I gave him both wings and both thighs. He asked no more questions but looked at me so closely, staring and turning away, that I told him my name and age, explained that I was a stranger in his state, and asked him how to get to Griffinsford.

"Ah, the curse of it! That was my village, stripling, and sometimes I go there still to see it. But nobody lives in Griffinsford these days."

I felt that could not be true. "My brother and me do."

The bearded man shook his trembling head. "Nobody at all. Nobody's left."

I knew then that the name of our town had not been Griffinsford. Perhaps it is Griffin—or Griffinsburg or something like that. But I cannot remember.

"They looked up to me," the bearded man muttered. "Some wanted to run, but I said no. Stay and fight, I said. If there's too many giants, we'll run, but we got to try their mettle first."

I had noticed the word *giants,* and wondered what might come next.

"Schildstarr was their leader. I had my father's tall house in those days. Not like this. A big house with a half-loft under the high roof and little rooms behind the big one. A big stone fireplace, too, and a table big enough to feed my friends."

I nodded, thinking of houses I had seen in Irringsmouth.

"Schildstarr wasn't my friend, but he could've got into my house. Inside, he'd have had to stand like I do now."

"You fought them?"

"Aye. For my house? My fields and Gerda? Aye! I fought, though half run when they saw them comin' down the road. Killed one with my spear and two with my ax. They fall like trees, stripling." For a moment his eyes blazed.

"A stone . . ." He fingered the side of his head, and looked much older. "Don't know who struck me, or what it was. A stone? Don't know. Put your hand here, stripling. Feel under my hair."

His hair was thick, dark gray hair that was just about black. I felt and jerked my hand away.

"Tormented after. Water and fire. Know it? It's what they like best. Took us to a pond and built fires all 'round it. Drove us into the water like cattle. Threw brands at us 'til we drowned. All but me. What's your name, stripling?"

I told him again.

"Able? Able. That was my brother's name. Years and years ago, that was."

I knew it was not my real name, but Parka had said to use it. I asked his name.

"Found a water rat's hole," he said. "Duck and dig, come up to breathe, and the brands, burnin' and hissin'. Lost count of the duckin's and the burns, but didn't drown. Got my head up into the water rat's house and breathed in there. Waited 'til the Angrborn thought we was all dead and went away."

I nodded, feeling like I had seen it.

"Tried to climb out, but my shadow slipped. Fell back into the pond. Still there." The bearded man shook his head. "Dreams? Not dreams. In that pond still, and the brands whizzing at me. Tryin' to climb out. Slippery, and . . . And fire in my face."

"If I slept here tonight," I suggested, "I could wake you if you had a bad dream."

"Schildstarr," the bearded man muttered. "Tall as a tree, Schildstarr is. Skin like snow. Eyes like a owl. Seen him pick up Baldig and rip his arms off. Could show you where. You really going to Griffinsford, Able?"

"Yes," I said. "I'll go tomorrow, if you'll tell me the way."

"Go too," the bearded man promised. "Haven't been this year. Used to go all the time. Used to live there."

"That'll be great," I said. "I'll have somebody to talk to, somebody who knows the way. My brother will have been mad at me, I'm pretty sure, but he'll be over that by now."

"No, no," the bearded man mumbled. "No, no. Bold Berthold's never worried about you, Brother. You're no bandit."

That was how I started living with Bold Berthold. He was sort of crazy and sometimes he fell down. But he was as brave as any man I have ever known, and there was not one mean bone in his body. I tried to take care of him and help him, and he tried to take care of me and teach me. I owed him a lot for years, Ben, but in the end I was able to pay him back and that might have been the best thing I ever did.

Sometimes I wonder if that was not why Parka told me I was Able. All this was on the northern reaches of Celidon. I ought to say that somewhere.

CHAPTER 3

SPINY ORANGE

Bold Berthold was ill the next day and begged me not to leave him, so I went hunting instead. I was not much of a hunter then, but more by luck than skill I put two arrows into a stag. Both shafts broke when the stag fell, but I salvaged the iron heads. That night while we had a feast of roast venison, I brought up the Aelf, asking Bold Berthold whether he had heard of Aelfrice, and whether he knew anything about the people who lived there.

He nodded. "Aye."

"I mean the real Aelfrice."

He said nothing.

"In Irringsmouth, a woman told a story about a girl who was supposed to get married to an Aelfking and she cheated him out of her bed. But it was just a story. Nobody thought it was real."

"Come here, betimes," Bold Berthold muttered.

"Do they? Real Aelf?"

"Aye. 'Bout as high as the fire there. Like charcoal most

are, like soot, and dirty as soot, too. All sooty 'cept teeth and tongue. Eyes yellow fire."

"They're real?"

He nodded. "Seven worlds there be, Able. Didn't I never teach you?"

I waited.

"Mythgarthr, this is. Some just say Land, but that's wrong. The land you walk on and the rivers you swim in. The Sea . . . Only the sea's in between, seems like. The air you breathe. All Mythgarthr, in the middle. So three above and three under. Skai's next up, or you can say Sky. Both the same. Skai's where the high-flying birds go sometimes. Not little sparrows and robins, or any of that sort. Hawks and eagles and the wild geese. I even seen big herons up there."

I recalled the flying castle, and I said, "Where the clouds are."

Bold Berthold nodded. "You've got it. Still want to go to Griffinsford? Feeling better with this good meat in me. Might be better yet in the morning, and I haven't gone over to look at the old place this year."

"Yes, I do. But what about Aelfrice?"

"I'll show you the pond where they threw fire at me, and the old graves."

"I have questions about Skai, too," I told him. "I have more questions than I can count."

"More than I got answers, most likely."

Outside, a wolf howled.

"I want to know about the Angrborn and the Osterlings. Some people I stayed with told me the Osterlings tore down Bluestone Castle."

Bold Berthold nodded. "Likely enough."

"Where do the Angrborn come from?"

"Ice lands." He pointed north. "Come with the frost, and go with the snow."

"Do they come just to steal?"

Staring into the fire, he nodded again. "Slaves, too. They didn't take us 'cause we'd fought. Going to kill us instead. Run instead of fight, and they take you. Take the women and children. Took Gerda."

"About Skai—"

"Sleep now," Bold Berthold told me. "Goin' to travel, stripling. Got to get up with the sun."

"Just one more question? Please? After that I'll go to sleep, I promise."

He nodded.

"You must look up into the sky a lot. You said you'd seen eagles up there, and even herons."

"Sometimes."

"Have you ever seen a castle there, Bold Berthold?"

Slowly, he shook his head.

"Because I did. I was lying in the grass and looking up at the clouds—"

He caught me by the shoulders, just the way you do sometimes, and looked into my eyes. "You saw it?"

"Yes. Honest, I did. It didn't seem like it could be real, but I got up and ran after it, trying to keep it in sight, and it was real, a six-sided castle of white stone up above the clouds."

"You saw it." His hands were trembling worse than ever.

I nodded. "Up among the clouds and moving with them, driven by the same wind. It was white like they were, but the edges were hard and there were colored flags on the towers." The memory took me by the throat. "It was the most beautiful thing I ever saw."

* * *

Next morning Bold Berthold was up before me, and we had left his hide-covered hut far behind before the sun rose over the treetops. He could walk only slowly, leaning on his staff; but he lacked nothing in endurance, and seemed more inclined to talk while walking than he had been the night before. "Wanted to know about the Aelf last night," he said, and I nodded.

"Got to talking about Skai instead. You must've thought I was cracked. I had reasons, though."

"It was all right," I told him, "because I want to know about that, too."

The almost invisible path we had been following had led us to a clearing; Bold Berthold halted, and pointed Skaiward with his staff. "Birds go up there. You seen them."

I nodded. "I see one now."

"They can't stay."

"If— One could perch on the castle wall, couldn't it?"

"Don't talk 'bout that." I could not tell whether he was angry or frightened. "Not now and maybe not never."

"All right. I won't, I promise."

"Don't want to lose you no more." He drew breath. "Birds can't stay. You and me can't go at all. See it, though. Understand?"

I nodded.

He began to walk again, hurrying forward, his staff thumping the ground before him. "Think a bird could, too? Eagle can see better than you. Ever see a eagle nest?"

"Yes, there was one about five miles from our cabin."

"Top of a big tree?"

"That's right. A tall pine."

"Eagle's sitting there, sitting eggs, likely. Think it ever looks up 'stead of down?"

"I suppose it must." I was trotting behind him.

"Then it can go, if it's of a mind to. The Aelf's the same." One thick blue-veined finger pointed to the earth. "They're down there where we can't see, only they can see us. You and me. Hear us, too, if we talk loud. They can come up if they want to, like birds, only they can't stay."

After that we walked on in silence for half an hour or so, I pursuing almost vanished memories. At last I said, "What would happen if an Aelf tried to stay here?"

"Die," Bold Berthold told me. "That's what they say."

"They told you that? That they couldn't live up here?"

"Aye."

Later, when we stopped to drink from a brook, I said, "I won't ask how they've been wronged, but do you know?"

He shrugged. "Know what they say."

That night we camped beside the Griffin, cheered and refreshed by its purling waters. Bold Berthold had brought flint and steel, and I collected dry sticks for him and broke them into splinters so fine that the first shower of yellow sparks set them alight. "If there wasn't no winter I could live so all my life," he said, and might have been speaking for me.

Flat on my back after our meal, I heard the distant hooting of an owl, and the soughing of the wind in the treetops, where the first green leaves had burst forth. You must understand that at that time I believed I would be home soon. I had been kidnapped, I thought, by the Aelf. They had freed me in some western state, or perhaps in a foreign country. In time, the memories of my captivity would return. Had I been wiser, I would have stayed in Irringsmouth, where I had made friends, and where there might well be a library with maps, or an American Consul. As it was, there might be some clue in Griffinsford (I was not yet convinced that was not the name of our town); and if there were none, there was nothing to keep me from returning to Irringsmouth.

Half destroyed, Irringsmouth remained a seaport of sorts. Maybe I could board a ship to America there. What was there to keep me from doing it? Nothing and nobody, and a ship sounded good.

"Who-o-o?" said the owl. Its voice, soft and dark as the spring night, conveyed apprehension as well as curiosity.

I too sensed the footsteps by which someone or something made its way through the forest, although one single drop of dew falling from a high limb would have made more noise than any of them.

"Who-o-o comes?"

You would get married, and I would be in the way all the time until I was old enough to live on my own. The best plan might be for me to stay out at the cabin, for the first year anyway. It might be better still for me not to come home too quickly. Home to the bungalow that had been Mom and Dad's. Home to the cabin where we had gone to hunt and fish before snow ended all that.

Yet it was spring. Surely this was spring. The stag I had killed had dropped his antlers, the grass in the forlorn little garden of Bluestone Castle had been downy and short. What had become of winter?

A lovely, pointed face lit by great lustrous eyes like harvest moons peered down into mine, then vanished.

I sat up. There was no one there except Bold Berthold, and he was fast asleep. The owl had fallen silent, but the night-wind murmured secrets to the trees. Lying down again, I did my best to recall the face I had glimpsed. A green face? Surely, I thought, surely it had *looked* green.

The old trees had given way to young ones, bushes, and spindly alders when Bold Berthold said, "Here we are."

There was no town. No town at all.

"Right here," he waved his staff, "right there's where the street run. Houses on this side, back to the water. On that other, back to the fields. This right here was Uld's house, and across from it Baldig's." He took me by the hand. "Recollect Baldig?"

I do not remember what I said, and he was not listening anyway. "Uld had six fingers, and so'd his daughter Skjena." Bold Berthold released my shoulder. "Pick up my stick for me, will you, stripling? I'll show where we met 'em."

It was some distance away, through bushes and saplings. At last he stopped to point. "That was our house, yours and mine. Only it used to be Pa's. Recollect him? Know you don't recollect her. Ma got took 'fore you was ever weaned. Mag, her name was. We'll sleep there tonight, sleep where the house stood, for the old times' sake."

I had not the heart to tell him I was not really his brother.

"There!" He led me north another hundred yards or so. "Here's the spot where I first seen Schildstarr. I'd boys like you to shoot arrows and throw stones, but they run, all of 'em. Some shot or threw first, most just run soon as the Angrborn showed their faces."

He had stayed, and fought, and fallen. Conscious of that, I said, "I wouldn't have run."

He thrust his big, bearded face into mine. "You'd have run too!"

"No."

"You'd have run," he repeated, and flourished his staff as if to strike me.

I said, "I won't fight you. But if you try to hit me with that, I'm going to take it away from you and break it."

"You wouldn't have?" He was trying not to smile.

Having convinced myself, I shook my head. "Not if they had been as tall as that tree."

He lowered his staff and leaned on it. "Wasn't. Up to that first big limb, maybe. How you know you wouldn't run?"

"You didn't," I said. "Aren't we the same?"

Long before sundown we had cleared a space to sleep in where the old house had stood, and built a new fire on the old hearth. Bold Berthold talked for hours about the family and about Griffinsford. I listened, mostly out of politeness at first; as the shadows lengthened, I became interested in spite of myself. There had been no school, no doctor, and no police. At long intervals, travelers had crossed the Griffin here, wading through cold mountain water that scarcely reached their knees. When the villagers were lucky, they had sold them food and lodging; when they had been unlucky, they had to fight them to protect their homes and herds.

If the Angrborn had been giants, the Osterlings who sometimes came in summer had been devils, gorging on human flesh to restore the humanity they had lost. The Aelf had come like fog in all seasons, and had vanished like smoke. "Mossmen and Salamanders, mostly," Bold Berthold confided. "Or else little Bodachan. They'd help sometimes. Find lost stock and beg blood for it." He bared his arm. "I'd stick a thorn in and give a drop or two. They ain't but mud, that kind."

I nodded to show I understood, although I did not.

"You was here with me then, only you didn't talk so high. Pa raised me, and I raised you. You got to feeling like you was in the way, I'd say, 'cause of me runnin' after Gerda. Prettiest girl ever seen, and we had it all planned out."

I did not have to ask what happened.

"You went off, and I thought you'd be back in a year or two when we got settled. Only you never come 'til now. How'd you like it where you was?"

I tried to recall, but all that I could think of was that the best times in my life had come when I had been able to get out under the sky, out on a boat or among trees.

"Nothing to say?"

"Yes." I showed him the arrowheads I had saved. "Since we'll have a few more hours of daylight, I'd like to fit new shafts to them."

"Old ones broke?"

I nodded. "When the stag fell. I was thinking that if I could find more wood of the same kind as my bow, my new shafts wouldn't break."

"You'd cut one, for a couple arrows?"

I shook my head. "I'd cut a limb or two, that's all. And if I could find one of last year's fruits, I'd plant the seeds."

Laboriously he climbed to his feet. "Show you one, and it ain't gone."

He led me into the brush, and kneeling felt through the grass until he discovered a small stump. "Spiny orange," he said. "You planted it 'fore you went away. It was on my land, and I wouldn't let nobody cut it. Only somebody done, when I wasn't looking."

I said nothing.

"Thought it might have put up shoots." He rose again with the help of his staff. "They do, sometimes."

I knelt, took one of the two remaining seeds from my pouch, and planted it near where the earlier stump had grown. When I rose again, his face was streaked with tears. Once more he led me away, then stopped to wave his staff at the wilderness of saplings and bushes that stretched before us. "Here was my barley field. See the big tree way in back? Come on."

Halfway there he pointed out a speck of shining green. "There it is. Spiny orange don't drop its leaves like most do. Green all winter, like a pine."

Together we went to it, and it was a fine young tree about twenty-five feet high. I hugged him.

It seems to me that I should say more about the spiny orange here, but the truth is that I know little. Many of the trees we have in America are found in Mythgarthr too—oaks and pines and maples and so on. But the spiny orange is the only tree I know that grows in Aelfrice too. The sky of Aelfrice is not really strange until you look closely at it and see the people in it, and (sometimes) hear their voices on the wind. Time moves very slowly here, but we are not conscious of it. Only the trees and the people are strange at first sight. I think the spiny orange belongs here, not in Mythgarthr and not in America.

CHAPTER 4

SIR RAVD

Lad!" the knight called from the back of his tall gray. And again, "Come here, lad. We would speak to you."

His squire added, "We'll do you no hurt."

I approached warily; if I had learned one thing in my time in those woods with Bold Berthold, it was to be chary of strangers. Besides, I recalled the knight of the dragon, who had vanished before my eyes.

"You know the forest hereabout, lad?"

I nodded, giving more attention to his horse and arms than to what he said.

"We need a guide—a guide for the rest of this day and perhaps for tomorrow as well." The knight was smiling. "For your help we're prepared to pay a scield each day." When I said nothing, he added, "Show him the coin, Svon."

From a burse at his belt the squire extracted a broad silver piece. Behind him, the great bayard charger he led stirred and stamped with impatience, snorting and blowing through its lips.

"We'll feed you, too," the knight promised. "Or if you feed us with that big bow, we'll pay you for the food."

"I'll share without payment," I told him, "if you'll share with me."

"Nobly spoken."

"But how can I know you won't send me off empty-handed at the end of the day, with a cuff on the ear?"

Svon shut his fist around the scield. "How do we know you won't lead us into an ambush, ouph?"

"As for the cuff at sunset," the knight said, "I can give you my word. As I do, though you've no reason to trust it. On the matter of payment, however, I can set your mind at rest right now." A big forefinger tapped Svon's fist; when Svon surrendered the coin, the knight tossed it to me. "There's your pay for this day until sunset, nor will we take it from you. Will you guide us?"

I was looking at the coin, which bore the head of a stern young king on one side and a shield on the other. The shield displayed the image of a monster compounded of woman, horse, and fish. I asked the knight where he wanted me to take him.

"To the nearest village. What is it?"

"Glennidam," I said; I had been there with Bold Berthold.

The knight glanced at Svon, who shook his head. Turning back to me, the knight asked, "How many people?"

There had been nine houses—unmarried people living with their parents, and old people living with their married children. At a guess, three adults for each house . . . I asked whether I should include children.

"If you wish. But no dogs." (This, I think, may have been overheard by some Bodachan.)

"Then I'll say fifty-three. That's counting Seaxneat's wife's new baby. But I don't know its name, or hers either."

"Good people?"

I had not thought so; I shook my head.

"Ah." The knight's smile held a grim joy. "Take us to Glennidam, then, without delay. We can introduce ourselves on the road."

"I am Able of the High Heart."

Svon laughed.

The knight touched the rim of his steel coif. "I am Ravd of Redhall, Able of the High Heart. My squire is Svon. Now let us go."

"If we get there today at all," I warned Ravd, "it will be very late."

"The more reason to hurry."

We camped that night beside a creek called Wulfkil, Svon and I putting up a red-and-gold tent of striped sailcloth for Ravd to sleep in. I built a fire, for I carried flint and steel now to start one, and we ate hard bread, salt meat, and onions.

"Your family may worry about you," Ravd said. "Have you a wife?"

I shook my head, and added that Bold Berthold had said I was not old enough yet.

Ravd nodded, his face serious. "And what do you say?"

I thought of school—how I might want to go to college, if I ever got back home. "A few more years."

Svon sneered. "Two rats to starve in the same hole."

"I hope not."

"Oh, really? How would *you* support a family?"

I grinned at him. "She'll tell me how. That's how I'll know when I've found her."

"She will? Well, what if she can't?" He looked to Ravd for support, but got none.

I said, "Then would she be worth marrying?"

Ravd chuckled.

Svon leveled a forefinger at me. "Someday I'll teach—"

"You must learn yourself before the day for teaching comes," Ravd told him. "Meanwhile, Able here might teach us both, I think. Who is Berthold, Able?"

"My brother." That was what we told people, Ben, and I knew Bold Berthold believed it.

"Older than yourself, since he advises you."

I nodded. "Yes, sir."

"Where are your father and mother?"

"Our father died years ago," I told Ravd, "and my mother left soon after I was born." It was true where you are, and here as well.

"I'm sorry to hear it. Sisters?"

"No, none," I said. "Our father raised my brother, and my brother raised me."

Svon laughed again.

I was confused already, memories of home mingling with stories Bold Berthold had told me of the family here that had been his and was supposed to be mine. It was all in the past, and although America is very far from here in the present, the past is only memories, and records nobody reads, and records nobody can read. This place and that place are mixed together like the books in the school library, so many things on the wrong shelf that nobody knows what is right for it anymore.

Ravd said, "You and your brother don't live in Glennidam, from what you said. You'd know the name of Seaxneat's wife, and the name of her new child, too, since there are only about fifty people in the village. What village do you live in?"

"We don't live in any of them," I explained. "We live by ourselves, and keep to ourselves, mostly."

"*Outlaws,*" Svon whispered.

"They may be." Ravd's shoulders rose and fell by the thickness of a blade of grass. "Would you guide me to your house if I asked you, Able?"

"It's Bold Berthold's, not mine, sir." I was glaring at Svon.

"To your brother's then. Would you take us there?"

"Gladly. But it's no grand place, just a hut. It's not much bigger than your tent." I thought Svon was going to say something; he did not, so I said, "I ought to become a bandit, like Svon says. Then we'd have a nice house with thick walls and doors, and enough to eat."

"There are outlaws in this forest, Able," Ravd told me. "They call themselves the Free Companies. Do they have those things?"

"I suppose they do, sir."

"Have you seen them for yourself?"

I shook my head.

"When we met, Svon feared you would lead us into an ambush. Do you think the Free Companies might ambush us in sober fact? With three to fight?"

"Two to fight," I told him. "Svon would run."

"I would not!"

"You'll run from me before the owl hoots." I spat into the fire. "From two lame cats and a girl you'd run like a rabbit."

His hand went to his hilt. I knew I had to stop him before he drew. I jumped the fire and knocked him down. He let go of the hilt when he fell, and I drew his sword and threw it into the bushes. We fought on the ground the way you and I did sometimes, he trying to get at his dagger while I tried to stop him. We got too close to the fire and he broke loose. I thought he was going to draw it and stab me, but he jumped up and ran instead.

I tried to clean myself off a little and told Ravd, "You can have your scield back if you want it."

"*May.*" He had never stirred. "*May* governs permissions, gifts, and things of that sort. You speak too well, Able, to make such an elementary mistake."

I nodded. I had not figured him out, and I was not sure I ever would.

"Sit down, and keep my scield. When Svon returns, I'll have him give you another for tomorrow."

"I thought you'd be mad at me."

Ravd shook his head. "Svon must become a knight soon. His family expects it and so does he. So do His Grace and I, for that matter. Thus, he will. Before he receives the accolade, he has a great deal to learn. I have been teaching him, to the best of my ability."

"And me," I told him. "About *can* and *may* and other things, too."

"Thank you."

For a while after that, we sat with our thoughts. Before long I said, "Could I become a knight?"

That was the only time I saw Ravd look surprised, and it

was no more than his eyes opening a little wider. "We can't take you with us, if that's what you mean."

I shook my head. "I have to stay and take care of Bold Berthold. But sometime? If I stay here?"

"You're very nearly a knight now, I believe. What makes a knight, Able? I'd like your ideas on the matter."

He reminded me of Ms. Sparreo, and I grinned. "And set them right."

Ravd smiled back. "If they need to be set right, yes. So tell me, how is a knight different from any other man?"

"Mail like yours."

Ravd shook his head.

"A big horse like Blackmane, then."

"No."

"Money?"

"No, indeed. I mentioned the accolade when we were talking about my squire. Did you understand me?"

I shook my head.

"The accolade is the ceremony by which one authorized to perform it confers knighthood. Let me ask again. What makes a man a knight, Able? What makes him different enough that we have to give him a name differing from that of an ordinary fighting man?"

"The accolade, sir."

"The accolade makes him a knight before the law, but it is a mere legality, formal recognition of something that has already occurred. The accolade says that we find this man to be a knight."

I thought about that, and about Ravd, who was a knight himself. "Strength and wisdom. Not either one by itself, but the two together."

"You're closer now. Perhaps you are close enough. It is honor, Able. A knight is a man who lives honorably and dies honorably, because he cares more for his honor than for his life. If his honor requires him to fight, he fights. He doesn't count his foes or measure their strength, because those things don't matter. They don't affect his decision."

The trees and the wind were so still then that I felt like the whole world was listening to him.

"In the same way, he acts honorably toward others, even when they do not act honorably toward him. His word is good, no matter to whom he gives it."

I was still trying to get my mind around it. "I know a man who stood his ground and fought the Angrborn, with just a spear and an ax. He didn't have a shield, or armor, a horse, or anything like that. The men with him wanted to run, and some did. He didn't. Was he a knight? This wasn't me."

"What was he fighting for, Able?" It was almost a whisper.

"For Gerda and his house. For the crops he had in his fields, and his cattle."

"Then he is not a knight, though he is someone I would like very much to count among my followers."

I asked if he had many, because he had come into that forest alone, except for Svon.

"More than I wish, but not many who are as brave as this man you know. I'd thank every Overcyn in Skai for a hundred more, if they were like that."

"He's a good man." I was picturing Bold Berthold to myself, and thinking about all that we would be able to buy with two scields.

"I believe you. Lie down now, and get some rest. We'll need you well rested tomorrow."

"I want to ask a favor first." I felt like a little kid again, and that made it hard to talk. "I don't mean anything bad by it."

Ravd smiled. "I'm sure you don't."

"I mean I'm not going to try to steal it, or hurt you with it either, or anybody. But could I look at your sword? Please? Just for a minute?"

He drew it. "I'm surprised you didn't ask when we had sunlight, when you could have seen it better. Are you sure you wouldn't prefer to wait?"

"Now. Please. I'd like to see it now. I promise I'll never ask again."

He handed it to me hilt first; and it seemed like a warm, living thing. Its long straight blade was chased with gold and double-edged; its hilt of bronze and black horsehide was topped with a gold lion's head. I studied it and gripped the sword to flourish it, and found with a sort of shock that I had stood up without meaning to.

After a minute or two of waving it around, I positioned the blade so that the firelight fell on the flat, just ahead of the guard. "There's writing here. What does it say?"

"Lut. You can't read, can you?"

I knew I could. I said, "Well, I can't read this."

"Lut is the man who made it." Ravd held out his hand, and I returned his sword. He wiped the blade with a cloth. "My sword is Battlemaid. Lut is a famous bladesmith of Forcetti, the town of my liege Duke Marder. Your own duke, Duke Indign, is dead. Did you know?"

"I thought he must be."

"We're attempting to assimilate his lands, and finding them a bit too much to chew, I'm afraid." Ravd's smile was touched with irony.

"Was that Duke Marder on the scield you gave me?"

Ravd shook his head. "That's our king, King Arnthor."

"What was that on his shield?"

"A nykr. Lie down and go to sleep, Able. You can save the rest of your questions for tomorrow."

"Is it real?"

"Sleep!" When Ravd sounded like that, you did not argue. I lay down, turned my back to the fire, and fell asleep as soon as I shut my eyes.

CHAPTER 5

TERRIBLE EYES

Something that sounded like a scuffle woke me up. I heard Svon's voice and Ravd's; and I decided that if I did not want to start another fight, the best thing might be for me to lie there and listen.

"I stumbled." That was Svon.

Ravd said, "No one pushed you?"

"I said I stumbled!"

"I know you did. I wish to discover whether you will verify it. It appeared to me that you had been pushed from behind. Was I wrong?"

"Yes!"

"I see. You have your sword again."

"I found it in the bushes. Do you think I'd come back here without it?"

"I don't see why not." Ravd sounded as though the question interested him. "If you mean you might need it to deal with our guide, it wasn't of great use to you an hour ago."

"We might be attacked."

"By the outlaws? Yes, I suppose we might."

"Are you going to sleep in your armor?"

"Certainly. It's one of the things a knight must learn to

do." Ravd sighed. "Many years before either of us was born, a wise man said that there were only three things a knight had to learn. I believe I told you a week ago, though it may have been more. Can you tell me what they are now?"

"To ride." Svon sounded as if it were being dragged out of him. "To use the sword."

"Very good. And?"

"To speak the truth."

"Indeed," Ravd murmured. "Indeed. Shall we begin again? Or would you prefer to omit that part?"

If Svon said anything, I could not hear it.

"I've been sitting here awake since you ran away, you see. Talking to our guide at first, and talking to myself after he went to sleep. Thinking, in other words. One of the things I thought about was the way he threw your sword. I saw it. Perhaps you did as well."

"I don't want to talk about it."

"Then you need not. But I will have to talk about it more, because you won't. When a man throws a heavy object such as a sword or spear for distance, he uses his whole body—his legs and torso, as well as his arm. Able did not do that. He simply flung your sword away as a man might discard an apple core. I think—"

"Who cares what you think!"

"Why, I do." Ravd's voice was as smooth as polished steel, and sounded a good deal more dangerous. "And you must, Svon. Sir Sabel beat me twice, once with his hands and once with the flat of his sword. I was Sir Sabel's squire for ten years and two. No doubt I've told you."

Maybe Svon nodded. I could not see.

"With the flat of his sword because I attacked him. He would have been entirely justified in killing me, but he was a good and a merciful knight—a better knight than I will ever be. With his hands for something I had said to him, or something I had failed to say. I never did find out exactly what it was. He was drunk at the time—but then we all get drunk now and then, don't we?"

"You don't."

"Because he was, I found it less humiliating than I would have otherwise. Perhaps I said that I cared nothing for his thoughts. That seems likely enough.

"Able flung your sword as a man flings dung, or any such object. I believe I said that. He merely cast it from him, in other words, making no effort toward great distance or force. If you were to cast a hurlbatte so, I would chastise you. With my tongue, I mean."

Svon spoke then, but I could not hear what he said.

"It may be so. My point is that your sword cannot have been thrown far. Three or four strides, I would think. Five at most. Yet I didn't hear you searching for it in the dark, and I expected to. I was listening for it."

"I stepped on it," Svon said. "I didn't have to look for it at all."

"One resolves not to lie, but one always resolves to begin one's new truthfulness at a later time. Not now." Ravd sounded tired.

"I'm not lying!"

"Of course you are. You stepped upon your sword, four strides southeast of where I sit. You uttered no grunt of astonishment, no exclamation. You bent in silence and picked it up. You would have had to grope for the hilt, I believe, since you would not wish to lay hands on a sharp blade in the dark. You then returned it to its scabbard, a scabbard of wood covered with leather, without a sound. After that, you returned to our camp from the west, tripping over something with such violence that you almost fell into the fire."

Svon moaned like one in pain, but spoke no word.

"You must have been running to trip as hard as that and come near to falling. Were you? Running through a strange forest in the dark?"

"Something caught me."

"Ah. Now we're come to it. At least, I hope so. What was it?"

"I don't know." Svon drew breath. "I ran away. Was your churl chasing me?"

"No," Ravd said.

"Well, I thought he was, and I ran right into somebody. Only I don't think it was really a person. A—a ghost or something."

"Interesting."

"There were several." Svon seemed to have taken heart. "I can't say how many. Four or five."

"Go on." I could not tell whether Ravd believed him.

"They gave me back my sword and brought me here, and they pushed me at our fire, hard, just like you said."

"Saying nothing to you?"

"No."

"Did you thank them for returning your sword?"

"No."

"Perhaps they gave you a charm or a letter? Something of that kind?"

"No."

"Did they take our horses?"

"I don't think so."

"Go now and see to them, please, Svon. See that they're well tied, and haven't been ridden."

"I don't—Sir Ravd . . ."

"Go!"

Svon cried, and right then I wanted to sit up and say

something—anything—that might make him feel better. I was going to say that I would go, but that would just have made him feel worse.

When he stopped crying, Ravd said, "They frightened you very badly, whoever they were. You're more afraid of them than you are of me or our guide. Are they listening to us?"

"I don't know. I think so."

"And you're afraid that if you confide in me they'll punish you for it?"

"Yes!"

"I doubt it. If they are indeed listening, they must have heard that you *didn't* confide in me. Able, you are awake. Sit up, please, and look at me."

I did.

"How much have you heard?"

"Everything, or nearly. How did you know I was awake?"

"When you were truly asleep, you stirred in your sleep half a dozen times, and twice seemed almost to speak. Once you snored a little. When you feigned sleep, you moved not a muscle and uttered not a sound, though we were talking in ordinary tones within two strides of you. So you were awake or dead."

"I didn't want Svon to feel worse than he did already."

"Admirable."

I said, "I'm sorry I threw your sword, Svon."

"Who caught Svon and returned him to us? Do you know?"

I had no idea. I shook my head.

Svon wiped his nose. "They gave me a message for you, Able. You are to be sure that your playmate is looking out for you."

I suppose I gawked.

Ravd said, "Who are these friends of yours, Able?"

"I think . . ."

"The outlaws?"

I shook my head. "I don't think so. Couldn't it be the Aelf?"

Ravd looked thoughtful. "Svon, did you intend Able's death?"

"Yes, I did." There were no tears now; he drew his dagger and handed it to me. "I was going to kill you with this. You may keep it if you want to."

I turned it over in my hands. The tip was angled down to meet a long straight edge.

"It's a saxe." Svon sounded as if we were sharing food and passing the time. "It's like the knives the Frost Giants carry. Of course theirs are much bigger."

I said, "You were going to kill me with this?" and he nodded.

Ravd asked, "Why are you telling us this now, Svon?"

"Because I was told to give their message to him as soon as he woke up, and I think they're listening."

"So you said."

"I was hoping you'd go to sleep. Then I could have awakened him, and whispered it. That was what I wanted."

"You'd never have had to tell me what happened."

Svon nodded.

"I don't want it," I said. I gave him his dagger back. "I have a knife of my own, and I like mine better."

"You may as well tell us everything," Ravd said; and Svon did.

"I didn't run into them like I said. I ran into a tree, and hit it hard enough that I fell down. When I could I got up again and circled around your fire, keeping it only just in sight. When I was on the side where Able was, I got as close as I dared, and that was pretty close. You said you would have heard me if I had found my sword. I don't think so, because you didn't hear that. I was waiting for you to go to sleep.

When I was sure you were sleeping, I was going to kill him as quietly as I could and carry his body away and hide it. I wouldn't come back until tomorrow afternoon, and you'd think he had simply run away.

"They grabbed me from behind, making less noise than I had. They had swords and bows. They took me to a clearing where I could see them a little in the moonlight, and they told me that if I hurt Able I'd belong to them. I'd have to slave for them for the rest of my life."

Ravd stroked his chin.

"They gave me that message and made me say it seven times, and swear on my sword that I'd do everything exactly the way they said."

"They had your sword?"

"Right." The kind of sarcasm I was going to get to know a lot better crept into Svon's voice. "I don't know how they got it without your hearing, but they had it."

Recalling things Bold Berthold had told me, I asked whether they were black.

"No. I don't know what color they were, but it wasn't black. They looked pale in the moonlight."

Ravd said, "Able thinks they might be Aelf. So do I. I take it they didn't identify themselves?"

"No, but— It could be right. I know they weren't people like us."

"I've never seen them. Have you, Able?"

I said, "Not that I remember, but Bold Berthold has. He said the ones who bothered him were like ashes or charcoal."

Ravd turned back to Svon. "You must tell me everything you remember about them, just as truthfully as you can. Or did they caution you not to?"

Svon shook his head. "They said to give Able their message when he woke, and never to hurt him. That was all."

"Why is Able precious to them?"

"They wouldn't tell."

"Able? Do you know?"

"No." I wished then that Ravd had not seen I was awake. "They want me to do something, but I don't know what it is."

Svon said, "Then how do you know they do?"

I did not answer.

"Our king was born in Aelfrice," Ravd told me, "as was his sister, Princess Morcaine. Since you didn't recognize his face on a scield, I doubt that you knew it."

"I didn't," I said.

"I don't believe my squire credits it—or at least, I believe he did not until now, though he may have changed his opinion."

Svon told me, "People talk as if Aelfrice were a foreign country, like Osterland. Sir Ravd says it's really another world. If it is, I don't see how people can come here from there. Or go there either."

Ravd shrugged. "And I, who have never done it, cannot tell you. I can tell you, however, that it's not wise to deny everything you can't understand. How were your captors dressed? Could you see?"

"They weren't, as far as I could see. They were as naked as poor children. They were tall, though—taller than I am, and thin." His breath caught in his throat. "They had terrible eyes."

"Terrible in what way?"

"I can't explain it. They held the moonlight and made it burn. It hurt to look at them."

Ravd sat in silence for a minute or two after that, his hand stroking his chin. "One more question, Svon, then we must sleep. All of us. It's late already, and we should be up early. You said that there were four or five of them. Was that the truth?"

"About that many. I couldn't be sure."

"Able, put a little more wood on the fire, since you're up. How many could you be sure of, Svon?"

"Four. Three were men. Males, or whatever you call them. But I think there may have been more."

"The fourth was female, I take it. Did she speak?"

"No."

"How many males did?"

"Three."

Ravd yawned, which may have been play-acting. "Lie down, Svon. Sleep if you can."

Svon spread a blanket for himself and lay down on it.

Ravd said, "I believe you will be safe, Able. From Svon, at least."

I suppose I nodded; but I was thinking how another world might seem like it was just another country, and about yellow eyes that burned with moonlight like a cat's.

CHAPTER 6

SEEING SOMETHING

We reached Glennidam about midmorning, and Ravd called the people together, all the men and all the women, and some children, too. He began by driving Battlemaid into a log Svon and I fetched for him. "You are invited to swear fealty to our liege, Duke Marder," he told them. "I won't make you swear—you're free to refuse if you wish to refuse. But you should know that I will report those who do not swear to him."

After that they swore, all of them, putting their hands on the lion's head and repeating the oath after Ravd.

"Now I would like to speak with some of you, one at a time," he said, and chose six men and six women, and had Svon and me watch the rest while he talked to the first one in the front room of the biggest house in the village. An hour went by while he was talking to that first one, and the ones who were waiting got restless; but Svon put his hand to his sword and shouted until they quieted down.

The first man came out at last, sweating and unable to meet the eyes of the waiting eleven, and Ravd called for the first woman. She went inside trembling, and the minutes ticked by. A shiny blue fly, big with carrion, buzzed around me until I chased it, then around Svon, and at last around a little black-bearded man the rest called Toug, who seemed much too despondent to chase anything.

The woman appeared in the doorway, her face streaked with tears. "Able? Which one is Able? He wants you."

I went in, and the woman sat down on a little milking stool in front of Ravd.

He, seated on a short bench with a back, said, "Able, this is Brega. Because she is a woman, I permit her to sit. The men stand. Brega tells me there is a man called Seaxneat who is well acquainted with the outlaws and entertains them at times. Do you understand why I asked you to come in?"

I said, "Yes, sir. Only I don't think I can help much."

"If we learn nothing from you, you may learn something from us." Ravd spoke to the woman. "Now, Brega, I want to explain how things are for you. In fact, I must explain that, because I doubt that you understand it."

Brega, thin and no longer young, snuffled and wiped her eyes with a corner of her apron.

"You are afraid that Able here will tell others what you've told me about Seaxneat. Isn't that so?"

She nodded.

"He won't, but your danger is much greater than that. Do you two know each other, by the way?"

She shook her head; I said, "No, sir."

"You have told me about Seaxneat, and of course I will try to find him and talk to him. Those people outside will know you've talked to me, and the longer we're together the more they will think you've told me. Do you understand what I'm saying?"

"Y-yes."

"Have you yourself, or your husband, ever been robbed?"

"They knocked me down." The tears burst forth, and flowed for some minutes.

"Do you know the name of the outlaw who knocked you down?"

She shook her head.

"But if you knew it, you would tell me, wouldn't you? It would make no sense for you to keep it from me when you have told me as much as you have. You see that, don't you?"

"It was Egil."

"Thank you. Brega, you've taken an oath, the most solemn oath a woman can take. You've acknowledged Duke Marder as your liege, and sworn to obey him in all things. If you break that oath, Hel will condemn your spirit to Muspel, the Circle of Fire. The sacrifices you've offered the Aelf can't save you. I take it you know all that."

She nodded.

"I am here because Duke Marder appointed me. If it were not for that, I would be sitting at my own table in Redhall, or seeing to my horses there. I speak for Duke Marder, just as if he were here in person. I am his knight."

She sniffled. "I know."

"Furthermore, the outlaws will avenge themselves upon you and your whole village, if they are left free to do so. Egil, who knocked you down, will do worse. This is your chance to avenge yourself, with words worth more than swords to Duke Marder and me. Do you know of anyone else here who is on good terms with the outlaws? Anyone at all?"

She shook her head.

"Only Seaxneat. What is his wife's name?"

"Disira."

"Really?" Ravd pursed his lips. "That's perilously near a queen's name some men conjure with. Do you know that name?"

"No. I don't say it."

"Does she? I will not use her name. The woman we are speaking of. Seaxneat's wife. Has she alluded to that queen in your hearing?"

"No," Brega repeated.

Ravd sighed. "Able, would you know Seaxneat if you saw him? Think before you speak."

I said, "I'm sure I would, sir."

"Describe him, please, Brega."

The woman only stared.

"Is he tall?"

"Taller than I am." She held her hands a foot apart to indicate the amount.

"A dark beard?"

"Red."

"One eye? Crooked nose? Club foot?"

She shook her head to all of them.

"What else can you tell us about him?"

"He's fat," she said thoughtfully, "and he walks like this." She stood up and demonstrated, her toes turned in.

"I see. Able, does this square with your recollection? Fat. The red beard? The walk?"

It did.

"When we spoke earlier, you did not name Seaxneat's wife. Was that because you didn't know her name, or because you were too prudent to voice it?"

"Because I didn't know it, sir. I'm not afraid to say Disira."

"Then it would be wise for you not to say it too often. Do you know what she looks like?"

I nodded. "She's small, with black hair, and her skin's very white. I didn't think her a specially pretty woman when Seaxneat was cheating Bold Berthold and me, but I've seen worse."

"Brega? Does he know her?"

"I think he does." The woman, who had been wiping her eyes, wiped them again.

"Very well. Pay attention, Able. If you will not listen to me about that woman's name, listen to this at least. I want you to search the village for these people. When you find either, or both, bring them to me if you can. If you can't, come back and tell me where they are. Brega will be gone by then, but I'll be talking to others, as likely as not. Don't hesitate to interrupt."

"Yes, sir."

"I want Seaxneat, of course. But I want his wife almost as much. She probably knows less, but she may tell us more. Since she has a new child, it's quite possible she's still here. Now go."

At the outskirts of Glennidam, I halted to search its sprouting fields with my eyes. I had looked into every room of every one of the village's houses, and into every barn and shed as well, all without seeing either Seaxneat or his wife. Ravd had said I was to interrupt him if I found them, but I did not think he would like being interrupted to hear that I had not.

And Ravd had been right, I told myself. A woman with a newborn would not willingly travel far. There was every chance that when she heard a knight had come to Glennidam she had fled no farther than the nearest trees, where she could sit in the shade to nurse her baby. If I left the village to look there . . . Trying to settle the matter in my own mind, I called softly, "Disira? Disira?"

At once it seemed to me that I glimpsed her face among the crowding leaves where the forest began. On one level I felt sure it had been some green joke of sunlight and shadow; on another I knew that I had seen her.

Or at least that I had seen something.

I took a few steps, stopped a minute, still unsure, and hurried forward.

CHAPTER 7

DISIRI

"Help . . ." It was not so much a cry as a moan like that of the wind, and like a moaning wind it seemed to fill the forest. I pushed through the brush that crowded the forest's edge, trotted among close-set saplings, then sprinted among mature trees that grew larger and larger and more and more widely spaced as I advanced.

"Please help me. Please . . ."

I paused to catch my breath, cupped my hands around my mouth, and called, "I'm coming!" as loudly as I could. Even as I did it, I wondered how she had known there was anyone to hear her while I was still walking down the rows of sprouting grain. Possibly she had not. Possibly she had been calling like that, at intervals, for hours.

I trotted again, then ran. Up a steep ridge crowned with dreary hemlocks, and along the ridgeline until it dipped and swerved in oaks. Always it seemed to me that the woman who called could not be more than a hundred strides away.

The woman I felt perfectly certain had to be Seaxneat's wife Disira.

Soon I reached a little river that must surely have been the Griffin. I forded it by the simple expedient of wading in where I was. I had to hold my bow, my quiver, and the little bag I tied to my belt over my head before I was done; but I got through and scrambled up the long sloping bank of rounded stones on the other side.

There, mighty beeches robed with moss lifted proud heads into that fair world called Skai; and there the woman who called to me sounded nearer still, no more (I thought) than a few strides off. In a dark dell full of mushrooms and last year's leaves, I felt certain I would find her. She was only on the other side of the beaver-meadow, beyond all question; and after that, up on the rocky outcrop I glimpsed beyond it.

Except that when I got there I could hear her calling still, calling in the distance. I shouted then, gasping for breath between the repetitions of her name: "Disira? . . . Disira? . . . Disira?"

"Here! Here at the blasted tree!"

The seconds passed like sighs, then I saw it down the shallow valley on the farther side of the outcrop—the shattered trunk, the broken limbs, and the raddled leaves that clung to them not quite concealing something green as spring.

"It fell," she told me when I reached her. "I wanted to see if I could move it just a little, and it fell on my foot. I cannot get my foot out."

I put my bow under the fallen trunk and pried; I never felt it move, but she was able to work her foot free. By the time she got it out, I had noticed something so strange that I was certain I could not really be seeing it, and so hard to describe that I may never make it clear. The afternoon sun shone brightly just then, and the leaves of the fallen tree (which I think must have been hit by lightning), and those of the trees all around it, cast a dappled shade. Mostly we were in the shade, but there were a few splashes of brilliant sunshine here and there. I should have seen her most clearly when one fell on her.

But it was the other way: I could see her very clearly in the shade, but when the sun shone on her face, her legs, her shoulders, or her arms, it almost seemed that she was not there at all. At school Mr. Potash showed us a hologram. He pulled the blinds and explained that the darker it was in the room the more real the hologram would look. So when we had all looked at it, I moved one of the blinds to let in light, and he was right. It got dim, but it was stronger again as soon as I let the blind fall back.

"I don't think I should walk on this." She was rubbing her foot. "It does not feel right. There is a cave a few steps that way. Do you think you could carry me there?"

I did not, but I was not going to say so until I tried. I picked her up. I have held little kids who weighed more than she did, but she felt warm and real in my arms, and she kissed me.

"In there we will be out of the rain," she told me. She kept her eyes down as if she were shy, but I knew she was not really shy.

I started off, hoping I was going toward the cave she knew about, and I said that it was not going to rain.

"Yes, it is. Haven't you noticed how cool the air has gotten? Listen to the birds. To your left a trifle, and look behind the big stump."

It was a nice little cave, just high enough for me to stand up in, and there was a sort of bed made of deerskins and furs, with a green velvet blanket on top.

"Put me on that," she said, "please."

When I did, she kissed me again; and when she let me go, I sat down on the smooth, sandy floor of the cave to get my breath. She laughed at me, but she did not say anything.

For quite a while, I did not say anything either. I was thinking a lot, but I had no control of the things I thought, and I was so excited about her that I thought something was going to happen any minute that I would be ashamed of for the rest of my life. She was the most beautiful woman I had ever seen in my life (she still is) and I had to shut my eyes, which made her laugh again.

Her laugh was like nothing on earth. It was as if there were golden bells hanging among the flowers through a forest of the loveliest trees that could ever be, and a wind sighing there was ringing all the bells. When I could open my eyes again, I whispered, "Who are you? Really?"

"She you called." She smiled, not trying to hide her eyes anymore. Maybe a leopard would have eyes like those, but I kind of doubt it.

"I called Seaxneat's wife Disira. You aren't her."

"I am Disiri the Mossmaiden, and I have kissed you."

I could still feel her kiss, and her hair smelled of new-turned earth and sweet smoke.

"Men I have kissed cannot leave until I send them away."

I wanted to stand up then, but I knew I could never leave her. I said, "I'm not a man, Disiri, just a kid."

"You are! You are! Let me have one drop of blood, and I will show you."

By morning the rain had stopped. She and I swam side by side in the river, and lay together like two snakes on a big shady rock, only an inch above the water. I knew I was all different, but I did not know how different. I think it was the way a caterpillar feels after it has turned into a butterfly and is still drying its wings. "Tell me," I said, "if another man came, would he see you like I see you now?"

"No other man will come. Did not your brother teach you about me?"

I did not know whether she meant you or Bold Berthold, Ben, but I shook my head.

"He knows me."

"Have you kissed him?"

She laughed and shook her head.

"Bold Berthold told me the Aelf looked like ashes."

"We are the Moss Aelf, Able, and we are of the wood and not the ash." She was still smiling. "You call us Dryads, Skogsfru, Treebrides, and other names. You may make a name for us yourself. What would you like to call us?"

"Angels," I whispered; but she pressed a finger to my lips. I blinked and looked away when she did that, and it seemed to me, when I glimpsed her from the corner of my eye, that she looked different from the girl I had been swimming with and all the girls I had just made love with.

"Shall I show you?"

I nodded—and felt muscles in my neck slithering like

pythons. "Good lord!" I said, and heard a new voice, wild and deep. It was terribly strange; I knew I had changed, but I did not know how much, and for a long time after I thought I was going to change back. You need to remember that.

"You won't hate me, Able?"

"I could never hate you," I told her. It was the truth.

"We are loathsome in the eyes of those who do not worship us."

I chuckled at that; the deep reverberations in my chest surprised me too. "My eyes are mine," I said, "and they do what I tell them. I'll close them before I kiss you, if we need more privacy."

She sat up, dangling her legs in the clear, cold water. "Not in this light." Her kick dashed water through a sunbeam and showered us with silver drops.

"You love the sunlight," I said. I sensed it.

She nodded. "Because it is yours, your realm. The sun gave me you, and I love you. My kind love the night, and so I love them both."

I shook my head. "I don't understand. How can you?"

"Loving me, couldn't you love some human woman?"

"No," I said. "I never could." I meant it.

She laughed, and this time it was a laugh that made fun of me. "Show me," she said.

She kicked again. The slender little foot that rose from the shimmering water was as green as new leaves. Her face was sharper, green too, three-cornered, bold and sly. Berry lips pressed mine, and when we parted I found myself looking straight into eyes of yellow fire. Her hair floated above her head.

I embraced her, lifting and holding her, and kissed her again.

CHAPTER 8

ULFA AND TOUG

When she had gone, I tried to find her cave again. It was not there, only my bow, my quiver, and my clothes lying on the grass. The spiny orange bow that had seemed very large to me was suddenly small, almost a toy, and I would have torn my shirt and pants if I had managed to put them on.

Throwing them aside, I drew my bow, pulling the string to my ear as I always had. The spiny orange did not break, although I bent it double; but the bowstring did. I flung it away, and got out the string Parka had bitten off for me from her spinning, the string whose murmuring voices and myriad strange lives had disturbed my dreams for so many nights. I tied loops in its ends and put it on my bow, and it sang there when I drew it to my ear, and sang again—a mighty chorus far away—when I sent an arrow flying up the slope.

I could not draw that arrow to my ear, it was too short by two spans; yet it sped flat as a bullet and buried half its shaft in the bole of an oak.

Naked, I returned to Glennidam at twilight, and struck the little, black-bearded man because he laughed at me, and laid him flat. When he could stand and speak again, he told me Ravd and Svon had left that morning.

"Then I can hope for no help from them," I said. "I must have clothes just the same, and since you are here and they aren't, you must provide them. How will you do it?"

"W-we have c-cloth."

His teeth were chattering, so I was patient with him.

"M-my w-wife will s-s-sew for you."

We went to his house. He fetched out his daughter, and I promised not to harm her. Her name was Ulfa.

"A knight was here yesterday," she told me when her father had gone. "A real knight in iron armor, with huge horses, and two boys to wait on him."

"That's interesting," I said. I wanted to hear what she would say next.

"He'd a big helm hanging from his saddle, you know how they do, with plumes and a lion on it, and a lion on his big shield, too, a gold lion with blood on its claws where they raked the shield, like."

"That was Sir Ravd," I told her.

"Yes, that's what they do say. We had to stand and wait his pleasure, and go in one by one when the boys said, only I didn't. Papa was feared his pleasure might be his pleasure." She giggled. "If you know what I mean, and I still a maid, so he hid me in the barn and pitched straw over me, only I got out and watched, and talked to some of them that had been in. Some of the women, I mean, for there was men, too, only I don't think he would, with them. Hold still while I pin."

Her pin was a long black thorn.

"They said he asked about the Free Companies, only they didn't tell nothing, none of them did, even if they all had to swear. Are you sure you don't want some mush? We've lard to fry in from the barrows Pa slaughtered last fall."

"I'll kill a deer for you," I promised her, "in payment for these clothes."

"That'll be nice." The black thorn was back between her teeth.

I drew my bow, reflecting that it had been all I could do to bring an arrow near my ear the day before. Talking to myself, I said, "A short arrow at that."

"Hmmm?" Ulfa looked up from her work.

"In my quiver. Two arrows I made for myself from spiny orange, and two I took from a boy I fought."

"One of the boys with him had splendid clothes," she confided. "I got as close as I could to look. Red pants, I swear by Garsecg's gullet!"

"That was Svon. What about the other boy?"

"Him? Oh, he was ordinary enough," Ulfa said. "About like my brother, but might be good-looking in a year or two."

"Didn't he have a bow like mine?"

"Bigger'n yours, sir." She had finished cutting her cloth and begun to sew, making long stitches with a big bone needle. "Too big for him was the look of it. Brother had one too, only it's broke. Pa says when a bow's not strung it oughta be no bigger than the man that carries it, and most is smaller of what I've seen. Like yours is, sir."

"I need longer arrows," I told her. "Does your Pa have a rule for arrows, too?"

Still plying her needle, she shook her head.

"In that case I'll give you one I just made. An arrow ought to reach from the end of the owner's left forefinger to his right ear. Mine are far shy of that."

"You'll have to find new ones."

"I'll have to *make* new ones, and I will. What if I were to tell you I was the boy with the big bow?"

The needle stopped in mid stab, and Ulfa looked up at me. "You, sir?"

I nodded.

She laughed. "That boy that was here yesterday? I could've shut my hand 'round his arm, almost. I doubt I could get both 'round yours, sir."

Pushing the trousers she had been making for me to one side, she rose. "Can I try?"

"May I try. Yes, you may."

Both her hands could not encircle my arm, but they could caress it. "You should be a knight yourself, sir."

"I am." My declaration surprised me, I think, much more than it surprised her; yet I recalled what Ravd had said—"We find this man to be a knight"—and it carried an inner certainty. "I am Sir Able," I added.

Hidden by her shift, her nipples brushed my elbow. "Then you ought to have a sword."

"Others have swords too," I told her, "but you're right just the same. I'll get one. Go back to your sewing, Ulfa."

When the trousers were finished and she had begun the shirt, I said, "Your father was afraid Sir Ravd would rape you. So you said."

"Ravish me." She nodded. "Only not because of his name. I don't think he knew it then."

"Neither do I. Isn't your father afraid I'll ravish you myself?"

"I don't know, Sir Able."

"A man intent on rape could do much worse. Have you no mother, Ulfa?"

"Oh, yes. By Garsecg's grace she's still among us."

"But being blind, or crippled in her hands, she can no longer sew?"

Ulfa bit her thread, waking a memory. "She can, Sir Able, I swear to you. She sews better'n I, and taught me. Only skillful sewing takes sunlight."

"I see. Who's in this house, Ulfa? Name them all."

"You and me. Ma, Pa, and brother Toug."

"Really? They're uncommonly quiet. I haven't heard a

voice or a step, other than yours and mine. Where is your mother, do you think?"

Ulfa said nothing, but I followed the direction of her eyes, and opened the door of a wretched little room that appeared to be a sort of pantry. A woman Brega's age was huddled in its farthest corner, her eyes wide with fright.

I said, "Don't worry, Ma. However this falls out, I'll do you and your daughter no hurt."

She nodded and compelled her lips to smile, and the pain of her effort made me turn away.

Ulfa joined us, eager to distract me. "Try it on now. I have to be sure it's not too small."

I did, and she ticked like a beetle in the wall, saying I had the shoulders of a barn door.

I laughed, and said I had not known barn doors boasted shoulders.

"You think you're ordinary, I s'pose, and the rest of us dwarfs."

"I saw myself in the water," I told her. "I had been with a woman called Disiri, and—"

"Disira?"

"No. Disiri the Mossmaiden, who I imagine must have given Disira her dangerous name. She wanted to lie in the shade, but she left when the sun was high. I happened to stand in the sunlight, and I saw my reflection. I was . . . I was held back once, Ulfa. Not allowed to grow with the years. She said something about that, and she undid that holding back." It hurt, but I added, "I would guess for her own pleasure."

Ulfa's mouth formed a small circle. She said nothing.

"Anyway I am as I am, and I have to make myself longer arrows."

Hesitantly, Ulfa said, "We try to stay on good terms with the Hidden Folk."

"Do you succeed?"

"Oh, a bit. They heal our sick sometimes, and watch the forest cattle."

"As long as you speak well of them, and put food out for them?"

She nodded, but would not meet my eye.

"Bold Berthold and I leave them a bowl of broth and a bite of ash-cake now and then."

"We sing songs they like, too, and—and do things, you know, in places we can't ever talk about." Ulfa's needle was fairly flying.

"Songs that can't be sung for strangers, and things you can't speak of even among yourselves? Bold Berthold told me something about it."

After a long pause, she said, "Yes. Things I can't talk about."

"Then talk about this. Is Disiri great among the Aelf?"

"Oh, yes." Ulfa rose, holding up the shirt for me to admire.

"A great lady?"

"Worse."

I tried to imagine Disiri worse. "Perhaps she punishes bandits and the like. Liars."

"Anybody that offends her, sir."

I sighed. "I love her, Ulfa. What am I do?"

Ulfa put her mouth to my ear. "I don't know 'bout love yet, Sir Able."

"And I won't teach you—or at least, not much. Give me my shirt. I promise to try not to get my blood on it."

I pulled it over my head and flexed my shoulders; it was as loose-fitting as I could have wished. "Didn't Pa tell you to make it tight, so as to bind me?"

Ulfa shook her head.

"He hadn't time to think of that, perhaps, or perhaps he thought I would not be wearing it. I suppose it must be easy to kill a man between a woman's legs."

"I—I wouldn't have a thing to do with . . . You know. With nothing like that, Sir Able. Queen Disiri my witness." Her small, strong hands caressed shoulders that thanks to her were no longer bare.

"I believe you," I told her, and kissed her.

A wolf howled in the distance, and in a strangled voice she said, "A Nornhound. It's a bad omen. If—if you was to stay with me tonight, I would stay awake to warn you."

I smiled. "I won't. But you're right, the hunt is on. Warn me of what? Your father and your brother?"

Wordlessly, she nodded.

"I thought they might burst in when I kissed you. Hoped they would, because it would be better to fight where I've got light. Let's try again."

I kissed again and held her longer. When we separated, I said, "So that's the taste of human women. I didn't know."

She stared but did not speak. I went to the window and looked out into the street. It was too dark to see anything.

"I know a little something about love now, Sir Able." She was rubbing herself against me, reminding me of grandma's cat. "There's something down here that's hot as the steam from the kettle."

"Your father and brother didn't rush in. You must've noticed."

"Your servant girl didn't notice a thing right then, Sir Able. Except for you."

"So it will be outside in the dark. But this house has a rear door. I saw it when we looked in on Ma."

I opened the door to the pantry, nodded to the cowering woman, and threw open the door in the opposite wall.

Outside were a boy with a spear and two men with brown bills. The men poked at me as if I were a burning log, but I caught a bill in each hand, snatched them from their owners (though I had to kick the larger), and broke the shafts over my knee. The boy dropped his spear and fled.

He did not get far. I snatched up my bow and ran after him, and caught him in a little meadow near the forest. "Are you Toug?"

Perhaps he nodded; if so I could not see him; and if he spoke, it was so softly I could not hear him. I pinned his arm behind his back and rapped his ear with my bow when he screamed. "You have to answer my questions," I told him, "and answer honestly. Promptly, too, and politely. Is this forest safe by night?"

"No, sir," he muttered.

"I didn't think so. We need each other, you see. While I'm with you, you get my protection—a needed safeguard, at least 'til the sun's back. I, on the other hand, need you to warn me of danger. Suppose I got annoyed and killed you."

He trembled, shaming me. He was only a little kid.

"I wouldn't get your warning then, and things might be bad for me. We've got to be careful. And look out for each other. Your name's the same as your dad's?"

"Uh-huh."

"That was his house?"

"Uh-huh."

"You've got to speak clearly, and call me Sir Able. I don't want you to duck my questions with uh-huh and huh-uh either, not any more, or even yes and no. You talk about every answer you give." I wanted to say like in school, but I changed it quick to, "Or else you'll get a broken arm."

"I'll try." Toug swallowed audibly. "Sir Able."

"Good. You were ready to kill me with that spear when I opened the door, but I'll forget it, if you let me. There were two men with bills with you. Who were they?"

"Vali and my pa, Sir Able."

"I see. I knocked your father down for laughing at me. I guess he resented it. His name is . . . ?"

"He's Toug too." We were crossing a moonlit glade, and Toug eyed its shadows as if he expected a lion in every one of them.

"You told the truth. That's good." I stopped, making him stop too. "And who's Vali?"

"A neighbor," Toug muttered.

I shook him. "Is that how you talk to a knight?"

"Our neighbor, Sir Able. Right next door."

"I expected you in the street. That was why I went out the back. How did you outguess me?"

"Pa did, Sir Able. He said he thought you'd sneak out the back."

" 'Sneak.' Well, that'll be a lesson to me. Suppose your father had been wrong?"

"Ma'd a' told us, and we'd a' gone 'round both sides a' the house, so one got behind."

"And put his bill into me?"

Toug nodded, and I shook him until he managed to say, "That's it, Sir Able, or if we wasn't in time we'd a' waited where the path goes through the alders."

"What about the other men in your village? There must be twenty or more. Wouldn't they help?"

"Huh-uh, Sir Able. They—they was afraid the knight'd come back. The other knight."

"Go on!"

"Only Vali and— And . . ."

"And somebody else." I let my voice drop to a whisper. "Who was it?" When Toug did not speak, I lifted his pinned arms.

"Ve, Sir Able! He's a little 'un, Sir Able, younger'n me."

"Is he Vali's son? He sounds like it."

"Uh-huh, Sir Able. Vali and Hulta only got the one, Sir Able, and he's not old enough to plow. He had to help. His pa told him to."

"Then I won't be hard on him, if he comes my way. And I won't be hard on you, because you were worried about him. I was younger than you are yesterday. That may be why it doesn't feel like bullying to do this. But maybe it is."

"You—you're twice as big as Pa, Sir Able."

"I didn't see a little kid with you when I opened the door, Toug. Where was he?"

"He run off into the woods, Sir Able."

"When I opened the back door? You were scared and ran yourself, but I saw you. Why didn't I see Ve?"

"He run 'fore I did, Sir Able."

I let go of his arms and caught him by the neck. "Have you ever been hit with a bow, Toug?"

"Uh-huh, Sir Able. I—I had this bow myself, and—and . . ."

"Your dad beat you with it. No, because you wouldn't mind telling me that. Your sister did it. Ulfa." I felt Toug nod, and shook him.

"That's the truth. Ulfa beat me with it."

"You deserved it, that's for sure. She beat you black and blue, I hope."

"Oh, yes, Sir Able. Real bad."

"So bad you couldn't stand afterward?"

"Uh—no, Sir Able. Not as bad as that."

"You're nearly as big as she is. You must have gotten even some way. What'd you do?"

"N-nothing. Pa wouldn't let me."

"We're going to walk again," I told him, "and I'm going to turn you loose. You keep in front of me so I can see you if you try to clear out. I'll catch you if you do, and when I catch you I'll beat you with this bow 'til you can't stand up." I let him go and gave him a push, and when he stopped walking I pushed him again. "What are you so afraid of? Bears? They'll eat you first, and maybe you'll fill them up so they won't eat me. What do you think?"

"N-nothing."

"I know. But you think you do, and that's sad. Toug, you'd better tell the truth, or I'll beat you this minute—beat you 'til you crawl. So tell the truth or get ready. You're afraid of something up ahead. What is it?"

"The Free Companies, Sir Able."

"The outlaws? Go on."

"He—Ve run to fetch 'em. His pa made him, Sir Able. Only—only . . ."

"Yes? Only what?"

"We wanted to tell Ulfa not to sew so fast, so they'd come 'fore you left. Only we couldn't."

"She knew what you planned?"

Toug said nothing, and I rapped his ear. "Out with it!"

"I dunno, Sir Able. Really I don't."

"She knew something was up, but she sewed very fast, and kept this shirt and my trousers as simple as she could. I thought it was because she was afraid of me. Maybe she was afraid *for* me. I hope so. But you've got nothing to be afraid of up there, Toug. If the outlaws were hiding in those shadows, we'd be full of arrows by this time. They could see us in this moonlight."

"They got spears 'n axes, mostly," Toug muttered.

I hardly heard him, because I was listening so hard to something else.

CHAPTER 9

A WIZARD KNIGHT

"Where are we?" Toug stared about him as he spoke, seeing (as I did) ancient trees thicker through than his father's house and lofty as clouds, and a forest floor decked with flowers and ferns, and laced with crystal rills. The soft gray light by which we grasped the nobility and heartrending beauty of all these seemed to proceed from the air itself.

I said, "In the world underneath, I think. In Aelfrice, where the Aelf come from. Now keep your voice down. It must have been your talk that betrayed us."

"This is Aelfrice?"

"I think I said that." I was not sure, but tried to sound sure, and angry, too.

"It isn't real!"

I put my finger to my lips.

"I'm sorry, Sir Able." Toug was near to choking on his curiosity. "Do you think they followed us?"

"I doubt it, but they might have. Besides, if you make noise here you might wake something worse."

"Such as I, Able?" The voice was Disiri's, filled with mirth, mockery, and music, sourceless as the light. I knew it at once. "Disiri, I—"

"Would fawn upon me, if I allowed it."

"Y-yes." I fell to my knees, somehow feeling it might keep me from stammering. "I would, beautiful queen. Have pity and show yourself."

She stepped from behind a tree, no taller than Toug, slender as the naked sword she held, and green. He knelt too, I suppose because I had.

"Is this your slave, Able? Tell him to get up."

I made an urgent gesture and Toug rose.

"I let you pay me homage, as a very great favor. It extends no further than yourself."

I said, "Thank you. Thanks very much. I understand."

"Now you ought to stand, too. In the future, you are to send him away when you wish to adore me. It is not fitting that my consort kneels while his slave lounges."

Toug retreated.

"Disiri, could we—" I was still on my knees.

"Take ourselves to some private place? I think not. Your slave might get into mischief."

"Then may I kill him?"

Toug gasped, "Sir Able!"

Disiri laughed. "Look at him! He thinks you mean it!"

"I do," I said.

"He wants to talk, see how his mouth moves." Delighted, Disiri pointed with the slender blade she bore. "Speak, boy. I will not let him strangle you—at least, not yet."

"My sister . . ."

"What of her?"

Toug drew breath. "I got this sister, Queen Disiri. Her name's Ulfa."

Disiri shot a glance at me. "I ought to have watched you more closely, dear messenger."

"She loves him, loves Sir Able. Or that's what I think."

I adjusted the position of the too-short arrow I had brought to Parka's string. "You can't know that. Or if you do, you have to know I don't love her."

"I was listening under th' window. My pa said to. I heard

how she talked. How she sounded." Toug paused to clear his throat. "I want to say if you kill me, Sir Able, you'll be killin' th' brother of a girl that loves you. You want to do that?"

I spoke to Disiri. "I'll kill him if you want me to."

She looked at me curiously. "Would not it trouble you afterward?"

"Maybe. But if you want him dead, I'll kill him for you and find out."

"You mortals," Disiri told Toug, "are often tender about such things. It is supposed to be a good example for us, and sometimes it is."

Wide-eyed, Toug nodded.

Disiri turned to me, seeming to forget him. "When was it we were together last, Able? A year ago? Something like that?"

"Yesterday morning, Queen Disiri."

"In so brief a time you have become a knight? And learned that I am a queen? Who told you that, and who gave you the colee?"

I did not want to say Ulfa had told me. "A knight with no sword," I said instead, "and I just made myself a knight. I was hoping it would make me somebody you could love."

She laughed. (Toug cringed.) "By the same measure, I am a goddess."

"I've worshipped you since I carried you to the cave, Queen Disiri."

"Your goddess," she told Toug, "but I do not dare ascend to the third world just the same. Did you know that, little boy?"

He shook his head, and seeing my eyes on him said, "No, Queen Disiri. We don't know nothin' 'bout things like that in Glennidam."

"Your Overcyns would destroy me as a matter of course.

Nor is the second much safer." She turned back to me. "It is an awful place. Dragons like Setr roaring and fighting. Would you follow me there?"

I said—and meant—that I would follow her anywhere.

"I can climb to your world, too, as you've seen."

I nodded. "Could I get to the third world the same way? I've been wondering."

"I have no idea." She paused, studying me. "You're a knight, Able. You say so, and so does this boy. You also say you have no sword. A knight requires one."

"If you say so, Queen Disiri."

"I do." She smiled. "And I *do* have an idea about that. A great knight, fit to be a queen's consort, should bear no common sword, but a fabled brand imbued with all sorts of magical authority and mystical significance—Eterne, Sword of Grengarm. Do not contradict me, I know I am right."

"I wouldn't think of it. Not ever."

Her voice fell. "Such swords were forged in the Elder Time. The Overcyns visited Mythgarthr more often then and taught your smiths, that you might defend your world from the Angrborn. No doubt you know all that."

I shook my head.

"It is so. The first pair of tongs was cast down to fall at the feet of Weland, and with them, a mass of white-hot steel. Six brands Weland made, and six broke. The seventh, Eterne, he could not break. Nor can the strength of the Angrborn bend that blade, nor the fire of Grengarm draw its temper. It is haunted, and commands the ghosts who bore it." She stopped to look into my eyes. "I have done an ill thing, perhaps, by telling you."

"I'll get it," I told her, "if you'll let me go after it."

Slowly, she nodded.

Just the thought of it had grabbed me the way nothing else

ever has except Disiri herself, and I said, "Then I'll get it or die trying."

"I know. You will try to wrest it from the dragon. Suppose I were to beg you not to."

"Then I wouldn't."

"Is that true?" She bent over me.

"As true as I can make it."

"Just so." She sighed. "You would be a lesser man after that, and your love would mean little to me."

I looked up, crazy with hope. "Does it mean a lot now?"

"More than you can know, Able. Seek Eterne, but never forget me wholly."

"I couldn't."

"So men say, yet many have forsaken me. When the wind moans in the chimney, O my lover, go into the wood. There you will find me crying for the lovers I have lost."

Trembling, the boy Toug came forward. "Don't send him after that sword, Aelfqueen."

Disiri laughed. "You fear he will make you go too?"

Toug shook his head. "I'm afraid he won't let me come."

"Listen to that! Will you, Able?"

"No," I said. "When we get out of here, I'm going to send him back to his mother."

"See?" Toug reached toward Disiri, though he did not dare touch her.

"More than both of you together." She straightened up. "Will you obey, Able?"

"In anything. I swear."

"In that case I have things to say to this boy, though he will have nothing to say to me. You need not fear he will return a man. There will be no such transformation." She raised her sword and struck my shoulders with the flat of its blade, surprising me. "Arise, Sir Able, my own true knight!"

A step or two, and she had vanished among tall ferns as green as she; like a dog too fearful to disobey, Toug hurried after her and vanished too.

I waited, not at all sure either would come back. The time passed slowly, and I found out that my new, big body was tired enough to die. I sat, walked up and down, and sat again. For a while, I tried to find two trees of the same kind. All were large and all were very old, for Aelfrice (as I know now) is not a place in which trees are felled. Each had its own manner of growth, and leaves of its own color and shape. I found one with pink bark and another whose bark was purple; white bark, both smooth and rough, was common among them. Leaves were red, and yellow, a hundred shades of green, and one tree was leafless, having green bark in place of leaves, bark that hung loose in folds and drapes so that it got more exposure to the light. Since that time alone in a forest of Aelfrice, it has always seemed to me that the spiny orange must have come from there, as I said earlier, its seed carried by an Aelf or more probably by some other human being as forlorn as I was, returning to his own world. However that may be, I took the last of my seeds from the pouch at my belt and planted it in a glade I found, a place of silence and surpassing beauty. Whether it sprouted and took root, I cannot say.

In that glade, I paused at my planting to look up, and saw the comings and goings of men, women, children, and many animals—not each step each took, but the greater movements of their days. A man plowed a field while I blinked, and returned home tired, and chancing to look in through his own window, saw the love his wife gave another. Too exhausted to be angry, he feigned not to have seen and sat by her fire, and when his wife hurried out, looking like a dirty bed and full of lies, he asked for his supper and kept quiet.

As I finished planting the seed, I thought about that, and it seemed to me that the things I had seen in the sky of Aelfrice were like the things my bowstring showed in dreams; I had unstrung my bow the way you do, but I strung it again and held it up so I could study my string against that sky, but Parka's little string vanished into the great gray sky, so that I could not make out its line. I did not understand that then and do not understand it now, but it is what I saw.

When I had tamped earth over the seed, I would have gone back to the spot where Disiri had left me if I could. Unable to find it, I wandered in circles—or at least in what I hoped were circles—looking for it. Soon it seemed to me that the air got darker with every step I took. I found a sheltered spot, lay down to rest, and slept.

I woke from terrible dreams of death to the music of wolves. Bow in hand, I made my way among the trees, then paused to shout "Disiri!"

At once an answering voice called, *"Here! Here!"*

I hurried toward it, feeling my way with my bow, entered a starlit clearing, and was embraced with one arm by a woman who clasped an infant in the other, a little woman who rushed to me weeping. "Vali? Aren't you Vali?" And then, "I'm so sorry! Did Seaxneat send you?"

It was a moment before I understood. When I did I said, "A gallant knight sent me to find you, Disira. His name is Sir Ravd, and he was concerned for you. So am I, if you are out here alone."

"All alone except for Ossar," she told me, and held her baby up so I could see him.

"Seaxneat told you to hide in this forest?"

She nodded, and cried.

"Did he say why?"

She shook he head violently. "Only to hide. So I hid and hid, all day and all night. There was nothing to eat, and after the first day I wanted to go back, but—"

"I understand." I took her elbow as gently as I could and led her forward, although I had no idea where we were or where we might be going. "You tried to find your way back to Glennidam and got lost."

"Y-yes." A wolf howled as she spoke, and she shuddered.

"You don't have to be afraid of them. They're after fawns, and the new calves of the forest cattle. They won't dare attack as long as I'm with you. I'm a knight too. I'm Sir Able."

She huddled closer.

At dawn we found a path, and in the first long beams of the rising sun I recognized it. "We're not far from Bold Berthold's hut," I told Disira. "We'll go there, and even if Bold Berthold has nothing for us, you and Ossar can sit by his fire while I hunt." Looking down at Ossar, I saw he was at her breast, and asked if she had milk.

"Yes, but I don't know if it will last. I'm awfully thirsty and I haven't eaten. Just some gooseberries."

We both drank deep at the crossing of the Griffin, and I shot a deer not a hundred strides after it, and merrily we came to Bold Berthold's hut.

He welcomed us and said he had thought, because of the wound that he had gotten from the Angrborn, that I was much too young to be his brother. Now he was glad to see I was as old as I ought to be, and bigger than I ought to be, too (I was much larger than he was), and felt sure he was getting well at last.

There was mead and venison (that some people would call tough, although we did not), and the last hoarded nuts to crack. Bold Berthold played with little Ossar, and talked about how life had been when his brother was no bigger than Ossar, and he himself (as he put it) only a stripling.

In the morning Disira begged to stay one more day; she was exhausted; her feet still hurt; and I, knowing how long our return to Glennidam was likely to be, said it would be all right.

I made myself new arrows that day, four for which I already had steel heads, and four more that I hoped to get heads for from the smith in her village. We slept under deerskins at Bold Berthold's, and she crept under mine that night when Ossar and Bold Berthold were asleep. I did not betray Disiri, although I know Disira expected me to; but I put my arms around her and kissed her once or twice. That was what she wanted mostly: to be loved by somebody strong who would not hurt her.

Next day we stayed too, because I wanted to try my new arrows and hoped to get something Bold Berthold could eat when we were gone. The day after that we did not go because it rained. As we sat around the fire, singing all the songs we knew and talking when we felt like it, I said something about your mother and mine, Ben, and Bold Berthold hugged me and cried. I had already started to wonder if America had ever been real and not trust the life I remembered there with you (school and the cabin, my Mac and all that) and this made it worse. I lay down, and to tell the truth I pretended I was asleep, wondering if I was not really Bold Berthold's brother Able.

I was almost asleep when I heard Disira say, "I was all alone out there, and he came from nowhere, calling me. He'd been with the Queen of the Wood. That's what he said."

Bold Berthold muttered, "Aye?"

"He calls himself a knight, but his bowstring talks to him

in the dark, and he talks while he's sleeping. He's really a wizard, isn't he? A mighty wizard. I see it every time I look into his face."

"He's a man like I was once," Bold Berthold said, "and better than I was, and my brother. Go to sleep."

So we slept, all four of us, until I woke up thinking that Disiri had called me. I got up as quietly as I could, slipped out, and wandered through the rain and the mist calling for her. I saw strange faces peer up at me from the swirling waters of the Griffin and from a dozen ring-marked forest pools. More peeped from behind bushes or looked down from the leaves of trees—faces that might have come in a flying saucer, green, brown, black, or fiery. Glass faces too, and faces whiter than snow. Once I nearly shot a brown doe that got all smoky and turned into a long-legged girl; and many times I heard the howls of wolves, and once the nearer baying of something that was never a wolf.

But Disiri, the green woman I love, I never found.

CHAPTER 10

FROST

Days had passed while Toug and I had knelt in Aelfrice. Now weeks slipped by while Disira, her baby, and I remained with Bold Berthold. I hunted and he trapped, for he was clever at making snares. Disira swept and cleaned, skinned the game we got, stretched and tanned the hides, cooked, and played with Ossar. We were not husband and wife; but I might have had her, I think, at any time; and no passerby (had there been any) would have guessed that we were not.

Seaxneat had treated her badly and had beaten her more than once while she was carrying their child, so that she had been in terror of a miscarriage. Moreover, he had been in league with the outlaws, just as Ravd had been told; and the longer she was separated from him, the less eager she was to go back to him. I learned a whole lot about them just by listening to her, for she knew much more than she believed she knew. I hoped for an opportunity to tell Ravd all that I had learned, though I never saw him and had no way of knowing whether he and Svon were nearby or back in his beloved manor of Redhall.

There came a morning—fine and sunny—on which the air was touched with something new. As I prowled the wood, a leaf, a single leaf, the broad leaf of a maple, fell at my feet. I picked it up (I still remember this very clearly) and examined it, and though largely green it was touched with red and gold. Summer was over; fall had come, and it would have been foolish not to plan for it.

First came the need to store food, and if we could, to buy more. We could take our hides to Irringsmouth this time. The trip would be longer, but we might get a better price, and might not be cheated. We could buy flour, salt, and hard bread, cheese and dried beans there, but we would need more meat to smoke, and more hides to sell. The nuts would ripen soon—beechnuts, chestnuts, and walnuts. Bold Berthold had taught me that we could even eat acorns if they were properly prepared, and it would be smart to lay in as many nuts of all kinds as we could manage.

Second, Disira. If she wanted to go back to Glennidam at all, she would have to do it now. Traveling with a baby would be hard enough; traveling with one in winter . . .

I began to hunt in the direction of Glennidam, something I did not do very often, telling myself it would serve two purposes. If I got game, well and good; but even if I did not, I would refresh my memory on the paths and turnings. I was near the Irring when I saw a head with a face that looked almost human above some little trees. Its glaring eyes swept over me, leaving me paralyzed—too frightened to run and too frightened to hide.

In half a minute, the whole monster came into view. I am going to have to talk about the Angrborn a lot, so let me describe this one to stand for his whole tribe. Imagine the most heavily built man you can, a man with big feet and thick ankles, massive legs, and broad hips. A great swag belly, a barrel chest, and enormous shoulders. (Idnn perched on King Gilling's shoulder the way she might have sat on a bench; of course Idnn was a bit under average size.) Top the shoulders with a head too big for them. Close-set eyes too big for the sweating face—eyes so light-colored they seemed to have no color at all, with pupils so tiny I could not see them. A big splayed nose with nostrils you could have shoved both your fists in, a ragged beard that had never been trimmed or even washed, and a mouth from ear to ear. Stained tusks too big and crooked for the thin black lips to cover.

When you have imagined a man like that and fixed his appearance in your mind, take away his humanity. Crocodiles are not any less human than the Angrborn. They are never loved, neither by us, nor by their own kind, nor by any animal. Disiri probably knows what it is in people, in Aelf, in dogs and horses, and even houses, manors, and castles that makes it possible for somebody to love them; but whatever it is, it is not in the Angrborn and they know it. I think that was why Thiazi built the room I will tell you about later.

Now that you have stripped all humanity away from the

figure you thought of as a man, replacing it with nothing at all, imagine it far larger than the biggest man you have ever seen, so big that a tall man riding a large horse comes no higher than its waist. Think about the stink of him, and the great, slow thudding steps, steps that shake the ground and eat up whole miles the way yours take you from our door to the corner.

When you have thought of all that, you ought to have a picture of the Angrborn that will do for the rest of the things I have to tell you; but remember that it is not quite true—that the Angrborn have claws instead of fingernails and ears too big for their heads—that their hands and arms, backs, chests, and legs are covered with hair the color of new rope, and that in the flesh they are worse than any picture could show.

As soon as I could, I ran. I ought to have put a couple arrows in its eyes. I know that now, but I did not know it then, and seeing it the way I had, with no warning, was a jolt. I do not think I ever really believed Bold Berthold the way I should have. No matter what he said about them, I kept thinking of them as about eight feet tall; but Hela was as big as that, and her brother was a head taller than she was. They were half-breeds, and real Angrborn call people like that Mice. Hela was not all that bad-looking, either, once I got used to her size.

I smelled the smoke before I ever saw the place where Bold Berthold's hut had been. It was the smell of burned leather, a lot different from wood smoke. As soon as I got wind of it, I knew I was too late. I had come to tell him that there were Angrborn around, and I was going to try to get him to hide, and going to hide Disira and her baby in a place I knew where there were big thornbushes all around. But when I smelled burning leather, I thought the Angrborn had been there already.

After that I found some footprints and knew it had not been Angrborn after all. They were human-sized, made by feet in boots—feet turned in, for one pair. After that I heard Ossar crying. I looked for him and found his mother. Dead, she was still holding him. I never found out why Seaxneat had not killed him too. He had hit Disira in the head with a war-ax and left his little son there to die, but he had not killed him. I suppose he lacked the courage; people can be funny like that.

I had to pry Ossar out of her hands, and I kept saying, "You have to let him go now, Disira." I knew it did no good, but I kept saying it just the same. I can be funny too, I guess. "You have to let him go." I tried to keep my eyes on her hands, and not look at her face.

Right after that, Ossar and I found the place where Bold Berthold's hut had been. They had taken what they wanted and burned the rest, a circle of smoking ash in the wild violets that had stopped blooming while it was still spring.

I took off Ossar's diaper and cleaned him up as well as I could with river water, and wrapped him in a deerskin that had only burned at one edge. I looked everywhere for Bold Berthold's body, but I never found it. I wanted to bury Disira, but there was nothing to dig with. Eventually I cut a big stick and whittled it flat at the wide end. There was a stub I could put my foot on, and I dug a shallow little grave down by the Griffin with that, and covered her up, and piled stones from the river on her. I made a little cross by tying two sticks together to mark the grave. It is probably the only grave marked with a cross in Mythgarthr.

It was pretty late by then, but I started for Glennidam anyway. I had nothing but water to give little Ossar, and I knew I had to get him to somebody who had cow's milk or goat's milk in a hurry; besides, I thought I might find Bold

Berthold in Glennidam. I wanted to find Seaxneat, too, and kill him. That night, when it was so dark we had to stop, I heard something that was not a wolf howling at the moon. I knew it wasn't a wolf and I knew it was big, but I had no idea then what it was.

Here is something I cannot explain. I am tempted to leave it out altogether; but if I leave out everything I cannot explain I will be leaving out so much you will get no idea of what it is like here, or what my life has been like since I came here. One was the doe. I saw a doe and a fawn the next day, and I was hungry and I knew I had better get some meat and cook it—for me, because I was getting weak, and so I could chew some up good and give it to little Ossar before he starved to death. He had not had anything but water since his father killed his mother. So when I saw the doe I knew that I ought to shoot her or the fawn, but I remembered the brown girl, and somehow I knew this was her again, and I could not do it. I found blackberries instead, and mashed them, and gave them to Ossar; but he spit them up.

I had been hoping to get to Glennidam before night. We did not, and I think I knew we would not. Glennidam was an easy two days from where Bold Berthold's hut had been, but I had not had two days, only three or four hours the first day, and a day after that, and Ossar had slowed me down. So we camped again, and I could see he was getting weak. I was, too, a little, and although I had eaten all the blackberries I could find, I was hungry enough to eat bark. I wanted to go out looking for something to eat; but I knew it was a waste of time in the dark, and the best thing for us to do was sleep if we could and hope no bear or wolf found us, and get to Glennidam as fast as we could in the morning.

CHAPTER 11

GYLF

"Sir Able?"

I sat up, suddenly wide awake, shivered, and rubbed my eyes. A north wind was in the treetops, and there was a full moon that seemed almost as bright as the sun, with no warmth at all in it. I stared up at it the way you do sometimes, and I thought I saw a castle floating in front of it, a castle with walls and towers sticking up out of all six sides, merloned walls and pointed towers with long, dark pennants streaming from them.

This is something else I cannot explain, although I did it myself. Disira was dead, Ossar was likely to die, and Bold Berthold was gone; and all that hit me then, harder than it ever had before. I did not know who owned that castle that had brought me here, or why I ought to ask for anything from him. But I raised my arms and shouted for justice, not just once, but maybe twenty times.

And when I finally stopped and put some more wood on our little fire, I heard somebody say, *"Sir Able?"*

There was nobody there but Ossar, and Ossar was too young to talk, starved and worn out and sound asleep. I picked him up and told him we were leaving, night or not. With the moon as bright as it was, I knew I could follow the path, and maybe three or four more hours would get us to Glennidam.

Just as we started out, a little voice right behind me said, "Sir Able?"

I turned as fast as I could. Getting big as suddenly as I had made me clumsy, and I still was not entirely over that. I was pretty fast just the same, and there was nobody.

"There is a lamb."

This time I did not look.

"There's a lamb," repeated the little voice. It sounded as if he were right in back of me.

"Please," I said. "If you're afraid of me, I won't hurt you. If you want to hurt me, just don't hurt the baby."

"Upstream? A wolf dropped it, and we thought . . . We hope . . ."

I was trotting upstream already, with my bow in one hand and Ossar in the other. I found the wolf first, just about tripping over it in spite of the moonlight. If there was an arrow in it, I couldn't see it. I laid Ossar down and felt around. No arrow, but its throat was torn. Hoping that the person who had told me about it had come with me, I said, "We could eat this, but the lamb would be better. Where is it?"

There was no reply.

I picked up Ossar, stood up, and started looking for it. It was only a dozen steps away, just harder to see than the wolf because it was smaller. I put it behind my neck the way I did when I killed a deer, and carried it back to our fire. That had almost gone out, and by the time I had built it back up and skinned the lamb, the sky was getting light.

"There is something we have to give you."

Without looking around, I said, "You've already given me a lot."

"He is rather large." The speaker coughed. "But not valuable. I do not mean *valuable*. Well, he *is*, but not like gold. Or jewels. Nothing like that."

I repeated that he did not have to give me anything.

"Not only me. All of us, our whole clan. I am our spokesman."

A new voice said, "And I am our spokeswoman."

"Nobody appointed you," the first protested.

"I did. We want to make it plain that it is not only the Woodwives, just as it is not only the Woodwives in the wood. We are in this too, along with them, and we are *not* powerless."

"Well said!"

"Thank you. Not powerless no matter what anybody says. We do not have to hide, either."

"Be careful!"

"He has seen me twice, and he did not shoot either time, so what are we frightened of?"

"Suppose he does not like it?"

"He is too polite to give it back."

"Well, it *is* of the best breeding. A whelp from the Valfather's own pack."

I froze. "What can you tell me about him?"

"Nothing!" (That was the male voice I had first heard.)

"Nothing at all, really." (This was the female voice.) "You know much more about him than we do. A lot of you think him the Most High God."

"Thus they know less. We cannot remain after sunrise, you know."

I said, "Bold Berthold says he's master of the flying castle, and it's in Skai."

"Really?"

"We have never seen it." The male speaker cleared his throat. "Besides, we wish not to talk about it. Here, Gylf! Here boy!"

"What do you want to do? Hide behind him?"

"If necessary, yes. Sit! Good boy!"

I said, "May I look around? I won't hurt anyone."

"Did I not say you could?"

She was tall, so slender she seemed like a collection of flexible sticks about the color of milk chocolate. He was a lot shorter, brown too, with an enormous nose and beady eyes; but at first I did not see him all because of the dog.

It was the biggest dog I ever saw, very dark brown with a white blaze on its big chest, and smiling. You know how dogs smile? It had soft ears that hung down, a head as big as a bull's, I-can-take-care-of-myself eyes, and a mouth I could have put my whole head in.

"This is Gylf." For a minute I thought the dog was talking, but it was the male voice coming from behind him.

The brown woman said, "He is a puppy, really."

"But he can—you know."

"Would you like us to take care of the baby?"

"We will have time on our hands now, you know." The owner of the male voice peeped cautiously around Gylf as he spoke. He was terribly ugly. "It is not as if we have never raised your children before."

"*I* will do the work," the brown woman said, "and *he* will take the credit."

"The sun will be up any moment."

I said, "You'll feed him? And—and . . . ?"

"Educate him," the brown woman said firmly. "You shall see."

"Only not soon. He will be in Aelfrice."

"Well, so will he!"

I wish I could say why his saying that made me decide, but it did. Partly I was thinking that if I left Ossar in Glennidam Seaxneat might kill him when I was gone. Partly I was thinking of something I could not remember, something I knew even if I could not remember it. "Take him!" I said.

She did, cradling him in her arms and crooning to him.

Immediately both Aelf began backing away. Instead of sloping up, the riverbank was sloping down, and they went down that slope into a mist. "Have no fear," the brown woman called, "I will teach him all about you."

"About Gylf," the owner of the male voice said, "it happens all the time. After a storm, someone finds such whelps."

"As we did," the brown woman added.

"But they are his."

"We are to take care of them until he whistles."

"Which we have. . . ."

They were gone and little Ossar with them, and the riverbank sloped up normally again.

I was looking at the dog, I suppose because there was nothing else left to look at. "Those were Bodachan, weren't they? Earth Aelf?"

He seemed to nod, and I grinned at him. "Well, I'm an earthman. See how brown my arms are? It shouldn't be too much of a change for you."

He nodded again, this time unmistakably, and I said, "You're a real smart dog, aren't you?"

He nodded and smiled.

"Were you really the Valfather's? I think that's what they said."

He nodded the same way he had before.

"I see. Somebody's trained you to nod when you hear a question. Is there any question that wouldn't make you nod?"

As I expected, he nodded to that too. He also looked inquiringly at the lamb I had skinned, and then back at me, cocking his head.

"You're right, I ought to cook that. I'll give you some meat, and all the bones, okay?"

Of course he nodded.

In a few minutes more I had a whole leg-of-lamb roasting on a pointed stick. It was not until I smelled it that I found out how hungry I was. My mouth watered, and it seemed to me I had never smelled anything as good as it was going to be.

The dog came closer, lying down next to me. I said, "Gylf? Is that your name?"

He nodded as if he had understood every word.

"You're a hunting dog, or that's what it sounded like. What do you hunt?"

He nuzzled me as if to say *you.*

"What? Me? Really?"

He nodded.

"You're putting me on!"

Eyeing the sizzling meat, he licked his lips. His tongue was Day-Glo pink in the firelight, and about as wide as my hand.

"I'll give you some, but we'll both have to wait before we eat any. It'll be very hot." I took it from the fire while I was talking to him; you can cook meat more if it needs it, but if you cook it too much, you cannot cook it less. When it was clear of the fire, I petted the big dog that had become mine so fast. His flat brown coat was soft, and thicker than it looked. "You'll be nice to sleep with on cold nights," I told him.

He nodded and licked my knee. Big as it was and rough as it was, his tongue was warm and friendly.

"When we're through eating, we'll go to Glennidam. I want to find Seaxneat and kill him, if I can. Besides, Toug may be back home by now. I hope so. We'll see about that. If you stay with me, you're my dog 'til the Valfather comes for you. If you don't you're not, but I wish you luck just the same."

I touched the meat, and licked my fingers, then waved it around on its stick to cool it. "Are you as hungry as I am?"

He nodded, and I noticed he was drooling quite a bit.

"You know, I've been wondering what killed that wolf. That was dumb of me, with the answer lying right next to me. It was you. You don't have to nod, Gylf. I know it was."

He nodded anyway.

"Then you left the lamb for me, instead of eating it yourself. Maybe the brown girl had something to do with it, but it was nice of you anyhow." I tore the lower part of the lamb's leg from the upper and gave it to him.

He held it down with his forepaws, the way dogs do, and tore it with teeth that would have surprised me in a lion's mouth. Seeing them, I wondered why the wolf had not dropped the lamb and run. "Well, how is it?" I asked him.

And he grunted, "Good!"

CHAPTER 12

OLD MAN TOUG

Glennidam looked just about the same. There was a kid in the street who tried to beat it when he saw Gylf and me, but Gylf headed him off and I caught him. "Is your name Ve?"

He looked scared and shook his head. He was quite a bit younger than I used to be, if you know what I mean.

"You know him, though."

He nodded, although I could see he did not want to.

"Don't gape at me. You've seen strangers before."

"Not nobody big as you."

"My name's Sir Able," I told him, "and you and me will get along much better of you use it. Say, yes, Sir Able."

"Yes, Sir Able."

"Thanks. I want you to find Ve for me. Tell him I'll be at Toug's house, and I've got to talk to him."

Gylf sniffed the kid's face, and he shook like Jell-O.

"Tell him I'm no enemy. I'm not going to hurt him, and neither is my dog here." I let him go. "Now go find him and tell him what I told you."

"I, um—uh . . ." the kid said, then he managed to add something more that might have been, "Sir Able."

"Out with it, if it's important. If it isn't, find Ve and tell him."

The kid touched his chest with a grimy finger and bobbed his head.

"You *are* Ve."

"Y-y-y . . ."

I made him come with me, saying I wanted to talk to him and Ulfa together.

The house was right down the street. I rapped the door with my bow and grabbed the father by the front of his dirty shirt when he answered it, shook him as I pushed him in, and ducked under the lintel. "Where's your daughter?"

She must have heard me, because she looked in from one of the little rooms in back.

I wished her good morning. "Get your mother, please, and both of you sit down."

Her father's hand was flirting with the hilt of a big knife. I saw it and shook him hard. "If you pull that, I'll kill you."

He scowled, and I was tempted to knock him down again; I shoved him down on a bench in front of the fire instead. I made Ve sit with him, and got Ulfa and her mother on a couple of stools.

"Now then." I sat on the table. "Ulfa, I took your brother with me the last time I was here. Maybe your father told you."

She nodded, looking scared.

"I don't have him anymore. Disiri took him. I doubt that she's going to hurt him, but I have no idea how long she'll keep him. She didn't say what she wanted with him. You may see him again today. You may never see him again, and I have no way of telling which way it might go. If I see her, I'll ask about him. That's all I can do."

I waited for one of them to talk, stroking Gylf's head but keeping my eyes on them. After a minute or two, I said, "I'm sure all of you have questions. Probably I can't answer them. But I'll listen, and answer if I can. Ulfa?"

Her chin went up. "How long was he with you?"

"Less than a day. We were in Aelfrice for part of it, and it's not easy to tell how long things take there, but a little less than a day should be about right."

"Did you hurt him?"

"I twisted his arms enough to make him squeal once when he wouldn't obey, but I did no permanent damage. Neither did anybody else while we were together." I took a long look at Ulfa's mother and decided she was not the kind to speak to a scary stranger.

Her husband said, "He's in Aelfrice?"

"I don't know where he is. That's where he was the last time I saw him. He may have come back here—to this world or planet or whatever you call it. I don't know." As you can see, I was thinking then that Mythgarthr was probably not just some other country. For one thing, nobody called the country Mythgarthr—the country was Celidon. Another thing was that I was pretty sure that other countries on Earth did not have Aelf. I felt like I would have heard about them.

But there was a lot against that idea, too. One was that the moon in Mythgarthr looked exactly like ours, and if the stars were different, I could not tell it. The Big Dipper was still there, and the North Star, and some other things I was really sure of.

About then, Ulfa said, "You let Disiri take him." It was not a question.

"I wouldn't have stopped her if I could," I told Ulfa, "and I couldn't if I'd wanted to. Yeah, I let her take him."

"Will you try to get him back? He's my brother."

"If I can, sure. Now I've got questions of my own for all of you. Is Seaxneat here? By here, I mean here in this village or near it, right now."

Ulfa's father shook his head. "Out lookin' for his wife."

"He found her. That's why I'm here."

Ulfa said, "What happened?" very softly. I think she guessed.

"I'll tell you in a minute. First I want to tell you about Ossar. I want to tell you—that's Ulfa and Ve—particularly. Ossar's in Aelfrice too, and I put him there, or I pretty much did. I left him with the Bodachan, the little brown Aelf. My brother" (that was what I said) "used to help them sometimes, and they used to help him. He said they were nice and pretty harmless unless you got them mad. Anyway, they wanted Ossar and said they'd take care of him, and I had no milk to give him and no food he'd keep down. So I gave him to them."

Nobody said anything.

"Time goes slower in Aelfrice, so he might show up again in twenty years, still a little kid. It could happen. If it does, I want you to remember that he's Disira's son just the same, and look after him." I made all four of them promise they would.

Then I said, "Seaxneat killed Ossar's mother, and I'm going to kill Seaxneat for it if I can. But maybe I can't, and maybe he'll be here when Ossar comes back. Tell him Ossar's been nursed by the Aelf, and they're likely to get even for anything Seaxneat does to him. That may help. I hope so."

Ulfa's mother spoke. I think it was the only time she did. "By the queen who took my son?" she wanted to know. "By Disiri?"

I shook my head. "One of the Bodachan, I never learned her name. Ve, your dad sent you to get the outlaws the night I took Toug. It can't have taken you very long, since they were after us the same night. Where did you go?"

"You mean my father? I—I'm not supposed to say. Sir Able."

Ulfa's father rasped, "Tell him!"

I said, "I can get it out of your father if I have to, Ve, but I might have to hurt him. It'll save a whole lot of trouble for you both if you tell me now."

Ve gulped. "He's not here, Sir Able."

"Is he off looking for Seaxneat's wife too?"

"I d-don't know, Sir Able."

"But you know where he told you to go to find the outlaws. You'd better tell me."

Gylf growled, and Ulfa's father got Ve's arm. "Your father's away," he told Ve, "and I'm here in his place. I say to tell him. It's on my head, not yours."

"To the c-cave. The big cave."

I nodded. "I see. Do they stay there often?"

"S-some do, Sir Able. One of the Free Companies."

"Where is it?"

"Th-that way." Ve pointed. "You t-take the path to the little pond and go 'round it through the b-beeches, only turn at the big stump—"

Ulfa's father said, "I'll show you."

It took me by surprise.

"You'd make the boy do it, and maybe get him kilt. With me there'll be two men, if they're there."

Gylf growled again, louder this time.

"Dog thinks I might turn on you," Ulfa's father said. "Maybe he will, but I won't."

I thought about that. "You sent Ve for the outlaws when I was here before."

He shook his head. "Vali did. Not me. I wanted to kill you myself." He paused to stare at the floor, then looked up to meet my eyes. "If I'd of believed you was a real knight, it'd of been different. Only I didn't and thought me and my boy could do for you, and with Vali we could do it sure. Only he wanted to fetch Jer's Free Company and sent his boy, and I didn't stop him."

"You don't like them?"

Ulfa's father shook his head.

Ulfa started to speak, but I raised a hand to silence her. "What's your name?"

"Toug. Same as my boy."

"That's right, I remember now. What is it, Ulfa?"

She said, "They make a lot of trouble, and take anything they want. Sometimes they trade with us, and sometimes they give us things, but it's mostly Seaxneat, the trading and the giving, too."

Old man Toug added, "Vali'd like to be him."

"I see." I was still studying him, and wishing I could see under that black beard. "How many outlaws will there be in the cave, assuming they're still there?"

He shrugged. "Five, could be. Could be ten."

I asked Ve how many there had been when he went to fetch them.

"S-seven, Sir Able."

"Will you run to warn them as soon as we leave? You look fast, and you know the way. You may get there before we do."

"No, S-Sir Able. Not unless you say t-to."

"I can't risk it. Ulfa, you and your mother will have to hold him here. Two hours should be enough. Will you do it?"

Ulfa's mother nodded. Ulfa herself said, "I'll do it for your sake, Sir Able, as well as my father's."

He stood up. "We can be there in a hour or not much over. You broke my bill."

I nodded.

"I still got my spear, though, and my knife. All right if I take 'em?"

I said yes, and he went into one of the back rooms and returned with the spear his son, Toug, had dropped when he ran from the fight.

Ulfa said, "Tell us what happened to Disira."

"Don't matter," old man Toug muttered. "Dead now."

"Well, Pa, I'd like to know, and Sir Able said he'd tell us."

I nodded. "Your brother and I went to Aelfrice, as I said earlier. Disiri took him, and I returned alone. I wanted to find Disiri again, and called her name. Disira answered, thinking I had been sent to search for her. She and Ossar had been hiding in the woods, probably for the second time and maybe more than that. She was hungry and worn out, scared, and lost. I should have taken her back here, but I didn't. For one thing, Bold Berthold's was closer and I thought I could get her something to eat there. For another, the outlaws had been after Toug and me. It seemed to me that there was more risk of their finding me here than at Bold Berthold's hut."

I stroked Gylf's head and waited for one of them to speak until Ulfa said, "I understand. Go on."

"She and Ossar stayed there with Bold Berthold and me.

She was afraid of Seaxneat. He had treated her badly, and I believe she thought he might hurt Ossar when they came home. A couple of days ago, I went out to hunt and saw one of the Angrborn—"

Old man Toug said, "Where?"

"By the river, quite a way upstream. I thought I ought to warn Bold Berthold and Disira, so I went back to the hut. It had been burned, and at first I thought the Angrborn had done it. I found footprints made by men our size, though. One had walked with his toes turned in. I thought that was Seaxneat, and I still do. I heard Ossar crying, and found Disira's body—she'd been hit with an ax. That's easy to say, easy for me to talk about in here, where I don't have to see her. But it was pretty horrible. I didn't like to look at it, and I don't like to think about it."

Ve whispered something to Ulfa. She nodded and said, "He's afraid to ask you, but he'd like to know why you took Disira to a hut, if you're a knight. Aren't you supposed to have a big house?"

"Because I'm not a wealthy one," I told Ve. "Not yet, anyhow. But I'm a slow one, sometimes, and way too fond of talking, which isn't the way a true knight ought to be." I put my hand on old man Toug's shoulder. "Not so long ago you wanted to kill me."

He nodded reluctantly.

"I broke your bill, and could have killed you with the head of it. I didn't."

"I 'preciate that."

"You say you want to be my follower. I'll be loyal to you as long as you're loyal to me, but no longer."

He nodded. "I got it."

We left after that, I motioning for him to come with us.

CHAPTER 13

CAESURA

Side by side we went down the village street, through fields, and into the forest; and Gylf trotted ahead of us, exploring every thicket and clump of brush before we reached it. Soon the path narrowed, and I went before old man Toug with an arrow at the nock; but even then, Gylf ranged ahead of me. Near Glennidam the trees were small and mean, the better ones having been cut for lumber and firewood. Farther on, they were bigger and older, though there were still stumps where men had felled them for timber. Beyond those lay the true forest, the mighty wood that stretches for hundreds of miles between the Mountains of the Sun and the sea, and between the Mountains of the North and the southern plowlands—trees that had been old when no man had walked among them, trees thicker through than the biggest house in Irringsmouth, trees that push their pleasant green heads into Skai and nod politely to the Overcyns.

Springs well from their roots, for in their quest for water those roots crack rocks deeper than the deepest well. Wildflowers, small ones so delicate you cannot see them without loving them, grow around the springs. The north sides of the trunks are covered with shining green moss thicker than bear fur. Every time I saw it I thought of Disiri and wished she was with us, but my wishing did not bring her, not there or anyplace else, ever.

To tell the truth, I was afraid I was going to choke up, so I said, "Now I see how it is that the air in Aelfrice seems full of light. This air looks full of light too."

"Ah," said old man Toug, "this what Aelfrice's like?"

"No," I said. "Aelfrice is much more wonderful. The trees are bigger and of incredible kinds, strange, dangerous, or welcoming. The air doesn't just seem to shine, it really does."

"My boy can tell me 'bout it, maybe, if I get him back."

I asked whether he had given his son his name because he wanted his son to be like him, or because he wanted to be a boy again; and now I cannot help wondering what he thought of the young knight who came back to him wounded, and what each said to the other.

Not long after that, a white stag, already in antler, darted across the path; Gylf did not bay on its track, nor did I loose an arrow. We both felt, I would say, that it was not a stag to be hunted.

"Cloud buck," said old man Toug.

"What do you mean by that?"

"What they call 'em," said old man Toug, and nothing more.

The land rose and fell, gently at first as it does in the downs, then more abruptly, making hills like those among which I found Disiri. The trees sank their roots in such stone as a dog, a boy, and a man might walk upon.

At last we climbed a hill higher than any we had seen before, and its crest was bald except for wisps of grass; from its top I could make out, to the north, peaks white with snow. "Not far now," old man Toug told me.

Gylf whined, and looked back at me. I knew he wanted to talk, but would not talk as long as old man Toug was with me; so I told old man Toug to go forward until he could no longer see us, then wait until we caught up with him. Naturally he wanted to know why, but I told him to do it or return to his wife and daughter, and he did it.

"They know," Gylf cautioned me.

"The outlaws?"

He nodded.

"How do you know that?" I asked him.

"Smell it."

Thinking about what he said, I remembered your telling me dogs could smell fear. I asked Gylf if they were afraid, and he nodded again.

"How did they find out we were coming?"

He did not answer; as I got to know him better, I came to understand that it was the way he generally reacted when he did not know the answer to a question (or thought the question foolish). Probably they had lookouts. I would have, if I had been their captain.

"Thought you wouldn't catch up," old man Toug said when we overtook him.

I told him we had wanted to see whether he would tell the outlaws about us.

"You and the dog did?"

I nodded.

"Kill it straight off, they will."

"I suppose you're right, if he finds them before we do."

"I seen a knight once that had one of them shirts of iron rings for his dog, even."

"I'll try to get one for Gylf, if he wants one," I said, "but from here on I want you to stay back with him, and make him stay back with you. I'll go first."

"You only got eight arrows. I counted 'em."

I asked how many he had and ordered him to stay well in back of me. After that, I told Gylf to keep back and to keep old man Toug with him.

* * *

Until now, I have been recounting what I did and what others did, and reconstructing what we said. Now I think I had better call a halt to that, and explain how I felt then and later, and why I did what I did. I have been a general, sort of, and I can tell you that good generals march hard, but they do not march night and day. There is a time for marching, but also a time for halting and making camp.

I went forward alone, as I told you, with my bow strung and an arrow already on the string, listening to the murmur of the many, many lives that made up that string—to the noise of the people, if I can say it like that. To life. Those men, women, and children who made up Parka's string knew nothing about me, nothing about my spiny orange bow, nothing about the arrow they would send whistling at some outlaw; but they sensed all of it, I think, sensing that their lives had been drawn tight, and the battle was about to start. There was fear and excitement in their voices. They sat at their fires or did the work they did each day; but they sensed that there was going to be a battle, and how it came out would depend on them.

It was not much different for me. I knew that I would probably have to fight half a dozen men, and that they would have bows, too, with plenty of arrows, and swords, axes, and spears. If I turned right or left, I would save my life; and Gylf and the man with him would know nothing about it unless they turned too, because they would both die when they got to the outlaws. If I turned back, they would know but I would save their lives as well as mine. Saving the lives of the people with you is supposed to be the big thing, and killing the people who are trying to kill you (and them) does not really count.

I went forward anyway.

If you ever read this, you are going to say it was because of what Sir Ravd had said. You will be mostly right—that was a lot of it. I wanted to be a knight. I wanted to be a knight more than I ever wanted to make the team or make the honor roll. I do not mean that I only wanted to call myself a knight the way I had been doing, or make other people call me one. I wanted to be the real thing. There were a couple of people on our team who were there because we could not find anybody good. There was a person on the honor roll who was there because his whole idea was to be there. He took gut courses, and if he did not get an A, he went to the teacher and argued and begged and maybe threatened a little until she raised his grade. The rest of us knew it, and I did not want to be a knight like that. This was the big test. This was one behind in the ninth, two out, and a man on second. It was not the way I would have chosen if I could have chosen, but you never get to choose.

That was only the smallest part of it, though. Let me tell you the truth right here. I thought Bold Berthold was dead. I thought his body was someplace around where his hut had been and I just had not been able to find it. I might not have found Disira's if it had not been for Ossar, and there would not have been anything like that to tell me where Bold Berthold was. If I had been there, I might have run away when the outlaws came, and I might have tried to get Bold Berthold to run away too; but I knew Bold Berthold pretty well by that time, and he would not have done it.

The Angrborn had hurt him so much it seemed like he should be dead. He could not stand up straight. His hands shook, and sometimes it was so bad he could hardly feed himself. He could be kind of crazy, forgetting things that had happened a little while ago or remembering things that had never happened. He had been so sure I really was his brother Able that I had to answer to his name, and sometimes he had almost made me think it was true—and he thought I was still Able when I came back older-looking and bigger than he was.

All that was true, and there was more; but you could not scare him. The outlaws could have killed him, and I thought probably they had, but they would have to. They would not have scared him, and he would have protected Disira and Ossar until he died.

So Bold Berthold was dead.

He had taken me in when I had no place to go. He had loved me like his brother, and taught me everything he knew—how to farm, how to handle cattle and horses and sheep. How to hunt, and how to set snares. How you fought with a spear if a spear was all you had, and how you fought with a club if a club was all you had. He had not known a lot about shooting a bow, but he had taught me what he knew about that, too, and he had understood when I practiced and practiced, and helped me every way he could. When you have to hit what you are aiming at if you want to eat, you get to be a pretty good shot pretty quickly. When you have got to hit it or somebody who loves you will not eat either, you learn all the other stuff: how to get in a little closer, how to miss that branch without missing the deer, and how to follow a wounded deer even when it seems like it is hardly bleeding at all, because sometimes they bleed inside.

How to guess where it will go before it decides itself. Once I had a wounded deer go to a hiding place where I was hiding already and get so close I could grab it and throw it down. I had learned all that fast, like I said, and I owed it to Bold Berthold, every bit of it. The guys who killed him were going to have to deal with me, and I was not old or sick.

There was Disira, too. I had never been in love with her. I loved Queen Disiri, always, and nobody else; and if you do not understand that, you will never understand all the things I am going to tell you at all, because that was always the main thing. Just about everything else changed as time went on. I made new friends and lost old ones. Sir Garvaon taught me how to use a sword, and Garsecg showed me how I could be stronger and quicker than I had ever known—quiet sometimes, or so fierce and wild that brave men who saw me ran. But that never changed. I loved Disiri and nobody else but Disiri, and there was never a minute in the whole time when I would not have died for her.

There was one other thing, and I am going to talk about it, too. I knew I was just a kid inside. Toug always did think that I was a man, even when I told him I was not. His father thought I was a man, too (and so did Ulfa), younger than he was, but a man, and I was a lot bigger. I knew it was not true, it was just something Disiri had done, and I was really a kid. There were a lot of times when I wanted to cry. That time when I was coming up on those outlaws and looking for men hiding behind rocks or up in the trees like Aelf with every step I took, that was one of them. There was another one when I really did cry, and I'll tell you about it in a minute. When you are a kid and you are in a tight place like I was you cannot ever admit it, because if you ever once admit it everything is going to come loose.

So I did not. I just kept going toward the big cave, one slow step at a time, and thinking, well, if they kill me they kill me and it will all be over.

But the main thing was still Disiri. That is how it has always been with me, all through going to Jotunland and the River Battle and everything that happened. I loved her and I wanted her so bad it tore me up.

If you do not understand about Disiri, it will not matter what you understand, because you will not understand a thing. The outlaws were between me and her, and anything that came between us was going to get shoved out of the way and stamped into the mud, and that was the way it always was, the whole time.

CHAPTER 14

THE BROKEN SWORD

I had told Gylf to keep way behind me, and I had told old man Toug to stay back, too; but neither of them were very good at it. The first thing I knew old man Toug was right beside me (and scaring me so much I just about put an arrow through him) trying to whisper something. And when I turned around to see what it was, Gylf sneaked past me, not making hardly any noise but going fast.

"See the black rock?" Old man Toug pointed with his spear. "When we get there, they'll see us if they're there, and we'll see them."

I pointed behind us. "You see that round rock off to one side?"

He nodded.

"You go back there and wait, or I'll take away your spear and stick it up your nose. Get going!"

He did, and I stood there and watched until he was all the way to it.

About then Gylf came back. He did not say anything, but I knew from the way he looked and the way he had come back so fast, that the outlaws were right up ahead. I made him get behind me, but he would not go back to the round rock. As soon as I started going forward again, he was right behind me.

Pretty soon something happened that I had not figured on at all. One of them stood up on a big rock maybe fifty paces ahead and asked who I was and did I want peace or a fight. I pulled the arrow back to my ear and let it go so fast he had no time to duck down. It got him in the chest and went right through, and he fell off his big rock.

I still had not seen the rest of them, but they had seen him, and I heard them yell. I ran to the black rock because it looked like I could climb it, and went right up it like a squirrel, scared half to death the whole time and thinking I was going to get an arrow in my back. When I got up on top I lay down flat, sort of hugging the rock.

They came around it, and it was not six or seven like we had been talking about, it was more like twenty. They saw old man Toug standing back there where I had told him to wait, and they went for him, shouting and waving spears and swords. He dropped his spear and ran like two hares, and I got up fast, shot the last one, and got two in front of him, all in a lot less time than it takes me to write the words. The last had a bow and a quiver, and when I saw the quiver I jumped.

It was a long jump. When I think back, I am surprised I did not break a leg, but I did not—just landed with my feet together and fell down. I got his arrows and put them in my own quiver with the ones that did not have heads, and I pulled my arrow out of the dirt and rocks and put the nock to the string. That arrow had blood on it, and the feathers did not look as nice as I would have liked, but the point had not bent and I knew it would still work.

I took back my other arrows, too. One of the men was still

alive, but I did not kill him. I could see he was going to die anyway and pretty quickly, and I left him where he lay. The first had not been Seaxneat, and neither of these were, either.

After that I followed the ones chasing old man Toug. I could still hear them yelling, so it was not hard. Pretty soon I found a man almost as big as I was with his head torn off. It was dead, but the fear was still on his face. He had been so scared when he died that I felt sorry for him, although I would have killed him myself.

Maybe I ought to talk about that. Where you are, people kill people all the time just like they do here. Then they talk like it was the worst thing in the world. Here it is murder that is bad, and fighting is just fighting. Our way, people do not feel bad about doing what they had to do; Sir Woddet killed so many Osterlings once that it made him sick for a long time, but killing Osterlings never did bother me. How can you feel bad about killing somebody who would cook and eat you? Killing outlaws never bothered me either.

When Gylf and I found old man Toug, they had hung him upside-down and were throwing their knives at him. I told Gylf to get around on the other side where he could get them if they ran. When he did, I started shooting. They rushed me, and I ran back almost to where the round rock was, and got up on another rock. I stood up straight then and waited for them to catch up, feeling Parka's string with my fingers. It seemed like it was no thicker than a thread—so thin it almost cut me; but it whispered beneath my fingers with a thousand tongues, and I knew that no matter what happened it would never break.

An outlaw came out of the woods that had a bow too. I let him shoot, and his arrow hit the rock right where I was standing. A couple more outlaws had come out of the trees by that time. I held my bow over my head and shouted, "I am

Sir Able of the High Heart!" (Because that was what Parka had said.) "Give up! Swear you'll be loyal, and I promise not to hurt you!"

The one with the bow had another arrow out, but so did I. I shot him as he was pulling back the bowstring, and my arrow cut his string, went through him, and split a sapling behind him, and it scared the others halfway to Muspel. I was proud of that shot, and I still am. I have made others just about as good as that since, but I have never made a better one.

"Don't have to stay with me," old man Toug whispered when I had cut him down and freed his hands and feet.

I told him I was going to anyway, and I cut up the shirt his daughter had made for me for bandages.

"They kill the dog?"

"No," I said. "Didn't you see him?"

He tried to smile. "Guess I wasn't lookin'. Somethin' troublin' you?"

"My dog."

" 'Fraid he won't come back?"

I was afraid he would, but I built a fire for us there. I could have carried old man Toug back to Glennidam, but it was getting dark and I would have had to put him down fast if we had been jumped. It seemed to me that if he could rest overnight, he might be able to walk in the morning. That would be a big help.

When the fire was burning pretty well I brought him water, carrying it in his hat; and when he had drunk it he said, "You ought to go to their cave. Might be treasure in there."

I doubted it because it seemed to me that the outlaws had probably spent whatever they got as soon as they got it; but I promised we would go in the morning.

Gylf came with two rabbits, fading away into the night as soon as he laid them down. I skinned them and rigged a spit of green shoots the way Bold Berthold had showed me; when I had them cooking, old man Toug said, "Your dog looked different. Firelight, maybe."

"No," I said.

"Still your dog?"

I nodded.

"One time you asked if I wanted my boy to grow up like me, or did I want to be a boy again myself. I wanted him to be like me, only now I'd sooner be like him." He sighed.

I told him I had been a boy myself not very long ago.

"Know what you mean."

"When I found out I'd been turned into a man, I was scared, but after that I was so happy I jumped all around, yelling. Tonight I'd go back, if I could."

"That's it."

"I told you how your son and I went to Aelfrice. We met Disiri there, and she took him. When I was a boy, I spent years in Aelfrice, but when I had gone I couldn't remember what had happened there, and I looked the same way I had when I got there. All those years hadn't changed me at all."

"Happens," old man Toug muttered.

"But when I was there alone, when I was waiting around for Disiri to return with your son, some of it began to come back. I can't remember exactly what it was now, but I can remember remembering it. Do you know what I mean? And it was happy. I had been really, really happy there."

"You ought to of stayed and remembered more."

"I didn't mean to leave. But I think you may be wrong. Terrible things have been nibbling at the edges of my mind. Maybe that's why I went looking for Disiri. I wanted her to reassure me. To tell me everything was all right after all."

A new voice said, "I can't do that, but I can help nurse my father."

I looked around. It was Ulfa.

Old man Toug said, "Followed us, didn't you? Thought you might. Ma couldn't keep you?"

"I left while she was busy with Ve, Pa. I didn't even ask her." Ulfa turned to me. "You frightened poor Ve half to death."

I said I had not meant to. I had just wanted to scare Ve enough to make him do what I told him, because I did not have any money, and I could not think of any other way to keep him from warning the outlaws.

"Kindness might have done it."

"I suppose."

I do not think old man Toug had been listening, or at least not paying much attention, because right about then he said, "Gold, Ulfa! Real gold! There's treasure in the cave. You'll see."

"Will Sir Able let you share in it?"

I said, "Yes, if there's any to share."

Old man Toug said, "I kilt two out 'a Jer's company, Ulfa. Two! Believe that?"

She sighed, and shook her head. "I've been stumbling over bodies for—I don't know, Pa. It seems like half the night. If you only killed two, Sir Able must have killed two score."

I told her that Gylf had killed more than both of us.

"His dog," old man Toug explained. "I kilt and run and kilt and run, and then they put a arrow in my leg. Hung me on a tree. He cut me down, cut me loose. Got water for me and everythin'." Tears spilled from the corners of old man Toug's eyes, soaking the matted hair that barred them from his ears. "I said, you go off. You get that gold. He wouldn't go, stayed here with me."

I turned the rabbits one last time and took them off the

fire, waving them to help them cool. Neither Ulfa nor old man Toug spoke, but I saw the way they looked at them, and as soon as I could I tore off a hind leg and gave it to old man Toug, cautioning him that it was still hot.

"What about you, Ulfa? You must be hungry."

She nodded, and I gave her the other hind leg. We were eating when she said, "Don't you need money?"

I wiped my mouth on the back of my arm. "Sure. I need it more than you or your father do. I have plenty of arrows now, and a really good bow. The knife I used to skin these rabbits, and my dog. But I need everything else a knight ought to have. A charger to fight on. A good saddle horse to get from place to place, and a pack horse to carry all the stuff I haven't got." I tried to grin to show her it was not getting me down. "Even a horse like that, a horse a knight wouldn't even get on, would cost a good deal. And I haven't got anything."

Ulfa nodded. "I see."

"You remember Svon—you told me how well dressed he was. He said one time that a charger like Blackmane costs as much as a good field. Svon didn't always tell the truth, but I don't think he was lying about that. And besides the three horses, I ought to have mail, a good shield, and five or six lances."

Ulfa nodded again. "A manor for your lady."

"My lady has her own kingdom. But you're right, I don't own enough land to grow a turnip." It was not hard to smile that time, because I was thinking how nice it was to have two friends to talk to and something to eat after all that had happened that day. "A dagger like the ones knights wear would be nice, and maybe a battle-ax." That brought back Disira with her hair full of blood. "No, a club. A club with spikes would be good. But as for a manor or anything like that, I can't even think about it. If you were to sew me a new shirt, that would be more than enough to make me happy."

"I'll try. What about a sword? When I made your other shirt, that was what you said you needed."

I shook my head. "Someone's seeing to that. I don't think it would be smart for us to talk about it."

When we had finished the second rabbit, we lay down to sleep; Ulfa and old man Toug were soon snoring, but I was still awake when Gylf returned with a hind in his jaws, and I lay awake another hour listening to him breaking the bones.

Dawn came. The light woke me, and I sat up rubbing my eyes. The Gylf who lay beside me seemed an ordinary dark brown dog, just bigger than any other dog I had ever seen.

We went to the outlaws' cave, walking very slowly because old man Toug could only limp along leaning on the shaft of his spear. Ravens had already been at the bodies of the dead outlaws we found, but Ulfa had brought a leather burse and she dropped such silver and gold as she could get from them into it; it was not a very large burse, but by the time we reached the cave it was heavy. I suppose I could have done that if I had to, but I would not have liked it. I did not even like to look at them.

"I see now why people turn outlaw," I told her when she showed me how much she had, "but if people can get that much by stealing from the kind of people you see around here, how much could a knight get from a good war?"

She smiled. "A manor house, Sir Able, and twenty farms."

The elder Toug snorted. "Pike head though the gut."

At the mouth of the cave you could see the ashes of a lot of fires; bones, spoiled food, and empty wineskins were scattered all around. Farther in we found some heavy winter coats wrapped up in oiled parchment, and some other clothes that had just been thrown down and walked on.

There were blankets, too, mostly rough forest wool, but thick and tight.

Beyond those there was a big jumble of silver platters and tumblers, some really good saddles and saddle blankets, harnesses of the best leather with copper or silver bosses, daggers (I took one), forty or fifty pairs of embroidered gloves, a hunting horn with a green velvet strap, and last of all, very hard to see because it was so dark back there and it had fallen between a couple of stones, a broken sword. It was Ulfa who found that, but I was the one who carried it out of the cave to look at in the light. There was a gold lion's head on the pommel, and up against the guard the blade was stamped *Lut.*

When I saw that, I cried.

CHAPTER 15

POUK

I need to get to Forcetti," I told a sailor. "Do you know if any of these ships are going there?" I had already gone to Scaur's house, but he was out on the boat, and Sha had not recognized me and was afraid to talk to me.

The sailor looked at me for a minute, then touched his cap. "You try th' *Western Trader,* sir."

When he looked at me like that, I saw he was blind in one eye; the eyeball was still there, if you know what I mean, but it looked like the white part of a fried egg. What was more important, I liked the other one, and how it looked. He was not scared of me, but he did not want to fight me or cheat me. I do not think anybody had looked at me like that since I had left the forest.

I said, "You're sure it's going to Forcetti, to the town where Duke Marder is?"

"I dunno, sir, but it's th' only 'un in port now what might. Depends on what they find here, an' you'd be part o' that, sir."

I thought about that, and finally I said, "I need your advice. If I give you a scield for it, will you give me the best advice you can?"

He touched his cap again. "An' carry your bags aboard, sir. What do you want to know?"

"How much I ought to pay to get this ship to take me to Forcetti."

He scratched his head. "Depends, sir. Think I could see th' color o' that scield?"

I got out a scield and showed it to him.

"Goin' to sleep on deck, sir?"

I had slept outside a lot since I got to Mythgarthr, sometimes with a fire and sometimes without, and I would have two blankets from the cave; so that would not have bothered me if I had not been carrying so much money. But Ulfa and old man Toug and I had sold things from the cave and split what they brought among us. My share was a lot. So I said I would have to have a room of my own, with a door that locked.

"If you was, I'd say three o' them like you showed me 'ud do it, sir, if you bargained 'em hard. Since you ain't, you got to find a officer what might share his cabin, sir, an' take a look at it."

I asked if they really had cabins on the ships, because I was thinking of our cabin back in America; then I thought I saw one and pointed it out to him.

"That there's a deckhouse, sir. Cabins is what you'd call

rooms ashore, sir. Officers has 'em. Only sometimes there's two or three sleeps in one. Depends on th' vessel, sir."

"I see. If I could find an officer who had a cabin by himself, he might share it?"

"Aye, sir. If th' price was right."

"How much, would you say?"

He looked thoughtful. "For a good 'un, a couple o' ceptres 'ud do it, most like, sir. For a bad 'un, mebbe eight, ten scields, dependin'. Between 'em," he shrugged, "a bit more or mebbe a ceptre. Goin' to bring your own rations, ain't you, sir?"

"Should I?"

"I 'ud. Even if they say they'll feed you right, sir, it's good to have a bit over, ain't it? An' you can always eat it after if there's any left."

I saw the wisdom in that. "Maybe you could tell me what I ought to take."

"Go with you an' help you pick it out, sir. Carry for you, too, like I said. You a fightin' man, sir? You look it."

"I'm a knight," I said; I always said that, because I knew I could never get people to believe me unless I believed it myself. "I'm Sir Able of the High Heart."

He touched his cap. "Pouk Badeye, sir. At your service."

We joined hands they way they do here, not shaking them but just squeezing. His hand was as hard as wood, but mine was bigger and stronger.

"A fightin' man can get a better price, sir, 'cause o' his helpin' protect th' vessel," Pouk explained. "Only I'd get a sword first, sir, if it was me."

Thinking of Disiri, I shook my head.

"Got 'un already back where you're stayin', sir?"

"No," I said. "I'm not going to get one here, either. An ax, maybe." You know what I thought of as soon as I had said that, so I said, "Or something like that." I knew how dumb it sounded.

"There ain't none but Mori that's a good armorer in Irringsmouth these days, sir. I can show you."

"Then let's go. I'll need food, too."

"Dried stuff, sir, an' smoked. Apples is good, an' we should be able to get 'em this time o' year. Small beer to drink. That don't spile in th' cask like water, sir."

"Wine?"

"Crew'll snaffle it, sir, 'less you watch it day an' night." Putting his thumb to his mouth, Pouk pretended to drink.

I said, "You'd know all about that, I bet."

"Do it myself you mean, sir? Not I." (As well as I could judge, his denial was entirely serious.) "Can I ask why you're bound for Forcetti, sir? Not that it's on my watch, just friendly like, sir?"

"To take service with Duke Marder, if I can. He'll need another knight, and if he doesn't want me he may be able to suggest somebody who might."

"Right there's Mori's, sir." Pouk pointed to a long dark shed from whose several chimneys smoke issued. "You could get a good sword there—"

"No."

"Or a ax, sir. Or whatever you fancy. Did you see somethin', sir?"

I shook my head, not knowing whether I had or not.

"You jerked around, like."

I pretended I had not heard that, and went into Mori's front room. It was big and dim, full of tables upon which weapons and armor were displayed. More covered every wall—swords, daggers, and knives of every kind, war-axes and half-axes, war hammers, morning-stars, and studded flails. Helms that covered the entire head, and helmets that left the face bare. Hauberks, gauntlets, and other mail. Buff-coats of wild-ox leather, byrnies of brass-studded leather, gambesons of quilted canvas, and much more—far too much for me to name even if I knew all the names. Bundles of lances, pikes, spears, bills, and halberts stood in corners. Through a wide door at the other end of the room I could see two brawny men in leather aprons working at a forge, one holding a glowing brand with tongs while the other hammered it.

After a time, an old man who had been watching them noticed us. "A knight, I see. We are honored, Sir . . . ?"

"Able of the High Heart. May I ask how you knew me for a knight, sir? By my clothes?"

The old man shook his head. "By your bearing, Sir Able. By the set of your shoulders, particularly. I confess there are some called knights these days I wouldn't have known." He sighed. "Knights used to guard the fords in my time. They'd help poor travelers, and fight any other knight who wanted to cross."

I said, "I don't believe I've heard of that."

"It went out, oh, thirty years ago. But 'twas a fine custom while it lasted, for it weeded out the fakers. A good custom for me, because they'd bring me the swords and armor."

Pouk chuckled. "Claimed th' salvage did they, sir?"

"Indeed they did, sailor. As is still done, in knightly combat. The winner leaves the loser his clothes and a nag to ride home on. But he takes the arms and armor. The charger if it lives, as it generally does. He takes its tack, as well—its saddle, its bridle, and the rest. A ransom, too, in many cases. Now if you want to buy something, I'll have my clerk take care of you."

"I'm wit' Sir Able. His servingman, like. Thing is, Master

Mori, I want him to get a sword. He don't have none an' says he don't want none, so I steered him to you."

I explained that I was expecting a sword from another source, and needed another weapon I could use until I got it.

"It ain't th' same! Th' skipper o' the *Western Trader* won't never believe you're a knight without you got a sword, sir."

Mori said, "Not all my swords are costly, Sir Able. I can show you a fine arming sword with a good plain grip—"

I raised my hand to cut him off. "Let's say I've sworn not to carry a sword." The next was hard to get out, but I managed it. "An ax might be more useful on a ship anyway. Isn't that right?"

Mori looked thoughtful. "Does this oath preclude the use of a falchion? I've a very fine one just now."

"There isn't any oath. I made it up. I just wanted to make you and Pouk here understand how I feel. I—if I take a sword now, I won't ever get the one I'm hoping to get, and if I don't get that one, I won't see the person who might get it for me. So no swords. Not any kind. Can't you show me some axes? What about that double-bitted one with the yellow tassel?"

"There ain't no ax that's a sword!" Pouk insisted.

Mori's eyes gleamed under his shaggy brows.

"What about this?" It had a long handle and a narrow blade. I picked it up and swung it over my head. "A cutting edge on one side and a hammer on the other, so it's an ax and a mace, too."

"If I say you're a knight an' th' skipper sees you with that, he'll laugh us both ashore!"

Mori laid his hand on my shoulder. "Will you listen with patience, Sir Able, to what an older man has to say? I am no knight, but I've had years of experience in these matters."

I said that I would be glad to hear him, but that I did not want a sword.

"Nor will I ask you to take one. Hear me out, and I'll tell you of another weapon which, though not a sword, is as good in some respects, and in others better."

I nodded. "Go on."

"Let me first address the utility of swords and axes. The ax is like the mace in that it finds its best employment against heavy armor. It will split a shield—sometimes—in the hands of a man as strong as you are. But let a man in light armor, or a man in no armor, fight an axman, and he will kill him inside a minute or two, if he has a good sword and knows the use of it. As for that war hammer, it would be valuable indeed on horseback against another rider. But for a man afoot—a man aboard a ship, for example—well, you might be better off with an oar or a handspike."

Pouk grunted with satisfaction.

"Socially, too, your man is quite correct. A sword is preeminently the weapon of a man of gentle birth. A man who bears one, who meets another similarly armed whom he thinks no gentleman, may challenge him, and so on."

I tried to nod as if I had known it.

"May I introduce a hypothetical? Say for the sake of argument only that your man and I conspired to introduce a sword among your baggage. A sword so cleverly concealed that neither you nor anybody else could see it. What good would it be to you, do you think, when you boarded your ship?"

"Not any. When I found it I'd drop it in the water."

Pouk groaned under his breath; Mori said patiently, "Before you found it, Sir Able."

"If I didn't know I had it, it couldn't be of use."

"Would not captain and crew acknowledge you a knight?"

I shrugged. "They will. But not because of a sword they never saw."

"Now we come to it. It is the seeing of the sword—the perception of it—that matters. Not the sword itself. Look here." Mori limped across the room, and from the table farthest from the door picked up a richly trimmed scabbard of white rayskin holding a weapon with a hilt of hammered steel. "What have I here, Sir Able?"

I knew there was some trick, but I was clueless about what it was. I said, "It looks like a sword. It's on the short side, I'd say, and from the way you picked it up it can't be very heavy. The blade's probably narrow." I waited for him to say something, and when he did not, I asked, "How are you fooling me?"

Mori chuckled. "As to its weight, I'm not as feeble as I may look to a man your age, and I've spent many a busy day forging blades."

Pouk had gone to check it out. "You're sayin' it ain't a sword at all?"

"It is not." Mori carried the weapon, still sheathed, back to me. "It's a mace, a mace of the Lothurings who live where the sun sets. I doubt that there is another on this side of the sea. Will you draw it, Sir Able?"

I did. The heavy steel blade was four-sided, only slightly wider than it was thick; its edges had never been sharpened.

"When it came into my hands," Mori said, "I thought it the strangest thing I'd ever seen. But I dug out an old great helm, one that was dented and had lost its clasp but was still good and strong. I set that helm on the end of a post and tried the mace you're holding on it, and came away a believer. Two ceptres' weight in gold, if you want it."

Seeing my expression he amended his price. "Or a ceptre and ten scields, if you'll promise to come back and let me know how it served you."

"We'll take it!" Pouk declared.

CHAPTER 16

THE WESTERN TRADER

This here's Sir Able o' th' High Heart," Pouk explained to the mate of the *Western Trader.* "Him an' me's wantin' passage to Forcetti."

The mate touched his forelock to me. "You'd be wantin' to share a cabin, sir?"

I said I would have to see the cabin first. The cold squall that had come into the harbor to announce autumn had made me pull up the hood of my new cloak already; now a gust of rain wet it, and the *Western Trader* jerked at her cable, rolling and shuddering to let us know exactly how she felt.

"Foller me, sir."

The mate turned away, starting down a steep little stair. I told Pouk to go first, because I knew that if I left the open air I was going to be sick. For a minute or two I looked around at the ship—the reeling castles of brightly painted wood at the front and back, the deckhouse, the swaying masts, with long, slanted poles to spread the sails that were bunched around them now, and the rest of it. My face felt hot, and I was glad the wind was cold. I knew I might throw up any minute, and I swore that I would make Pouk clean it up if I did.

And kill him if he would not do it.

"Sir?"

It was him, naturally, looking up from the stairs.

"Trying to keep my bow dry," I said. I fiddled with the oiled leather bowcase we had gotten for it.

"Th' cabin's a mite small," Pouk said.

It was. With the mate, Pouk, and me in it, there was hardly room to turn around.

"This here's my bunk, sir." The mate seated himself on it, giving us a little more space. "Up there'd be yours."

The upper bunk looked dirty, and emitted a sour smell over and above the reek that seemed to be everywhere under the main deck.

"Captain's cabin's right up there," the mate announced proudly. " 'Cept for that, this here's the best berth on the ship."

Pouk had his back to the mate. He waggled one finger and winked.

I said, "Somebody's been sleeping up here already. Who is it?"

"Our second, sir. Nur's his name."

"If I'm going to be taking his bed, I ought to make my bargain with him."

Pouk grinned approval.

"I've the say, sir." The mate sounded angry. "As for bargainin', there won't be none. Two—"

I had made up my mind, and I cut him off. "You're right, we're not making any kind of deal. I wouldn't sleep in here if you locked me in. Show me the captain's cabin."

"He'd have to do it hisself." The mate sounded angrier than ever.

"Then let's go see him."

There was an awkward silence until I realized that I would

have to go out before Pouk and the mate could. I did, bumping my head on the top of the tiny doorway and turning sidewise to get my shoulders through it. The whole affair was awkward enough, and painful enough, that I forgot to be sick for a minute or two.

Back on deck, the mate rapped (timidly, I thought) on the captain's door while I took long breaths of cold salt air.

"Cap'n?"

There was no answer. I decided the gale had gotten worse, if anything. Cold rain slammed my face, and was very welcome there.

"Cap'n, sir?" The mate rapped again, a trifle louder.

"Be a long tunne a' money," Pouk whispered.

The sterncastle door opened. I glimpsed a middle-aged man's dirty face and bleary eyes before it closed again.

"You gotter come back," the mate announced with great satisfaction. "Come back tomorrer."

I pushed him to one side and pounded on the door. When the captain opened it, his face red with rage, I shoved him backward and went in.

After the mate's cabin, this one looked spacious indeed, a good four paces long and three wide, with a ceiling almost high enough and big windows on three sides. I pointed to one and said, "Open that!"

The captain (who was naked) only stared. Pouk hastened to obey.

I said, "I see only one bed. Where will you sleep?"

"You're a knight?" The captain took trousers from the back of a chair screwed to the floor.

"Right. Sir Able of the High Heart."

"I doubt it." The captain sat down on the cabin's one bed. "I've never heard of you."

"You'd be smart to act as if you had," I told him. By that

time I was really beginning to catch on to the way these people talk.

"You want to travel in my cabin." He snorted. "That's what Megister Kerl said."

"Right again. To Forcetti."

"If I permitted it," the captain seemed to weigh each word, "it would cost you seven gold ceptres. Good gold, too. Paid in advance, and not a copper farthing shy of the full seven. You'd sling your hammock over there, and by wind, rain, and sea you'd have it out of my way each morning before breakfast."

Kerl had come in behind me by that time. He chuckled.

The captain rose and buckled his belt. "Otherwise, I'd teach you, Sir Able of the Shy Fart, how the authority of a captain is to be obeyed. As it is, I won't let you have it at any price. I give you as much time as it takes to make sail to clear my ship." From under his mattress he pulled a curved sword of Osterling make. "Or we'll throw you in the bay."

I grabbed his wrist with my left hand and got hold of the pommel with my right. Before I could wrench the sword away, a punch from Kerl spun me half around.

The sword came free. I ducked another punch, and hit him in the chest. I still remember the sound of it, like a mallet pounding a tent stake. It gave me a moment to throw the captain's sword out the window.

As soon as it was gone he was on me, bellowing like a bull. That stopped the first time I hit him. He fell down, and I picked him up and shoved him headfirst out the window, catching hold of an ankle as it crossed the sill.

"Sir Able? Sir Able . . ."

I was looking down at the captain. A jokester whitecap had just washed his head. "You wouldn't do this if you were me, Pouk? I'm helping him out. He was knocked cold, and the water will bring him back and make him feel better."

"I got his knife, Sir Able. Mate's, I mean. Had it in his belt, he did. Likely you didn't notice, sir."

"Sure I did." I took the knife and glanced at it. "Give it back to him. It's his."

Pouk looked dubious. "Into th' drink might be better, sir. He's havin' trouble gettin' his breath, sir, only it won't last."

"He didn't try to stab me with it," I told Pouk, "so I'll let him keep it."

"Put it in your back, sir, like as not."

Kerl gasped, "N-No."

"We've got his word, Pouk." I took another look at the captain, who had started waving his arms and sputtering. A high-speed roll cracked his head against the side. "His word is good enough for us."

I looked around at the mate. "Megister Kerl."

Still gasping, Kerl contrived to say, "Aye, sir?"

"My baggage is out there where Pouk unloaded it. The boatman's there, too, waiting for his money. Pay him, and help Pouk carry it in here."

"Sir—aye aye, sir."

Pouk was already out the cabin door. Kerl struggled to his feet and followed him.

When it had shut behind them, I pulled in the captain. "Get up," I told him. "I might have to hit you again."

He tried and fell down. I picked him up and plumped him down on the table. "Can you talk?"

"I'm all right. Just dizzy. It'll pass off."

"We'd better settle this before those two come back," I told him. "I'm going to sleep in here, alone, until we get to Duke Marder's city."

He muttered, "Aye, sir."

"That's another thing. Don't say sir to me. I've let Pouk do it, and just now your mate did it too. But you're going to say yes, Sir Able. Every now and then you'd better say yes, Sir Able of the High Heart. When you do it, I'm going to listen really hard to the last two words." He did not answer, so I said, "Make it plain you understand me, or you're going out that window again."

"Aye aye, Sir Able of the High Heart." The captain straightened up. "I understand you perfectly, Sir Able of the High Heart."

"Swell. I'll pay you three ceptres for this room when we get to Forcetti. That's if I get the best food you've got, and you and your men treat me the way a knight ought to be treated. Make it clear you understand all that, too."

"Aye, Sir Able of the High Heart." Still shaky, he got up, holding on to the little table with both hands. It was screwed to the floor, like just about everything else. "I understand you perfectly, Sir Able of the High Heart."

"If the food's not good, or you and your crew call me names behind my back, I'm going to start knocking money off those three ceptres. I'll decide how much, and—"

There was a tap on the door.

"Just a minute!"

I turned back to the captain. "Do you understand what I've been telling you? About my deductions? Make it clear."

"I do, Sir Able of the High Heart. You can count on me, Sir Able."

"We'll see." I was feeling sicker than ever and felt like I was sure to chuck. "I'm going to move you out of here right now. Get all your stuff together—that means your clothes and personal things. Leave those blankets. Once you're out, there won't be anything to stop you from getting your crew together and giving out every kind of knife and stick you can find."

He looked scared, and I was glad to see it.

"Only remember this. It won't be enough to tell them to jump me. You'll have to get out in front." I opened the door. "Now beat it."

When Pouk and Kerl had brought my baggage, I chased them out too, pushing Pouk—he wanted to talk—right out the door and sliding the square iron bolt into the socket. After that I was sick out the window, but when it was over and I had cleaned up, I felt better than I had since I got into the big rowboat that had ferried us out to the *Western Trader.*

Before I go on, I ought to tell you a lot about boats and ships (which are different from boats, although I did not understand that then) and the coasting trade, and the high-sea trade. But the truth is that I do not know a lot about those things. The *Western Trader* was a big ship to them; only the biggest had three masts. In the summer it went west, just like its name said, and traded among the islands there. But in winter it just traded along the coast of Celidon, so it could duck into a port whenever the weather got too bad, and it tried to trade south.

The Osterlings were to our east, but they followed the coast south, west, and north, murdering and stealing. Duke Indign had tried to stop them, but they had killed him, and pulled down his castle. With him gone, they had looted and burned most of Irringsmouth.

CHAPTER 17

AT ANCHOR

Next morning the ship rolled and pitched in pretty much the same way it had all night and the day before, but once I had hopped out of bed (there was a dream I wanted to get away from) I felt fine and was hungry enough to eat an old shoe. Looking out the windows I could see we were still in the harbor, and the noises that had made me wake up showed that something heavy was being brought on board and was making a lot of trouble. There were bumps and rumbles and rattles, and bare feet running here and there, and a good deal of yelling. There was a squeaking noise too, that I thought might be some kind of bird.

What was better was the sunshine and the way the wind blew, one of those warm fall winds that make you want to throw a football. I pretended I was, and I knew that with the arms and legs and shoulders I had now I could play for the Vikings. After that I got dressed and buckled on the foreign mace we had bought from Mori. It hung from a belt like a sword belt. I checked on my bow and quiver. They looked fine, but I decided I'd leave them in the cabin for now, along with my boat cloak. When I had bad dreams—and I did, just about every night—it was generally because of Parka's bowstring. It was in the bowcase, and I had put that on the far side of the cabin; but I thought it might not have been far enough.

Out on deck, crates and barrels and boxes were being unloaded from a square-prowed barge with forty men leaning on the oars. There was a slanted pole on the biggest mast for it, with a wheel at the end and a rope run through the wheel. When you had a good load on it, that wheel made more noise than a flock of gulls, squeaking and squealing. They pulled the things up that way, one at a time, swung them over the hatch, and let them down.

Kerl came running, touching his cap. Pouk was right in back of him, and when I saw him I remembered I still owed him a scield.

"I hope the noise didn't bother you, Sir Able, sir." Kerl touched his cap all over again. "We figured you was probably roused, sir, only we didn't mean to bother you. Would you be wantin' breakfast, sir?"

I was still looking around, but I nodded.

"In your cabin that'd be, sir?"

That meant I did not have to eat in there, the way I saw it, so I thought about it and said, "I don't know much about boats like this, Megister Kerl."

He nodded, looking scared.

"You've got these wooden castles. One in front, and this one in the back that's really my room."

"That's right, sir, Sir Able. To fight off of, sir, if we got to fight. That 'un's the forecastle and this 'un's the sterncastle, sir."

"Are the roofs flat? They look it." It seemed like I might have a pretty good view of the ship and the harbor from up there, and wind and sunshine, too.

"Aye, sir." Kerl bobbed his head. "It's where the ship's steered from, sir. Where the wheel is."

Pouk added, "That's where you ought to be too, sir, an' not down here."

I nodded. "Lead the way. I want to see it."

Pouk led, with Kerl right in back of him. Some narrow steps they called a companionway led up to a solid deck with wooden walls, with square notches cut out of the walls to shoot arrows through or throw spears. That is what is called a battlement, and the broken wall I saw at Irringsmouth had them too, only that wall was stone. The steering wheel was on this deck. So was the lodestone, on a stand in front of the wheel.

And so was the captain, drinking small beer and eating eggs and bacon, fresh bread, and a salad made of radishes and shoots. He got up politely as soon as he saw me and said, "A good morrow to you, Sir Able of the High Heart."

I said good morrow too. "May I join you, Captain? I haven't had breakfast."

When he said yes, I told Pouk, "I need to talk to you after I eat. Have they fed you?"

He touched his cap. "Aye, sir, I et."

"Then get me a chair, and have a word with the cook."

Right away the captain put in, "Take mine, Sir Able. A pleasure." So I did.

Pouk said, "I'll fetch another for th' cap'n, if it's all right, sir. Only mate's got to tell cook, sir, an' I judge he's gone off to already."

Not very sure of himself, the captain said, "If you're hungry, Sir Able of the High Heart, you might want to sample some of this. I was saving my greens for last, Sir Able, and these two slices haven't been touched."

I said I could wait.

"If you'd prefer to be alone, Sir Able of the High Heart . . . ?"

I said no. "I've got a lot of questions, and I want to ask them while I eat my breakfast and you finish yours. The crew doesn't need you for what they're doing now?"

"Stowing cargo?" The captain shook his head. "Megister Kerl can see to it as well as I could."

"But you've got a nicer cabin. Or you did."

The captain did not answer.

"You give the orders, and Kerl does whatever you tell him to. What can you do that he can't?"

"In all honesty, Sir Able of the High Heart, he could make a stab at everything I do, and he might succeed with a good deal of it. I'm the better navigator, but Kerl can navigate a bit. I flatter myself that I'm better at getting us goods to trade, and a better trader. I don't think Kerl could show as good a profit, but he's a good seaman."

I had asked that because of the dream. In the dream I had been way down under the main deck. It had been pitch dark, but I had known somehow that our mother was not really dead at all—she was down there, tied up and gagged so she could not make any noise, and if I could find her I could cut her loose and bring her up on deck. Only the captain was down there too, and he had a rope he wanted to choke me with. He was moving around very quietly, trying to come up behind me and get it around my neck. I was trying to be quiet, too, so he could not find me. Only pretty often I would stumble over something or knock something over.

So I was thinking suppose I just killed him like we had the outlaws? He was being so nice this morning that I think he must have guessed what I was thinking. But underneath he hated my guts and wanted his cabin back, and I knew it. Kerl would not be half as much trouble, and he could take me to Forcetti just as well.

There had been somebody else down there with us in my dream, somebody that never moved at all or made any noise; but I did not know who it was.

Pouk came back with a chair for the captain. "I'll see to

th' bed an' tidy up your cabin if you don't need me right now, sir." I nodded, and he said, "Just sing out, sir, if you need anythin'. I'll be directly below."

The captain sat down. "A good servant?"

I did not know, but I said, "He's been useful, anyhow. He's spent most of his life on one ship or another, from what he says. When are we going to get going?"

"With the tide tomorrow night, Sir Able of the High Heart, if that's satisfactory to you."

"Why not today?"

"We must load our cargo. I mean, if you permit it, Sir Able. Today and tomorrow for that, if the loading goes well. Once it's secure below, we'll put out as quickly as we can." He had not started to eat again, waiting for my food to get there.

I said I had been wondering about that. Could he go right now without waiting for the tide?

He lifted his shoulders and let them drop. "It would depend on the wind, Sir Able. If Ran favored us, we could do it. But I can't always predict the wind. I know when the tide will run, however, and I know it will bear us out to sea if we let it."

He waited for me, but I was thinking.

"If you'd prefer I try earlier, I will, Sir Able of the High Heart. The risk of running aground will be greater, I warn you."

"You wouldn't ordinarily do that?"

The captain shook his head.

"Then don't do it tomorrow. We can wait for the tide, like you say. How long will it take to get to Forcetti?"

"That will depend on the wind again—"

Just about then the cook and his helper brought up my breakfast. I did not know much about ship's food back then, but I knew enough from Pouk to see they had fixed some of everything they could lay hands on. When the dishes had been crowded onto the little table and the cook and his helper had gone back to the galley, the captain said, "With fair winds we'll tie up in Forcetti within a fortnight, Sir Able of the High Heart. With foul—well, anything you care to name. A month. Two months. Never."

A fortnight is two weeks or half the moon, but I did not know that then. I said a fortnight seemed awfully fast and waited to hear what he would say to that.

"We can sail night and day," he explained, "and with a fair wind we can travel as fast as a well-mounted rider. When that rider would be eating and sleeping and resting his horse, we can sail on as if the sun were up."

I was eating.

"Then too, it will depend on how we go, Sir Able. Is it your wish to stay in sight of land the whole time?"

I swallowed and said, "It's my wish to get there as quick as I can without taking any silly chances."

"Landsmen usually want to keep sight of land," the captain explained, "because they don't see how we can find our way at sea." He chuckled. "Sometimes, neither do we. But we do it, mostly. And out at sea's quicker, and safer too. Osterlings and storms are dangerous everywhere, but inshore's the worst for both."

I nodded, and said I had seen Bluestone Castle.

"Exactly. They generally creep up the coast, landing here and there. Just where depends on how many men they have, and how confident they are. They want flesh, but they want gold, too, and sometimes they want one more than the other. If they see a ship, they'll take it if they can overtake it. But there's always more flesh and more gold ashore than at sea. Storms are equally likely in either place, but they blow a ship about, mostly. When they wreck one, it's generally by driving it onto rocks."

I said, "I doubt that I'll be much use in a storm, but I'll lead your men in a fight if they'll follow me." I did not think it would really happen. "You've got weapons for them?"

He nodded. "Pikes mostly. Boarding axes."

That explained Pouk's objection to a battle-ax.

The captain cleared his throat. "Speaking of weapons leads me to something I've got to ask you, Sir Able of the High Heart. You don't trust me, I know. And I don't blame you, but you can. I'll let bygones be bygones, if you know what I mean."

I said that was nice.

"We'll be sailing tomorrow night. May I go ashore and get myself another sword? I may need it."

Well, I wanted to say no. But I knew that he could get one of those boarding axes or something else like that. So I said all right.

CHAPTER 18

ALONE

When I had seen everything, I went back to the captain's cabin. Pouk had made the bed and swept and mopped the floor, and was unpacking things we had bought ashore and stowing them in chests and cupboards. I got out the scield I had promised him and put another one with it, saying that he had earned that much and more, which was the truth.

"Thankee, Sir Able. Thankee, sir." He bowed, touching

his cap at the same time, something I was going to see a lot of, although I did not know it then. "You don't have to give no more than the 'un, sir. Only I'll take 'em if you want to give 'em to me. Only I'll give 'em back if you need 'em for yourself, sir."

I shook my head. "They're yours. You earned them, like I said. You might be able to hitch a ride back to shore on that boat the sailors are unloading, but you'd better hurry. It's about empty now."

Pouk shook his head. "I'm stayin' on, sir, with your leave. I was lookin' out sharp for a berth when you spied me on th' wharf. I've dropped my hook, if you take my meanin'."

"You're planning to sail on this ship?" I sat down on my bed.

"Aye, sir. As your man, sir." Seeing the way I looked, he added, "You need somebody what will look out for you, sir. You're as good a man as ever I seen, an' smart, an' I'm sure you know lots out o' books. Only sometimes you're a green hand, sir. I seen it when we was fittin' up, sir. They'd o' cheated you twenty times over. So you need somebody bad—somebody that knows th' ways."

That made me mad. Not mad at Pouk—it was pretty hard to be mad at Pouk, usually—but mad at people, mad at a world where so many were out to cheat everybody. Maybe it was because of the time in Aelfrice; I do not know. "I was a boy not long ago," I told Pouk. "It hasn't been long at all, and in lots of ways, I still am."

"Course, sir. So that's me, sir. I ain't bad as they come, but I'm plenty bad enough. Try me, an' you'll see."

"As for books, I looked into some in Irringsmouth and the writing was just black marks on the paper. I can no more read than you can, Pouk."

"You know what's in 'em, sir. That's what matters."

"I doubt it." I took a deep breath. "I do know this, though.

I know I don't need a servant, and I can't afford to pay one, certainly not a scield a day."

"There you are, sir! A scield? That's wages for a month for a sailor or a stableman or just about anybody."

I said no, and I made it as firm as I knew how.

"So I'm set for a couple o' months, an' after that I'd let it ride a couple more. Only I don't want no pay, sir." He laid his two scields on the table. "Just let me stay on, an' I'll look out for myself. Why, I mixed my seabag in with your bags, sir, an' you didn't pay no mind."

I was worried about my gold, gold in the burse that hung from my belt and more in my old bag, which was hanging from my neck under my clothes. I told him he could not sleep in the cabin with me, and that was final.

He grinned, seeing he had won. "Why, I don't want to, sir. I'll sleep in front o' th' door, sir, like I done last night. That way can't nobody get in without wakin' me up."

"On that wooden floor?" I had slept on skins and dead leaves a lot by then, but I could not imagine Pouk or anybody sleeping on bare boards.

"Th' deck, sir? Sure thing, sir. I've slept out on deck many an' many a time."

"Knights sleep in their armor, sometimes," I told him. "What you do—what sailors do—must be worse. What will you do when it rains?"

"There's a bit o' set-in to your door, sir. Mebbe you didn't notice, but there is. That's what it's for, an' I've a bit o' canvas to wrap myself in."

I made a last try. "You'll serve me for nothing? I warn you, Pouk, that's what I'll pay you."

"Aye, sir! See them scields, sir? You take 'em. You won't hear a word out o' me."

"I said I wouldn't pay you, not that I'd rob you. I paid

them to you. They're yours now." Then I thought about the outlaws I had killed, Bold Berthold's hut, and some other things; and I said, "It seems to me, Pouk, that a true knight has to respect other people's things, if they came by them honestly. If somebody came to rob me, I'd fight him and I might kill him. But how could I do it if I'd stolen myself?"

"I judge you're right, sir. You always are, mostly."

"So put them away. If you leave them on the table, I'll take them, I swear."

He hesitated, then nodded and picked them up. "They tried to get me into th' search party, sir. Second did, sir. Nur's his name."

"What search party?"

"Searchin' th' ship, sir. I dunno if they found anythin'."

I thought I knew what they had been looking for, but I asked just the same.

"A dog, sir." Seeing my face, Pouk backed away. "Just a big dog, sir. Lookout seen it swim out to th' ship, sir, an' climb aboard. Last night it was, sir."

"But you don't know if they found it?"

"No, sir. Like I said, sir. Second was after me to help look, only I was movin' cap'n's things out so I could put yours in, sir. Food's in that 'un, sir, an' beer's in th' corner there, an'—"

I held up my hand. "Just a minute."

"Aye aye, sir. Only I want to say, sir, that's another reason you need me, sir. Crew'll come in an' pinch it, sir, when you're not in here, sir. Food, particular. Only I'll be here an' they can't, sir."

"And you won't?" I tried to smile.

Pouk looked shocked. "Course I will. Only feedin' one's not like feedin' twenty."

"I suppose not. And you may find that you can steal less

than you think. They haven't found the dog, Pouk. I know that. But I want you to ask about him just the same. Find Megister Nur, or whatever he's called, and tell him I want to know."

"Aye aye, sir. Only I was wonderin', sir. When we was ashore an' you seen that big dog, sir, you—"

"Forget that." I felt tired and I wanted to be alone, even if it was just for a minute or two. "Go ask Megister Nur like I told you, and tell me what he says."

When Pouk had gone, I took out the foreign mace I had bought in Irringsmouth and looked it over carefully. The four corners of the blade were as sharp as broken glass. The end was cut off square, a diamond-shape that somebody had painted red. I thought I would file it sharp, like a spike, and went out and found a sailor. He said the carpenter might have a file, so I sent him to borrow it. He did, but when I tried to reshape the end of the blade the file would scarcely scratch it; so I told myself that if it were sharp the whole thing would be too much like a sword anyway. Disiri was going to bring me a sword, I thought, because I did not have one; and when she did, I would see her again. So I gave the idea up.

After that I barred the door, took out my gold, and stacked the coins on the table, all while wondering what I had stopped Pouk from saying. That the brave knight Sir Able had turned pale when he saw a half-bred mastiff? That he had started as if he had seen a ghost?

That big black shape I had seen when Gylf killed the outlaws, a dog as big as horse, with dripping jaws and fangs half as long as my arm, had been the Valfather's dog. One of the Valfather's dogs, and he had a whole pack of them. Nine or ten? Fifty or a hundred? For a minute I wondered about the Valfather. What was he like, what could he be like, if he had dogs like that? I still wanted to get to his castle in the sky. In Skai. It was crazy, but I did. I wanted to go there and take Disiri with me.

I still do.

After that I looked at all the coins, counting them and really looking at them, comparing one to another. They were gold ceptres, and when I had finished I still thought they were all the real thing. When we divided up the money, I had given Ulfa and her father the copper and brass and all the silver. All the foreign coins, too; there had been a good many of those, and a lot had been gold. I had kept only the gold ceptres for my share, and I was not sorry I had, either.

Some were a little worn, but a lot were new or nearly new. I took one of the new ones to a window where I could see it clearly in the sunlight. There was a big mace on one side, not like mine but a fancy club with a crown. On the other was the king with his face turned sidewise, just like that man on the quarter. There was writing underneath his picture, probably his name, but I could not read it. It was just a bunch of marks to me. I looked at the king and tried to think what he might be like because I knew that even if I worked for Duke Marder, Duke Marder worked for him. He was young and handsome, but he looked tough and maybe a something out past tough. Like he would do whatever he wanted, and if you did not like it you better get out of his way and keep your mouth shut.

After that, Pouk knocked on the door, and I put my gold away and let him in. He said they had not found the dog, and "Second" said it had probably jumped off the ship again, or else the lookout had been seeing things. Pouk said, "It's your dog, ain't it, sir?"

I said no, it was a dog I had been keeping for somebody else. That felt wrong as soon as I said it, and I did not feel right about it until I called Pouk back and said, "You were right, Pouk, he's really my dog, and I'm pretty sure he's still on the ship. I won't tell you to look for him. If they didn't find him you won't either. But I want you to put a bucket of fresh water down in the hold where it will be a while before anybody finds it."

He said he would, and went off to do it.

And that is all about that day, except that I stayed on the ship because I was pretty sure the captain would sail it away if I got off. That day and the next day I learned quite a bit about ships and the work sailors do, mostly by watching and asking Pouk and Kerl questions.

On the second day, a couple of hours after it got dark, we put out like the captain had said we would. Sitting in my cabin I watched the lights of Irringsmouth fade out behind us until there was nothing but dark, greasy-looking sea. Pretty soon I was going to understand it a lot better than I have ever understood people; but I did not know about that then. Then it was only something I loved, something beautiful and dangerous and tricky, like Disiri.

After that, I just sat in my cabin. Maybe I got out Sword Breaker again. I do not remember. I could not have seen it very well, because I kept the cabin dark, waiting for what I thought would be coming.

Finally I thought, well, there is no Mac and no TV and no books or magazines to read. But there are feather pens in the desk, and paper and ink. I could write myself notes or make lists or something.

So I lit one of the lamps and got the stuff out of the drawer and started writing down the most important things that had happened to me, like finding a spiny orange tree in the woods, Parka, and seeing the knight that blew away in that wrecked castle. I wrote up to Disiri leaving and me finding Disira and Ossar. Then I decided to give it up.

Only there was one other thing. When I picked up the list I had been writing, meaning to wad it up and toss it out the window, I looked at it. And all of a sudden I saw it was not the way we wrote at school at all. It was Aelf writing. I had not known I could do it, but I had done it and I could read it.

CHAPTER 19

THE CABLE TIER

Here is where I am going to make you mad. I know I am going to do it, and I do not like it, but I am. I am not going to tell you about the fight with the Osterling pirates. It still hurts, and it would hurt a lot worse if I had to write all about it. So I will not. That it happened is the main thing, and you already know that. We were only three days out of port.

The other main thing was that I got stabbed. I had bought a mail shirt and a helmet in Irringsmouth, and I was wearing them. The shirt was not a real hauberk like a knight would wear. It had short sleeves and came down a little bit below my waist; but I was proud of it, and while our crew was putting up the net I pulled it on and put on my helmet. When I got stabbed I thought the blade had come up under it. Only it had not. It had gone right through. I saw that later.

One night down in the cable tier, when they thought I was going to die, I dreamed the whole thing over again and kept looking around for a machine gun I had lost. And the truth is I remember that dream a lot better than the real thing, and maybe some parts are mixed up. I do not know.

We were sailing as fast as we could go, with sticks tied on

the yards and extra sails on them and the ship heeling way over and turning a streak of sea to cream, if you know what I mean. But the Osterlings were rowing hard and sailing too, and their ship was really narrow and had four masts, with the one in front raked way forward, and they must have had two hundred men at the oars. In a gale we might have outsailed them; I know that now. But it was pretty calm, just a good breeze, and we did not stand a chance.

I asked Kerl what they wanted, and he said, "They want to cook you and eat you." That was just in my dream, I am pretty sure, but it is the truth anyway. They wanted all of us. That is the way it works here. What you eat makes you more like it, and the closer it is to you, the more it moves you that way, if you know what I mean. You take Scaur and Sha. They ate a lot of fish, but it did not make them very much like fish, just quick and graceful, and knowing a lot about the sea. They never said their hands were cold either, or tried to warm them in front of the fire. But when they touched you, their hands were as cold as seawater. Deer are closer, and if you eat a lot you smell things more and your ears get sharper and you can run faster. That is how it works, and sometimes I think it must be mostly in the blood, because when I drank Baki's blood it healed me a lot in just a day or so, and in certain ways I was more like one of the Aelf. I guess I still am.

That had not happened yet. At the time I am telling about it was the Osterlings that mattered. They are people, only they are not much like regular people, especially lower down. The Caan and the princes and so on are pretty human, I guess because they can get whatever they want. But the more ordinary Osterlings have faces like skulls and horrible eyes that look like they are burning holes in you.

Here I am going to say something that maybe I should not say. They are thin, too. You can count their ribs and see where all the bones are underneath their skin. In America we liked people to be really thin and all the girls I knew were always trying to lose weight. West of the mountains it is not like that, and I think it is because of the Osterlings. Men are supposed to have muscles and wide shoulders and big, thick arms and legs, sort of like football players. (We are not supposed to have thick heads too, but pretty often that is the case.) Women are supposed to have big round breasts like grapefruits, two-balloon hips, and lots of meat on their arms and legs. Idnn was not like that, which could have been one reason she was not married already. But Gaynor always made me think that she ought to lose about twenty pounds, only I could not decide what parts I would like smaller.

So that was the way most people were in Celidon, which is where we were until we put out to sea, and it just made the Osterlings want to kill us that much more. But the fact was (I did not know this back then) that they would kill just about anything and eat it: horses and dogs, rats and cats.

The net I was talking about was made out of good-sized ropes and it was there to keep people out. It was a good idea, because the ropes were hard to cut and I could shoot arrows through the holes, which I did. But they could be cut after a while, which the Osterlings did, wanting to get at us, so chain would have been better.

In my dream I could see the one who stabbed me, and see the dagger's blade coming at me, and all that. After I was stabbed I lay on the deck of the Osterling ship and bled and bled, and after a long, long time our captain came, shuffling his feet, and when he was standing beside me he kicked me in the face. But I do not think that really happened.

I woke up, and I had not been kicked. It was Pouk, and for a minute I did not know where I was (I thought I was back in my bedroom at home) or who Pouk was. You know how it is, sometimes, when somebody wakes you up from a dream.

"It's me, sir, Pouk Badeye. I got some water here, sir, thinkin' you might like it."

I took it, the kind of wooden mug they call a cannikin.

"It ain't good water, sir, but you can drink it. I been drinkin' it. They feedin' you, sir?"

It was hard to remember. Finally I said, "I don't think so. I've been sleeping most of the time. Dreaming." Back in a corner of my mind I was still trying to figure out how my bed had turned into a big coil of rope.

"I didn't think so. I'll try an' get you somethin', sir. Cook'll give me somethin' if he knows it's for you."

It was so dim in there that I could just barely make out Pouk's face. That was when I asked Pouk where I was, and he told me, "Cap'n wanted to kill you, sir, only we wouldn't let him. We'd o' mutinied, sir, if he'd tried it. He was goin' to, sir. He come up to where you was layin' an' raised up his sword, sir, and I felt it go all though the ship, men standin' up that had been sittin', an' feelin' for axes an' knives an' pikes. So he couldn't, sir, not then. He had some carry you down here, sir, with Nur to watch 'em. Only I got to go, sir, 'fore I'm missed."

Pouk had become another dream. I heard him say, "I'll bring you somethin'. I will that." But the Osterlings were gaining on us, their thin black ship leaping across the sea, and the arrow was at my ear.

A friend came and licked my face.

* * *

Next time I woke up I was myself again. Weak, and scared when I saw how weak I was. It was damp in the cable tier; my wound was hot, but I shivered there for hours.

"Here y'are, Sir Able, sir. Sprat dumplin's, sir."

I looked up at the sound of a stranger's voice. It was too dark to make out his face, but metal clinked on metal and there was a good smell. In another second or so it was under my nose, crisp outside and soft inside, full of flavor, greasy and wonderful. I chewed and swallowed and had to fight to keep from swallowing without chewing. When I had finished, I asked who he was.

"Cook, sir. Hordsvin's me name." He gulped. "Fought next ta ya wi' me cleaver, Sir Able. Had me napron on but warn't hog's blood on it. Me helper fought, ta, sir. Surt's his name. He's watchin' out fer me na. Had me big knife."

A warm thing was pushed into my hand. I took it, bit off too much, and choked.

"Drink this, sir. Your man come, Sir Able, only he'd of et it hisself, I was afeerd. So I brung 'em, sir. They's me specialty, Sir Able, sir. I'll leave th' pan wi' th' lid on so's th' rats don't get 'em."

After that I rationed them out to myself, and thought about what I would have to do.

The next time Pouk came, I told him, and he said, "You can't fight him, sir. He'll kill you an' we'll kill him, but it won't do no good. So wait up, sir, till you're stronger."

"What if I'm weaker? I'll make peace if I can, but if I can't shake his hand I'll break his neck. Did he really want to kill me?"

"Aye, sir." Pouk's voice had become a shamed whisper. "I shoulda killed him then, only I didn't. You'd of, an' no countin' costs. Only I'm not you, sir, an' I know it."

"I'm not you, either. I'm no seaman. Help me up."

"You're too weak, sir."

"I know." I felt like I ought to be angry, but I was not. "That's why I wanted you to help me." He did, taking my hands and pulling me up. "I'm a knight," I said. "We fight when we're weak."

"Why's that, sir?" Pouk sounded like he was a million miles away. I said I could not explain, there was not enough time. I tried to take a step and fell down.

After that I was in bed, and a nurse came in and said I had fought the hijackers, and everybody was so proud of me they could bust. There was a dog in the hospital, that was why she was there, and had I seen it?

CHAPTER 20

SWORD BREAKER

There were shouts outside the cable tier. The door opened, and a seaman looked in. "Cap'n, Sir Able. Nothink ter worry h'about, sir. We're watchin' an' won't let 'im h'in."

I said I wanted to talk to him, but the door had already closed.

It got quiet again, just the creak of the timbers and the slap of the waves on the side of the ship, things I had been hearing so long I hardly heard them at all.

I had a blanket and a bottle of brandy. The blanket had

been one of mine, Pouk said, and he had pinched the brandy from the captain's private stock. I had drunk some; it made me terribly dizzy, and I swore I would not drink any more.

"I'm just a kid," I told Pouk between mouthfuls. He did not understand *kid,* so I said, "A boy who's supposed to be a man after one night with a woman."

"Aye, sir. I've felt th' same many's a time."

Right here I want to stop everything and say something like this has happened to me a lot. I have tried to tell other men about Disiri and me and how I changed. And they have said the same thing happened to them. I do not think it did, really. They *felt* like it did. I felt like it did too, but I felt that way because it really did. Of course they would say the same thing.

"Just a boy," I told Pouk. "A boy who thought he was a brave knight."

"I ain't never seen no braver man nor you, sir." Pouk sounded ready to fight anybody who contradicted him. "Why, when them Osterlings got through the net, who was it went for 'em?"

I stopped eating to consider the question. "The dog, I'm sure. The dog Megister Nur couldn't find."

"No, sir! It was you. The rest o' us come after, an' if you hadn't gone, we wouldn't o' gone at all, sir. Them Osterlings, they didn't never think we'd have no knight aboard. You had 'em beat 'fore anybody caught breath. Time you went down, they was cuttin' free."

It took a while, but I nodded. "I remember. Or anyway I think I might. Enemies in front of me and on both sides. Striking them with the mace we bought from Mori. Where is that, by the way? Do you know what happened to it?"

"Cap'n got it, prob'ly, sir."

"Find out, if you can. I'd like to get it back." I stopped talking for a while to eat and scratch my head. "I need something for my left hand, Pouk. A shield, or at least a stick I could use to stop blows. I had to do it with the mace."

"Aye aye, sir. I'll keep my eye out for somethin'."

"Then look for my bow and quiver while you're at it. And for the dog. Is the dog still on board?"

"Wyt seen it last night, sir. Mighty thin it looked, Wyt says, and slavered like to eat him."

"At least the captain hasn't got him."

Pouk coughed. "Speakin' of Cap'n . . . As we was, sir, 'cause he's prob'ly got 'em. Speakin' o' him, I've learnt what he's plannin', sir. He told Mate, an' Mate told Second, and Njors heard him an' told me. When we get to port, sir, he'll pay off the crew and let 'em go ashore. He thinks everybody'll go, only I won't, sir. Him an' Mate'll come down here to do for you then, only I'll be with you."

I said no. "I won't wait for them. How long before we get to port?"

Pouk shrugged. "I ain't no navigator, sir. Could be five days. Could be ten."

"Forcetti?"

"No, sir, Yens, sir. That's what they say. If you're through eatin', sir—"

"No." I got to my feet, without help and without a lot of trouble. "Let me take that back. I'm through eating, but I'm not through with this stewed beef you brought me."

"I wouldn't talk quite so loud, sir. First might be around."

I had not even noticed that I had raised my voice, but I raised it some more. "I've been trying to keep quiet, like you said, but what good is it? The captain's made his plans. I've got to stop him from following through. I want my bow, as soon as you can get it. The bow and the bowstring—the string's very important. My quiver too, and all the arrows you can find, if you can find some."

"Aye aye, sir."

I opened the door of the cable tier. "Gylf!" I made it loud, but it had not been loud enough. *"Gylf! Here, Gylf!"*

"Sir? Who's-?"

"My dog. He really is my dog, Pouk, until his old owner wants him back. I didn't want him because I was afraid of him. I tried to get rid of him before we forded the Irring. I made him go and told him never to come near me." I took a deep breath. It hurt bad, but I took it. *"GYLF! Come here, Gylf!"*

I think Pouk would have run if I had not grabbed him. "I thought I'd shaken him when you and I got on this ship."

I stopped to whistle.

"It's night now, isn't it? That's why it's so dark in here—no sunlight leaking in."

"Aye, sir."

"I'll talk to the captain tomorrow, after he's had his breakfast. I owe him that much. You can tell him, if you want to."

I heard the scrabble of dull claws out in the hold, and I opened the pan Pouk had brought and put it on the floor for Gylf.

I knew that cabin, and I knew there was no way to lock the door if you were not inside. If the captain had eaten in there, I was going to go in when Hordsvin's helper came in to clear away the dishes; but it did not happen like that. He ate on the roof of the sterncastle, which was what I had been expecting, and Gylf and I just came up out of the hold and walked into the cabin like we belonged there. Which we did.

By the time he came in, I had found the foreign mace I had gotten in Irringsmouth and strapped it on. He opened the door and saw us, yelled for Kerl, and then (I guess because I was sitting down and had not pulled out my mace) shut the door and barred it. His sword was under his mattress, like before. I had found it already and left it there. I could have stopped him from getting it, no problem, but I did not.

When he had it I said, "Don't you trust Kerl?"

The captain just looked at me, not saying anything. I told Gylf to let him see him then, and he did. He had been lying in a corner where it was dark and he came up out of there like brown smoke but all solid and snarling.

"I can kill you if I want to," I told the captain. "I beat you before, and I can beat you again. Gylf could kill you, too, and you won't stand the ghost of a chance against both of us. Do you own this ship? Some of the crew told me you did."

"Half."

"Fine. I don't want it. I never did. I don't want to kill you, either." I stood up and held out my hand. "Put that sword away. I don't think we can ever be friends, but we don't have to be enemies either."

He stood there looking at us for maybe half a minute. Then he laid the sword down on his bed and sat down beside it. "You don't object to my sitting in my own cabin?"

"It's my cabin," I told him, "but only until I get off at Forcetti."

"I'm sitting, so you can sit down again. Go ahead. Your wound can't have healed already."

I did. "I want my bow and I want my money. Somebody told me you had them, but he was too scared of you to come in here and get them for me. So I'm here to get them myself. You've got that sword, which is yours, and you'll have some money of your own. Go get it, and give me mine. All I want is what belongs to me. Give it to me, with my bow, the case, and my quiver, and you can go away without fighting."

He shook his head.

"I didn't think you would. All right, here's my last offer. Gylf and I will go out on deck. Before the next watch, you clear out of this cabin, leaving all my stuff—money, bow-case, armor, and so forth—where I can find it. Twenty-two gold ceptres, most of them new and all real gold, plus my other stuff. Will you do that?"

He stood up and Gylf growled. I was afraid he was going to grow into the black thing that had killed the outlaws, and I told him not to.

"You'll return my ship and its cargo to me when we reach port?"

"Sure," I said. "But I don't want them in the first place. I don't—"

He was grabbing his sword. I got the mace out just in time to block the cut. It sounded like a big hammer hitting an anvil. The next cut would have lopped off my head, but I blocked it too. I never had stood up. I was on one knee in front of the chair. The third cut came very fast and broke his sword blade. That was when I decided to call my mace Sword Breaker. Gylf jumped on the captain as soon as his sword broke and pulled him down, and I hit him with Sword Breaker thinking I would knock him out. I hit him too hard, though, and the diamond-shaped blade went deep into his head instead. It came out with blood and brains all over it. I just stood there looking at it, and thinking of Disira and saying, "Good lord, good lord," about twenty times. Then Gylf said, "Shall I eat him?" and I knew he was right and we had to get rid of the captain. So I wiped Sword Breaker on his coat and pushed him out a window, and we cleaned up.

After that I went out on deck and talked to Kerl. I told him he was captain now, and Nur was the first mate. I said that the captain had jumped me, and told him what had happened after that. I said if he wanted to tell somebody when we got to Forcetti, that was all right, but they would probably keep the *Western Trader* there a long time for the trial and so on.

He said it might be better if everybody just said the captain had died on the voyage, and we had buried him at sea. I said that was fine with me, and it really was the truth or pretty close. So he got the crew together and told them, and nobody seemed to mind very much.

After that I thought maybe Head Breaker or something, but somebody was sure to ask whose head it had been, so I stuck with Sword Breaker. Later I gave Sword Breaker to Toug and he called her that too, because that was what I told him.

CHAPTER 21

SEEING THEM

That night Gylf and I talked things over in our cabin. He did not say much, not then and not ever, but he was a good listener and when he did say something it was a real good idea to listen close and think about it afterward. The thing was, I was afraid my wound was not getting any better, and I thought it might be getting worse. It felt as hot as fire, and when I pressed it blood came out, mixed with other stuff.

I was scared. I know I have not said a lot about being scared, but I was scared pretty often the whole time I was in Mythgarthr. I am not going to go back now and tell you about all the times, there would be no point in it. And besides, some of the worst times were times I have not told anything about, like when I was out hunting just after Bold Berthold took me in and I shot the bear and it chased me up a tree. I had not thought a big bear like that could climb trees, and it was brown anyway and not black. I guess the bears in the Forest of Celidon are different from the bears we have at home, because it could climb quicker than I could. When it got really close I stuck an arrow down its throat and it fell out of the tree and went away. I was so scared I could not climb down. I just held on and shook for a long time. I had dropped my bow when I ran, and the bear had just about bitten my hand off when it snapped down on the shaft.

Anyway, I was scared and Gylf and I talked about my being wounded and what might happen. He said those deep wounds were the worst because you could not lick them clean. I laughed because I could not have licked there. I would have washed it. Only I thought about the kind of water we had on the ship, and he was right. Licking would have been better.

After a while I remembered Bold Berthold's telling me that the Bodachan would fix up sick animals sometimes, and they had helped him as much as they could. Then too, Disiri was an Aelf, and I was sure she would help me if she knew I was hurt. So I said what we needed to do was get in touch with some Aelf that might help us, and were there some on this boat?

Gylf put his head down between his paws, and I could see he was holding something back. So I said, "Well, if you know where some are, how about if you try to get them to help me? If they won't I won't be any worse off than I am right now."

He just looked at me for a while, then he went to the door

and scratched it so I would let him out. I did. It was dark by then, and the moon and the stars were out, and we had just enough wind to fill the sails; that was my favorite time on the ship, every time I was on it.

Then Gylf pushed past me, because the door was pretty small, and ran across the deck and jumped over the rail. When he came back and we had talked, I went out on deck again and asked Kerl if he was afraid of the Aelf.

He scratched his head the way I do sometimes. "I dunno, Sir Able. I never seen one."

"You will," I said. I pointed to the sailors who were on that watch. They were asleep on deck except for the helmsman and the lookout. I told Kerl to wake them up and send them below, and said he could give them any reason he wanted to.

He looked kind of surprised. "Do I have to give them a reason, Sir Able?"

I said no, and he started yelling at them to wake them up. I told one to find Pouk when he went below and send him to me. We had him steer and sent the helmsman below. The way that wind and that sea were, I could have steered the ship myself, or we could have tied the wheel. Pouk had no idea what was going on then, and neither did Kerl.

Once the watch had gone below, Gylf jumped over the side again. After that there was nothing to do but wait, so I sat down in one of the crenels. Kerl was scared. He came up to me, very quiet. "He's no ordinary dog, is he, sir?"

I said no.

"He's comin' up to breathe, mebbe, where we don't see him, sir?"

I said yes, and pretty soon he went away. The moon was a narrow crescent, just beautiful. After a while I could see it was really a bow, and see the Lady holding it. I did not know a thing about her then, but I saw her anyway; she is the Valfather's daughter, the most important one. Bold Berthold had always said Skai was the third world, and the people up there were the Overcyns. Seeing her like that I wondered about Number Two and Number One. I had asked him about those one time, but he only said nobody knew very much.

I blinked and the Lady was gone. I remembered then that Bold Berthold had told me they went a lot faster up there and what we saw was years to them. They get killed sometimes (I found that out later) but they never get old and die the way we do.

Then I thought about the highest world, Number One. It seemed to me for that living way up there and looking down on the rest of us would make him proud. After a while I saw where that was wrong, and under my breath I said, "No, it wouldn't. It would make you kind instead, if there was any good in you at all." As soon as I had said it, I knew Pouk had heard me, but I do not know what he made of it.

What I had thought was what if it was me and I was all alone up there, with just rabbits and squirrels? Or the only grownup, and the rest were little kids? Sure, I could strut around and show off for them, but would I want to? If one was bad, I could smack him and make him cry. But I was a knight. What kind of victory would that be for a knight?

I decided I would just take care of the kids as well as I could, and I would hope that someday they would get older and be people I could really talk to.

Maybe I nodded off then, or maybe I had already. Anyway I dreamed I was a kid again myself asleep on a hillside. In my dream, the flying castle crossed the sky over my head and made me remember how I used to live in a place where there were swords and no cars.

I woke up because I had been about to fall and went to

stand by Pouk. There was a dark cloud way in the west, and I saw a man riding down it. He looked really small because he was so far away, but I saw him as clearly as I have ever seen anything, a man in black armor on a big white horse—the horse's neck stretched out, and its open mouth and wild eyes. Its hooves just flying. Down the cloud and across the sea, lower and lower until it seemed like it was running over the crests of the waves.

"Look!" I yelled. "A man on horseback, there in the lowest stars. See him?"

Pouk looked at me as if I had gone crazy.

Kerl sighted along my arm. "The Moonrider, Sir Able? You seen him?"

"I see him now."

"I never have." Kerl squinted and peered. "Some do, they say."

"Right there, two fingers above the water, where the bright star is."

Kerl peered again, then shook his head. "I can't, sir. I've had Nur point like you and say he seen him plain as day, but I'm not one that has the second sight."

"I'm not, either."

From the wheel, Pouk said really soft, "You are, Sir Able, sir."

I started to say how plain he was and anybody could see him, but all of a sudden I could not see him myself. After that I kept looking and looking. The moon was still like a shining bow, but it was only like it. It was not one, not really. The stars were still there, reflected in the sea, and there were a few clouds and it was really beautiful. I sort of thought I would say here that there was nobody there, that it was all just empty. That would not be true. I knew there was somebody there, maybe a lot of somebodies. Only I could not see them.

I must have looked for about an hour, and then the Aelf came. They were as solid and real as anybody there in the night, some with fishes' scales and some with fishes' tails. They were blue, dark blue, but it was not like a certain sky or anything. It was not navy blue or midnight blue or blue black, or anything like that. It was more like the color of deep, deep water than anything else, but that was not it either. It was their own color, and their eyes were like the yellow fire of the sun reflected in ice. They had lonely, lovely, piping voices, and they called out to each other, and to the sea and the ship. I knew most of the words they used, but I could not understand what they were saying and I cannot write it down, either.

I stood up, balancing on a merlon, and waved to them, yelling, "Over here! I'm Able!"

They called to one another, pointing, and swam over to the ship, diving in and out of the water and leaping free of it, sometimes as high as the mainmast. Spreading fins like wings. I told Kerl to hang a rope over the side or something and he did, but not many of them used it. They just climbed up the sides, or else jumped up on the deck until there was a crowd of them there.

I pulled off my shirt and the bandage so they could see my wound, and they came up on the sterncastle deck to look at it, asking questions without waiting for answers.

I had to guess at what to say; so I said I wanted to be cured and I would do anything for them if only they would do it. And if they could not, I would still do anything they wanted me to.

"No," they said. And, "No, no!" And, "No, no, no, brave sir knight. We could not ask you to fight Kulili for us until you were well and strong. Ill and weak you would surely die."

Another was almost like an echo. "Will surely die . . ."

Then an old Aelf came; he looked like a man of thin blue glass, with wild white hair and a tangled blue beard to his knees. All the others stood aside—you could tell he was somebody. He took my face between his hands and looked way down into my eyes. I could not help looking into his when he did that, and it was like looking into a storm at midnight.

When he finally let my face go, it seemed like it had been a long, long time. Hours. "Come with us to Aelfrice" was what he said. "The sea shall heal your wound and teach you to be the strongest of your kind, a knight against whom no knight can stand. Will you come?"

I could not talk, but I nodded.

As soon as I did, there were eight or ten Aelfmaidens tearing at my clothes. They took off my sword belt and Sword Breaker, and everything else, too, and as soon as they got down to bare skin they kissed it, giggling and elbowing each other and having a fine time. One grabbed my right hand and another one got my left, and one jumped up onto my shoulders. It seemed like she weighed no more than a few drops of water, and the long, thin legs she wrapped around my neck were as cold as dew.

All four of us jumped into the sea then. I did not mean to, but I did anyway. It was all really strange. There had been this greasy swell up where the ship was, but before we hit the sea was tossing waves, and they looked as clear as crystal—chimerical, like ghosts in sheets of snow-white foam, ghosts spangled all over with moonlight and reflected stars. There was a shock as if we were jumping into a cold shower, and a roar like a big wave hitting another head-on, and then we were down under all those waves.

"You will not drown," the one on my left told me, and giggled. I had not even been worrying, but I should have been.

"Not as long as we are with you, Sir Knight." That was the right-hand Aelfmaiden; she laughed, and the sound of it was like little naked kids playing in some pool the tide had left.

"But we will leave you!" It was the one on my shoulders who said that, and she pulled my hair a little bit to get me to pay attention. "It is what we do!"

All three of them laughed and laughed at that. There was nothing cruel about the way they laughed, but there was nothing kind about it either.

"Garsecg will make us!" they said.

Strange fish swam all around us. Some of them looked dangerous and some looked very dangerous. I did not know who they belonged to then. Deeper down we lost the moon and the starlight, and the whole world of suns and moons and winds seemed really, really far away. I guess it was the way an astronaut must feel; he was so used to those things that he never thought they could be taken away, and when they are he must wonder how he got into this.

I know I did.

Some of the fish down there had teeth like big needles, and a lot had spots or stripes on their sides that glowed red, yellow, or green. I saw an eel that looked like a rope on fire, and some other scary things, and finally I asked the Aelfmaidens if this was where they lived, because it did not seem to me that anybody would if they could live anywhere else.

"We live wherever we are," they said, "and Kelpie is our name." They lit up for me then, slender, pretty girls that seemed like they were made of blue light. They made me look at their gills and tails, and they had long curved claws that looked as sharp as the fishes' teeth.

CHAPTER 22

GARSECG

At the mouth of an underwater cave we found the old man who had promised to cure me. He made the Kelpies go away, and I was kind of glad. I wanted to know where we were, and he said it was Aelfrice. "I am not the oldest of my kind," he told me, "nor the wisest. Yet I know many things. I am Garsecg." Later I found out it was not his real name; but then I believed him, and I still think *Garsecg* when I think of him; so it is what I am going to call him. I asked how he was going to cure me.

"I cannot. The sea will heal you. Come with me, and I will show you." He took my hand, and the two of us swam to a place where the sea bottom was as warm as water in a bathtub, and steam bubbles blew mud and sand out of crevices. "You have a rent in your side," Garsecg told me. "Have you ever seen a rent in the sea?"

I said no.

"Watch."

The bubbles came faster, and stones were thrown up, and there was a rumble underneath the stone like thunder. White-hot rock roared up from the seafloor so that great white clouds of steam belched up and all the fish and crabs and things ran away, everything except us.

That went on for a long time; gradually all the noise trailed off into a sound like a giant asleep, like Gilling dying down there in a bed as big as a lot of people's houses. The rock stopped flowing up and got hard. We went up to look, and it was a whole island of rock with a sort of basin in the middle. Some seabirds had started nesting there, and the sea lapped at the gray-rock beach all around it like a cat laps cream.

Grass started growing there, then trees. The trees sent roots way down deep looking for fresh water, following little cracks and splitting them. For maybe a second I saw Disiri running naked through the trees. I wanted to run after her, but Garsecg held me and we sort of fought about it. That was the only time we ever fought.

New birds—birds Disiri had brought—nested in her trees, nuts fell off them, and crabs came ashore to eat the nuts. Garsecg caught one and ate it the way you would eat a praline, but I was worried about their pinchers.

The island got more and more beautiful, and smaller and smaller, until it sunk in the sea and the waves closed over it, and it was like it had never been there at all. "Now you have seen a rent in the sea," Garsecg told me. "Have you seen a crag die?"

I said no, and we swam again. When we got to the crag that was going to die, we climbed up it, up the sheer rock, and stood on the top.

There had been a wind the whole time, getting worse all the time. Pretty soon it roared so loud you could not hear yourself think. The waves got bigger and bigger until every wave that hit the crag was like a railroad train, and the spray hit us too, and sometimes the water at the top washed right over us. The crag shook, and there were boulders in those big waves, boulders that hit like hammers and then fell back into the sea for the next wave to pick up. Once on Halloween I had thrown gravel at windows; this made me think of that, but when I was doing it I had never known how horrible it really was, and now I felt like I was out there under the sea, still a kid throwing rocks. It got so bad we had to back off the crag, way back onto solid land. Even there the wind made me think of a knight, a big knight on a big horse riding among little ordinary people like Garsecg and me and slashing left and right. I know it sounds crazy, but that is the way I thought.

The water came up, the same way it had a hundred times before. It covered the crag, but when it went away this time the whole crag was gone.

I went out to the edge and looked down. It was not easy to keep my balance in that wind, but I did it—I had to—and down at the bottom you could see what was left, a little less each time a wave smashed into the beach. Garsecg came and stood beside me. After a minute he held out his hand, cupped, so I could see what was in it. At first I thought there was nothing. It was water. Just water. He asked if I understood.

I said, "I think so."

He waited a long time before he said, "The island?"

"I have to be like the sea, isn't that right? It waits, it runs out the clock and closes over the torn part."

"The crag?"

"Water is nothing, but water with energy is stronger than stone. Is that the right answer?"

Garsecg smiled. "Come with me."

We went back to the sea, swimming up at the top this time, jumping with its waves or letting its currents carry us. "Your blood is the sea," Garsecg told me. I did not get that for a long while, but as we swam on and on it began to make sense. First I thought it was crazy, then I thought he might be right after all, then I knew he was right—I could feel the sea inside of me exactly like I felt the sea outside of me. After that we kept on swimming, until knowing that the sea and I made one thing became part of me. It is still part of me, and still true. The Kelpies and the other Sea Aelf say it is like that for them too; but they are lying. For me it is really true, like it is for Kulili. I can be all sunny and smiles for a long, long time. But I can rise up like when we fought the Angrborn at the pass. Giants ran from me then and the ones that did not died.

Finally I said to myself, "By the power of the sea life left the sea. They were able to leave it because they took it with them. I was a sea-creature in Mother's womb, and she was a sea-creature inside her mother, and I will be a sea-creature as long as I live. The king must know, exactly the way I do, because he put a nykr on his shield."

"He is my brother," Garsecg said.

We were both swimming hard, but I looked around at him, surprised. "Can you hear my thoughts?"

"Sometimes."

"You're an Aelf. Isn't the king a human man?"

"He is."

I thought about that for a long time, and got nowhere with it.

Garsecg must have been able to hear some of it, because he said, "When a man of my kind takes a woman of your kind, she may bear a child."

Still not understanding, I said, "All right."

"Every child has something of its father and something of its mother as well; save for monsters, every child is of the male kind or the female kind nevertheless."

We stopped to rest, floating on our backs in the clear sea. I said, "I took an Aelf woman—a woman I really truly love like nobody else on earth."

"I know it."

"Will we have children?"

"I cannot say."

"Suppose we do." These were things I had not thought about before. "If it's a boy, will it grow up to be a human man?"

"Or an Aelf man. Until the child is born, there is no knowing."

"What if it's a girl?"

"The same. The king's royal father lay with a woman of my race, even as you with your Aelfmaiden."

I saw then that Garsecg did not really know everything, and to tell the truth I felt good about it.

"Of their union three children were born, one of my kind and two of yours."

"Three?"

Garsecg nodded. "Our sister's name is Morcaine."

When we started off again, I thought we were going to swim a long way like we had before. Now I can see Garsecg wanted to rest before we got where we were going. He knew about the stairs, and he knew we might have to fight. The Khimairas would not recognize him, and he would not be able to tell them who he was. Anyway, I was just getting warmed up again when he stopped and pointed. "That is the isle your mariners call Glas," he said, and pretty soon we were there and climbing over slick sharp rocks that shone crimson, gold, and scarlet in the sunshine, with a lot of other colors, more beautiful than I could ever make you believe it was.

"Do they call it Glas because it's made of glass?" I asked him.

He shook his head. "It is not, but of fire opal."

"The dragon stone."

He would not look at me. "Who told you that?"

It had been Bold Berthold, and I called him my brother. "He's dead now, I think."

"Wise Berthold. If you do not know him dead, let us hope that he lives."

I told Garsecg how I had searched for Bold Berthold's body without finding it.

"Many have searched for this isle, but those who search for it never find it. More than a few have sighted it by chance, however, and a handful of mariners have landed here."

I had the feeling Garsecg knew more about that than he was telling, so I asked what happened to them.

"Various things. Some returned safely to their ships. Some perished. Some remain with us, and some went to other places. Do you see the tower?"

I did, and it was huge. Somebody had built a skyscraper all by itself way out on that little island, and at first I thought why did they have to make it so high? Because there was nothing else out there to crowd it. Only there was. It was the sea. The island was not really very big, so if you wanted to put a big building on it, it had to go straight up.

It did. It was round, and only a little wider at the bottom, and it went up and up like a needle, taller than the tallest mountain.

"The builder was of the sixth world, which is Muspel," Garsecg said. "My people build nothing like it unless they must. Would that they did! From this tower Setr sought to overawe this sphere, which you call the World Below."

I said we called it Aelfrice mostly.

Garsecg nodded. "He built smaller towers as well, his strongholds on many coasts. My sister dwells in one when she chooses."

"But you don't?"

"I could if I wished." Garsecg stood up on what I had

thought was just another slick rock, and walked away. When I could not see him, I heard him say, "How is your wound?"

I felt for it, but I couldn't find it.

"Healed?"

When I caught up with him, I said, "There's a scar, but it's closed and it's not sore."

"The scar will fade. For a time, a gull might have seen rocks below the water."

"I get it. Am I really the strongest knight in the whole world now?"

"That is for you to say."

"Then I am." I did not feel any stronger when I said it, but I knew I was very, very strong and very, very fast. Exactly how strong and how fast I did not know. I also knew that some of that was what Disiri had done, and some came from the sea—from learning how it was, and that it was in me, tides of blood pounding the beaches of my ears. But some was just me, and in fact the part about the sea was just me, too; that had been there all the time, although I had not known it.

I stopped thinking about all that stuff because I had seen the stair. On that skyscraper it looked like a cobweb, stretching up and up to a sort of crevice way up high. The sun on that stair and the wall made them look like they were on fire. You wished you had really dark sunglasses or maybe welding glasses. I squinted and shielded my eyes and all the rest, but it did not bother Garsecg.

"Here Setr gathered all the greatest weapons of our world, in order that we might not resist him. He who could sunder mountains would not permit us so much as a dagger. Yet in the end we drove him out."

I wanted to know if Garsecg thought he would come back.

"He does return at times, then flies again before we can muster our forces. Would you drive us from your Middle World if you could, Sir Able?"

I thought of Disiri, and I made my no as strong as I could get it.

"Many would. Many strive against us even now. Yet we would return someday. It is the same for Setr."

"All those weapons you were talking about, are they still there?"

Garsecg nodded. "We have been pillaging his trove a thousand years, and the weapons we have taken from it are scattered throughout the worlds."

"Then they're gone."

The next time Garsecg said something, his voice was so low I could barely hear him. He said, "The trove is hardly diminished."

CHAPTER 23

ON THE STAIR

"You will recall," Garsecg said when we got to the base of the stair, "that I told you truly that I could not heal your wound, but that the sea would heal it if only you would come to Aelfrice with me."

I nodded, feeling my wound again to see if it was still gone.

"I promised also that you would be the strongest of all your kind. You are, but it was not my doing but yours, and the sea's."

I said, "Are you trying to get me to bitch about all this? I won't. I owe you. I'll owe you for the rest of my life."

He shook his head. "Am I not an honorable man? You owe me nothing whatsoever. I want to make that entirely clear."

It was not easy to grin at Garsecg, and that may have been the only time I pulled it off. I said, "Okay, I don't owe you a thing. Only I'd like for you to owe me, because I might want another favor from you sometime. What would you like me to do?"

"Put your foot on the first step."

I did. "There you go. Now watch this." I ran up the next hundred or so, then stopped and turned around to look down at him. "Aren't you coming with?"

"I am," he called, "but you must go first, and I must warn you that we go into danger."

I said sure, and climbed some more. And right here I had better stop and make a lot of things a lot clearer.

First off, a couple of hundred steps was nothing on that stair. It went right straight at the skyscraper until it hit it about a quarter of the way up, and it just got steeper and steeper all the time. It was curved about the way a string with a little slack in it would be. There were thousands and thousands of steps.

Second, nobody had to tell me it was dangerous. The steps were hard fire opal, polished like a jeweler would have polished them and so slick you could see your reflection in them. They were about two and half feet end-to-end, and there was no rail.

The third one is really tough for me to get out, but here it is. I kept thinking that Garsecg had really done me *three* big favors. I had promised Gylf I would never try to ditch him again. I had meant it, and I never did. But he still scared me.

Pretty soon I will tell about Mani. He could be scary, too. But no matter how scary he was, he was still a cat. A big cat and a tough cat, but just a cat that could talk. Gylf was plenty big enough to scare people the way he was regular, and I had already guessed that regular was just the way he looked so he would not scare us. The black thing with fangs like daggers, the thing as big as Blackmane, was the real Gylf. Okay, I had not tried to ditch him. But he had stayed on the boat (this was what I thought) when I went off with the Kelpies, and that was fine with me.

Garsecg caught up to me. "I carried you to this isle in order that you might choose some storied weapon for your own, before we asked service of you. You are still young, thus I hoped your eagerness to blood your treasure would lead you to accept the challenge."

I said sure. I would do it, whatever it was.

"I feared you might consider that trickery, and so I make haste to explain myself. I am glad you do not. Even so, you speak too quickly."

"No way," I said. "Those Kelpies told me you wanted me to fight somebody called Kulili. I knew what I was getting myself into." I had tried looking over the side a while back and I had not liked it. I was keeping my eyes straight to the front. Sort of under my breath I said, "Going down is going to be a lot worse."

Garsecg said, "Going down may be infinitely easier, Sir Able. Look above you."

I did. "The black birds?"

"They are not birds. They are Fire Aelf—or they were. These Fire Aelf are Khimairae now."

"Bad news?"

"They serve Setr. We are shapechangers, we Aelf."

I remembered Disiri and how she had been a bunch of different girls for me, and I said, "Yeah, I know."

"Setr cast those into the shape you see. He is a shape-changer himself, so potent that he can lend great strength to others. As they are, he made them. They cannot break his spell."

High above a shrill voice screamed, *"Will not!"*

"They guard his tower still," Garsecg told me, "or try to."

I was thinking it was like a big video game, except I was on the screen. Or virtual reality maybe. I sort of felt my head for the gear, but there was not any and just then a Khimaira swooped down at me, pulling up just before I could grab it, a little starved body, mostly black but red at the cracks, with claws and jaws and black bat wings.

"They hope to convince you that they pose no serious threat," Garsecg muttered. "Now that you have seen them, they fear you will turn back."

"I don't think so."

"When we have climbed higher, they will cast us from the stair. If we fight, we will surely fall. Shun them, and climb as fast as you can. In the tower we will not be safe from them, yet the tower is to be preferred."

I stopped and looked back at him, thinking about how old he was. "Aren't they going to try to kill you too?"

"These Khimairae have sought my life before," he said.

I went up about a hundred more steps, and one whished past so close I could smell it. Another went in back of me, and its wing brushed my head.

"Look about you," Garsecg warned me. *"Heeeeaaaar!"*

I looked back at him instead. Only he was gone, and where he had been there was a kind of alligator with horns, as big as a cow, and ten or twelve legs. The legs had suckers, and all the suckers were grabbing on to the steps. It lashed its tail and raised its head and roared at the Khimairas, snapping at any that came close. Just then one blindsided me. I fell and barely caught the edge of the stair with the fingers of one hand. They were slipping, and I knew I was going to die when a sucker closed around my wrist and heaved me back up onto the steps.

I was still grabbing and shaking when the alligator's mouth opened and I saw Garsecg's face inside it. He said, "Recall the sea. And run!"

I was so scared I could hardly stand up, but as soon as I did, a big wave caught me from behind. Do you know what I mean? My legs ached too, but that did not matter. I went up those stairs like I was flying, three steps at a time. They kept hitting me, or trying to, and once I stumbled. But I never stopped until one dropped down on the step ahead of me with a sword in each hand. It was black and all bones and wings, and its lips would not quite cover its teeth. But the eyes seemed wrong. They were those yellow-fire eyes all the Aelf have, even the Kelpies and the ones who gave me Gylf, the same kind of eyes Disiri used to have even when the rest looked just like a human girl. When I looked at them all I could think of was her.

It opened out its wings when it saw I had stopped. With those big black wings open it looked as big as a house. "You musst fight usss." Its voice was mostly hiss, but you could understand. "Ssee? I have sswordss for uss both."

It held one out hilt first, but I did not take it. I hit the pommel with the flat of my hand instead and drove the sword backward into the Khimaira's chest. Its eyes got big and scared then, and stuff that was not quite blood spurted out of the wound, and it fell off the stair. I thought that had been pretty easy, but before I could take another step, five hit me all at once, not to knock me off but grabbing me and lifting. I had one on each leg and one on each arm, and one had its claws in my hair. They flew with me so fast it was like falling up in a hurricane. I saw there were windows and balconies and arches and torn places in the sides of the skyscraper, and way up above us but getting closer and closer was Mythgarthr: trees and people, animals and mountains.

About then the one that had my left ankle yelled like it was scared and let go and peeled off, and I figured they were going to drop me, so I wrenched around and grabbed the wrists of the ones holding my arms. After that I kicked off the one that had my other leg. Their wings went even faster, but we started losing altitude. The one who had my hair said, "We fall!" and I told him to land me on the steps, but he let go instead.

After that, the one that had been holding on to my left arm screamed we were going to die. I kept yelling land on the steps, and we did, coming down too fast and crashing on them. It was not easy to keep hold of the Khimairas the way I did, but I did it, and as soon as I got my breath I banged the two of them together until they begged.

I stopped. "You guys work for Setr?"

"Ssetr iss henss."

I banged them together some more. "That's not what I asked you. Do you work for him?"

"Yess!"

"Okay. Quit. From now on you're going to work of me."

"We cannot renounsse Ssetr!" They both said that.

"Then you're gonna die. I'm gonna break your wings and throw you off this thing."

Garsecg came up behind me, not being the alligator anymore. "They are evil creatures, Sir Able, but I ask you to spare them."

That was crazy, and I said so.

"Yet I ask it, Sir Able, for the sake of the good I have done you."

I threw one down and got my foot on its neck, and I bent the other one backwards over my knee. I was still hurting from the fall and still scared silly, and I would have killed it then and there for two cents. I leaned down on it, and heard its back creak like a gate in the wind.

"She cannot renounce Setr," Garsecg said to my back.

I did not answer, just leaning down some more on the Khimaira.

"Do you owe me nothing?"

I owed him a lot and I knew it, but he was beginning to bug me. I thought about things a little, and then I said, "I owe this whateveryoucallit, too. If it hadn't been for him, I'd be dead. So I'm going to take him away from Setr so he doesn't have to look like this anymore."

After that I bent the Khimaira some more, and it said, "I renounsse him!"

I eased up a little. "That's good. Say it again."

"I renounsse him."

"Say the name. Who are you renouncing?"

"Ssetr. I renounsse Ssetr forever."

I kind of looked over my shoulder at Garsecg. "What do you think of that?"

He shrugged. "Are you pleased with a breath?"

"You don't think it means it?"

"I do not know. Nor does it matter—anyone can say anything. She cannot renounce Setr, as I told you. If a prisoner renounces his chains, do they fall from his wrists?"

"What could she swear by that would make it real?"

Garsecg shook his head. "There is nothing."

So I thought about that, and finally I said, "How does Setr make them do whatever he wants?"

"Who knows?"

"Well, she does." I put more pressure on the Khimaira and said, "You listen up. Tell me how he's got you, or I'll break your back this minute."

Garsecg said a lot more then, but I am not going to write it down here. He wanted me to let the Khimaira go.

"Sslay me," she said. "End my life and end my agony."

I let her off my knee and grabbed her by the neck. "You swore by Setr, didn't you? Admit it!"

"Yess."

About twenty were buzzing us by then, and I decided we had better get inside quick. I let the other one up and grabbed her too. I made them fold their wings, tucked one under each arm, and ran for it. They did not weigh a lot, and the sea was surging all through me. Even so, it was tough going, and when we got inside I was ready to quit. I lifted them up and threw them down, and I made them shut up until Garsecg got there and I caught my breath. It was a really big, huge room, pretty dark, that stunk of rotten meat and mold, and it was so quiet you could listen to your heart beat. The throne at the far end must have been twenty-five feet high and fifty feet wide.

"Here Setr plans to judge our world," Garsecg said when he got there. "Forcing us to live virtuous lives."

I was still mad. I said it sounded like a tall order to me, that even though there were a lot of things I liked about the Aelf I had met, everybody said you could not trust them and they could lie birds out of the trees. I thought Garsecg was going to climb all over me for that, but he looked kind of sad and nodded.

I said, "Well, we're not exactly the most honest people in the whole world either."

Then he said something that surprised the heck out of me. He said, "Yet you are the gods of Aelfrice."

I had never heard anything like that before. (Okay, really I had, but I did not remember it.) I knew he was serious from the way he said it, and I did not know how to react. I did not want to show it, and I wanted time to think about it, so I grabbed one of the Khimairas and asked again if she renounced Setr, and when she said yes, I told her to go back to being a regular Aelf, because I liked that shape a lot better. She tried, but she could not.

I told Garsecg he had been right. "You probably know Disiri," I said. "I know her too, and she did some shape changes for me once. It didn't seem like it was hard at all for her. Was it hard when you turned into the alligator with all the legs?"

He shook his head. "It is a matter of concentration, Sir Able. Observe." Before he said that last word he had started to melt and flow. I know you do not know what I mean, even if you think you do. But that is the only way I can describe it. You know about Claymation? It was like that, like somebody I could not see was molding him between shots. He started looking like me. (I mean the way I looked after Disiri got through with me.) He looked more and more like me until he would have fooled everybody on the ship. There was no smoke, but I did not think about that.

That was when I first noticed his eyes. I have probably said a couple dozen times that all the Aelf had those yellow fire eyes. Up until then it had not bothered me that Garsecg did not. Before, he had bushy blue eyebrows, and the eyes deep in. The alligator's eyes had been really small, and I guess I had not paid a lot of attention. When he looked like me, his eyes were easier to see and I looked at him harder. And he did not have Aelf eyes at all. He did not have human eyes, either. Or cat eyes or dog eyes or anything like that. His eyes were a high wind on a dark night.

I had been scared plenty already, and that scared me a lot more. I pretended I had not noticed, but I was shaking inside. To cover up, I told the other Khimaira to renounce Setr.

She would not, and I said, "Even if he made you look ugly and stay there? What did he ever do for you?"

"We ressieved nothing," the first one said, "ssave thesse sshapes. We were promissed great benefitss, alwayss to be paid when the nexst tassk wass done."

The one I had been talking to nodded. "Alwayss another tassk."

Garsecg stepped between them and me. "That being so, as I know it is, why will you not renounce Setr as your fellow did?"

That one stepped around him and knelt to me. "Lord, I will sserve you in all thingss whatssoever. Iss that not enough? I ssaved you jusst as Baki did. Assk what sservice you wissh, and you sshall resseive it."

I needed thinking time, so I said, "What's your name?"

"Your sslave iss Uri, Lord."

Garsecg was changing again, going back to the way he had usually looked. "You must not suppose, Sir Able, that those are their true names, of use in weaving spells."

"Yess, yess!" they said. "They are!"

Well, I had wanted to think. And sometimes I really do. I had been wondering about certain things, like why Garsecg's eyes did not look right and why he wanted me to let those two khimairas go. So I said, "It's not always a real good thing to throw around real names, is it? Like, Able's just what everybody calls me here. Is it all right if I use your real name? Or should I just keep on saying Garsecg?"

Garsecg said, "You are correct. Do not speak my true name, even when we are alone."

"Fine. I guess you know these two whateveryoucall 'ems just about killed me."

He shook his head. "I would have saved you." If he was lying, he was a good liar. Which he was.

I said I would not argue, but I felt like he owed me.

"I will repay you by letting you claim a storied weapon all the world will envy."

"Are you talking about Eterne?"

"No. It is not here, and I am surprised you know of it."

I sort of shrugged. "That's the only one I want, and you were going to let me take something anyhow, so I could fight Kulili for you. I think I'll take these two instead. They're quitting Setr, so they ought to take off his uniform. That's how it seems to me."

"One has renounced Setr, as you say, and the other has sworn to serve you. Will you fight Kulili?"

"I said I would. I don't go back on my word, Garsecg."

"Then there is no reason you should not have these two to assist you—if you really want them. Make no mistake. When a man owns a slave, the slave owns a master."

I said I could live with that.

"Never say you were not warned. Their new uniform will be . . . ?"

"Their natural shapes," I said, "their Aelf shapes. If they won't change for me here, I'm taking them to the top of this skyscraper. That ought to do it."

Garsecg did not like that at all. He wanted me to let them go, and go straight down to the armories with him like he had planned. I would not do it, and when he got us over to the inside stairs the Khimairas and I went up instead of down. Finally he said all right, he would meet us up there.

CHAPTER 24

SUNSHINE

If I told everything that happened after that on the stairway that went up the inside of the skyscraper, and what I said to Uri and Baki, and what they told me in the way that they told it, it would use up a stack of paper as high as the stairway was. So I am not going to. Here are the main things.

I wanted to know why the Aelf had driven Setr out, and it was because he wanted to be king of all of them. Some of the kings and queens they had already had not liked that.

Then I wanted to know why some of them were for him, Uri especially. It was because of Kulili. They hated her, and Setr had been trying to kill her. He had raised a big army, all the Sea Aelf, all the Fire Aelf, and some others. They had tried to mob her, and she had killed about half of them and chased the rest. I tried to find out why they wanted her dead, too, but I never got to the bottom of that. It was the same when I asked what she looked like. She looked all kinds of different ways, so she was a shapechanger too. She lived in the sea, like the Sea Aelf, but in deeper water.

We did not get to the top that day, or even the day after. I probably ought to say that, too. Uri and Baki knew where food might be as you went up, so we would stop whenever we got near a place, rest, and eat, if there was anything. Maybe we would find a room we could barricade. We did that both times when we slept.

Only I sort of lost track of the days, and it was night when we finally got to the roof garden. There was no moon, but there was bright starlight and it showed fruit trees with a lot of fruit on them. We were ready to eat anything, and that was great. Baki flew up a date palm and brought me a bunch of ripe dates. I had never eaten those before, and they are the best fruit in the world. There were oranges, too, not exactly like our oranges at home, but not exactly like tangerines either. Small and sweet.

When we were full I made Uri and Baki lie down and said I would keep watch. I did it because the closer to the top we got the less they had wanted to come up here, and I was afraid they would run if I put one of them on watch.

So they sacked out and I sat up with my back against a tree and blinked and yawned, and tried to stay awake. I got to looking at the stars, too, and thinking about the man that Kerl called the Moonrider. And pretty soon, sure enough, the moon came up.

That was when it hit me. You could never see the moon or the stars or the sun or anything like that in Aelfrice. I never had when Toug and I went there, and I never had either when Garsecg and I were swimming all over, watching the island be born and live and die, and watching the crag die, and all of that. If you were lucky, what you saw was the place I had come from, the place where the *Western Trader* was, and Irringsmouth, and a lot more. You saw Mythgarthr, and people living their lives up there, kind of the way you see somebody's whole life in a movie. (It was not really like a movie, it was longer and more detailed, and you lost sight of somebody and went to somebody else, but you know what I mean.) So this was not Aelfrice at all. The bottom was in Aelfrice all right, but the top was in Mythgarthr, the same way that our moon and our stars were really in Skai.

So I had been right, and if anything could have kept me

awake, it was that. But it did not. Pretty soon I went to sleep anyhow. I could not help it.

The moon climbed up the Bowl of Skai and got brighter and brighter, but that was not what woke me. What woke me was Garsecg. He came flapping up like a big flying dinosaur, bigger than a plane. His wings fanned me and made as much noise as a storm, and I jerked awake. He was still shrinking back into Garsecg when he said, "This may kill them." He pointed to Uri and Baki. "Do you know that?"

I was yawning; I said, "I guess. Only I don't much care. Maybe I ought to but I don't."

"They would not obey you?"

"I had to drag them a little, and a couple of times I had to smack them around some. I didn't like that, but I did it. I tried not to hurt them too bad."

Garsecg nodded, really looking like himself now. "They know they may die."

"I don't think so," I said. "What I think is that Setr ordered them not to come up here, and they still can't do it even if they want to. He enchanted them, or put a spell on them, or whatever you want to call it."

Garsecg smiled. "Why would he do that? Do you know?"

"I think so," I said. "Did you get a chance to rest?"

"I have had far more rest than you, I am sure."

"Then stand watch for us. Wake me at dawn."

"Sunup?"

He was testing me to see if I knew where I was, but I did not care. I said, "Whatever," and went back to sleep.

It was the middle of morning when I woke up. I thought Garsecg had gone, but after I had splashed in the little creek I saw him (like you would see a ghost) sitting in deep shade under a big tree. I sat down beside him, not sure if I ought to be mad at him for letting me sleep.

"This is a durian," he said, and held up a funky-looking fruit. "Would you like it?"

I said sure and took it, and he picked up another one for himself. "The smell is unpleasant," he told me, "but the flesh is wholesome and delicious."

It had a thorny peel on it, and I could not get it open.

"You found no weapon on your climb?"

I told him no. "They're all down below in the armories. That's what Uri said. By the way, what happened to getting me up at sunrise? You said you would."

"I did not." Garsecg was peeling his durian. "You suggested that I awaken you at the first light. I asked whether you intended the rising of the sun. You said you did, and slept. Did you dream?"

I nodded. "How'd you peel that thing?"

"This is a good place for dreaming. It may well be the best place. What dream had you?"

"I had mail and a helmet, a shield and a sword." It was hard to remember already. "I rode down out of the sky like the Moonrider. I think I came to do justice on earth, only the earth swallowed me. What does it mean?"

"I have no idea. Nothing, perhaps."

"You know. You know all about all that stuff."

He shook his head. "I do not, and resist disturbing you with my speculations."

"Like you resisted waking us up. Can I try a bite of yours?"

He passed it over. I sniffed it like Gylf would have, and it stunk. It made me think of stinky cheese, though, and I like stinky cheese.

I bit into it. "It's good. You're right."

"You will find that I generally am. What woke you?"

I gave him his durian back. "The sun in my face."

"I take it that it has not touched your slaves."

"They aren't slaves. Not yet, or I don't think so."

"We will know when it does, I believe."

I looked for them and they were right where they had lain down. There was a big flower bush between them and the sun. I said, "Do you really think they'll die?"

"They may."

Garsecg sat quiet, fingering his beard while I tried to open my durian with my nails. Finally he said, "Before that happens—or does not happen—there are a dozen things I ought to tell you. Let me get through a few of them. First, I let you sleep because you must fight Kulili. You would fight, I know, even if you were exhausted. But you would be killed, and that would be of no help to me."

I said, "I'd like to think I'd win anyhow."

"Perhaps you do, but I cannot afford such follies."

He waited for me to argue, but I did not.

"Second, I lied to you. I told you I knew no oath that would bind an Aelf."

I looked over at him. "What is it?"

"The Aelf are bound when they swear by their old high gods."

When he said that I got a funny feeling that the flying castle was going over us. I looked up, but there was just a lot of blue, with a few big, solid-looking clouds. "You mean the Skai people, the Overcyns?"

"Yes," Garsecg said, "and no."

"I don't get you."

He nodded like he had known it. "It is not likely that you would. The old high gods of the Aelf were indeed their sky people. That is, they were the people seen in the sky of Aelfrice."

"You mean—? Wait a minute."

"Gladly."

"Are you talking about—about Bold Berthold or Kerl? About the guys on the ship? People like that?"

Garsecg nodded.

"You're saying I'm a god, too. That's crazy!"

"Not to yourself, but to the Aelf. If they swear by you, they are bound."

"I'm not a god!"

"You own a dog." Garsecg smiled. "I have spoken to him. He differs from the Aelf in that they have rebelled against you, but not otherwise."

That got me to thinking about Gylf, the way he had followed me from the ford, and swum out to the ship, and hidden there starving. I said, "I guess you're right, but sometimes he scares me."

"The Aelf worship me now." Garsecg smiled again. "Many do, and all will. There have been many times when they have frightened me."

I thought about that, too. And it seemed to me that it was one of those things that sound like they make sense, but really do not. After a while I hit on it, and I said, "The Overcyns are immortal, Garsecg. They live faster then we do, that's what Bold Berthold said. Whole years of life in one of our days. Only they never die."

Garsecg nodded. "The old high gods of the Aelf are likewise immortal. What will become of your spirit when you die?"

I tried to remember.

"Will it die too?"

"I don't think so."

"Mine will." Garsecg pointed to the Khimairas. "So will theirs. You have been aboard a ship, Sir Able. What becomes of the wind, when the wind dies?"

Right then one them screamed, and I got up and went to look. Behind me, Garsecg called, "Was that Uri or Baki?"

I could not tell, but the second one screamed too as soon as the sunlight touched it, so it did not matter. They were shaking, and their jaws were working, and their eyes looked like they were going to pop right out of their heads. I watched them a little while and called out to Garsecg, "Come look! Their wings are getting smaller!"

He did not say anything, so I said, "Aren't you going to come?"

One of the Khimairas was trying to say something. Her tongue was hanging out to where it could have licked her belly, but she was trying to talk just the same. The black stuff was falling off, too, and under that she was red. She made me think of a log in a fire. You whack it with a fresh stick, and the old burned stuff falls off, and you see the fire that was inside.

"They've got tits!" I called to Garsecg.

They did, and they did not have claws anymore, either. Their lips covered up their teeth, too.

Finally I went back to Garsecg. "This is really hurting them a lot," I said. "Is it just about over?"

He shook his head. "It has hardly begun."

"I've been thinking . . ."

He laughed. "It is good for you, provided you do not carry it to extremes."

"I love Disiri. How can I, if I'm a god to her?"

"By being yourself."

"She's never worshipped me, and I wouldn't want her to. *I* worship *her.*"

Garsecg looked at me the way that Ms. Collins used to sometimes. "Would she say the same, Sir Able?"

Before I could answer, one of the Khimairas stood up,

only she was not a Khimaira anymore. She was red all over, and her hair floated up from her head like there was a wind blowing up, just for it. It waved and snapped. She looked right at us, but you could see she did not see us. Pretty soon she stumbled away.

"She will throw herself off any cliff she reaches," Garsecg told me. "She is trying to fly back to Aelfrice. Will you stop her?"

I got up and caught her, no problem, and carried her to the durian tree. "Is it all right to lay her in the shade?"

Garsecg nodded, so I laid her down where I thought she would be comfortable. She was the color of a new penny all over, very slender and good-looking.

When I sat down next to Garsecg again, I said, "You know this was going to happen."

"I feared it would be worse, that she would die. I still fear they both will, though that seems less likely now."

"One time Disiri and I were playing in the water," I said. I was thinking how Disiri's foot changed when the sunlight hit it, but when I said "water" Baki must have heard me, because she started begging for water. The creek was right near there, so I carried her a little bit, cupping it in my hand.

Garsecg pointed. "You'll find a better container over there, if you want it." I started looking, and he said, "Under the lime tree, with some other things."

That was farther away. I asked if he would take care of the red Aelf girls while I was gone, and he said he would.

It seemed to me then like that garden up on the roof of the skyscraper was the most beautiful place I had ever been in. The jungle that had grown up on the new island had been pretty too, but this was better and I was in it. There were fruit and flowers everywhere.

At first it seemed like there was nothing but grass underneath that lime tree. When I did find something, it was a white bone. Pretty soon I saw more, ribs and leg bones, and little bones that might have come from hands or feet. When I saw the skull I went over to pick it up, and I stepped on a tube that looked like thick green glass. My foot was bare, like the rest of me, and did not break it. I picked it up and took out the cork, and there was a long sheet of paper rolled up inside. I carried it to a sunny spot to look at.

CHAPTER 25

THE FIRST ITEM

When I went back to the durian, the Aelfmaidens were lying side by side, so quiet except for their hair that I was afraid they were dead. I called them Aelfmaidens instead of Khimairas because that was what they were. There was no Khimaira left in them. When I saw they were still breathing, I showed Garsecg the goblet I had found under the lime tree and asked if it was what he had meant. He said it was, and I said, "Should I bring them some water now?"

"It can do no harm, provided you rinse it well."

When I got it to the creek I took sand off the bottom and rubbed the inside with it. It had been sort of dull and stained-looking, but pretty soon I had it shining. Then I washed it out good and filled it with clean, cold water.

I propped one of the Aelf girls up, Uri I think, and held the goblet to her mouth. Garsecg was watching, not smiling or frowning or anything. Just watching. I said, "When Disiri's foot got sunshine on it, it didn't seem to hurt her."

He nodded. "Thus you thought that it would do them no harm to bring them here. You would break Setr's hold, and restore them to their proper shapes. I understand all that. But how did you know that the summit of this tower reached into your Mythgarthr?"

"Well, when they grabbed me and flew away with me, I thought this was where they were going," I said. "At first I thought it was just to drop me and kill me, but they could have done that without taking me up any higher. So I figured the top was where they roosted, and when we got there and they tried to eat me I might be able to outfight them. Only one got scared and let go of my leg, and when I got over being scared myself I sort of wondered what had gotten into it. I remembered about sunlight, and I knew it would fall if it turned back into a regular Aelf. Only there isn't any sun in Aelfrice, so if it thought we were getting too close to sunlight it had to be because we were getting too close to Mythgarthr."

Baki sat up. Back then, I was not too sure which was who, but now I know it was Baki. She said, "It is wonderful to fly." Her voice was pretty weak, and she kept her hands pressed to her temples. "Will I ever fly again?"

"You may resume the Khimaira-shape whenever you choose," Garsecg promised her, "and shed it, too, when you choose."

I could see she did not understand, so I said, "You're free again," and let her hold the goblet of water.

"No, Lord." She tried to smile, and seeing it like that I just about cried. "Not free, nor do I want to be. I have a new master."

"Your slave," Garsecg explained, "as I warned you."

"I don't believe you ever promised to work for me," I told

her, "or if you did, it was just a promise. You never swore or anything."

"L-Lord, you are wrong. I swore it in my heart, where you could not hear me."

After that I wanted to know about sailors, because I was still thinking about the bones I had found. I asked Garsecg if they saw the island the same way he and I had, and if they climbed way up here.

"This is the island they see." He waved his hand to show me what he meant.

Without sitting up, the other Aelfmaiden said, "You d-did not see all when you were in A-Aelfrice, Lord."

"Okay, not the top or the other side, but I'm not sure that makes a lot of difference. Do you Aelf leave bones when you die, the way we do?"

Both of them said no, and Garsecg wanted to know why I was asking about it.

"When I carried Disiri I thought she was just a regular human woman. Did I tell you about that?"

"No," Garsecg said. "Nor did your dog, who confided that you had spoken often of your love for her when I was loath to come and heal you."

"Did you think I'd be afraid of you?" I asked him.

"No, I feared you would attack us, as so many of your kind do."

"Well, I didn't. Anyway, I never had carried a woman before, and I thought she'd weigh a lot more than she did. She wasn't much heavier than a little kid, even though she was . . . You know." I made curves with my hands.

Garsecg smiled. "You shape a viola d'amore of air."

"If you say so. The thing is, I liked it and the real Disira wasn't anywhere near as nice. I liked it a lot."

"You were intended to."

"I guess. Only just now I found bones over there where you sent me to get the cup, and I thought it must have been one of the sailors you'd talked about, because the Aelf are so light and change shape. But I wanted to make sure."

Garsecg said, "I doubt it."

"Well, if they're human bones . . ."

"They were the bones of a woman. Before you woke, I found the pelvis. The pelvis always settles that question."

"I wouldn't think you'd know about that."

"Because we see no human bones? I wish that you were correct. Do you also suppose that though your men sometimes enjoy Aelfmaidens, we in Aelfrice are never favored by human women?"

Baki wanted water too, and I brought her some. Her hands shook too bad for her to drink until I held the cup for her. I was thinking about Garsecg and what he had said and how he had sounded while she was drinking, and when she was finished I said it was none of my business, but maybe he had known some human girls?

"Yes, and seen their bones."

I said, "I'm sorry." I did not know what else to say.

"So am I. You are still young, Sir Able. You'll find that life is a cruel business."

"Let's not make it any worse. Were you wanting to go down to those armories now?"

Garsecg shook his head.

"That's good, because I'm not going to leave them until they feel better."

When I said that, Baki whispered, "I'll go with you."

"As far as the armories, maybe. I think that ought to be all right."

"Wherever you go, Lord." Baki's voice was so weak I could hardly hear her.

A voice like that should not scare anybody, but it scared me. I said, "Are you talking about going to fight Kulili? That's crazy."

"Wherever you go . . ."

Garsecg said, "Do not argue with her, Sir Able. You'll tire her."

"All right." I had way too much to think about, but I was trying to think about it just the same. "You said I was still young, and you're right. I'm younger than you probably think. I don't know if I told you I'd been to Aelfrice twice before, only one time I don't remember it. We're going to have lots of time now, it seems like. So I'd like to tell you."

"Then do so."

"Like I said, I don't remember it. It's not like I lost track of the time, I lost track of everything. I don't know who I talked to, or what I did. I told a lady named Parka about it when I got back. It seemed like she was one of the Overcyns or something. Do you know her?"

He shook his head.

"She said I was supposed to know about the wrongs of the Aelf so I'd tell people up here. Did you know me when I was in Aelfrice before?"

"No. Do you think the Aelf stole your memories?"

"I guess they must have."

"I cannot be certain," Garsecg said thoughtfully, "but it seems more probable this being you call Parka did it. Why should the Aelf complain to you and cause you to forget it?"

"I told her I didn't like them. It didn't make her mad or anything."

His eyebrows went up. "Do you still feel that way?"

I shook my head.

"That is well. I was going to explain that it would be pointless of the Aelf to rob you of your memories when there was something they wished you to remember."

"Can you do it? Take memories away?"

"I cannot. Some say I am wiser than any Aelf, but I do not know a way to do that. What memories would you like to discard?"

"About America. My real name, and living there."

Uri said, "Is America your real name?"

"It's a place where I used to live. That was before I went to Aelfrice the first time."

Garsecg said, "A bad place, since you would forget it if you could."

"Not really. Only . . ."

"Only what?"

"Only I'm like that girl in the movie. I can't get it out of my head. I'm not going back, not even if I find the ruby slippers, because Disiri's here and not there. But I wish I could just forget about it. Sometimes I think Bold Berthold was my real brother, you know? He wasn't, but I think he was. I love him like he was, but I know he wasn't."

"Which you would like to forget."

"Right. He used to be a big strong man with a big black beard. He's told me about it, and he thinks I remember it. Then the giants came. The Angrborn. They hurt him really, really bad, and I don't think he'll ever get over it. I used to think that when people got sick, someday they'd be well. I may just be a kid, but I know better now."

"You miss the man you never knew."

"Yeah, sure. He was strong and smart and brave. We used to sit in his little hut at night—this is before Disiri—and he'd talk about things that had happened before he got hurt, and I could see what he had been like. I kept thinking it would be wonderful to be like that, only I never could be, not really."

Baki sat up. She still looked pretty shaky. "You could never be what you are now?"

I tried to smile. It was not easy, but I tried and I guess I did it. "Oh, I'm plenty strong. Garsecg showed me all about the sea, so probably I'm stronger now than Bold Berthold ever was. But I'm not brave, and I'm not smart. Inside I'm still a kid. Outside I'm a man, I guess, or anyhow I look like one. But I was scared to death when we fought the Osterlings."

Nobody said anything then, so I asked Garsecg if I had told him about that.

"No, but your dog did. You fought like a hero, and received the wound that the sea has healed."

"But I was scared. I was scared to death. Our sailors were fighting them through the rope net we'd put up, and I shot through it until all my arrows were gone."

"Slaying many."

I nodded.

"Then that was the best thing you could do. My Sea Aelf do not use the bow, which is of no value under water; but your Disiri's Moss Aelf are expert with it, and I have seen what slaughter one fine archer can make among his foes."

"They cut through the net." I was remembering a lot more than I was listening. "They were made of good tough ropes thicker than my thumb, but they cut them and our men were running. There wasn't anything else I could do."

Garsecg smiled. "It required no courage, I am sure."

"That's right. I had to. I had Sword Breaker, and I yelled and jumped off the castle and one stabbed me and I fell down."

"Thus your ship was taken, and is now in the hands of the dreaded Osterlings." Garsecg shook his head like he felt sorry for me. "I failed to notice any when I went aboard, but it was due to my inattention, I feel sure."

"No, we chased them back onto their own boat. They cut the ropes and left some hooks behind, and—and went away."

Uri rolled her head to look at me. "Why, Lord?"

"I guess they were afraid we'd take it and kill the rest of them. We might have, too, if they hadn't cut the ropes."

Garsecg said, "Then you have omitted something from your account. I suspected it all along. You spoke of your fear, Sir Able of the High Heart."

"Yeah."

"And of leaping from the sterncastle, sword in hand."

I explained about its not being a sword.

"Sword Breaker in hand, in that case. After that you spoke of being stabbed. Through your armor, as I understand it from your dog. You fell, I suppose to the deck."

I said yes.

"Yet your being stabbed and falling to the deck cannot have taken place immediately after your leap. What did?"

I said I had hurt some people, hitting them with Sword Breaker and so on.

"Some Osterlings."

"This isn't what I wanted to talk about," I told him, "this isn't it at all. I want to say how brave Bold Berthold used to be, and how strong. Only when I knew him he wasn't like that anymore. He was bent over, and sometimes he didn't think quite right. His beard had white in it, and he didn't want to go back to Griffinsford to stay. Not ever. He just wanted to live in the forest where they couldn't find him. But they did. They found him, and now he's gone." I had to wipe my eyes with my fingers then, and after a while I said, "I'm sorry."

"For mourning the loss of your brother? The strongest may weep at such a time."

"This is what I wanted to say. I think what Disiri did was to make me grow up the way I would have if I hadn't been in Aelfrice."

Garsecg did not seem to want to say anything about that.

"It seems like ten years. I mean thinking about how I was before that night when she made me grow, and the way I am now. About ten years."

"Or less."

"Only Bold Berthold, he's maybe thirty, forty years older—"

Uri said, "I feel better now, Lord. I think I can stay up if you'll help me."

I did, and she sort of snuggled.

Baki said, "You just wanted his arms around you."

Uri grinned at her. "They're very nice arms."

Kind of under my breath, I told Garsecg, "Sometimes I dream about the Osterlings."

"So do I—they sacrificed to us while they held the Mountain of Fire. Do you want my opinion on these matters?"

I said yes, I would really like it.

"I do not believe you will. Or at least I doubt that you will be willing to accept every side of it." For a minute Garsecg seemed to be thinking about where to start.

"The first item, the Osterlings. You believe you lack courage because you feared them. Do you imagine that your brother would have felt no fear?"

"He fought the giants."

"And you the Osterlings, Sir Able. You were afraid, but you mastered your fear. Do you imagine they were not afraid of you? If you do, we will find a pool in which you can look at your reflection. You had armor?"

"A mail shirt and a steel cap. I bought them before we went on the boat."

"And Sword Breaker in your hand. Besides all of which, you were the man who had laid waste to them with the bow. Believe me, Sir Able, they feared you from the moment they laid eyes on you."

"Well, they sure didn't act like it." I found the durian I had been trying to eat and started all over again trying to get it open with my fingernails. It was just as bad as it had been the first time.

"Did you act as though you feared them?"

There did not seem to be anything I could say to that.

"I was not present, yet I know the answer. So do you, who were present. You mastered your fear until you fell wounded. They mastered theirs—for a time. When a knight is on a ship, that ship flies his pennant from its foremast. Did yours do that?"

I shook my head. "I don't have one, and I didn't know about it anyway. Maybe that's why the captain didn't think I was a real knight."

"In most cases, the Osterlings will not attack such a ship. They must have been surprised, and frightened, when they found you were on board."

I said all right, what about the rest?

CHAPTER 26

THE SECOND ITEM, AND THE THIRD

"Very well, let us move on to the next item. You brought a glass tube, as well as the goblet, back from the lime tree. Certainly it must have struck you that I would see it sooner or later. Are you going to let me examine it?"

I said, "After we had talked about the other things, I thought." It had been pretty well hidden in the long grass, and it was green anyway. But I picked it up and passed it to Garsecg. "There's a paper rolled up inside."

He nodded. "Did you break the seal?"

I told him there had not been any, and Uri leaned over to look. Baki came over so she could see better. They did not have anything on, then or after, and it was hard for me not to look at certain places, but I did it.

Garsecg pulled out the stopper and took out the paper. "It is a scroll," he told us. "A kind of book." He was untying the strings.

"I untied them too," I said, "but they were tied just like that."

"Did you read it?"

I shook my head. "I looked at it, but I can't read that kind of writing."

"Nor can I. This is the script of Celidon, presumably."

He handed the scroll to Baki, who said, "Huh-uh. I can read our writing, but not this stuff."

Uri snuggled closer. "If Baki cannot, I cannot."

Garsecg took the scroll from Baki, rolled it up again and tied it, and put it back into the tube. "This may be the testament of the woman whose bones we found, but I have no way of knowing. You may keep it if you like, Sir Able, or return it to its place."

After I had put it back under the tree, I asked if he thought she knew she was going to die.

Garsecg pointed to the goblet. "When one finds a cup beside a body, one assumes poison. That was why I advised you to rinse it thoroughly, although it has certainly been weathering here for a long time. If she was poisoned, she may have poisoned herself, and grasped her testament until she died."

I tried to imagine why a woman would kill herself in such a beautiful place.

"You may have more questions about this. Ask them if you like, but I confess I have no more answers."

"You said you'd seen the bones," I reminded him. "Did you see that glass tube too?"

He shook his head. "I looked around, but the sun was only just coming up. I did not see it."

"You were talking about a big war when the Aelf drove out Setr." I said it like that because I thought Garsecg did not want Uri and Baki to know who he really was. So I felt like I was being smart, but Uri started shaking and I had to promise her I would not say the name any more.

"We were supposed to die," she told me. "If we came up here, we were supposed to die." Baki said that, too.

"He forgives you," Garsecg told them. I could see they did not understand, but the way he said it made them believe it, or almost.

"A thousand of your years have passed since that war," Garsecg told me. "I can give you a wealth of detail, if you want it. But do you?"

"I guess not. Only I was thinking about that woman. Those bones can't have been here that long, can they?"

"In this well-watered place? Certainly not."

"Then the person who built this skyscraper we're on didn't put her up here?"

"Who can say? A thousand years here might be a hundred in Aelfrice, or even less."

Baki said, "Besides, he comes back. Let's not talk about him at all."

I was thinking hard. For one thing it seemed to me like the woman might have been shipwrecked, but if she had been, why did she kill herself? I asked Garsecg again about the top of the skyscraper being an island in Mythgarthr, and he said again that it was. Then I said, "All right, if it's an island, why don't I hear the sea? I haven't heard the sea the whole time we've been up here."

"When it is calm, as it often is, it makes no great noise."

"Well, I'm going to look. You stay here with these sick girls."

Really humbly Baki said, "Uri and Baki, Lord. I am Baki." That was when I got them straight. I never did get them mixed up again after that.

Garsecg shook his head, meaning he was not going to stay, but I did not pay any attention. The sun was still only halfway up the sky, so to keep it out of my eyes I turned my back to it and went west. I broke twigs and let them hang every hundred steps or so, and after a while I heard Garsecg behind me. He said, "Why do you do that?"

I did not look. "So I can find my way back, of course."

"And why do you want to go back?"

"Because those girls are sick, and we ought to be taking care of them. I was hoping you'd stay with them and do it."

"The Aelf have struggled to free themselves from the monster called Kulili throughout their history. You are their last hope, and their best. I am not letting you out of my sight—no, not for ten thousand puking maidens."

I had stopped to look at a tree of a shade of green I had never seen before. I am sure it came from Aelfrice, but it was so fresh and new-looking that it seemed like God had just made it. Like He had planted it a minute before I got there. It had blue and purple flowers, and the long feelers or whatever you call them inside the flowers were bright red. I have never seen another one like it, and I have remembered it all this time.

Anyway, I heard Garsecg laugh behind me, but I still did not look at him. But when I started walking again I asked if we were going the right way.

"I have no means of knowing. Or say, rather, that I know that any direction will prove right if we cleave to it long enough. This may be the shortest way. It may be the longest. In any event, it will take us to the sea in the end."

"I still don't hear any waves."

"Nor do I. But if we continue as we have begun, we will hear them if there are any."

I thought about that, and the weather. There was hardly any wind, and so I said, "That's right, it's pretty calm."

"It is, and it is in just such weather as this that this isle is most often sighted by seamen. It is a thing of heat and calm, most often seen at twilight."

"If it's too calm to sail, couldn't they row here?"

"They could, and some do."

I had been pretty mad at Garsecg because he had gone

away and left Uri and Baki to take care of themselves. But I got to thinking about all the things he had done for me, and how I had left them just as much as he had. So I stopped and motioned for him to catch up to me, and we walked together a little. We were in the shade of the trees all that time.

Before long we came to where the shade was only spotty, sunshine coming through the leaves in bright patches, sort of dappled. Then it seemed like something a whole lot bigger than Garsecg was walking beside me. Only it was not.

It was not really like a snake, and it was not really like a bird either. But I have to write those because they are as close as I can get. It was beautiful, and terribly scary. I do not remember all the colors and they changed anyway, but the thing was that whatever colors there were, were the darkest those colors could ever be. The blue was darker than black usually is, and so was the gold, a sort of brown gold with a deep, deep luster you felt like you could fall into. And dark, like you had seen something gold in the middle of a storm, but nowhere near as real as smoke.

I could hardly see Garsecg at all right then, but he looked like he was about to laugh. I told him I liked him better when he was Garsecg.

"I know."

"That's what you really are, isn't it? You're Setr. Are you really from the world under Aelfrice?"

"I am. Will you turn aside for a step or two now, Sir Able? There is something to be seen here more important than any view of the sea, and if you will consent I will show it to you."

I felt like I had already seen something important, but I said I would.

CHAPTER 27

KULILI

There was not any path, just soft grass and ferns underneath the big trees, down, around, and down again until it brought us to a little toy valley that could not have been more than a hundred yards long and wide. It was so pretty down there it took your breath away. There were tiny little waterfalls coming out of the rocks, and a pool in the middle with white lilies growing all around it, and some other kind of white flower that was prettier than the lilies. More ferns, too. The ones I had seen before had been little, but there they were huge, like the ferns were in Aelfrice. They arched up over my head so high I could have ridden a horse under them and never taken my helm off. It was dark shade there and Garsecg looked completely real, so real I knew if I touched him I would not feel the thing he really was at all.

Where the shade was thickest there was a white statue. It was a naked woman, but where it was in that dark shade it sort of loomed out at me like a ghost. One hand looked like she wanted to cover up her breasts, and the other hand looked like she was begging for something.

I was naked myself, as I guess I have already said, and when I saw that statue something happened that had happened at school when I watched the girls play volleyball. I did not want Garsecg to see it, so what I did was to jump right into the pool. It worked, too, because the water was good and cold. When I came up I tossed my hair out of my eyes the way you do and tried to grin.

Garsecg bent over to look at me. "Why did you do that?"

"To cool off and wash away my sweat. Aren't you hot after all that walking? I was."

He gave me his hand, and I swam over and climbed out.

"Look. Wait until the ripples die, and look carefully."

"You said you wanted to show me my reflection," I said, "so I'd know why the Osterlings were scared of me. Only I don't think they were. Is that all this is?"

"No. Look deeply into the pool, Sir Able."

I did. It looked like that pool went down forever but kind of crooked and off to the side, and I said so.

"Like many such waters, it is a gate to Aelfrice," Garsecg told me. "I am showing it to you so that you will know how such gates look. Could you not tell, when the Kelpies carried you to me, that you were entering Aelfrice?"

I shook my head.

"Does it not seem to you that you should be peering down into the topmost story of the Tower of Glas?"

It had not hit me before, but he was right. The dirt on the island could not have been more than ten or twelve feet deep. I really stared after that; and I remembered that even though I had sunk down quite a way when I jumped in, I had never touched bottom.

"Here one may stand in Mythgarthr and scrutinize the gate," Garsecg said. "Remember what you are seeing. Fix it in your mind. In times to come, what you learn may be of value to you."

I could not believe that pool went down to Aelfrice, and I said so. It did look funny, very funny, down there. But I had jumped in already, and the only thing that happened was what I had wanted to happen. (I still could not look at the statue. It made Uri and Baki look like boys.) I said, "Are you telling me I could get to Aelfrice like that, if you were with me so I wouldn't drown?"

"You will never drown," Garsecg told me. "You are one with the sea—more than you know."

The way he said it, I knew he meant it. And all I could think about then was that Disiri was in Aelfrice. I want her more than I have ever wanted anything in my life, and I dove right in. I would do it again.

It did not even feel very cold the second time, and as soon as I started to slow down I began swimming hard. I had been a pretty good swimmer even back in America, and while I had been with Garsecg I had gotten so good you would think I was putting you on if I told you how good I was. I went down and down.

It should have gotten darken and darker, only it did not. There was beautiful blue light, like I had seen under the sea before, and seeing it before did not make it any less beautiful now. After a while I decided I could use a little rest, and I just let myself float in it while I tried to figure out which way was up. It probably seems to you like that ought to be pretty easy, and the fish always know, but when there are no fish in sight and you cannot see anything but that beautiful blue haze, you have to think about it.

I floated there a long time, or anyhow it seemed long to me. There was a little current that turned me slowly, around and around, and carried me along, and that felt great. I was thinking about Disiri and the statue, and they got mixed up in my mind, and I started wondering if I was really real at all. It seemed to me this might be what it was like when you were just a memory, and maybe Disiri was remembering me, and would always remember me, would always love me like I would always love her, and this was me in her mind.

I am Kulili. It was not really a sound in my ear at all. It was more like a sound in the bones of my skull.

Down. Come down.

I did, and I knew which way down was because that was where her voice was coming from. The blue light went purple, then everything went black. Fingers touched my face, only I knew they were not really fingers at all. It seemed sort of not fair, and I said, "I can't see you."

You shall, by my will.

"Who are you?" I said. All of a sudden it seemed to me I did not even know who I was. Was I really just a kid from America? A knight? Bold Berthold's brother?

I am Kulili. You are the man who has sworn to fight Kulili.

"Able," I told her. "My name's . . . Able."

Will you fight me?

"I don't know." It did not seem to matter much either way. "I suppose I'll have to try. I promised."

So I judge. Your honor is sacred to you.

"You're a monster. That's what Garsecg said." It had been really, really dark up until then, but when I said that there was a green light off in the distance. I thought, what the heck is that?

A luminous fish. They come here sometimes.

"It's hard to think." I don't know why I said that, but it was true. "Why is it so hard to think here?"

My water is cold.

"Why did you bring me here?"

She did not answer.

"Is it okay if I swim back up? I'd like to get warm again."

Before you kill me? She was laughing at me, but it did not make me mad at all. I kind of liked it.

"You could kill me real easy down here if you wanted to."

I will not.

"You killed the Aelf when they came to kill you. That's another thing Garsecg said."

This world was mine. Mine in a time when there were no Aelf. They drove me from the land into the water, and from the water into these depths. I can be driven no farther. Would you see me?

Like somebody had just dropped it there, there was a clear picture in my mind. It was the statue, only alive.

You looked into the pool. What you saw was yourself, as you are to others. What you see now I am, in the eyes of others.

I could not imagine anybody hating anybody so beautiful. I asked why the Aelf hated her.

Ask them.

"Well, why do you hate them?"

I do not, but I must fear them as long as they fear me.

The beautiful woman was gone. Instead I saw a strange forest. There were trees like phone poles, with a few big leaves at the top. There were pools of water all over, and down where the roots were, something really big was getting bigger and sending out feelers everyplace. The trees talked to this woman under them, and the little plants did too; she answered all of them, one at a time, and was great. She saw them all, and she saw their souls, because each of them was wrapped in a soul like a man would wear a cloak. Their souls were beautiful colors, and no matter what color they were, they sort of glowed.

Insects ate the leaves and spilled their sap, and there were all sorts of animals that would eat the bark and kill the trees. So the woman underneath them made protectors for them, taking little bits of their souls and little pieces of herself, pale gray wisdom that gleamed like pearls. Sticks, leaves, and mud, too, and fire and smoke and water and moss. All sorts of stuff.

At first the protectors were sort of like animals too, but the big woman under the roots looked up into the sky and saw Mythgarthr, and people up there plowing, and planting flowers and tending orchards. So she made the protectors more like them. They were a lot like scarecrows, but they got better and better and got so they could change their shapes to make themselves better yet.

Some still protect, even from me. Do you know them?

I saw Disiri, and it choked me up. I felt like I was going to die if I could not touch her and talk to her, and I said, "Yes. I love her."

Kulili said, *So do I.* Then Disiri was gone. *Would you see me now? With your eyes of flesh?*

I think I said yes.

We waited then. It was not like ten minutes or ten seconds. It was the time they had before somebody built the first clock. I hung there in the cold seawater, turning and waiting, and that was all I did. White, yellow, and green lights went around and around me, and hay-colored lights, and sky-colored.

Our lamp.

They came together, and I saw they were really fish. There were little orange fish that glowed like the flames of candles, black fish with huge heads and bad-dream teeth that hung red and blue bait in front of their own mouths, long silvery fish with gills and tails like light bulbs, and big blue fish with rows of blue lights down their sides, and a lot more kinds that I forget. All sorts of reds and yellows and pinks and every kind of color.

Only they were not important. What was important was down under them, and it was white thread, a big, big tangle of white thread, all of it alive and sort of groping. When I first saw it I thought it did not have any shape, but as soon as I thought that, it did. There was a mouth that could have swallowed the *Western Trader,* and a nose like a hill. Only it was a beautiful nose and a beautiful mouth, too. Pretty soon there were eyes, white eyes that looked blind. They blinked, and they had pupils I could have dived into, and they were blue eyes, and there was color in the cheeks just like roses were blooming there. It was the woman the statue had been made like. Only the statue is usually bigger than the person. Way down in the dark seawater was the real person, and she could have worn the statue around her neck on a chain.

Will you kill me? Still?

In the first place, I did not want to. In the second place, I did not think I could. I said, "I'll have to try, Kulili. I'll have to try my best, because I promised I would. But I hope you get away. I hope I won't be able to do it."

Now?

"No. These fish of yours could kill me pretty easy, and I haven't even got a sword."

May it be long before we meet again.

CHAPTER 28

THREE YEARS

It was a long swim to the surface. It is funny, but when you have been way deep down it always seems like you are closer to the top than you really are. It is black down where you are, darker than any real night ever gets. You swim up quite a way, and it gets light, you can see things and you think you are only ten or twelve feet down. So you keep swimming up, maybe twenty-five feet, maybe fifty or a hundred. And you do not get to the top and nothing much changes. I felt like I was almost there half a dozen times probably before I really got there.

When I did, it was sort of a shock. For one thing I had not been breathing, and I was used to it. My head came out in the trough between two waves. I breathed out hard, and water ran out of my nose and mouth, and down my chin. And then a big wave hit me in the face. I choked, and when I got my head into the air again, I was making noises like a coffeepot. When I could breathe, I started to laugh.

After that I swam in and out of the waves and had a big time. Probably I played like that for half an hour.

I could see the sun, so I knew I was back in Mythgarthr again, and not in Aelfrice. I also knew that when I had been way deep down with Kulili, that had been Aelfrice. I figured I was pretty close to the island, and whenever I wanted to I could swim over that way and see about the two Aelf girls and Garsecg, and tell Garsecg it was going to take a whole lot more than a spear or a battle-ax for me to kill Kulili, and I really did not want to anyway. When I thought about it, I started hoping that I could trade him another favor for that one. Maybe a couple of them, or three.

Pretty soon I decided that was enough fun, and anyway it might be a long swim to the island, so I had better get started. I jumped up out of the water the way that fish do sometimes and had a look around. After the first one, I did it again, and again after that. The island was nowhere in sight. In fact there was no land anywhere. The only thing I could see was a ship about a mile away. I decided to swim for that because it would at least get me up higher. There was quite a bit of wind then, but the ship was headed toward me on a slant, so all I had to do was cut across to where it would be and wait. I could swim faster than it was sailing anyhow, so catching it was bound to be pretty easy.

I did not recognize it until it was close. A lot of paint had flaked off the forecastle, and some of the gold was missing from the wooden woman with the basket in front. But it was the *Western Trader* just the same. I could not believe it, even when I climbed up the side.

The lookout yelled something (I do not know what) and slid down the forestay, dropping off it in front of me. He sort of goggled at me, then he got down on his knees. "Sir Able! I didn't know 'twas you, sir. I didn't know what 'twas, sir. I'm sorry, sir. I never meant no offense, sir. By wind an' water, I never done."

"Nor gave any," I told him. "No sweat. If—wait a minute! You're Pouk!"

"Aye, sir."

"You've changed. It's the beard. How long have I been gone, Pouk?"

"Three year, sir. We—I thought you wasn't never comin' back, sir. Cap'n didn't, neither. Nobody done."

"The captain? I thought I killed him."

"Cap'n Kerl, sir, what was Mate. I—I signed papers, sir, 'cause they wouldn't feed me less'n I done it. An'—an' I been here ever since, sir. Topman o' the main now, sir, an' I've had worse berths."

I shook his hand and told him I was proud of him.

"Only I won't be no more, sir, if you'll have Cap'n strike me off articles, sir. Your man again, Sir Able, same as before, if there's no feelin's about me doin' somethin' else while you was gone." Pouk paused and gulped. "Or even if there is, sir, if you'll have me just th' same."

I did not know what to think of him, and I said, "You've got a good job here. You just said so."

"Aye, sir."

"I can't pay you or feed you. Look at me. I don't even have a pair of pants."

"I'll lend you 'un o' mine, sir. Only they'll be too small, maybe."

"Thanks. But you're right, I'd be sure to split them. Probably I couldn't even get them on. We'll have to talk to the captain. Captain Kerl?"

"Aye, sir." Pouk nodded.

"I know that you can't take yourself off duty, and you shouldn't even be talking to me. But before I go looking for Kerl I want to know why you'd quit your job to work for me, when you know I haven't got any money."

"Selfishness is all 'tis, sir." Pouk would not look me in the face.

"What do you mean, selfishness?"

"Crew's got to stick together, sir. You're s'posed to stick

to your shipmates, see? But—but it's my big chance, sir. Likely th' only 'un I'll ever get. I'm goin'." He turned away so I could not see his face.

I patted his shoulder and went to look for Kerl. There was a little runway of deck alongside the forecastle, and as I walked along that I wondered what the rest of the crew would make of me.

As soon as I rounded the corner, I found out. I had not taken two more steps before I was surrounded by cheering men. "Below there!" a new mate shouted from the sterncastle deck. "What's that gabble? Stations, all of you! Stations!"

A sailor I did not remember yelled, "It's Sir Able, sir! He's back!"

Somebody else yelled, *"Give a cheer, men!"* They did it, and all the noise brought Kerl out of his cabin. He started asking questions, then he saw me in the middle of a bunch of sailors, and he just gaped.

It was not real easy to push through all of them without hurting anybody, but I did it. I got to him and told him we needed to talk, and the two of us went into the cabin.

"By Ran's ropes!" he said. "By Skai, wind, and rain!" Then he hugged me. I have been really, really surprised a lot in the time I have been in Mythgarthr and Aelfrice, but I do not know if I have ever been any more surprised than I was when Kerl hugged me, unless it was by that one knight with the skull for a crest I fought up in the Mountains of the Mice. I do not believe there has ever been a human man that could squeeze me hard enough to break my ribs, not even Hela's brother Heimir, and Heimir was not strictly human. A lot of people would say he was not human at all, and as soon as it got to be hot summer he would sweat like a horse even sitting under a tree.

Only Kerl came pretty close. I could hear them creak.

"I've been in Aelfrice," I told him when he finally let me go. "I don't know for how long. I mean, I don't know how many of their days."

"Sit down! Sit down!" Kerl got out a bottle and pulled the cork, and found glasses for us.

I was thinking about the island that had come up out of the tear in the sea, the one where I had seen Disiri, and how I had watched the trees grow on it. So I said, "Maybe it was years there, too. I don't know if they have years, really. They talk about them, but maybe it's just because we do."

"Drink up!" Kerl shoved a glass at me. "This calls for a celebration."

I shook my head, because I was still thinking about Garsecg and that had reminded me of Uri and Baki and the whole thing with the Isle of Glas. I sipped the wine, though, and it was really good wine, the best I had ever tasted up to then, and I told Kerl so.

"Gave somebody that needed 'em a couple casks of water." He grinned. "He gave me five bottles of this. Hard not to have three or four glasses with my dinner every night, but I don't let myself do it. This is different. It's a special occasion, and I wouldn't want to die and leave one of those bottles wet."

"I'm lucky you feel like that." I drank some more. "Can you take me to Forcetti? Will you?"

"Aye! We're way down south here, and headin' back. We can stop off there." Kerl's grin faded. "I'm goin' to have to make some stops on the way though, sir. That all right?"

I said okay. I had been going to Forcetti because Duke Marder would probably need another knight, and sitting there naked in that cabin it hit me that if he had needed somebody to take Ravd's place he probably had him already, and I was going to need a lot of stuff when I got there. Like clothes. So

I asked Kerl if they had anything on the ship that I could wear.

That brought the grin back. "We kept yours for you," he told me. He opened a chest and held up Sword Breaker, still in her scabbard, and the scabbard still on my old sword belt. "I don't guess you've forgotten this?"

That made me smile. "I remember it pretty well."

"Clothes, too." Kerl lifted out a double armful. "Saved 'em all for you. Put cedar shavin's on 'em to keep the moths off, and they ought to be good as new." He put them on the bed for me to look at.

I thanked him, and told him how much I meant it (and I really did) and said I would sleep on deck and do whatever work I could to pay for my food.

"You'll sleep right here, sir." Kerl sounded like he meant that, too. "This here's your cabin just like these here are your boots, sir. Your cabin 'til you get off at Forcetti, sir, and I'm proud to give it to you."

"I can't pay—wait just a minute. I left money here when I went away with the Aelf. If you kept it for me too—"

Kerl could not meet my eyes. "I spent it, Sir Able. I had to. We was stove off Needam, and laid up seven weeks for repairs, sir. I'll pay it all back, I swear. Only I can't pay you back but a little right now."

He opened his strongbox for me and showed me what he had, and there was so little in there, just copper and brass and four pieces of silver, that I almost let him keep all of it. Only I knew I was going to have to have something, and I took half.

A couple of days after that we came in sight of the Mountain of Fire. I was curious about it because of what Garsecg had said, and I asked Kerl and some people in the little port nearby, where we sold some cloth Kerl had not been able to sell farther south. It had belonged to the Osterlings, and they had pushed people into the opening at the top because it bypassed Aelfrice and went straight to Muspel where the dragons are. If it had just been their own people, we probably would not have cared, but they raided, and ate people they captured the way they do, and pushed in the ones they would have liked to eat most so the dragons would help them.

King Arnthor had taken the Mountain of Fire, fortified it, and left a garrison there. Some of the men-at-arms were in the town when we were, drinking and trying to pick up girls. They were the first men-at-arms I had seen, and I was anxious to see knights. There were donkeys for rent at the stable, but I had very little money and Pouk had none, so we decided to walk.

CHAPTER 29

MY BET

If I had known what was in store for us, I would never have gone. And if I had gone anyway, there is no way I would have let Pouk come with me. As it was, we had a nice time of it, setting out early in the morning before the sun was hot, and holding walking races for forfeits. It got warmer and we slowed down a lot, basically walking from shade to shade if you know what I mean. We were lucky, because there was a lot of shade, but we were unlucky, too, because there were a lot of bugs. The bugs were not so lucky themselves, though. We must have swatted about a hundred, and I got to wishing I could put them all together in one big bug and shoot arrows at it.

I was trying to figure out some way to do that when a farmer came along with a cart full of fruit he was taking to the Mountain of Fire. He gave us a ride, and let us eat mangos as we rode along. We promised to help him unload when he got to the mountain, but when he found out I was a knight he would not let me. When we got there, Pouk had to unload for both of us.

While he was doing that, I was talking to some of the men-at-arms there about the walls and towers and so on, and who was there. Lord Thunrolf was in charge of everything. We were already inside the first wall, a kind of little one but long, that walled off the whole side where the mountain could be climbed. I told them I was a knight, which I was, and said I wanted to go on up the road and see the big walls and towers up higher, and maybe even climb on up to the place where the smoke was coming out. Kerl had said the smoke came from Muspel, and I thought that was pretty tough to believe and it was probably just a story somebody had told him, so I wanted to see for myself.

They said I could not go up unless Lord Thunrolf said it was all right. I said fine, where is he? Of course he was up quite a ways in the castle they called the Round Tower, so I got to see a lot while they were taking me up to him. It was beautiful and scary, both at once. You looked up and up, and what you mostly saw was towers and more towers, and walls one on top of the other, and big spaces of bare rock. There were flags on the tallest towers, the king's flag, and Lord Thunrolf's, and the banners of some of the knights that were knights banneret, and the pennants of the other knights. There were shields hung on the battlements of the towers, too, with each knight's arms on them. The stone everything was built of had been quarried right there on the mountain, and it was of all sorts of colors, mostly red and black and gray. And up above everything was the top of the mountain, with snow on it and smoke coming up out of the snow. Black smoke that drifted up and up into Skai as if the dragons of Muspel were trying to smoke out the Valfather and the other Overcyns. I will never forget it. It was a steep climb, but after a while it got cooler and there was a lot more wind, and before we had gone halfway I felt like I understood why Thunrolf bunked up there where he did instead of down in the lowlands. There were no more bugs, either.

With only one road going up to the top, it was pretty clear the Osterlings could not take back the Mountain unless they took all the fortifications along that road, one after another, or starved out the garrison. I never even tried to find out how much food and water they had up there, but Thunrolf told me there were big cisterns cut into the rock, and since it rained a lot they were generally full. But storming the walls and towers looked about as bad to me as storming the Tower of Glas. Back then I did not know that the Osterlings were going to take it away from us, or that we were going to take it back. If you had told me I was going to be the one that gave the order to give it up and retreat south, I would have said you were crazy.

Building more walls and more towers was the main thing Thunrolf and his men did there when Pouk and I were there the first time. They built up all the walls more and built new ones. The men-at-arms had to work on them some, and they had hired local people too. The knights bossed the job, and Thunrolf bossed the knights. Knights are not supposed to work with their hands, just fight and train to fight. I thought I knew about that from certain things I had picked up on in Irringsmouth, but I never really knew how strong it was until we got to Forcetti.

Anyway, they were taking every place where the road was narrow and the mountainside was really rough, and building walls with gates for the road, and towers so archers could shoot down on everybody. They had started at the bottom, and they were working their way up.

We got to the big tower and climbed four or five flights of stairs to get to the floor where Thunrolf was. Then we had to wait and wait. We had eaten a couple of mangos each on the cart, but that seemed like it had been years ago. We were both hungry, and really thirsty.

Every so often somebody would come and talk to one or the other of us, asking who we were and what we wanted. I was tired and did not pay a whole lot of attention when they were talking to Pouk, and maybe that was a mistake. Finally I told him to go off and find us some food and something to drink, and after that I waited by myself. It got later and later, and I wondered whether Thunrolf or somebody would let us stay overnight and give us a place to sleep.

I was about to try leaving to see if anybody would stop me when a servingman came out and told me to come in. I had seen him before, he had been in and out of that room where Thunrolf was half a dozen times. But this time he had a kind of smirk when he looked at me. I did not like it, but I could not do anything about it, so I followed him inside.

Thunrolf was sitting at a table with a bottle of wine and some glasses on it. I had told the servingman my name, and he told Thunrolf. Thunrolf told me to sit down and motioned to the servingman to pour me some wine, which I thought was nice of him. He was a tall man with long legs. Most men his age have beards or mustaches, but he did not, and looking at him I decided he probably drank too much and did not eat enough.

"So, you're a knight."

I said yes.

"Here on a ship bound for Forcetti. You've come a long way out of your way."

I tried to make a joke out of that. "I generally try to go

straight to the place I'd like to get to, but I don't seem to be good at it."

He frowned. "Has no one taught you to say *My Lord* when you speak to a baron?"

"I'm sorry, My Lord. I guess I haven't been around barons very much."

He waved his hand like it did not matter and drank some wine, which gave me the chance to drink a lot of mine. My mouth felt like the inside of an old shoe, and the wine was cool and tasted great.

"You wish to go to the summit of my mountain and look over the countryside."

I said, "Yes, My Lord. If it doesn't put you to a lot of trouble."

"It might be arranged, Sir . . . ?"

The servingman had told him, but I said, "Sir Able of the High Heart."

"So now you want to carry your heart high, and the rest of you, too." Thunrolf laughed at his own joke. His laugh did not make me like him better, but pretty soon he said, "Have you supped?"

"No, My Lord."

"You're hungry? You and the man with you?"

"We sure are."

"I see. You might sup with us, Sir Able, but if you do, two points must be settled before supper. The first is the rank of your companion. You told Master Egorn that he was a friend."

I nodded.

"Not another knight?"

"No, My Lord. Just a friend. Knights can have friends that aren't knights, can't they?"

"Not a man-at-arms?"

"No, My Lord. Pouk's a sailor."

"I see." Thunrolf drank some more wine.

I did, too, but then I decided I had better stop. My lips felt funny.

"Say, rather, that I don't see. Your friend told Atl he was your servant. I sent Master Aud to speak with him, and he told Master Aud the same thing. One of you is lying."

I tried to smooth it over. "Pouk is afraid people won't think I'm very important, My Lord, and of course I'm not. He wants them to think I am, so he says that. Maybe it would be true if I could afford to pay him, but I can't."

"You're poor?"

"Very, My Lord."

"I thought as much. Here is the other difficulty I mentioned. We have a custom here. I ought to say my knights do. Barbaric, if you ask me, but the custom is the custom." Thunrolf belched. "A new knight—you are a knight?"

"Yes, My Lord. As I told you."

"I know you did. I hadn't forgotten that. A new knight must fight their champion. With blunted swords, on the table before supper. He must fight him—excuse it—for a wager of one ceptre. You look stricken, Sir Able. Are you afraid to fight?"

"No, My Lord. But . . ."

"But what?"

From the way he was looking at me, I knew he thought I was scared and I did not like that, but there was not a lot I could do about it. I said, "Well, for one thing, I don't have a ceptre, My Lord."

He opened a drawer in the table and rummaged around in there and pulled one out. "I do," he said. He held it up. "Should I lend it to you?"

"Yes, My Lord. Please. I'll pay you back if I win, I promise."

"And if you lose?" He was looking at me with his eyes almost closed. "Because you will lose, Sir Able. Never doubt it."

"I won't be able to." Talking about bets like that, I remember the forfeits Pouk and I had paid with when we raced. I said, "Maybe I could do you a favor instead, My Lord. I'd do just about anything you wanted."

"*Anything,* Sir Able?"

I was pretty sure I was getting into trouble, but right then I did not care much. "Yes, My Lord. Anything."

"Well and good." He tossed me the ceptre. "I have been nurturing a little notion. We will have to go to the top of my mountain, which should suit you very well. A good plan, you see. Good plans fit together, like—oh, stones in a wall. That sort of thing. So you will get to go to the top of my mountain, as you wish, and I will have my plan, as I wish." He poured me some more wine and made me clink glasses with him.

I drank a little bit more. "There's another problem, My Lord, only I don't think it's as bad. You said blunted swords, and I won't use a sword. Can I use this instead?" I took out Sword Breaker then and showed her to him.

He held it for a minute and sort of waved it around the way you do, and gave it back. "I am afraid not, Sir Able. It's a mace. You said so yourself."

I said okay.

"Which makes it much too dangerous. I don't want to see anyone killed. I will find something else for you. Have you got a shield, by the way?"

I said no, and he said he would see about that, too.

It was already time for supper, so we went down to the hall. There were a lot of people there already and a lot more coming in, and we were standing there watching them when Pouk found us. He said he had not found anything for us to eat or drink, either, but maybe somebody there would let us have something. So I explained that we could eat with the others as soon as I fought up on the table like Thunrolf wanted.

Thunrolf pointed to a place and made Pouk sit down. Then we went up to the head of the table and he explained to me that knights sat up front close to him at the high table. A knight's friend that was not a knight himself ought to sit at the far end of the high table with the men-at-arms, so that was where he had put Pouk. Servants sat at the low table that was close to the door, and did I want to change anything? I said no.

Somebody, I guess Master Aud, brought us the blunted swords. They were just regular old swords, pretty plain with the points and edges ground flat. The knight that was going to fight me took one, and I explained again about how I was not going to use a sword, even one like that, that was not sharp. So Thunrolf sent somebody for the chief cook, and he came, and Thunrolf explained and told him to bring me a shield and something I could use that was not a sword. That was when they took Sword Breaker and my bow.

The chief cook came back pretty quick, and for a shield he had one of those pewter covers they put over a dish, and for a sword a long iron spoon. I did not like it, but I had to get up on the table and take them. Everybody was telling me to by then and yelling and laughing, and to tell the truth they picked me up and set me up there. I thought, all right, I am bigger and stronger than this guy and I am going to show them.

Right here let me get rid of the excuses. I had drunk too much wine with Thunrolf and I was none too steady. That is the plain truth. Also they were grabbing my ankles and trying to trip me. That is the truth, too. Only neither one of those was what really did it. He was a swordsman, a good one, and I was not. Until I tried to fight him, I did not even know what a good swordsman was or what one could do. I hit his shield hard enough to bend my spoon, and so what? He never hit my serving dish cover at all. He hit around it, and he could make me move it whenever he wanted, and wherever he wanted. He was probably a pretty nice guy, because I could see he felt sorry for me. He hit me three or four times, not too hard, and then he knocked me right off the table. I got up and gave him the ceptre I had borrowed, and that was the end of our bet.

Thunrolf was laughing, everybody was, and he slapped my back and made me sit by him. There was beer and more wine, and soup, meat, and bread. There was a kind of salad, too, that had cut-up roots in it or something crunchy like that, and oil and salt fish. That was pretty good, and so was the meat and bread. Afterward there was fruit, I think the same mangos we had ridden on that morning. I ate a lot, but Thunrolf did not eat much at all. He just kept drinking, but he never seemed really drunk. Later I got to know Morcaine, and she was like that, too. She drank brandy instead of wine, and she drank quite a bit of it. It put a lot of color in her face and she swayed sometimes when she walked, but she never sang or got silly or passed out. I never understood why she drank so much, or why Thunrolf did either.

CHAPTER 30

THE MOUNTAIN OF FIRE

When supper was about over, Thunrolf stood up and banged on the table with one of those silver glasses until everybody quieted down. "Friends!" he said. "True knights, brave men-at-arms, bold archers." He sort of stopped and looked hard at them before he said, "Loyal servants."

He kicked over his chair and went down to the servants' table, and his voice got slow and serious. "I have reason to believe that offense has been given. Given to us all, but to you loyal servants most of all."

He spun around after he said that, and came close to falling down, and pointed to Pouk. "Aren't you a servant? Sir Able's servingman?"

Pouk jumped up. "Aye, sir!"

The other servants sort of growled at that, and so did the men-at-arms Pouk had been eating with.

"You have pushed in among your betters," Thunrolf told him, "and turned your back on your comrades. If I left your punishment to them, you would get such a beating as would cripple you for life. Would you like that?"

"No, sir," Pouk said. "I just—"

"Silence! I will spare you the beating. Is the smith here?"

He was with the men-at-arms too, and stood up. Thunrolf whispered to him, and he went out.

"I want six intrepid knights. Six in addition to Sir Able

there." He named the ones, and said that anybody else could come who wanted to see it.

Thunrolf had a horse, and so did his knights, but Pouk and I had to walk, and so did most of the ones that came with us. The road got steeper and steeper, and finally there was a long flight of stairs where the ones that had horses had to leave them, and then more road, and then more stairs with snow and ice on them clear to the top. Some people stopped there and went back, but there were men-at-arms watching us, and we did not try. I told Pouk it was not much to somebody who had climbed to the top of the Tower of Glas, and he told me it was not much to somebody who had climbed to the top of the mainmast as often as he had. We cheered each other up like that, but the truth was that it was a stiff climb, and when I had gone up the stairs in the Tower of Glas with Uri and Baki we had stopped to rest every so often. Going up the Mountain of Fire, nobody stopped at all.

We got to the top, and it was beautiful, just beautiful. Down in the lowlands it was already night and you could see lights in the towers along the bottom wall, and here and there out past it, out in the jungle, where somebody had a little house or maybe just a campfire. Up where we were, there was a fresh cool wind and it was still sunset. The clouds over the sea were gold and gray, and I looked at some and thought, you know, a bunch of knights might ride down that valley any minute. And when the sun got just a little lower some knights did. They were tiny and way far away, but I could see their flags and the gleam of their armor and it was just beautiful. I will never forget it.

Only I never got to see where they were going, because I heard a hammer and looked around to see what it was. The smith had locked a gyve (a kind of iron ring) around Pouk's ankle, and he was pounding a staple into a big rock so that Pouk would be chained to the rock.

When he was through, Thunrolf told Pouk to pick the rock up and carry it. Pouk tried, but it was so heavy he had to drop it after a couple steps. Finally one of the servants who had come along to watch helped him carry it, and we all went up to the very top. There was a sort of stone terrace there, shaped like a fingernail-cutting, that the Osterlings had built. When you stood on the edge you could look down into the Mountain of Fire. It was not straight down, but a steep slope with rocks jutting out of it in places. It went down and down. You could see way down deep because it was lit up by fire at the bottom. The opening up where we were standing was a long bowshot across, or a little more. But it got narrower as it went down.

Thunrolf made Pouk come over to the edge, and I kept telling myself he was not going to throw him in, because that was what the Osterlings did. I believed it, too. Then the servant who had been helping carry let go and Thunrolf gave Pouk a little push, and he went over the edge.

He rolled and banged around down the slope and tried to grab on to things and hold on, but the rock always pulled him loose. That was when I went for Thunrolf.

The men-at-arms would have killed me then if he had let them, but he made them stop. I had knocked down one and broken the arm of another, but the other knights were holding on to me so I could not fight, and there were too many men-at-arms between me and him. They had the points of their pikes and halberds up against my face and my chest. The knights were holding me, and all they had to do was shove them in. Thunrolf got the smith to put a gyve on my right hand. There was another gyve on the other end of the chain, and he held it up and showed it to the knights.

"Now then, bold Sir Able," he said. "Do you still maintain that man is your friend, and not your servant?"

I said, "Yes. I told you the truth."

"My Lord." Thunrolf sort of smirked when he said that.

The knights that had my arms were trying to twist them, but the strength of the sea was building in me like a storm. I could hear the surf and feel the pounding of the waves. I did not want them to find out they could not twist them, not even with three holding each arm, so I said, "My Lord," very quick. "I told you the truth, My Lord. He's my friend."

"That's better." Thunrolf smiled at me. He was still holding up the empty gyve, and he was having a good time. "If he is really your friend, he has been wrongly accused—accused by his own tongue, but wrongly still. Look down, can you see him?"

The knights let go so I could go over to the edge and look. I could not see Pouk at first, but pretty soon I did. The rock he was chained to had gotten stuck on an outcrop, and he was trying to get it loose. I yelled to him to stay where he was, that I would climb down and get him out.

Thunrolf said, "Ah!" You could tell he liked that a lot. "You will if I permit it. Not otherwise."

I was about ready to rush him again, just trying to get a clear shot at him, but I said, "Please, My Lord, please let me. He hasn't done anything wrong. Let me go down and bring him back up."

Thunrolf nodded. "I will, Sir Able, if you mean it. You are willing to risk your life in my Mountain of Fire to save your friend?"

I said, "I sure am, My Lord," and started to climb over the edge.

He motioned to the other knights, and they stopped me. I felt like pushing them in, and I could have done it, too.

"You may go," Thunrolf told me, "but not alone. You shall have a companion, another bold knight to help you with your friend and the stone. Who will volunteer?" He held up the gyve again.

Nobody said a thing.

"Let me have a volunteer. Any knight present." Thunrolf waved the gyve.

I was like him. I thought that two or three would, and maybe all of them, and he would have to choose. But none of them did and you could see some of them backing away a little bit. I did not say anything, but I knew Sir Ravd would have volunteered, and I wanted to tell them.

Thunrolf got mad then. He called them poltroons and cowards, and I could see they wanted to kill him for it, but even so there was no one who would let him put the other gyve on him.

About then I looked down again, and Pouk was gone. I could not see him at all, and I knew he had gotten his rock loose and tried to climb up holding on to it, and had fallen down deeper than ever.

I grabbed on to Thunrolf's arm then. "I'm going," I told him. "You can put the other one on me."

"No," he said, "one of these cravens must go with you. I want to see—and I want them to see—who turns back first."

They would not even start, and I told him so and climbed over the edge. He still had the other end of my chain and one of the men-at-arms grabbed it too, and they stopped me. It was going to be a tough climb with two hands, and I knew that if I tried to pull them in, more would grab hold.

"This is your last chance," Thunrolf told his knights, "your final opportunity. Speak now."

I stuck my head up over the edge and yelled, "Put it on my other hand! I'll go!"

I have been awfully surprised here, and more than just once or twice. I know I have said that already, and it is the truth. That was one of them, because Thunrolf put that gyve on his own wrist and snapped it shut, gave his knights one last look, and climbed down with me.

As we went deeper and deeper the air got hotter and hotter and it was harder and harder to breathe. There was smoke in it, and we coughed a lot. I knew there was a good chance we would both die, and I did not want to.

(This is one of those places where it is hard to tell the truth. It may be the hardest of all. I think it is. I went outside and walked around and looked at the sea and the mountains and the beautiful place where we live. If Disiri or Michael had been there I would have talked to them about it, but they were not, and I had to decide for myself. I have, and this is the truth.)

If the Mountain of Fire had been a volcano like we have back home I would never have done it. I knew it was not, and that was one thing that kept me going. I knew that there was another world under Aelfrice, and that it was the sixth world and was called Muspel. I knew that the hole in the middle of the Mountain of Fire went there, and that was where the fire we saw was, and where the smoke was coming from.

So that was one thing. The other one was that I did not think we would have to go clear down to Muspel. Pouk had stopped partway the first time, so I thought he had probably stopped partway again, which was wrong. When Thunrolf got to coughing bad and wanted to go back up, I kept hustling him along. I knew he was trying to tell me that he would have me killed, and sometimes he was able to get most of it out. But I pretended I could not understand and kept pulling the chain on our wrists and telling him to keep moving.

After a while the hole started opening out again, and we were not climbing down the inside of a mountain anymore, we were climbing down a cliff. Thunrolf fell again. He had fallen a dozen times, but that was the worst. I caught the chain, and he was hanging by it. While I was trying to work him over where he could find a toehold, I saw Pouk far below us, with one of the dragons of Muspel coming for him.

I do not believe any two men ever went down a cliff any faster than Thunrolf and I did after that. We got to the bottom and I yelled to Pouk, and I yelled at the dragon, and that was when Thunrolf drew his sword and tried to kill me. I caught his wrist and bent his arm back and he dropped the sword.

This is hard to put down on paper because it happened so quickly. I could not watch the dragon while I was wrestling Thunrolf, but I knew it was coming for Pouk and coming fast. I wanted that sword. I knew I had been saying I would never use one until I got the one Disiri was going to find for me, but I wanted it anyway. That sword seemed to be our only hope, and if Thunrolf had it instead of me he was going to kill me with it and not the dragon.

He dropped it, as I said, and it fell into a crevice in the rock. There was fire coming out of that crevice, and it had fallen so far in I could not see it. I turned as quickly as I could, and the dragon had Pouk pinned under one of its forefeet. Think of a big snake, a crocodile as big as a boat, and one of those flying dinosaurs. Mix all the worst parts together and that is the way a dragon looks. It is worse than any of them, and worse than all of them at once.

I picked up a stone. It was almost too hot to hold, but I

threw it. The dragon hissed like a steam pipe and opened its mouth wide, and Garsecg's face was in there instead of a tongue. He said, "Sir Able, why war you against me?" It was still his voice, but it sounded like a whole rock band.

I explained that Pouk was my friend, and said that if he killed Pouk he was going to have to kill me, too.

"If I do not?" Garsecg smiled, there in the dragon's mouth. His face was three times the size that it had been.

"Then I'll be alive to keep my promise. I said I would fight Kulili for you, and I will."

At that he opened his wings. I had thought that he was big before, but with his wings open he was bigger than any airplane I have ever seen. He took off, and the wind was a hurricane. It blew sand and rocks and fire and us, knocking us down so that we were rolling across level ground as if we were falling down the inside of the Mountain of Fire.

Then he was gone. I looked up, and I could see him high in the sky, and his wings were so big that he looked big even up there. It was a terrible sky, red with dust and lit by the fires below. But up above it, where we see the highest clouds, you could see Aelfrice, beautiful trees and mountains and snow and flowers, and Kulili deep in the cool blue sea.

I could not break the chain that held Pouk to the rock, but I stood on it with both feet and pulled the staple out. If I had not, I do not think that Thunrolf and I could ever have carried him up the cliff and up the inside of the Mountain of Fire.

We almost failed anyway. Sometimes we stopped to rest a little, coughing and choking. We were both so thirsty that we could hardly talk, but I tried to explain to him that the time we had been in the Mountain of Fire might seem like just a few days to us, but it was going to be a lot longer when we got out of it.

"If we get out, Sir Able," he said, and he picked up Pouk and slung him over his shoulders the way I had carried him, and started climbing again. Pouk's legs were broken, and sometimes he was conscious and sometimes he was not. Thunrolf could carry him a little, then he would get shaky and I would have to carry him again; but Thunrolf never once asked me to. Not once. After a while I noticed that.

We climbed and climbed. It seemed something was wrong, we could not have climbed down as far as we had climbed up already, and we were noplace near the top. We were no longer in Muspel, but in another world of rock and stone and heat and smoke, one bent around us. I knew that we were going to die, and I could drop Pouk and dying would be faster for him and easier for me. I was too stubborn to do it. That went on so long it seemed like forever. It seemed to me that I had never been anybody's kid brother in America then, that I had never gone looking for a tree or lived in a hut in the woods with Bold Berthold. That there had never been anything for me, really, but climbing and choking and weariness.

I felt a cool wind. It smelled wrong and tasted wrong, but it was cool and I had burns everywhere, and I had been hot so long I did not notice anymore. I looked up, trying to see where it was coming from and how tough the slope was going to be up above, and I saw stars. I will never forget that, and I can shut my eyes right now and see them again. You do not know what stars are, or how beautiful they can be.

But I do.

CHAPTER 31

BACK TO SEA

A brighter, nearer star burned some distance below us—a campfire where the lower stair began. We made our way down to it, moving very slowly and snatching mouthfuls of snow, I carrying Pouk and supporting Thunrolf when he needed it. We were not far from the lowest step when Thunrolf said, "Aud!"

The men sitting around the fire sprang up, and Thunrolf stumbled down the last few steps to hug them, and cried. I laid Pouk near the fire and cut away his breeches, and was very happy to see the broken bones had not poked through the skin. Bold Berthold had warned me about that when I fell out of a tree, saying that when it happened the person generally died.

"This is Aud, my steward," Thunrolf told me, "and this is Vix, my body servant." Tears were running down his face. "I have never been happier to see two rogues in my life."

They had wine and water, and we sat with them, drinking it and coaxing Pouk to drink. He was dizzy and sick, and seemed not to know where he was or who we were.

"It was a year ago this day, Your Lordship," Aud told Thunrolf, "that you went into the Mountain of Fire. We came tonight to remember."

Vix said, "We were going back to Seagirt, Your Lordship. Leaving tomorrow. Lord Olof would give us places, but we didn't want them."

"So there's a new lord in the Round Tower." Thunrolf seemed to speak only to himself. "I don't care. I don't care at all. I am out."

"The king sent him, Your Lordship," Aud said.

"Then I can go home. We'll go home." He shook himself, and drained his cup. "I'm so tired—you'll have to help me up. Able, too. Sir Able. Help him too. Wilt journey to Seagirt with me, Sir Able? You shall be my chief knight, and my heir. I'll adopt you."

I thanked him, but explained that Pouk and I had been on our way to Forcetti to take service with Duke Marder.

"I'm going to sleep here. Cover us, Vix." With that Thunrolf lay down and shut his eyes, and Vix covered him with his cloak.

They had come on donkeys, and Aud rode to the Round Tower to fetch a leech. I was asleep myself before he came, and it was one of the few sleeps I had in Mythgarthr in which my dreams were not troubled by the people whose lives wove the bowstring Parka bit through for me. Nor did Setr trouble me, though he troubled many dreams of mine afterward.

I have never been less willing to wake, or less willing to rise than I was the next morning. The sun was high when I sat up, for the leech had covered our faces with muslin. "Your friend has been carried to the Round Tower," the leech told me. "I've done what I can for him, splinted his legs and his arm, and salved his burns. I've salved yours, too, and of course Lord Thunrolf's."

I had not even known that Pouk's arm was broken.

"Lord Olof agrees that you should not be moved until you're ready."

Probably our voices awakened Thunrolf. He pulled the

muslin off his face and tried to sit up. Vix and Aud ran to help him.

"I don't know whether I can walk," he told the leech, "but if you can get me on a horse, I think I might ride."

"That won't be necessary, Your Lordship. We have litters for you, and for Sir Able as well."

"In which I will not ride," Thunrolf declared. "No. Not if I must die here. Help me up, Aud. Where's my horse?"

There was no horse but the leech's. Aud and I helped Thunrolf mount, and I walked next to him holding his stirrup strap. I was afraid he would fall off, and I think he was afraid that I would fall down. When we were nearly there, he said softly, "A boon, Sir Able. You owe me none, I know. I crave one anyway, and you'll not find me a worthless friend."

I explained that I did owe him one. I had borrowed a ceptre and lost it, and promised any service I could perform.

"I'd forgotten that. Very well. I ask that you forgive me. Will you?"

I looked up at him. "Yes, My Lord, but that's no boon. I'd done it already."

"It is the boon you owed. Now I ask another, Sir Able. May I have it?"

"Sure."

"Let me speak when we reach the Round Tower. Agree with what I say, and say nothing that will disgrace me."

I was still trying to think of something polite, when half a dozen knights met us. Some were his, and some were Olof's, but they had all caught on that something was going on and come out to see what it was. Thunrolf's could not believe their eyes.

"We encountered a dragon," he told them, "and I lost my sword. I would like to get that back, but not at the cost of another dragon. Had you seen a dragon before, Sir Able? I had seen them pictured, but the pictures are nothing."

I said, "Once before, My Lord, but that didn't help. I don't think anybody ever gets used to them."

He smiled. It was a twisted smile because of the burns, but a smile just the same. "I will not, if I have anything to say about it."

Then we got the chain taken off; there was a lot more after that, but I am going to cut it short. He left pretty soon, going down to the port and getting a ship home. Nearly all his men had left already, going overland because of their horses. Pouk and I stayed until Pouk could walk, and Olof was very nice to us. He had Sword Breaker and my bow and quiver, and gave them back along with a lot of presents. When we left he loaned us horses, and sent some of his men with us to bring them back.

We stayed in an inn for three nights, I think it was, and did not like it much. After that, Pouk found an old man and his wife who would put us up cheaper than the inn, and better, too. The old man had been captain of a ship, but he had to quit when his eyes got bad. He knew a lot of stories. They were all worth listening to, and lots of them were worth remembering. We stayed with those people for over a month.

During the day I would practice with my bow, or with Sword Breaker, or I would go to the stable and get a horse. It was all day for a copper bit, or two for a better horse. I would ride around the country and gallop and trot, and so forth. I thought I was getting to be a good rider, too, but I was just getting started.

Pouk would go down to the docks and watch for a ship for us, and talk to the sailors and longshoremen. One day I came back and he was at the house, all smiles. He said there was a ship in port that was going to Forcetti, and it would take us there.

I said, "Fine! Let's go and see how much they want. You think it's a good one?"

"Aye, sir! That I do. Only I already booked, sir, by your leave. A snug cabin, sir, and straight up the coast to Forcetti."

I wanted to know how much. Thunrolf had given me a lot of money, but I knew there were a lot of things I would have to get in Forcetti. A knight's mail is not cheap, and a horse like Blackmane (that was Sir Ravd's) costs the world.

"You'll like the price, sir." Pouk was grinning like a monkey.

"You mean you paid it yourself? I was going to pay for us both."

He laughed a little. "Aye, sir. I did."

"Then I'll pay you back."

"Oh, that's all right, sir. I paid wit' what th' dragon give me."

I knew perfectly well that Setr had given him nothing but bruises.

It was the *Western Trader*, and I know you guessed it a lot quicker than I did. It did not look much better than it had a year ago; but it did not look much worse either, and when we went on board and had a chance to look around I saw that most of the sails were new.

Kerl and I hugged, and he told me how he had gone to the Round Tower looking for Pouk and me. That had been a week after we had gone down inside the Mountain of Fire, and he had been told we were dead, and Thunrolf was dead, too. So I told him most of what had happened, just saying that Thunrolf had wanted to shame his knights, which was true, and leaving out his trying to kill me when he saw Setr and I would not run.

I got the old woman to sew a pennant for me while we were waiting for the *Western Trader* to unload and load and get ready for sea again. It was silk and made of scraps left over from when she had made a gown for the daughter of the Captain of the Port. It was made of green silk, and she cut hearts out of red silk and sewed one on each side. Kerl flew it on the foremast for as long as I was on board. Later I put it away and sort of forgot it until I made a lance out of spiny orange. Then I remembered it and got it out, and put it on that lance. It was on there when that lance was hewn through.

Pouk and I stayed on shore with the old captain and his wife until the ship was ready. First, because we had gotten very comfortable there. And second, because I wanted to let Kerl keep his cabin for as long as I could. He was not going to charge me anything and would not hear of our paying, but I had decided that when we got to Forcetti I would leave behind the Osterling knife Olof had given me. It had a silver hilt and a silver scabbard, both set with corals, and so it was pretty valuable, but it was too close to being a sword for me to like it.

I did that, too.

It seemed like we were never going to sail. The big spar broke, and Kerl had to find a long piece of good wood so the carpenter could make a new one, and he had to make it, and after that they had to load the rest and get everything stowed. Back when I was living with you, I read stories about sailing ships and pirates, and fighting Napoleon and all that, but it had never really gotten through to me how slow everything was. How long everything took. There are about a thousand things that have to be ready all at once, and when everything else is set you load the water, because the water starts going bad the minute it gets in the casks. Small beer is nicer, like Pouk said, because it keeps better. But it costs, and water is free.

Pouk and I had small beer in our cabin. Wine, too. The wine there is not real wine because they cannot grow grapes.

But they make other stuff out of fruits they can grow, the same way we do cider. It had been cheap there in the little port town where the Mountain of Fire is, and we had gotten used to it. We had ship's bread too, and cheese and jam, and three different kinds of salt meat, two kinds of smoked fish, and a lot of other stuff. The old woman had fixed a basket for the first day: sandwiches and fruit, and all kinds of pickles. There was so much in it we ate it for the first three days. The old captain gave me his brass marlinspike that he had in the seabag he carried onto his first ship. He said I ought to learn to splice rope while I had the chance. It was a handy thing to know, and I might need it sometime. So I did.

Because we finally did put to sea. When it happened we had been waiting so long it did not seem possible.

Most people here have never been on a ship, and some of them have never seen the sea. (Disira had not.) People in America are the same way, and it does not bother them. So there are some things I ought to explain, and one is about bread and cooking and so on. There is a stove in the galley, and the cook bakes bread for the crew when he can. But he never lights his stove in bad weather because some coals could spill out and burn the whole ship. In bad weather you get ship's bread and cold meat. Everybody does, even the captain. In good weather the cook boils your meat in seawater to get some salt out. But any cooking he does costs firewood, and there is only so much of that. In cold weather there is no heat except for the galley stove. None. It got colder and colder as we went north up the coast. Winter was about over, but it was still cold north of Kingsdoom. I had been gone about three years with Garsecg in Aelfrice, and one year exactly with Thunrolf in Muspel. Time always runs slower in the worlds underneath Mythgarthr, but you can never be sure how much. Sometimes it is just a little slower, but sometimes it is a lot.

When I think back on those days, all the days and weeks and months after we got out of the Mountain of Fire there are two things I remember more than any of the rest. One is how bad Pouk looked after we got him out. When he was lying on the rock waiting for the leech, and later in his bed in the Round Tower. He was not what anyone would call handsome, besides being pretty small. He had a big hook nose and a big lantern jaw. His blind eye looked terrible, and his good eye was little and squinty. But he looked so pitiful when he was hurt so bad, and he was so brave about it. When Thunrolf told him he would never do anything like that to him again, he just said, "Thankee, sir. Thankee." And shut his eyes. I never knew how much I liked him until I saw him suffering like that, hurt so bad and trying to smile. He drank too much sometimes, but I could never get mad about it like I should have.

He was with me, on and off, until Disiri and I went away. After we had gone I saw what he had meant about my being his big chance. He was important (and Ulfa was, too) just because he had been with me so much. He was Master Pouk then, and worked for the king.

The other thing that I will never forget is seeing the Isle of Glas. The sun was almost down, and I was up on the sterncastle deck talking to Kerl. I thought I saw something and borrowed his big brass telescope.

And there it was. The tall, proud trees and the waves lapping a beach of blood-colored sand. I looked and looked, and pretty soon I started to cry. If I could tell you why, I would, but I cannot. Tears ran down my face, and I could not breathe right. I took the telescope down and wiped my eyes and blew my nose. And when I looked again, it was gone. I never saw it again until I went into Thiazi's Room of Lost Loves.

So those are the things. But I ought to say right here that I did not know Uri and Baki were looking for me. I had no idea, and of course my going to Muspel had made it really hard for them. They had searched the *Western Trader* three or four times, and had given up on it a long time before Pouk and I boarded it again.

CHAPTER 32

THE MARSHAL'S TOWER

"Keep your hand from your sword," the man-at-arms behind me whispered, "and none of your cheek." More loudly he said, "This here is Able, Master Agr."

I said, "*Sir* Able, sir."

"He says he's a knight, Master. He wanted His Grace, so I thought I'd better let you see him."

That was what I got for not buying a proper warhorse in Forcetti. I had planned to get one, and Pouk and I had looked at a few that they had for sale. None of them had really suited me, and even though Thunrolf had given me a lot I could not have bought one of the pretty good ones.

The thin man behind the big table nodded and stroked his little mustache. He looked smart. He also looked like he did not like what he was seeing very much, meaning me. It always seemed to me that people ought to see right away that I was not really a man, just a boy that Disiri had made look like one. Only they could not. Pouk had not been able to, and neither had Kerl. Neither had Thunrolf. Now it seemed to me like I had stumbled into somebody that would.

"I am the duke's marshal," he said. He did not give a damn what I thought about him, and the way he talked showed it. He was telling me the facts. "I keep order among his horses, among his knights, among his servants, and among any others who happen to be here in Sheerwall."

It did not seem like a good time to talk, so I just nodded.

"If it is needful that you speak to the duke, I will see that you gain audience. If it is not, you may speak with me. Or I will direct you to the correct person. Have you a wrong to lay before the duke's court?"

I said, "I seek service with Duke Marder."

"As a knight."

"Yes. That's what I am."

"Really." He smiled, and it was not a very nice smile. "From whom did you receive the accolade?"

"From the Queen of the Moss Aelf. From Queen Disiri."

"Make your japes over wine, Able."

"Sir Able, sir, and I'm not joking."

"You're a knight. We can leave the Aelfqueen out of it for the time being."

"That's right."

"You have the build for it, at least. As a knight, you are an expert rider? It's the management of the charger that distinguishes a knight from other men. I'm sure you know that."

"It's his honor that distinguishes a knight," I said.

Agr sighed. "But the management of the charger is the fundamental skill of knighthood. Have you a charger?"

I started to explain, but he cut me off. "Have you funds to buy one?"

"Not enough for one I'd want."

"I see." He smoothed his mustache again. He probably did not know he was doing it. "Have you a manor from which you draw support? Where is it?"

I said I did not have one.

"I thought not." Agr stood up and went over to his window

to look out. "His Grace has need of fighting men. Sir Able. On what terms would you serve him?"

I had not even thought about that, or how to explain how I felt about it. After about a minute I said, "I want to be his knight, or one of them, anyway. I didn't come to ask him for money."

I could hear steel hitting steel outside, and Agr leaned out his window so he could see what was happening. When he turned around again he said, "No monthly stipend? Merely to cover your expenses?"

I shook my head. "I've got a servant, Master Agr. Pouk is his name." When I had told Thunrolf about Pouk I called him my friend and got us in trouble. I was not going to do that again.

"I don't pay Pouk and sometimes I can't even feed him or get him a place to sleep. He looks out for himself then." I thought about when I had been hurt so bad, and lying in the cable locker, how little bits of light came in through cracks and how the rats came smelling my blood. "Sometimes Pouk looks out for me too, when I can't look out for myself," I said. "If I were one of Duke Marder's knights, I would be ashamed to treat him worse than Pouk treats me. If he wanted to give me something, I'd take it and say thank you. If he didn't, I'd try to serve him better."

That was the first time Agr looked at me like I was a real human being. He said, "That was well spoken, Sir Able. There's a baron with the king who prattles of the Aelf in his cups. I think he's as mad as a hare in spring, and I think you are too. But I cannot help wishing you were sane. With a little training you might make a first-rate man-at-arms. Can you use that bow?"

I said, "Yes, sir. I can."

"There's another master out there in the practice yard. His name is Master Thope. He's master of arms, and if you address him as 'sir,' as you have been addressing me, he'll break yours. Do you know what a master of arms is?"

I said, "No, sir. I don't."

"He trains our squires and men-at-arms in the use of weapons and the management of horses. I provide him with horses for that purpose. They are not good enough for a knight to ride in war, you understand; but an inferior horse can actually be better training for a rider than a good one, as well as making a young man appreciate a good one more. I want you to joust with Master Thope."

He saw that I did not understand, because he added, "To ride against him with a practice lance. He'll lend you a horse, a shield, and so forth. If you do well, we'll see how well you can shoot that bow and what you know of swordcraft."

After that, the man-at-arms who had brought me to Master Agr took me down to Master Thope. He was as big as I am, but going gray. I told him who I was and why I was there, and explained that I was supposed to joust with him. He squeezed my arms. He had pretty big hands, and they were strong.

"That's muscle," he muttered, "not fat. Can you use a lance, young 'un?"

"I can try," I said.

"All anybody can do."

He got me a practice shield. They are a lot heavier than the real ones because they are a lot stronger, too. "I'll aim for that," he told me while I was adjusting the strap, "and you aim for mine. Nothing tricky."

I said, "Okay."

My horse was a fat chestnut gelding that was sweating already. It knew all about jousting, and it did not want to do that anymore. I did not have any spurs, and I had the shield on one arm and my practice lance in my other hand, so it was not very easy to get it into position. That would not have been so bad, but one of the other knights that were watching called, *"Prick him with your lance!"* and I looked at the end of it before I remembered it was not sharp. They thought that was really funny, and I started getting mad.

The place where you joust is called the lists. It is not really a list of anything. Those are thin wooden things that make the fence for it. Each jouster rides with those lists to his left side, so that the two will meet shield-to-shield. It is like football. You are not supposed to want to hurt anybody. Jousting is about as dangerous as tackle, and the person you are jousting with will be on your side in a real battle.

Like I said, I had quite a bit of trouble with my horse, and once I got him into position he knew exactly what was up. He was scared and trying to be brave, just like me. I tried to say something that would make him feel better. None of it was his fault, but he was the one who had to run and carry me and the big jousting saddle, and he knew he could get hurt.

I was not feeling any too sure myself, and while I was talking to him I said, "I wish you'd paw the ground a little like Blackmane." Talking to a horse like that, a horse that did not understand me or care what I said, made me think of Gylf and how much I missed him. He had never come back to the *Western Trader*, and nobody seemed to know where he was. I would have liked to go back to Aelfrice to look for him and Disiri, but I did not know how to get there.

There was a boy with a trumpet pretty close to the place where we would hit. He blew on it, my horse trotted for a minute, then cantered, and Master Thope's lance hit my shield hard and drove it back into me. I remember turning over in the air and hitting the ground really hard.

I also remember lying there hurting, and all the other knights yelling, *"Try again!"*

So I jumped up, even though I did not feel like jumping,

and I found my lance and picked it up, and caught my horse, and got back in the saddle.

That was when Master Agr came to talk to me. Up until then, I had not known that he had come down to watch. Quiet, so the others would not hear, he said, "You don't have to go again. You're no knight."

I had been spitting blood because I had hurt my lip, but I grinned at him anyway. (I am still proud of it.) I said, "I am a knight, just one who's not real good with a lance. I want to."

Master Thope did not have on a helm or helmet any more than I did, but he must have heard us. He made a motion like pushing up a visor and sort of smiled.

We did it again, and it went exactly like the first one. I had thought that I would at least hit his shield with my lance, but I did not. That really bothered me, and when I got up, I was yelling at myself inside. Only I tried not to let it show, and thanked Master Agr for helping me up.

"I would do the same for anyone." He had one of those hard, cold faces, and it did not look any different when he said, "It's good training, I know. But I'm sorry I got you into this."

I said, "Well, I've got to learn."

That was when one of the other knights called, *"You're no knight, boy!"*

I looked at him for a minute. Then I said, "I am a knight, but you aren't." It sort of shut him up.

I had been watching Master Thope when he rode at me, so that third time I bent down in the saddle the way he did, and I concentrated on hitting his shield with my lance. Before I had been worrying about his lance hitting me. Now I put that clear out of my mind. I had to hit that shield. It was the only thing that counted.

I did, too. I hit it and my lance broke. And his lance hit my shield the way it had before, and knocked me right out of my saddle like I was a doll or something, and down I went. Hard. Only this time it was one of the knights who had been laughing that helped me up, and when I was on my feet again he hit me in the mouth.

Up until then I had not been able to feel the sea in me. It rose all at once, as fast as the fastest storm, breaking bones like spars and tossing men around like the timbers from wrecks. That first one I hit may have been the one whose jaw I broke. I do not know. I think I hit him more on the side of the neck, but wherever it was it knocked him kicking and the whole bunch jumped on me. Fights usually do not take as long as it takes to tell about them, but it seemed like they always had four or five new men.

CHAPTER 33

DRINK! DRINK!

I thought I was in the cable locker. Not that I had been put back in there, really, but that I had never left it. It was dark and I hurt bad, and I was not really thinking at all.

After a while it got through to me that I was in a bed instead of lying on rope, but for a while I thought the bed was in a hospital. The moonlight came through the window, and I saw it was a window shaped like the point of a sword, and it seemed like I was not in the cable locker or the hospital at all, but I did not know where I was, or care.

A long time after that I tried to get out of bed. I was going to look out and see whatever there was to see, I think. But I fell down.

* * *

Then I was back in the bed, and it seemed like the room was full of sunshine. It was really a pretty dark room, like all of them were, but the sun was coming in right through the window and it seemed bright to me. There was a little table next to the bed and a goblet on it, and I remembered the one I found on the Isle of Glas. It had been poisoned once, and I was afraid to drink out of this one.

After a while I could smell the ale, but it was a long time yet before I sat up and drank it. It was not cold or even cool, but I liked it, and there was a trencher there, too (it means a wooden plate), with bread and meat and cheese. I could not even think about eating, but I drank the rest of the ale and lay back down and went to sleep.

When I woke up I felt like I had been sleeping a long time, but I did not know how long. It was pretty dark again. By-and-by a woman in an apron came in and talked. I could not understand her, or even pay attention. She got to taking bandages off me and putting new ones on, and she said, "I've got food for you too, sir, if you want it. Think you might eat a little now?"

I said there was some there already. Really I whispered it. I had not meant to whisper, but I did.

"That? Oh, that's all dried up now, sir. I'll give it to the dogs. I brought you some fresh, some nice hot broth."

She wanted to sit me up, but I would not let her. I got myself up instead, and it hurt. I took the spoon away from her too, but I let her hold the bowl while I ate.

"Well, you're doing wonderful, sir. Poor Sir Hermad's like to die, they say, with every rib broke. An' Sir Lud's puking blood." She tittered. "He'll die, too, some says. They're taking wagers in the kitchen, sir."

"Sir Able's my name. If you really care about me, call me Sir Able."

She stood up fast and bent her knee the way women do here. "Yes, Sir Able. I didn't mean no harm, Sir Able."

Just hearing the words made me feel better. I said, "Of course you didn't. Sit down again. What's your name?"

"I'm Modguda, Sir Able."

"Am I still in Duke Marder's castle, Modguda?"

"Yes, sir. In Sheerwall, Sir Able. 'Cept you're in Master Agr's tower of it. Master Agr's the only one has a whole tower of it, 'cept Her Grace. She's got one, too, the Duchess's Tower is what we call it, Sir Able. 'Cept that's not where you are, you can't even see it from your window. This's the Marshal's Tower we're in, 'cause Master Agr had his men take you 'cause they'd beat you with the lance you broke is how I heard it. So this's where you are."

I nodded and found out that my head did not want me to do that. "If we're in Master Agr's tower, he must be your boss."

She did not understand, and I had to explain. Then she said, "That's right, Sir Able . . . sir."

I smiled, and that did not hurt at all. "Hey, out with it. What are you scared to say?"

"Well, you're a knight, sir."

"Right," I told her.

"And you knights don't much care for my master, sir, 'cause you've to do what he says, 'cept he's not one of you, like. Or not a baron or something neither, Sir Able. 'Cept the duke, he's behind him. He's the duke's man, sir, so you knights got to."

"You're dead wrong about that," I told her. "I'm not down on Master Agr. Not a bit."

"Well anyhow, that's what I was getting myself set to say,

sir. You shouldn't be, 'cause they had knocked you flat and their swords was out ready to kill you. 'Cept Sir Woddet didn't want to, sir. And Squire Yond—he's Sir Woddet's squire, sir—Squire Yond, he throwed himself right down over you, sir, and that's when my master's guards come that he'd called when him and Master Thope couldn't stop the fight and they stabbed Master Thope, sir. That's when his guards come. And then—"

"Wait a minute. Did you say Master Thope got stabbed? By Master Agr's guards?"

"Oh, no, Sir Able!" She looked shocked. "Master Agr wouldn't never tell them to do that, sir. It was one of the knights, maybe, or one of those squires. Then some varlets come to fight too, so it could of been one of them. Anyway Master Agr and Master Thope were trying to get between you and the knights sort of like what Squire Yond did. That's when Master Thope got stabbed, Sir Able, trying to help you like Master Agr. The guards finally got you out, sir."

My head was whirling. "Is Master Thope dead?"

"No, sir. Only he's hurt bad, Sir Able. That's what they say."

"I ought to go see him, Modguda, since he got hurt trying to help me."

"Yes, sir. Only you're not going to do much walking for a while, Sir Able." She got up and bent her knee as before. "He'll be pleasured to see your face, sir, I'm sure, and I'll show you where when you're ready, sir."

I was thinking, and one thing I was thinking about was what she had said, that it might be a while before I was up and around. "Can you take a message into town?"

"I'll try, sir, or send a boy."

"Good. I've got a servant named Pouk. We were staying at an inn in Forcetti. It had a bottle and seashell on the sign. Do you know where that is?"

"Yes, sir, Sir Able. That's the Dollop and Scallop, sir."

"Thanks. Tell Pouk I've been hurt, please, and where I am."

"Yes, sir. Is that all, Sir Able? They'll be wondering where I've got to."

I waved my hand, and she hurried out.

After that I ate some bread and a bite of cheese, not sure whether eating was a big mistake or not. I drank all the ale and lay down to sleep again, pretty dizzy.

In my dream Garsecg and I were in the throne room in the Tower of Glas. There was a big blue dragon on the throne, and it hissed at us and opened its mouth just like Setr had down in Muspel, and Garsecg's face was in the dragon's mouth. So I looked over at Garsecg to see if he had seen it too, and it was not Garsecg at all. It was Bold Berthold.

I woke up feeling cold, and this time I was able to get to the window. There was no way to close it, it was just a hole in the wall, really. Bats were flying around outside, bigger ones than we have at home. They were after bugs, the way bats do, diving and zooming and all that, and yelling and yelping so high you could only just hear it. Way up toward the moon I thought I saw Khimairas, just for a minute.

On the other side of my bed was a little fireplace, only there was no wood and I did not have any way to start a fire anyhow. I decided I would have to ask Modguda about that, or get Pouk to get me something when he came. After that I got back into bed and hunkered down under the blankets, hoping I would not have any more dreams like that last one.

* * *

"Lord? Lord?"

This time I was back on the Isle. I looked around and saw a lot of trees and flowers and birds.

"Lord?"

There were no spiny oranges, though. I wanted to find one and let it thank me for planting it, but I knew it could not hear me, and there were not any anyway. What there was, was big red snakes. They were wrapping themselves around my legs, but that was good because my legs were cold and they felt hot.

"Bite me, Lord. Bite me and kiss the bite, and your kiss will make you strong again."

That woke me up fast. The room was as dark as it could be. There was a really skinny woman in bed with me, sort of tangled up with me and holding on to a part of me that other people were not even supposed to see. Her hands were holding my head, too, and pushing my mouth against her neck. *"Drink! Drink!"*

"Drink! Drink!" The other hand sort of squeezed and slid around. That was when I caught on that there were two of them.

I really did not mean to bite her. That is the truth, and I will swear to it any time. Only something way down deep inside me took over and I did.

It was like I was starving hungry and here was a roast about one minute out of the oven. What I got in my mouth was steaming hot and sizzling. Greasy and dirty and hot as hell. It tasted wonderful.

"Enough." One was pulling and one pushing to get my mouth away. Pretty soon they did it, and I just lay there panting and thinking how good it had tasted. When I got my breath, I hit the blankets with my hand and said, "Stop that, you!" What she had been doing felt wonderful, but it felt *too* wonderful, if you know what I mean.

Under my blankets where I had hit her there was somebody a lot warmer than I was. She said, "I am Uri, Lord. I meant no harm."

It was dark in there like I said, so that when the other one stuck her head up beside mine and kissed my cheek I could not even see her face. She said, "You have drunk of Baki, Lord." And like she had just won the game "Who can take you from me now?"

"Drink of me, too!" Uri came up then, squirming in between us. "I have found you at last!"

I said, "Ash Aelf in the dark. Bold Berthold talked about this sometimes."

"Fire Aelf!" One laughed. "Did he tell you how lovely we are? Or how lovely you are? Your skin has taken on all sorts of beautiful colors."

"Those are bruises," I said. "If there's some way you can see them down there in the dark, isn't there some way I can see you?"

They glowed then. It was like they were copper or maybe brass, with a fire inside. They were not hot enough to burn me, but they were plenty hot. Uri jumped out of bed and sort of posed. "Look at me! Am I not beautiful?"

"He prefers me," Baki told her. Baki still had me wrapped up.

I guess I did, because I went to touch her face and she licked the tips of my fingers.

"I have sacrificed myself to you," she explained when she was through licking, "to make you stronger, and my lord forever. Sit up and you'll see."

"I will too," Uri told me. "Bite me. Anywhere!"

I sat up and found out Baki was right. I also found out I

was sweating and the room was freezing. Or anyway it felt like it was freezing. It was still spring, and pretty early spring, too, and the nights were cold. So I asked them to bring some firewood and tinder, and when they said they would I said to bring my clothes, and Sword Breaker, and my bow and quiver too. After I told them what Sword Breaker was, they promised to look.

For just a minute it seemed like the room was full of bats. Then the door opened. I saw a little red light out there, and the door closed again pretty hard, and I got up out of bed and wrapped a blanket around me. I did not feel good, but I did not feel that bad, either, except that I sort of felt like I had gone crazy. I opened the door, and the red light that I had seen had come from what they call a cresset. I did not know the word then, but it means an iron basket you can burn whatever you have in for light. There was one next to my door, and I found out later that they were all over the castle. I was glad to see it, because it meant I could light my wood there if I got any. So I went looking and found a room that had a woodbox next to the fireplace. I picked up the whole thing and carried it back to my room, and by the time Uri and Baki got back I had a nice fire going.

CHAPTER 34

BEING A KNIGHT

When I woke up next morning, Uri and Baki had gone. That was generally the way it was any time that they were with me, so I might as well explain it now, and later I will not say much about it. They did not like our sun. Sunlight hurt them, and if they stood in it you could hardly see them. So they went back to Aelfrice, mostly, when it got light, unless it was a dark day with lots of clouds. If they had to stay, they stood in the shadows or tried to. I did not understand that then, and thought I might have dreamed them.

I was going to get out of bed to see if Sword Breaker and my bow were really under it, when there was a knock at the door. I said, "Come in!"

He was bigger than I am, really huge, and blond, with a thick mustache that was not a lot darker than his hair. I liked him right away, because I could see he wanted to be friends but he was not too sure how to go about it. (I am like that pretty often myself.) He said, "I didn't wake you, I hope."

I was not sure whether he had or not, because he might have knocked before, but I said no. Looking at how bright my room was and sort of smelling the air, I decided it was the middle of the morning.

"I'm Sir Woddet of East Hall." He held out his hand.

I sat up and took it. "Sir Able."

"I'm not supposed to be here." He looked around and found a little stool. "All right if I sit?"

I said sure.

"No visitors by order of His Hungryhunks, but that's because he's afraid somebody will kill you." Woddet shoved out his lower lip and pulled his mustache, something I saw a lot of afterward. "Someone might, too. Not me, someone else."

About then I woke up enough to remember what Modguda had said. "You saved me."

"I tried to. So did some others."

"Your squire threw himself on top of me so they wouldn't hit me. That's what somebody said. I don't remember it."

"You were down by that time." Woddet pulled at his mustache some more. "That's the trouble with a fight like that. No gentle right. Not that they'd have accorded it to you, I'm afraid."

I did not know what he was talking about, but I said, "I guess not."

"I was fighting you, too. You got me right here." He pointed. "Knocked the wind out. By the time I could stand straight again, they were going for you with swords. I shouted stop, and that's when Yond threw himself on you."

I said, "I owe you. I owe my life."

"No, you don't." He shook his head. He was really big, and all that tow-colored hair made his head look about a size eleven. "Master Thope and Master Agr were trying to protect you, too. Some wretch put his blade into Thope's back for striving to preserve the honor of His Grace's household."

"Yeah, I heard about that. I'm going to pay him a visit today."

Woddet looked surprised. "Glad to hear you're up to it. I never wanted to kill you. Just thrash you, and I tried. You are a man of your hands, Sir Able."

"Only not of the lance."

Woddet grinned. "No."

"Not yet, but I will be. Why'd you want to thrash me?"

He looked at me, trying to size me up. "Are you of gentle blood?"

"Is that like noble? No."

He shook his head. "Noble blood means an inherited title, and lands. Knighthood's not inheritable. Gentle blood simply means your ancestors were never in trade or worked with their hands."

I explained that our grandparents had been farmers, and our dad had run a store. "I'd really like to tell you I'm some king's lost kid," I said, "but there wouldn't be a word of truth in it."

He had trouble looking at me. "Well, you see, Able, when someone is of gentle blood—"

"Sir Able," I told him.

"All right. But when someone is of gentle blood, as I am and the others, and someone else who isn't claims it, or claims to be a knight when he is not, for instance . . ."

"For instance what?"

"Well, we're supposed to beat him. Not kill him, thrash him. Or if he says someone who is of gentle blood hasn't got it, that's the same thing."

"Okay. There was somebody there that said I wasn't a real knight, and I said I was but he wasn't."

Woddet nodded. "We couldn't be certain you weren't a knight yourself, though none of us believed you. But when you said Sir Hermad wasn't, that loosed the string."

"I see. I really am a knight. If you don't believe me, we'll fight."

Woddet smiled. "With lances?"

"Here. Right now. You've got a sword. Are you too scared to use it?"

"Not I!" He drew his sword faster than he stood up, and he stood up fast. It was just a blur of steel and the point was pricking my throat. He said, "You declare yourself a knight, however. I can't kill an unarmed knight. Gentle right."

"I told you about my folks. I haven't got gentle blood."

"But I do." Woddet sheathed his sword almost as quickly as he had gotten it out. He was trying not to grin. "I'll have to ask His Grace's herald."

I said I would rather we were friends.

"I've given you my hand." He shrugged. "Still I wish you had ancestors, Sir Able. It would make everything much easier for both of us."

"I'm an ancestor," I told him.

I went to see Master Thope after that like I had said I would. I was nearly back to my room when I ran into Master Agr and a tall man with a white beard and a red velvet cloak. Master Agr was surprised to see me up and around, and said, "Here he is, Your Grace!"

I knew then that the other man was Marder, so I bowed. I would probably have guessed it from his clothes anyway. I had learned enough about clothes by then to know that they had cost a lot of money.

Marder smiled at me. "I'd heard you were bedridden, young man."

I said, "I was, Your Grace. I'm better today."

"Much better."

"Yes, Your Grace."

Agr said, "We came looking for you, and found an empty bed. I was afraid someone had killed you and made off with the body. Where have you been?"

I explained that I had gone to thank Master Thope. "I wanted to thank you, too, Master Agr, only your man said you were with His Grace. I—you did me a big favor. Anytime you want one from me, a boon or anything, just let me know. I'll probably never be able to pay you back, but I'll try."

Marder cleared his throat. "You know who I am, young man. I know only what Master Agr has told me concerning you, and I'd like to hear what you say about yourself. Who are you?"

"I'm Sir Able of the High Heart, Your Grace. A knight who will serve you gladly and loyally."

"Moneyless, too," Agr added under his breath.

"Not exactly, but I haven't got a whole lot."

Marder nodded. He looked serious. "You have no land? And very little money? What have you got?"

"These clothes and some others, if my servant hasn't run off with them. Some presents Lord Olof and Lord Thunrolf gave me." As soon as I said that about Pouk my conscience started hurting me, so I said, "I'm wronging my servant, Your Grace. He wouldn't do that, and I ought to learn to keep my mouth shut."

"Nothing else?"

"A shirt of rings, only it's torn, Your Grace. We left it at a place in Forcetti, to be fixed. A steel cap. Sword Breaker, my bow, and some arrows."

"I have his weapons locked away," Agr told Marder.

"Return them to him whenever he asks, Master Agr."

"I shall, Your Grace."

Marder had been studying me. "Should I accept you, you will have no easy time of it, Sir Able."

"I didn't come here looking for a bed, Your Grace."

"You will be sent against my foes. When you return, you will be sent against others. Do you understand me?"

I nodded. "I know what you mean, Your Grace. I was a friend of Sir Ravd's."

I saw Marder's eyes open just a little bit wider. "Were you with him at the end?"

"No, Your Grace. I was just a boy then, but I would have fought for him. I guess I would have died with him, too."

Marder started to say something else, then bit it back, and I noticed Agr was looking pretty uncomfortable. I said, "He died fighting for you, Your Grace."

Agr cleared his throat.

Marder said, "It has been four years—a long time, I realize, for a man your age. Yesterday you were struck down with the butt of a lance. So I hear."

"I got knocked in the head, Your Grace. That's all I know."

"Sir Ravd was my most trustworthy knight, Sir Able. I thought of him as a son."

I said that was no surprise to me.

"His squire reported that he himself had his head broken on the field. When he came to himself, he said, wolves were tearing the corpses. Now you say you were a friend of Sir Ravd's?"

"Yes, I was, Your Grace. I was Sir Ravd's guide in the forest." When I had said that, I thought that there probably were other forests, so I added, "Northeast of Irringsmouth."

"You were not with him when he died?"

"No, Your Grace. I was doing something else."

"In that case, you must have spoken with someone who informed you of his death. Who was that?"

"No one." All of a sudden I felt like something had me by the neck. "I found his sword, Your Grace. That's all. It was broken. We killed some bandits, Your Grace. My dog and I did, and a man named Toug. The broken sword was in with their loot. I saw it and picked it up . . ."

"I understand. There were only two of you? You and the man-at-arms that you mentioned?"

"Toug isn't a man-at-arms, Your Grace. Just a peasant."

"How many outlaws did you say there were?"

I had not said, and when he asked I was not sure I could remember. I told him that, and I said, "Ulfa counted them, Your Grace. Counted their bodies. She's Toug's daughter. I think she said twenty-three."

Agr snapped, "You expect His Grace to credit that?"

"I'm a knight," I said. "I wouldn't lie. Not to him."

"Pah!"

Marder motioned for him to shut up. "I hoped you might be able to tell me something about Sir Ravd's death."

"I've told you everything I know, Your Grace."

"About his squire's account, too," Marder said. "He is of an age to be knighted."

I said, "I think he's probably telling the truth, Your Grace, but I don't know."

"He is Sir Hermad's squire now. Sir Hermad, I believe, is disabled?" When he said that, Marder looked over at Agr.

Agr nodded, looking pretty gloomy.

"Well then, he can see to his master for a time. It will give him occupation. Since you guided Sir Ravd in the forests of the north, Sir Able, you must have guided Squire Svon likewise."

I said I had.

"You have no more than that to tell me?"

You can guess what I was tempted to tell then. Only I did not. "Nothing I haven't said already, Your Grace."

"You yourself were stunned in the lists. No one told me about the incident," Marder gave Agr a quick, hard glance, "until I noticed blackened eyes and missing teeth. Not to mention Sir Vidare's broken nose. I made inquiries."

Nothing I could think of seemed safe to say.

"You wish to serve me, Sir Able?"

"Yes, Your Grace." That one was easy.

"Without payment, though you have scarcely a scield."

"I've got some, Your Grace. It isn't like I don't have anything."

"You mentioned a manservant. How will you recompense him?"

"Yes, Your Grace, I did. His name is Pouk. He serves me without payment, Your Grace."

"I see. Though he may not. Is he blind? Crippled? Lame? A skin disorder, perhaps?"

"Blind in one eye, Your Grace."

Agr muttered, "And cannot see with the other, I'll wager."

"No, sir. Pouk has sharp eyes—a sharp eye, I mean. You and His Grace want to know why he serves me when I can't pay him, and I'd tell you if I knew. But I don't."

"In that case there can be small profit in discussing it. Has Master Agr explained my policy to you? My policy regarding taking knights into my service?"

"No, Your Grace."

"If the knight is of high repute, I admit him to my service at once. He must swear fealty to me. There is a ceremony."

"I'll gladly take that oath, Your Grace."

"No doubt. When a knight of less reputation offers his fealty, I either reject him outright or accept him informally and provisionally until he has had a chance to prove himself. I will accept you now on those terms, if you wish it."

I said, "I do, Your Grace. Thank you very much."

"Kneel!" Agr whispered. "One knee."

I dropped to one knee and bowed my head. It was sort of like being knighted. "You accept me just to try out, Your Grace, but I accept you as my lord . . . my lord—" What threw me off was either Uri or Baki. One of the two was watching us and laughing. Marder and Agr could not hear her, but I could. "My lord and master, even unto death." That was how I finished it, but it was pretty weak.

"That is well. You have small equipage, Sir Able."

I got up. "I'm afraid that's the truth, Your Grace."

"I intend to send you against my foes, so that you may prove yourself—as I feel sure you will—but for my own honor I cannot and will not send you unarmed."

"I have heard, Your Grace, that it used to be customary for knights to wait at a bridge and challenge any knight who wanted to get across. If I could do that, I could get armor, a lance, and a good horse. All I need."

Agr snorted. "Without horse, lance, or shield? You'd be killed."

I raised my shoulders and let them drop. "Just the same, I'd like to try it."

Marder said slowly, "I tried it in my youth, Sir Able. I suppose I was about your age. It is no tournament with blunted weapons. I could show you the scars."

"Well, I haven't, Your Grace. But I've got a scar to show anyway, and a bunch of bruises."

"I had them too, in my time."

I said, "I'm sure you did, Your Grace. That was your time, like you just said. Now it's my turn, and I'd like to try it."

For a second, Marder frowned at me. The frown faded and he roared with laughter. "From a raw stripling with a broken head!" He nudged Agr. "Want to send those shoulders against the Angrborn? He'd go, I swear!"

Agr nodded gloomily. "He would, Your Grace, if you'd give him a horse."

I said, "On foot, Your Grace, if you will not."

"Now hear my judgment." Marder had stopped laughing. This was dead serious. "For a fortnight you are to remain here at Sheerwall to mend. When that time is done, Master Agr will furnish you with whatever you may require. Go to some remote bridge, ford, or mountain pass as you have suggested, and take your stand. Remain at your post until winter—until there is ice in the harbor. When winter has set in, return to tell us how you fared."

Agr said, "Suppose that he loses his first combat, Your Grace. Everything I give him will be lost as well."

"Look at his smile, Agr."

Agr did, although he did not like it much.

"He will be risking his life. We can risk a few horses, some lances, and a hauberk."

Pouk came that afternoon, finding me in the Practice Yard watching mock fights with quarterstaffs. He had brought clean clothes. "Tried to fetch along everythin', sir, only landlord won't let me 'til he's paid. Couple o' nights, an' tuck."

"We'll see about that this afternoon," I told him. "It's just out the gate and down the hill."

"Bit farther nor that, sir."

"Not much. Before we go, though, I want to get in a bit of jousting practice. Watch, and tell me if it seems to you that I'm doing anything wrong."

He did; and that afternoon, as we were riding back to Forcetti on borrowed horses, he said, "That's what knights do, ain't it? The way you an' Sir What's-his-name was riding at each other."

"Sir Woddet." I nodded. "Yes, it is."

"Well, it looks grand, sir, but I don't see the sense of any of it."

I started to explain, but he interrupted at once. "Say I was on foot. When I seen you comin' with your long spear—"

"It's a lance," I told him.

"An' your big horse, I'd jump out o' th' way, wouldn't I? I don't like horses nohow." He looked down at his own with marked disfavor. "An' if I was on a good 'un myself, I'd ride around behind."

"I'm not yet skilled with the lance," I told him, "but a knight who is will put the point through a swinging ring no bigger than the palm of your hand while riding at full gallop. So if you jump, you'd better jump far."

Pouk looked dubious.

"As for circling around behind, a well-mounted knight would catch you in the side ten times out of ten. You'd have no chance to defend yourself before you were spitted on his lance. That is, if you and he were alone."

"I suppose."

"In battle, there would be a long line of knights riding at you, with another line in back of theirs, if it were King Arnthor's army. Light horse made up of squires and men-at-arms would guard their flanks, and there would be footmen and archers to guard the wagon-fort. I know all this, you see, because I asked Master Thope the same questions. Knights can be beaten, of course, particularly in the mountains where the enemy can get above them to throw spears and roll down logs. But it's never easy."

Pouk nodded slowly. "Aye, sir. I hope you never are, sir."

"So do I. But I know that there are no safe battles. I hope for honor from Duke Marder, Pouk. Honor and good horses and much more. A manor of my own. Although I can never come to Queen Disiri as an equal, I'd like to narrow the distance between us. Lord Olof told me that queens have wed knights more than once. It's not unheard-of."

Pouk shook his head. "I hope you don't get yourself killed, sir. That's all."

"Thank you," I said, and for a while we rode through the hot spring sunshine in silence. My conscience was bothering me, however, and eventually it made me speak. "Remember what I said about the footmen back at the wagon-fort, Pouk? If you stay with me, you'll be one of them. You'll have an ax, a coat of boiled leather, and a steel cap, I hope. More, if I can afford it."

"No worse 'n fightin' them Osterlin's at sea, sir."

We were topping a rise just then; shading my eyes with my hand I saw a farmhouse in the valley below, a prosperous-looking place I remembered passing on my way to Sheerwall. I said, "There's a farm with a good well down there, Pouk. We can water the horses, and get a drink ourselves."

CHAPTER 35

THERE WAS OGRES

Pouk's mind was still on the imaginary battle. "If I'm goin' to be back at th' wagons, how'm I s'pposed to look out for you? S'ppose you're th' 'un gets stuck on somebody's lance, sir? How'm I goin' to get to you an' find you in all that?"

"That will be my squire's task, if I have one."

"An' I still don't think it makes no sense for knights to come at each other the way you do, you an' Sir—Sir . . ."

"Woddet."

"Aye. You never did hurt th' other 'un a-tall, just you knocked him off his horse."

I corrected the record. "He knocked me off mine, Pouk. Three times."

"Only twice 'twas, sir. That other time—"

"Which makes three. There are half a dozen holes in your argument, Pouk, and I doubt that it's worth our while to plug them all."

"If you say so, sir."

"Besides, we'll be at the farm before I could do it. But I ought to tell you that I've never been in a real battle in which knights fought on horseback. What I've said about them, and what I'm about to say about knights fighting, I learned from Sir Ravd, Master Thope, and Sir Woddet. From Master Thope particularly. He's a regular goldmine of information, and I could listen for hours."

"Looks a pretty decent place, sir," Pouk said, regarding the farmhouse. Its mud-and-wattle walls were whitewashed, and its thatch looked new.

"They're doing better than a lot of people I've seen." I paused, recalling Master Thope's impassioned growl. "Your complaint is that Sir Woddet and I didn't actually hurt each other much, much less kill each other. He knocked me off my horse, and once I got lucky and knocked him off his."

"Aye!" The syllable bore a world of satisfaction.

"The first thing, the main thing you've got to get, is that Sir Woddet and I weren't trying to kill each other, or even trying to hurt each other. In a battle the knights are out to kill one another."

Pouk nodded reluctantly.

"We used practice lances made of wood not strong enough for real ones. You don't want a practice lance to be strong. Somebody might get hurt or killed. A real war lance is as strong as it can be made. It has a sharp steel head, too. Ours were blunt. By hitting me hard with a stout dagger, one of the Osterlings was able to stab through my mail, remember? His stab opened a couple of rings, and that was enough."

"Aye. We was a-feared you'd die, sir."

"I just about did, and maybe I would have eventually if it hadn't been for Garsecg. Now suppose instead of a dagger that mail was hit by a heavy war lance, with the weight of a knight and a galloping horse behind it."

Pouk scratched his head. "Go through it like it was cheese, sir."

"You've got it. What's more, Sir Woddet and I aimed at each other's shields. The shield's what's generally hit with a lance in a real battle."

"An' what good does that do? It's just like what I was sayin', sir."

"Pretty often, none. But the shields used in battle are a lot lighter than our practice shields, and the lance-point will go through sometimes. Even if it doesn't, the knight whose shield got hit may get knocked out of his saddle the same way I was. Remember what I said about a second line of knights behind the first? Now pretend you're a knight who's been knocked off his horse, pretty well stunned by the fall."

We had reached the house. Pouk said, "If it's all th' same to you, sir, I'd just as soon not." He dismounted, by that act alarming several ducks and a goose. "Maybe I ought to run in front, sir, an' tell 'em who you are."

A middle-aged farmwife had appeared in the doorway. I called, "We're harmless travelers looking for water for our horses and ourselves. Let us have that, and we won't ask for anything else."

She did not answer, and I added, "If you'd rather leave us thirsty, say so and we'll go."

Pouk trotted toward her, leading his horse. "This here's Sir Able, the bravest knight Duke Marder's got."

She nodded, and seemed to weigh me with her eyes. "You look brave enough. 'N strong."

"I'm thirsty, too. I've been jousting, and riding without a hat. May we have some water?"

She reached a decision. "We've cider, if you want it. It'll be healthier. Maybe a couple hard-boiled eggs 'n some bread 'n sausage?"

I had not known I was hungry, but when she said that I found out quick. I said, "We can pay you, ma'am, and we'll be glad to. We're going into Forcetti to pay an innkeeper what we owe him, and we can pay you as well."

"No charge. You come in."

She ushered us into her kitchen, a big sunny room with a stone floor and onions hanging in braided strings from the rafters. "Sit down. We get you knights up 'n down the road every day, almost, 'n that's good. The robbers don't bother us, only the tax man. But most knights don't stop here. Or speak, neither, when we wish them good morrow."

"They're not as thirsty as we are, maybe."

"I'll fetch the cider right away. Keg's in the root cellar." She bustled out.

"Hard cider, it might be." Pouk licked his lips.

I agreed, but I was thinking about the woman, and what she might want from us.

She came back with three basswood jacks, which she set on the table. "Fresh bread. Nearly fresh, anyhow. I baked yesterday." She took a sausage from the pocket of her apron and laid it on a trencher, where it fell in thick slabs under the assault of a long knife. "Summer sausage. We smoke it three days, 'n after that it keeps if it don't get wet."

I thanked her and ate some sausage, which was very good.

"Sir Able? That's you? You seem like a down-to-earth person, for a knight."

I interrupted my cider drinking to say I tried to be.

"You really the bravest knight the duke's got?"

"Aye!" Pouk exclaimed.

"I doubt it," I said, "but I don't really know. To tell you the truth, I don't believe there's a knight in Sheerwall Castle that would hesitate to cross swords with me. But I wouldn't hesitate to cross swords with them, either."

"Scared of ghosts?"

I shrugged. "There's no man I'm afraid of, and it doesn't seem likely that a dead man would be worse than a live one."

"Not a man." She glanced at Pouk, who had drained his mug and was looking unwontedly sober. "Little more of that?"

He shook his head.

"If it's a woman's ghost," I said, "she may be after some property or something she thinks is coming to her. I talked to an old lady down south who knew a lot about ghosts, and she told me that women's ghosts generally mean the woman was murdered. More often than not, justice is all they want."

"Not a woman." The farmwife got up to fetch a loaf of bread.

"A child's ghost? That's sad."

"I wish 'twas." She sawed her bread with exaggerated care, I thought to keep her feelings under control.

"Are you talking about the Aelf? They're not ghosts."

"Guess you know how you knights got started?"

I admitted I did not, that I had never even wondered about it, and added that I would like to hear the story.

"No story. There was ogres all around here in the old time. Dragons, too. Monsters. These here giants that's in the ice country now. Lots of them. A man that killed one, he was a knight, only after a while they was all killed off, so it had to be other things."

"You still haven't told me what the ghost is."

"A ogre. Must have been one killed right here, 'cause it's been haunting my farm."

Pouk looked around as if he expected to see it.

"You don't have to worry," the farmwife told him. "He don't come but at night."

I said, "In that case we can't help you. We've got to go to Forcetti." I took another piece of her summer sausage, thinking she might pull it out of reach soon. "We can't stay in Forcetti tonight, though. Or here, either. I promised Master Agr he'd get his horses back tonight."

Her face fell.

"It will be late, I suppose, when we pass your house again. Dark, or just about. We could stop in for a moment, just to make sure everything was okay."

"Me 'n my sons would be pleased as pigeons, Sir Able. We'd give you a bite to eat then, 'n your horses, too."

I snapped my fingers. "That's right, the horses haven't been watered. See to them, please, Pouk."

"Not good to give 'em too much, sir."

"That's when they're warm from galloping. They can't be hot now, they've been standing in the shade whisking flies while we ate. Give them all they want."

"Aye aye, sir." He hurried out.

The farmwife said, "Me 'n my sons work this farm, Sir Able. They're strong boys, both of them, but they won't face the ghost. Duns did, 'n it almost killed him. He was bad for more'n a year."

I said I would not have thought just being scared could do that.

"Broke his arms, 'n just about tore one off."

As soon as I heard that, I wanted to talk to the son, but he was out seeing to something or other; it stuck in my mind, though.

CHAPTER 36
THE DOLLOP AND SCALLOP

In the tap of the Dollop and Scallop (it was a big, plain, dirty room where you smelled the spilled ale), the innkeeper gave me his bill with a flourish.

"I can't read," I told him, "or not the way you write here. I wish I could—I'd like to learn, but you'll have to explain this to me." I spread the bill on the top of a table. "Now sit down and tell me about this. I see the marks on the paper, but I don't know what they mean."

He scowled. "Want to make a fool of me, don't you?"

"Not a bit. I can't read and neither can Pouk, but I'd like to know what I'm being billed for."

He stood beside me and pointed. "This right here's the only part that matters. Five scields up and down."

"For three days? It seems like an awful lot."

"Three days' rent of the best room I got. That's right here." He pointed. "And food here, and drink."

Pouk would not meet my eyes.

"And food for your dog. That's here."

I caught his arm. "Say that again. Tell me about it."

"Food for your dog." The innkeeper looked uneasy. "A big brown dog with a spike collar. Shark's teeth, the spikes was. We give him bones from the kitchen, couple old loaves with drippin's on 'em, and meat scraps and so forth, and I don't charge you for none of that. Only he stole a roast, too, and that cost."

"I didn't have a dog when I checked in." I tightened my grip because I had the feeling he was going to bolt if he got the chance. "But I used to have a dog. Pouk knows him. You showed him to Pouk, didn't you? And asked Pouk if he knew who he belonged to?"

Pouk shook his head violently. "He never showed me no dog, sir, I swear. Nor never talked about none neither."

"I was going to punish you," I told him, "for drinking at my expense when you knew I didn't have much money. But if you're lying about Gylf, I'm not going to punish you at all. If you've lied about Gylf, you and I are finished right now, and you had better keep out of my way from here on."

Pouk drew himself up. "I never seen no dog in this here inn, nor heard tell o' 'un, sir. Not from him, an' not from nobody here at all—not your dog Gylf what jumped over th' railin' that time we both remember, an' not no other dog neither."

The innkeeper was trying to pull away. I said, "Why didn't you show the dog to Pouk?"

"I tried to, but he was asleep."

"Last night, full of your ale. Did he tell you I had agreed to let him drink as much as he wanted?"

The innkeeper said nothing.

"You said the dog stole a roast. Why didn't you show him to Pouk after that? Wasn't Pouk here until Modguda came to get him?"

"She sent a boy on a horse, sir," Pouk explained. "Him and me rode back together, me sittin' behind o' him, like."

I said, "It's clear that Pouk was awake this morning, since Modguda's boy found him and spoke to him."

"We couldn't catch that dog, Sir Able. He's a bad one."

"So are you." I thought about the bill and the few gold ceptres that remained to me. I could pay; but when I had, that much more would be gone forever. "I won't pay for the roast. You wouldn't have fed this dog that other stuff after he had stolen a whole roast, so you knew he was here, and you did nothing to keep him from taking a big piece of meat that must have been left lying around in the kitchen. You were careless, and the roast is the price you've got to pay for it."

"All right," the innkeeper said. "Let go of my arm and I'll take it off."

"How much did you charge me for it?"

"Three cups. I'll take it off. I said I would. Let me go."

I shook my head, and stood up. "Not yet. I'm going to make you an offer. I'll pay the three cups," with my free hand, I fished big brass coins out of the burse at my belt, "if you'll show me the dog, right now, and it's mine. I'll let you go, too. Will you do it?"

"I can't. It run off."

I swept up my coins again. "In that case I'm not going to pay you anything for the dog's food. You let it run away instead of informing my servant. Neither will I pay a single copper for what he drank. Strike those off, and we'll talk about the rest. If you haven't cheated me on that, I'll pay it all."

"It's five scields," the innkeeper insisted. "Five, less the three cups for the dog's food. That much—or I call the watch."

I picked him up, turned him over, and dropped him. "I'm living at Sheerwall Castle now. You can go to Duke Marder for justice, and I'm sure you'll get it if you do. Only first, it might be smart for you to think about whether you really want it. Sometimes people don't."

We left him lying on the floor and went up to the room that had been ours, washed and shaved there, and packed up everything we had brought off the *Western Trader.*

When we went downstairs again, there was a knight in a green surcoat lying in wait in the taproom. He cut at my head; when I ducked, his blade bit into the doorframe. I rushed him before he could get it out, knocking him off his feet. With the point of his own dagger sticking him under the chin he begged for mercy.

I said all right, and got up and dusted myself off. "I'm Sir Able of the High Heart, and I claim your armor and your shield, your weapons except for your sword, your horse or horses if there's more than one, and your burse. You can keep your clothes, your life, and your sword. I'm not going to ask any ransom for you. Give me those things, and you can go."

"Sir Nytir of Fairhall am I." He got up and bowed. "Your offer is generous. I accept it."

Pouk said, "Pah," and I gave him a look that meant *shut up.*

Nytir unbuckled his shield and leaned it against the bar, took off his steel cap, and pulled off his mantle of mail, his surcoat, and his hauberk, piling everything on the nearest table. "My helm is on my saddlebow," he said. "May I keep the surcoat? It bears my arms."

I nodded.

"Thank you." He untied his burse and handed it to me. "Five scields and a few coppers. You said I might retain my sword. Does that extend to the scabbard and sword belt?"

I nodded again.

"The innkeeper called you a brigand. I shall have words with him, by-and-by."

"So will I," I said, and I told Pouk to have a look at the horse for me, adding that he should report on all of them if there was more than one.

"There are three," Nytir said. A smart pull freed his sword. "You might tell my squire to come while you're about it, fellow."

Pouk hurried out.

I made the mistake of looking at Pouk as he left, and Nytir's thrust almost spitted me. I jumped, half falling, and the point twitched the front of my tunic. The overhand cut that followed it would have killed me, I believe, if the point had not raked the low ceiling. As it was, I got Sword Breaker out and thrust with her, driving the flat end of her blade into Nytir's face. He was sitting on the floor trying to stop the bleeding by the time his squire came in. The squire hurried over and tried to help him, but Nytir would not take his hands away to let the squire examine his wound. Neither would he speak.

"Your horses are mine," I told the squire. "Pouk, is there a charger among them?"

"There's a good 'un what he rode," Pouk said. "Don't know if I'd call it a charger, but it's a good 'un. Then there's his," Pouk gestured toward the squire, "an' a pack horse, like."

"Whatever goods are on that pack horse are mine too," I told the squire. "I'm keeping that horse, and the one your master rode. Is the one you rode your own? Or does it belong to him?"

"It's Sir Nytir's, Sir . . . ?"

"Able."

"Sir Able. I—I . . . You have no armor."

"I do now. I'm giving you the horse you rode. Pay attention. It was Sir Nytir's. I took it from him when I beat him, and I just gave it to you. Now that you own it, I want you to put him on it and lead it someplace where they've got a doctor."

The squire nodded. "He has a house here, Sir Able. I . . . You are a true knight. I hope to be a true knight myself, soon."

I wished him luck.

"I must tell you that I was one of those who pummeled you in the practice field. You needn't give me Stamper, and you should not."

Nytir said something, indistinctly.

"I won't take Stamper back," I told the squire. "He's yours. Get your master up on him, and get him out of here."

Pouk and I went outside and watched them go. When they had vanished around the first bend in that crooked street, Pouk asked if I wanted him to look into the pack horse's load. I shook my head and told him to find the innkeeper.

"Here, sir? He'll be outward bound under all sail."

"Look for him anyway. There must be help of some kind here, a cook and so on. Look for them, too. I'll be in the tap trying on Sir Nytir's mail."

Nytir's sword was in there, too. I did not want it, but I was glad to have a chance to look it over. It was a little bit bigger than Ravd's, and a bit heavier too, although I did not think it was quite as good. Wanting to see what it would do, I drove it into the top of the bar. It went through five or six inches of wood and stuck, so I left it there.

I had Nytir's hauberk on and was fastening the lacings (that can be tough when you are wearing the hauberk) when Pouk came back with a stout red-faced woman. "This's the innkeeper's wife," he announced, "and this here's my master, Sir Able o' th' High Heart."

She bent her knee, and I explained that I had rented a room for three nights.

"Upstairs, front," Pouk added.

"I know this one." The innkeeper's wife jerked a thumb at Pouk. "Only I didn't never see you up to now, Sir Able. He tolt me his master was a knight, only I never more'n half swallowed it. He's a sailor, sir, and there ain't much truth in 'em."

"Sailors see things other people won't believe." I shrugged. "Would you believe him if he were to tell you of the Isle of Glas?"

"No, sir!"

"I don't blame you. But I've seen it too, and even walked through its glades. Seamen lie just as we do, of course, and for the same reasons. But I'm telling you the truth when I say that."

"Far be it from me to give *you* the lie, Sir Able."

"Thanks. Don't lie now, and we can be good friends. Do you know where your husband is? I'd like to talk to him."

"I haven't no notion, Sir Able. He's gone out, seems like."

"Yeah, it does. Before he left, he told me about a dog that came here. He said it was a big brown dog with a spike collar."

She nodded. "And a bit of chain hanging off it, where it had broke."

"I see. Your husband thought it might be mine, and I've been hoping he was right. I lost my dog a while ago. Do you know where it is?"

"No, sir. I seen it yesterday, only I don't know where it's got to. We was all chasing it and trying to get the roast it took back, and it run off. Real big, it was, drop ears and thick in the chest."

"That sounds like Gylf. If he comes back, be nice to him and send word to me. I'll be at Sheerwall Castle."

"I'll try, sir." The innkeeper's wife's attention had strayed to Nytir's sword.

I told her who it belonged to; and I said that she and her husband were to leave it where it was until he came back to get it, at which she bent her knee again.

"I know it will be in the way—" I began.

She shook her head. "They'll come in to see it, Sir Able, and have one or two while they gawk and we tell about it. It'll be money in our pocket."

"I hope so. But when Sir Nytir comes back, you'll have to let him take it. Tell him that I didn't want it and left it there for him."

"Is he a friend of yours, Sir Able?"

Pouk laughed.

"He had it in for me," I told her. "He must've followed me here, and he seems to have scared your husband away before we had it out. Did you notice what we did to the doorframe?"

Reluctantly, she nodded.

My bill was where I had left it. I got it and showed it to her. "Your husband and I were talking this over. He made it five scields. I didn't think that was fair."

She examined it. "He goes too far, sometimes, Sir Able, Gorn do."

"No doubt we all do. Can you write?"

She nodded.

"Then I'll pay you four scields in good silver if you'll write 'paid in full' across this and sign your name. You'd better date it, too."

She hurried away to fetch ink, sand, and a quill.

CHAPTER 37

A GREEN KNIGHT

I'd been riding a lot that day; I was sore, but I got my left foot in the stirrup and swung myself into the saddle almost as if I knew what I was doing. The horse Nytir had ridden was a cobby bay stallion with a big white blaze, nervous and energetic, but not big enough or strong enough for a charger. A green lance (with pennant flying) still towered above the beautiful green-leather fighting saddle.

The bay skittered sidewise, iron-shod hooves clattering on the cobbles.

"Glad you got to ride him an' not me," Pouk said, as he finished tying Nytir's shield onto the pack horse's pack.

"Be careful with that," I told him. "It's the only piece that fits."

"Got his mark on it though, sir." Pouk was tightening the last knot.

"His arms, you mean." I held the bay hard.

"Aye, sir. A sheep with big horns, sir, only they wasn't big enough."

"We'll have it painted over. Three streets up the hill, and four west."

Pouk nodded, looking dubiously at his own mount. "Sign o' th' Hammer an' Tongs, sir."

"Can you lead two horses, Pouk?"

"If they'll tow, I can, sir. Some will an' some won't, an' you never know 'til you try."

The armorer with whom we had left my mail shirt was larger, younger, and slower of speech than Master Mori. He held up my new hauberk, whistled to himself, and carried it to a window where the light was better.

I said, "I got it from Sir Nytir, if that's of any help."

"Double mail. Not our work, but 'tain't bad."

"If you can let out the shoulders and the arms—"

" 'Deed I can, Sir Able. But it'll cost."

"Those mail trousers. I don't even know what you call them. I'll give them to you if you'll let out the hauberk for me."

He gave me his hand. "I got to take your measures, Sir Able. I'll give you a final fittin' when you come get it, 'n have it done that day if you come in the mornin'."

Pouk said, "Ask him 'bout this shield, sir. You say you like it."

"I do." I took it from him and held it up. "Can you paint out the ram without making it look bad?"

"'Deed we can." The armorer accepted and examined it. "Leather over willow. Pro'ly double willow." He looked up at me. "Grain up-'n-down 'n crosswise so's not ter split. Only I'd have to get the leather off ter see for sure. He was a nice workman, though, 'n wouldn't 'a used single. I won't look 'less you want it, just repaint the face. What you want 'stead a' the ram?"

When I did not reply, Pouk said, "What about a heart, sir? A heart wit' th' sun under. That oughta do it."

I shook my head.

"Charges up or down," the armorer said, "dependin' on the design. Harder my artist's got ter work, the more I got ter charge. There was one wanted three hearts 'n three lions, all on the one shield. We done it, but it cost the world."

I said that I would never use a lion.

"Well, what would you? That's the question."

I thought about stars and stripes, and I remembered that all the teams at school had been Bobcats, but nothing seemed right.

Pouk had wandered over to the wall and taken down a long knife. Its blade was black, and Pouk examined it curiously.

"Aelf work," the armorer told him. "Only one like that I got. You ever see anythin' like this, Sir Able?"

"No, but I'd like to."

Pouk passed me the knife.

"They like them leaf-shaped blades. Drive me crazy."

"Looks all right to me," Pouk said.

I was turning the black blade this way and that to get as much light as I could on it. "There are swirls in the steel, like the currents in a creek."

The armorer nodded. "Mixed metals. We try ter mix metals 'n they run together like you'd mix water 'n vinegar. Aelf got some way ter mix 'em like oil 'n water. They mix, only they stay separate. See what I mean?"

"I do," I said. "I'm looking at it." I was not sure I ought to say more, but I did. "You believe in the Aelf. A lot of people don't."

The armorer shrugged. "I know what I know."

Pouk began, "My master—"

I shut him up with my hand. "His master does too. You must know a bit about swords. Have you heard of one called Eterne?"

"Famous. Poetry about it."

"Do you know where it is now?"

The armorer shook his head. "Fire Aelf work, like that knife. King a' 'em made it, 'n he put magic in it. Can't break, can't bend. Need a dragon's claw ter sharpen it, only it don't never have ter be sharpened. Famous men's owned it, kings 'n knights 'n like that, 'n come back if you draw it. Only I don't know who's got it. It's somewheres in the Aelf world, pro'ly."

Pouk said, "That's called Aelfrice, ain't it, sir?"

The armorer nodded again. "I know. Only I didn't think you would. This here's Mythgarthr. Know that?"

Pouk shook his head.

"Figured you didn't."

I ventured, "You said Eterne had been made by the King of the Fire Aelf. I was told that a man like us made it, a man called Weland."

"That's his name all right," the armorer said, "only he was King a' the Fire Aelf like I told you. King Weland. Dragon got him, but people still talk about him."

"That is true," a soft voice behind me whispered. "We speak of him and mourn him, even now."

I nodded to show that I had heard. Out loud I said, "The shield I brought you. Will you paint it green?"

"Green now, sir. What do you want on it?"

"Plain green," I told him. "I want nothing on it. Paint out the ram so that you can't see it at all."

It felt cooler when we left the armorer's shop; and at first I thought the change—a great improvement—was due merely to our getting away from the heat of the forges. As Pouk and I rode out of the city, however, a west wind sent the bay's long mane flapping around his eyes and made my cloak billow about me like a sail until I closed it and tied the cords. That wind was chilly, and no mistake; it came pretty close to cold.

"Skai help them what's at sea," Pouk muttered.

He was looking behind us, and I turned to look too. Black clouds reached for the sun back there. While I watched, one was shot with lightning.

I clapped my heels to the bay. There is one thing you cannot ever take from a knight you beat even if you kill him. That is a pair of gold spurs. I had wanted Nytir's, and bad; and yet I had never said a word about them, because of the law. I wanted them because they are the sign of knighthood, but as we rode out of Forcetti I wanted them because they were spurs. "We've got to shake a leg," I yelled to Pouk, "or we'll get soaked."

He slapped his mount's withers with the ends of the reins, kicked it, and swore until it broke into a pounding trot that nearly shook him out of the saddle. "I need to cut me a stick, sir, an' I'll stop off an' do it first likely bush I see. I'll catch up after, never fear. You feel like talkin'?"

I reined in the bay for Pouk's sake. "Not particularly, but I don't feel like not talking either. What do you want to talk about?"

"You was in a brown study, sir, if I can say it, so I didn't want to fash you. Only I wanted to say, sir, there ain't much point to ridin' fast. That blow back there'll hit long 'fore we get to th' castle. Only it won't be so nice to ride in as what this is, sir, so there's sense in hurryin' after all. Only they'll be waitin' dinner on us, sir. We told 'em we was comin'."

I snapped my fingers. "That farm. That's right! I wanted to talk to Duns."

"Naturally you'd forget, sir, thinkin' hard like you was. Another thin', sir. Time we eat it'll be pourin' fit to founder us an' a wind to knock you down. You really think Master Agr'd mind if we stopped overnight, like, and kept his horses out a' th' blow?"

"Probably not. He'd overlook it, I'm sure, even if he didn't okay it."

"That's my feelin' too, sir. It's landsmen, sir, what think you ought to sail in all weathers. From what I seen a' them at the castle, they're not landsmen when it comes to horses, if you take my meanin'."

Pouk cleared his throat. "There's one other thin' I been itchin' to ask, sir, an' no offense meant, but why'd you tell that smith to do a plain green shield? Don't say nothin', sir, if you don't feel like it."

"It's no big secret, but once I thought of it I could see it was the thing to do. Look here." I took the helm from my saddlebow and held it up. "I should tell you I took the little wooden ram off the top and threw it away. That was yellow, but what color is this?"

"Green, sir."

"Right. It would cost to have it repainted, cost money we can't afford to spend. The steel cap you packed for me is enameled, too. Maybe you noticed."

"Aye, sir. Only I'd not thought about it."

"A design on my shield would cost quite a bit, even a simple one like the heart and sun you suggested. Or the mossy tree I was thinking about myself. So plain green—my lady is Queen of the Moss Aelf."

CHAPTER 38

THE WIND IN THE CHIMNEY

It was raining hard by the time we reached the farm. One of the sons opened the barn for us, and we rode in and tethered our horses in a crowded herd. I told Pouk he had to unload the sumpter so it could rest while we ate.

"Ya won't get no fancy meal," the son warned me. "We's plain folk here."

"So am I, and so is Pouk." I offered my hand. "I'm Sir Able."

The son wiped his hand on his soaking trouser leg. "Duns' my name, sar. 'Tis wet 'n I begs your pardon fer it."

"So is mine," I told him. We shook hands, after which he shook hands with Pouk.

Uns joined us after that. At first I thought him only a shorter version of Duns; later on, when I got a look at him in a better light, I saw there was something the matter with his back.

I asked our hostess's name, and Duns said, "Mother's Nukara, sar, on'y she's cookin' 'n can't come out ta talk 'til it's ready, 'n when 'tis we'll eat."

"I understand. If this rain keeps up, we may be begging you for beds as well as a meal, if you've got any to spare."

"Won't last ta moomrise," Uns muttered. "Wind's gonna die, rain keep a-goin' awhile." He was an excellent weather prophet, as I was to learn.

Duns nodded. "We got da 'un bed 'n that's aw, sar, on'y I kin give ya mine."

"I'll sleep on deck, sir," Pouk put in hastily. "You know I'm one what's done it many's a time."

Seeing through him, I grinned. "At my door, to keep the ghost from killing me in my sleep."

"Aye, sir. Try, sir."

"Tomorrow we'll have to ride back to Sheerwall, storm or no storm," I told him. "I'm landsman enough for that. But we may stay here tonight, if our hostess is willing. If we stay, we must remember to unsaddle these horses and see that they're fed. What do you think, Duns? Will Pouk and I catch sight of your ghost if we stay the night?"

"He's no joke, sar."

"Not to you, I'm sure. Maybe he shouldn't be one to me either. When we were here before, your mother told me he crippled you for a year."

Duns nodded, his homely, sunburned face grim.

"Suppose I wanted a look at him. What should I do?"

Duns glanced at Pouk, saw he had finished unloading the sumpter, and motioned for us to follow him. "Get inna house first, sar, 'n we kin dry off."

With Uns lagging behind, we followed Duns through the pelting rain to the front of the house, splattering ankle-deep mud at every step and ushered in by a roll of thunder loud enough to shake the walls. "Cap'n's whistlin'," Pouk said when we were inside and he could make himself heard.

I smiled and reminded him that most people would say that the Valfather was angry.

"Not at us he ain't," Duns declared. "We need this."

Uns caught my sleeve. "If ya was ta sleep inna kitchen, mebbe." He was answering the question I had asked out in the barn, but it took me a second to realize that.

Duns ran his fingers through his hair and shook water from them. "He's a knight, ya coof! Knights don't sleep inna kitchen. I'll fetcha towel, sar. That way ya kin dry ya face, anyways."

Pouk edged close enough to whisper, "Be a big fire in th' kitchen, sir."

Shivering, and wet to the skin, I told Uns we wanted to say hello to our hostess, and promised we would not keep her from her cooking. He led us into the big, cheerful, tiled room, where we greeted her and warmed ourselves at the fire that was roasting our dinner.

As we ate it, Duns said, "Ya wanted ta know how ya could see it, sar, if ya was ta stay."

I nodded, and added that I would gladly sleep in the kitchen if it would get me a glimpse of the ghost.

Nukara shook her head.

"All I kin tell ya's what I done. I guess ma tolt what happent ta me."

I nodded again. "It seemed like it a very solid ghost."

Duns nodded ruefully, and his mother eagerly. Uns only stared down at his plate.

"What I done was sit up da 'un night, sit up quiet 'til I heard somethin'. Then I creept up quiet as I could. I kin show where I first seen it."

"Maybe later."

"'Twas hot 'n da winders open, 'n it jumpt out 'un, 'n I caught up inna sout' pasture. I'se a strong man."

I said, "I know you are. I remember your grip."

"I'se stronger den. On'y it's stronger dan me. Lot stronger." He was clearly shamed.

Nukara looked at me anxiously. "You're not goin' to

wrestle it are you, Sir Able? The way Duns done? I thought you'd—I don't know what."

"I don't—" I fell silent as the eerie howl of the wind filled the room, a ghost not nearly as substantial as the one I hoped to hunt down.

"Storm's gettin' worse," Duns muttered.

"Yes." I stood up.

Nukara looked surprised. "That was just the wind in the chimney, Sir Able."

I agreed, but I had recalled what Disiri had told me when we parted, and knew I had to go. Pouk rose too, but I made him sit back down and finish his food.

After that, I turned and went out, afraid that I would say or do something that would give my secret away. There was a covered porch at the back of the house, and I suppose I stood there for half a minute looking at the rain. That may have been why I missed her.

I do not know how long it took me to cross the fields and meadows and reach the woods on the other side. It was slow going and hard going, but I kept at it, head down, with the hood of my cloak pulled up as far as I could get it to give my face some protection. I started calling for her when I got close, and I was dumb enough to be happy that the wind had dropped and it seemed like she might hear me. The rain had slacked off by that time too, not stopped but not pouring the way it had been.

"If you simply want a woman," said a soft voice at my ear, "I know one who would be honored."

I jumped. It was a red Aelfmaiden taller than I am but as slender as a glowing poker.

"I am back, Lord," she said, "and I am Baki. Possibly you have forgotten me."

"To tell the truth, I've been wondering where you were," I said. "You got Sword Breaker for me, and my bow, and put them under my bed."

"After which you told me to go away and let you alone."

I really did not want to talk to her, although I felt I had to. I said, "You wanted to get under the covers with me again. You and the other one."

She tittered.

"Has anybody told you you sound like a bat?"

"Only bats, Lord."

"That was you, wasn't it, in the armorer's shop? I could hear you but I couldn't see you."

"Not I, Lord." She smiled. She had big white teeth, and they looked sharp. "It must have been Uri. Or your precious Queen Disiri, perhaps."

I sighed. "I ought to punish you for lying."

"I? Whose blood glutted you? You have not the heart, Lord."

"You're right, I don't." I started calling for Disiri again, though I felt pretty sure I was not going to find her.

"I need not look like this, you know." Smoke came out of her eyes. She shrank and faded, getting wider, white and gold. In about a minute, maybe less, there was a naked, shy-looking girl with golden hair and a big stick-out chest where Baki had been standing. Her eyes sucked up the smoke. "Do you like me better now, Lord?" Her head came as high as my chin.

I had thought only Disiri could do that, but I said, "I'm not exactly crazy about you either way."

"Your guilty slave grovels." The blonde bowed her head. "She would do anything to please you, Lord, and if you have no notions of your own, she can offer any number of exciting suggestions."

"Aren't you cold?"

"I am, Lord, and so are you. We can heat ourselves pleasantly by following one of my most exciting suggestions. First I will kneel—so! You—"

As quickly as I could, I said, "Have you been following me all day?"

The blonde shook her head, keeping her eyes down as she had the whole time. "Up here, Lord? Of course not. But I have watched you from Aelfrice. Will not you go there with me? It is not raining there."

Something too deep-voiced for a wolf howled in the distance. I stopped to listen before I said, "I spent quite a bit of time in Aelfrice with Garsecg. I don't remember seeing anybody I knew in this world then."

"Because you did not know how to look, Lord. Put your head right down here."

I shook it instead.

"You will not? Seriously, if you come to Aelfrice with me I will teach you to view Mythgarthr. It is not difficult. You can learn in a day or two."

"And afterwards I'll come back and find out I've been gone three years."

"Not that long. Or I think not, Lord. It is unlikely. Lord, if you will not sport with me, may I change?"

I did not answer because she had begun to change while she talked, looking up at me for the first time so that I saw the blonde had Aelf-eyes of yellow fire. Smoke poured from them, wrapping her in a robe of twilight and snow. When it returned to her, she was Baki again.

I said, "Are you really my slave?"

Still kneeling, she bowed to the rain-soaked fern. "I stand ready to serve my lord night and day, though night is preferable. He need only ask."

"Who's your lord?"

The white teeth flashed in that face of glowing copper. "You are. Who should be my lord but that most noble knight, Sir Able of the High Heart?"

"A knight," I said, "but not noble."

"I think otherwise, Lord."

"The armorer seemed to know about you Fire Aelf, and he said you were iron workers. Is that true?"

"Metal workers, Lord. Iron and other metals. Would you like to see a sample of my own work? What of a silver chain with but one end? Whenever you needed money, you could cut off a piece and sell it."

I shook my head. "Why did Setr choose metal workers?"

"You must ask him, Lord."

"I will, next time I see him. Why did your people persecute Bold Berthold?"

"Persecute is a terrible word, Lord. We may have teased him. Was he worse for our attention?"

"The years, the Angrborn, and you all hurt him. Why did you do it?"

A gust of rain hit us; the howl I had heard before came with it, deep but as lonely as the cry of a wounded bird.

Baki wiped cold water from the burning oval of her face. "Do you still care about this Berthold, Lord? Whom I have never set eyes upon, by the way. Or may we talk of something interesting?"

"I'll always care for him."

"Very well. It was not I. I was a Khimaira for Setr for a long, long time. It must have been centuries here. If Aelf teased him, I apologize on their behalf."

I was tired, and I knew by then that I would not find Disiri; but I was stubborn too. "I wish I knew why they did it."

"Which you will not learn from me, Lord, for I cannot know it. I might speculate, if you wish me to." Baki looked sulky.

"Go ahead," I told her.

"We like to tease you upper people. You think you are vastly superior and we do not matter at all. So we tease you, and if you prefer to say torment, go ahead. Usually we do no harm, and sometimes we help, especially when we think our help is going to surprise somebody we have been teasing. We Fire Aelf like to help smiths and such mostly, people like your armorer. We like them because they do the same kind of work we do in Aelfrice."

"Are you saying Disiri enjoys tormenting others? I won't believe it."

Baki stared at the ferns around her feet.

"Well, does she? Let's hear it!"

"Not she, perhaps, Lord. But the rest of us do. Mostly we choose people who are alone, because it bothers you more. You are not sure it is really happening. Was this Berthold all alone?"

"Yes." I nodded. "In a hut in the forest."

"Well naturally then. That's exactly the kind we like to play with."

"I have met Fire Aelf, Water Aelf, and brown Bodachan." I sighed, remembering Disiri. "Also the Moss Aelf, who have been very kind to me."

Baki stood, and suddenly she was so near that our cheeks touched. "I would be very kind to you too, if you would let me." Her long warm fingers toyed with the cord of my cloak.

I smiled—bitterly, I'm afraid. "Now it's my turn, isn't it? I'm alone among trees, just like Bold Berthold."

"You think I am going to pinch you and run? Try me, Lord. That is all I ask."

I shook my head.

"There is a great deal we can do without lying down on

this wet ground, you know. But look at how soft this fern is. It is wet, but we are wet already. Let us make our own fire."

I pointed. "I want you to go to the farmhouse I came from. Watch there. Watch all of them, but watch the younger brother most closely. Don't let anybody see you, and be ready to tell me everything they did when I come back."

"As you wish, Lord."

I waited until she vanished among the shadows of the trees, wondering whether she would do what I had told her, and whether I would ever see her again. Once she was out of sight, I called Gylf.

CHAPTER 39

MAGIC IN THE AIR

It was Gylf who found me, not me who found Gylf. When I had *gone* so far into the woods that I had begun to think I might get lost, I heard him trotting behind me. I stopped and sat on a log (it was no wetter than I was) and motioned to him in a way I hoped was friendly. He was bigger than I remembered, but you could count his ribs.

"You mind?" He came a step at a time, not too sure of me.

I said, "If I didn't want you I wouldn't have called you, would I?" and I smiled; and he came up to me then and let me scratch his ears.

After a while I said, "I know I tried to leave you behind before I got on that boat. I'm sorry I did that. Maybe I've apologized already, and if I have I apologize again. You must have thought I was doing the same thing when I didn't come back to look for you, but I didn't know you were waiting in Aelfrice. I thought you had probably gone back to the boat. I went there, and after I did I couldn't get back to Garsecg. Did he tell you what happened?"

Gylf shook his head.

"Maybe he didn't know." I thought about that. Garsecg was as smart as anybody I had ever met, and he knew a lot; but when somebody's like that you can overestimate them and maybe you convince yourself they know everything. Not even the Valfather knows everything.

I said, "I used to think he had arranged for me to meet Kulili, and for you and me to get split up the way we did. I can't be sure, but now I think that's probably wrong."

"Think so."

"Do you?" I thought about that for a minute or two. It seemed like Gylf had been waiting down where the Kelpies were for quite a while after Garsecg and I got separated, and if Garsecg had come back there Gylf might have heard something. Finally I started telling about the ogre, just because it was on my mind a lot and I wanted to talk it over.

I told Gylf how it had hurt Duns and scared Nukara. "I don't believe it's really a ghost at all," I said. "Why would a ghost run from Duns? It could disappear. Baki can disappear pretty well, and she's not even a ghost. People may think that all the ogres are dead, but there are still giants in the north, lots of them. I think this is a real ogre, still alive, and safe because everyone thinks the last ogre died a long, long time ago."

It took a while before Gylf nodded, but he did.

"I didn't come out here to look for it, I came to look for Disiri. But maybe I should have. It must live in these woods."

Gylf shook his head.

"It doesn't? How do you know?"

"Smell." Gylf yawned and lay down at my feet.

"Of course you don't smell it. How could you? It's still raining, and it was raining hard. Rain washes smells out of the air. Everybody knows that."

Gylf stayed quiet, but the way he looked up at me showed he was not convinced.

"Look here," I said, "everything fits, and you ought to be able to see it. The windows were open because of the hot weather. The ghost or ogre—I think ogre—could get in just by climbing through a window."

Gylf shook his head again.

"You think it's too big? It jumped out one when Duns chased it, so it could climb in one."

Gylf was too polite to say anything, but I could tell how he felt.

"A big thing like a snake shaped like a man. That's the way Duns described it, and Duns should know. Maybe we could come back when the weather's better. Then you could track it for me."

Gylf put his head down between his paws and closed his eyes.

I said, "Am I putting you to sleep? I hope you're not scared of it."

"No," Gylf said very distinctly.

"Because I'm scared of you. That's why I tried to leave you behind before we crossed the Irring."

He pretended not to hear.

"I like going around telling people how brave I am. What a jerk! I told that woman back at the farm that there wasn't a knight in Sheerwall I wouldn't cross swords with. Maybe it's the truth—I know I thought it was when I said it. But I saw how you changed when we fought the outlaws, and it scared me half to death. I wasn't scared when Disiri changed. Or when

Baki did, just now. I wasn't even very scared about Garsecg and what the sunlight showed he really was, even if I was scared of him later in Muspel. But what you did was different."

Gylf laid his head on his paws the other way, and sort of groaned.

"I'm sorry. I don't want to make you feel bad. I'm sorry too that I didn't have more guts. I'm a knight, and we're not supposed to be scared of anything. Besides, you're the best friend I've got."

"Dog." He looked up at me. He had brown eyes set deep in his brown face, and most of the time I did not notice them much; but when he said "dog" they looked straight at me, and I knew he was begging me to understand what he was and how he felt.

"Yes," I said, "you're my dog, and nobody ought to be afraid of a friendly dog. A knight shouldn't, for sure. Disiri said a dragon had the sword called Eterne—somebody like Garsecg, I guess. How am I supposed to fight a dragon if I'm afraid of my own dog?"

Gylf only looked up at me, his eyes saying he could not make himself any smaller than he was. (It was really pretty big, a lot bigger than any other dog I ever saw.)

"I'm supposed to fight Kulili, too." I wanted to hide my face in my hands as soon as I said that. "I gave Garsecg my word, and look at all he did for me. But I don't want to kill Kulili. The Aelf hate her because they're afraid of her, that's all. It's one of the things fear does to you, it make you want to kill things that haven't ever hurt you, just because they might. Like it made me try to leave you behind before I forded the Irring. I'm ashamed of that, too."

I waited a long time for him to talk because I did not feel like talking any more myself. Finally I asked, "Why didn't you come back to the boat? You went to get Garsecg, but when he came it was just him and some Water Aelf. Why didn't you come with them?"

"Chained me."

"That's right, the innkeeper's wife said you had a broken chain on your collar." I turned his spiked collar on his neck, and sure enough there were two or three links of chain hanging off it. There was no catch or anything, so I just undid the collar and threw it away. I think it may have been Aelf skin, but the spikes were shark teeth. After that I asked Gylf if he knew why Garsecg chained him up.

"Afraid of me."

"There it is again." I took a deep breath and let it out with a *whoosh!* "Well, I've apologized, and maybe Garsecg will too, eventually. He let you go free, though, once he and I had separated. I'm glad of that."

"Broke it," Gylf said succinctly.

"And came to Forcetti to wait for me?"

Uri stepped from behind a tree; it was as if she had been waiting there since Mythgarthr was made. "He came to search for you, Lord. He came to this wood looking for you, and to a good many other places besides. Baki and I would catch glimpses of him now and again while we were watching you."

"I don't like your doing that," I told her, "but since you were doing it anyway, why didn't you tell me?"

"You did not ask. You scarcely spoke save to tell us to steal your weapons back."

I did not buy that. "I've never noticed that you and Baki were shy about forcing your talk on me."

Uri bowed the woman way, spreading a skirt she did not have. "Because you are not sufficiently observant. We are diffident, Lord, whether you notice it or not."

"Then you must have a swell reason for elbowing in on me and Gylf."

"I do, Lord. Someone must explain to you that this is not the first time your dog has been in this wood. Far from it. You seem to think him newly come—"

"No!" Gylf said. It sounded a lot like he barked, but it was *no*.

"That he cannot wind this ogre you hunt because of the storm. The truth is that he has been here in many weathers. Have you ever winded him here, dog?"

Gylf eyed her with disfavor but shook his head.

I asked, "Have you ever smelled him at all? Anywhere?"

"No."

"Maybe you really have." I was testing him. "Maybe you smelled a strange smell, and you didn't know what it was."

He shut his eyes.

"He feels it is useless to talk to you since you will not believe him," Uri explained. "Baki and I often feel the same way, so I recognize the symptoms."

I stood up, swinging my arms to get warm. "Well, it's possible, isn't it?"

"It is not, Lord."

"He do you know?"

"Because he has said that he did not. I trust his word, and so should you. Perhaps this ogre is a ghost. I cannot say. I have never seen it, or smelled it either. But if it is a ghost it is not in this wood. I would know."

"What about Disiri? Is she here? I should've asked you before, and Gylf, too. Have either one of you seen her?"

Gylf rose, shaking his head. "Hungry?"

"No," Uri said. "I cannot declare she is not present, for her arts are greater than my own. But I would be as surprised if she were to step from behind a tree as you were when I did."

"Go home to Aelfrice," I told her. "Wait there until I call you."

She nodded and walked away.

"When we find this ogre," I told Gylf, "I'm going to fight him by myself. I'd like any help you can give me finding him, but once the fight starts you leave him to me."

Gylf looked unhappy.

I've got to prove myself to myself, I said, and it was only when I was through that I realized I had not said it out loud. Did I really like Kulili? Kulili was just a bunch of worms, something worms made when they got together. Maybe I just told myself I did because I did not want to fight her. When I beat Sir Nytir, was that one of those crazy things that happen when a team down in the cellar beats the division leader? I knew I was no good with a lance. Was I good at all?

I did not know, and not knowing was so bad I was ready to risk just about anything to find out.

By then the rain had stopped. The sun came out, and it was not the enemy sun that had pounded down on Pouk and me earlier that day, but a beautiful sun of new gold. East, a rainbow leaped in glory, the bridge that the Giants of Winter and Old Night had built for the Overcyns so they could climb up to Skai.

"There's magic in this air," I told Gylf. "I love it!"

He did not say anything, but I started whistling.

CHAPTER 40

A CITIZEN OF CELLARS

Supper was fresh bread hot from the oven, with butter and big bowls of good vegetable soup. Nukara had cleaned out a spare room for me, put clean blankets on the bed, and so on. While we ate she told me how nice it was.

I shook my head. "I've promised to get Master Agr's horses home tonight, and I know the duke wants me to spend every night at Sheerwall 'til he lets me go north. I thought the storm would give me a good excuse for staying here with you, but it's over. Pouk and I will have to say good-bye as soon as he gets our horses ready."

She stopped smiling; she had really wanted us to stay.

I said, "I think I may get a crack at your ghost just the same. If we're lucky, he may be gone forever by the time Pouk's finished loading our pack horse."

"So quick?" I could see she did not believe me.

I nodded and passed some bread down to Gylf. "If you'll lend me Uns. Will you?"

She looked at Uns, and so did I, but he just looked down at his soup. "He's shy," she said.

He still would not look up.

"You're not—will he get killed? Or hurt the way Duns was?"

I shook my head. "I'm going to fight the ogre, if Uns and I can find him. Uns won't get hurt."

Pouk cleared his throat. "I'd main like to watch, sir. With your permission?"

I was soaking bread in the soup for Gylf; it gave me an excuse to think things over before I answered. Finally I said, "You've got work to do. Uns and I will be going out into the fields to look for the ogre. Maybe into the woods. You'd probably get lost trying to find us. I think you'd better stay here."

Duns said, "Be dark soon, Sar Able."

I told him I was pretty sure the ogre would not show himself by daylight, so we had plenty of time to sit and talk and blow our soup. "When it's over," I said, "Pouk and I can ride home by moonlight. There'll be a good big moon tonight, and when we get there the sentries will let down the bridge for us." I kept waiting for Uns to say something, but he never did.

I left the house with Gylf trotting beside me and Uns lagging behind us. Knowing nothing better, I followed the narrow path that had taken me between fields and into the wood, the path Duns and Uns must have used when they cut firewood. When we came to the first trees, we stopped. I remember that the moon was just clearing the eastern peaks then. When Uns caught up, I told him, "I didn't come out here to hunt your ogre, and I know as well as you do that he's not here. I came so you and I could have a private talk."

I waited for him to speak, but he did not.

"I'm pressed for time. You know about that. It'll save some if you tell me everything now. I don't want to hurt you and I'll take it as a favor."

He opened his mouth, hesitated, and shut it. After a moment he shook his head.

"Whatever you want. After this, you're to ask nothing from me. I gave you fair warning, so you get no favors."

Gylf growled low in his throat.

"Before I came here," I said, "a couple of friends of mine came to wait for me. They call themselves my slaves, but they're really friends."

With his crippled back, it was hard for Uns to look up, but easy for him to look down. He took the easy way now, staring at his muddy feet.

"Gylf couldn't find a trace of your ogre in these woods. Gylf's my hound. I think I told you. He has a fine nose."

Uns nodded.

"But there really is an ogre. Your brother wrestled it and was laid up for a year. I don't know if I believe in ghosts, but I sure don't believe in ghosts that act exactly like they were alive. I got one of my friends to watch in your house while I was away. Do I have to tell you what she saw? This is your last chance, Uns."

Uns turned and ran. I nodded to Gylf, and he brought him down before he had gone ten yards.

"She saw you go into the cellar and talk to the ogre," I said while Gylf crouched over Uns snarling. "That's where it hides, I guess. I suppose it steals food from your mother's kitchen. You wanted me to sleep there. Was it so your ogre could kill me while I was asleep? Or was it to stop it from stealing for one night?"

Uns said, "Git him off!"

"In a minute. It's a live ogre, it has to be, if it's an ogre at all. Is it?"

"I dunno. Guess sa."

That was the first time he had admitted anything, and I thought it would be better to pretend I had not noticed. I pulled my chin and asked what it said about that.

"Don't talk much."

"But it does talk?"

"A li'l. I learnt him."

I smiled, although I certainly did not feel like it. "I guess you caught him young. What's his name?"

"Org. Git him off or I won't talk no more."

I told Gylf to let him go, and Gylf backed away, still growling.

Uns waited a minute, not sure Gylf would not take off an arm if he got up. Finally he did. It was not easy for him, because his bad back made it hard to keep his weight over his feet.

I said, "Maybe I sound like I know everything. I don't. What's important to me is that I don't know if I could beat your ogre in a fair fight. You can't tell me that, even if you think you could. Did you catch him young?"

"Din't ketch him a-tall," Uns muttered. "Da ma was dead, layin' inna woods wid arrows all over in her 'n Org starvin'. I ought ta let him. I knew. On'y I'se a mop ta 'n wanted him 'n I tooked him hum."

"You hid him in your mother's cellar?"

"Yessar, dere's a ol' storeroom ma's forgot, 'n dat's Org's place."

"I see."

Uns craned his neck to look up, seeking understanding. "He stinks, he do, from sleepin' in his shit, 'n sumptimes I wants ta turn him out. On'y he'd git stock. Dat got his ma kilt. Sa I don'. On'y I want ta, 'n I will, ta, 'un day."

I waited, pretty sure that he would keep talking if I gave him a chance to think about things.

"Learnt him ta talk a li'l, sar. Tried ta teach him ta say ogre 'cause he is. On'y he says org. Sa Org's wat I calls him, sar. He says yes 'n no 'n Uns. Li'l words like dat."

I nodded. "I suppose knowing you had him—a monster in the house that nobody knew about—made you feel like you were better than your brother. Maybe better than your mother, too."

"Made me good as dem, dat's aw, sar. Ma . . ."

"Go on."

"She's my ma, dat's aw, 'n sumptimes it's like I'se still a mop. 'N it's her farm, 'n she'll give it ta Duns when she passes."

I nodded to myself.

"Sa Org means I count ta."

"Can you get him from the cellar and bring him here without being seen?"

Uns hesitated, gnawing his lip. "Ya goin' ta kill him, Sar Able?"

"I'm going to wrestle him, if he'll wrestle me. Maybe he'll kill me, breaking my back or my neck. If he does—"

Gylf growled; you have heard the same noise, but you thought it was distant thunder.

"You and Gylf and Pouk will have to sort things out. Or I may kill Org, the same way. We'll see."

"Ya goin' ta wrestle him fair, sar?"

"Yes. Without weapons, if that's what you mean. Can you bring him? Don't let anybody see you."

Uns bobbed his head. "Yessar. Outta da cellar door, sar. Dey won't know."

"Then bring him. Bring him now, and I'll do my best to see that no serious harm comes to him."

Gylf wanted to go with Uns, but I would not let him. When Uns had gone, I took off my boots and my sword belt and laid them aside, with Sword Breaker and my dagger still in their scabbards. After that, I took off my clothes. They were still pretty wet, but I found I was a lot colder without them than I had been with them on. I had put my sword belt on my boots to keep it off the wet ground, sticking Sword Breaker and my dagger into the boots. Now I piled my clothes on top of everything, trying not to get them any wetter than they were already.

When I had stripped, I stretched the way they teach you to in gym, leaning right and left as I touched my toes. The swing of the sea was strong in me, and I called upon it as I loosened up my muscles. I was a big man, thanks to Disiri, a head taller than almost everybody, with big shoulders and arms thicker than most men's legs. I knew I was going to need all that, and the sea-surge most of all. The big waves pound, and drain away. They are strong, not stiff, and they swallow everything you throw at them and throw it back at you harder.

Gylf snarled, and from the sound of it I knew Org was coming. I took a good deep breath and let it trickle away.

Then I folded my arms and waited. This would be the test, and I had no idea how it would come out.

CHAPTER 41

ORG

"He bites, sar. I oughta tell you dat. 'N he's bigger now dan when Duns catched him."

I said okay, feeling a little sick. Standing in back of Uns in the clear moonlight, the ogre did not look much taller than he was, but its shoulders were huge. As well as I could tell its head was twice as big as his, but on those shoulders it looked too small. I could see the arms were so long they touched the ground, but I was too dumb to realize right away that it was walking on its knuckles.

"Quick, ta, Sar Able." Uns sounded proud. "You watch out, sar. Don' dink he's slaw jus' 'cause he's sa big. He's fas', 'n he'll hit wid his hands fas'. Slap ut ya, only dey don' feel like no slaps."

I said, "You sound as if you fought him too."

"Not like Duns done, sar. He beat me easy, on'y I made him see he had ta have me. Somebody ta take care a' him. I dink he was goin' ta eat me, dough."

"Well, he doesn't have to have me." I stepped a little closer. "He can eat me if he can."

Org's left hand slashed faster than any sword I have ever seen. I tried to duck, but the edge of it got the back of my head. I was half stunned, but knew I had to get inside those long arms before I was knocked out. I went in hard, slamming my shoulder against his great bow belly.

It was like hitting a boulder. I drove my fists into it, short jabs with the strength of big comers behind them, right and left, and right and left, again and again. His scales were ripping the skin off my knuckles, but I did not feel it until later. What happened next was that he picked me up and threw me. I ought to remember flying through the air, but I do not.

When I came to, I was lying on wet grass and feeling like I had swallowed soap. I knew I had gone to sleep when I ought to have been doing something else, something really important, but I could not think what it was. Pretty soon Bold Berthold would come and see I had not finished the job, and he would be too nice to say anything and I would feel like I ought to just kill myself and get it over.

But maybe I could see what the job was if I could just sit

up, and if I could I could start doing it and be hard at work when he came and that would be better. Then I heard a dog and I thought it was sheep or something, I had promised to watch sheep for somebody and fallen asleep. Except that it was dark, just moonlight all around and probably the sheep ought to be in a pen someplace and I had not penned them, and had gone to sleep before the sun went down.

The dog sounded as big as a bear.

Bold Berthold was most likely dead. Disira was dead too, and I had given little Ossar to the Bodachan when they gave me Gylf. I got up, dizzy and near to chucking. The grass was barley, high already but nowhere near ready for harvest.

When I found Org, Gylf had him by the throat and Gylf was black and as big as a horse. He was shaking Org like a rat, and Org was trying to get loose while a two-headed snake of fire and brass struck at his face. I yelled at the snake until it quit and changed into Uri and Baki in a cloud of smoke.

I made them help me get Gylf to let go. I do not think I have ever done any work rougher than that. Baki and I kept trying to pry his jaws apart, with him throwing us around when he shook Org and the sticks Uri found for us breaking. When we finally got him off Org fell down limp, and I knew just exactly how he felt. I told him I was sorry, that I had wanted for us to have a fair fight, and he had won it and I knew it. Maybe I should have offered him my armor and the horses, but I did not think of it then and he was not a knight anyway. I said that I would never claim to have won, and whenever anybody asked I would tell the truth.

Gylf did not want to go back to dog size, but I made him, and I helped Org get up and promised Gylf would not go for him. "I'm ready to fight again if you want to," I said. (I knew it was not true, but I thought Org probably felt worse than I did.) "If you need a few minutes to catch your breath, that's okay. But we can't take too long, because I've got to get back to Sheerwall Castle."

I have had some big surprises in my life, and that was one of the biggest. Org got down on the ground again and crawled over to my feet on his belly.

Uri said, "He yields, Lord. That is his surrender."

I said, "Is that right, Org? Are you saying you give up?"

He moaned, and put my foot on his head. It was colder than any rock.

Baki said, "He wishes to join us, beautiful naked Lord." Uri laughed at that, and I wanted to run off and hide in the barley.

"These two Aelfmaidens call themselves my slaves," I explained to Org. I had my hands over my privates, and I felt like the biggest fool in the world. "They think you want to be my slave too." I stopped for a minute, still dizzy and wondering whether he understood any of it.

Finally I said, "That's what they want us to think they think, anyhow. Is that what you want?"

He grunted twice.

"There!" Baki sounded like she had won the lottery. "You see, Lord? It says uh-huh."

I got mad. "No, I don't, and I don't know what he said. I don't believe you do either."

I found my sword belt and put it on; I was not sure I could crack that skull with Sword Breaker, but I was willing to try and I could not stop thinking about what the people back at Sheerwall would say if I killed the last ogre. With him lying on the ground the way he was, it was a terrific temptation; so I made him stand up.

He did, sort of crouching.

Uri ran her fingers up and down my back. "You have not accepted him, Lord. He fears that if he stands you will take it as a gage of battle."

I had my hand on Sword Breaker's hilt. "If you're my slave, Org, I can sell you. Do you understand that? I can, and I probably will. Is that what you want?"

He shook his head. The motion was not really right, but close enough that I knew what he meant. I said, "What do you want, then? I can't let you go back to Nukara's house. I promised her I'd get rid of you if I could. If I let you go free—well, Uns was afraid you'd kill cattle and sheep, but I'm afraid you'd kill people."

"Wi' you," he muttered.

I did not know what to say, so I got Baki to hold my sword belt while I pulled on my wet clothes again. When I had my cloak back on, I said, "You mean like Pouk? It's going to be really hard for me to keep people from killing you."

Org dropped down again and crawled over to the new place where I was standing. "Wi' you, Master."

"Okay, you can be my servant." I said that before I really thought about it, and there were times afterward when I wished I had thought it over more. "Only listen here. If you're going to serve me, you've got to promise you won't kill anybody unless I say it's all right. You mustn't kill livestock either, unless I say you can." I was not sure he understood *livestock,* so I said, "No horses or cattle or sheep or donkeys. No dogs and no cats. No fowls."

He looked up (I saw his eyes glow in the moonlight), and I think he was deciding whether I meant it. After a moment or two, he nodded.

"You'll get hungry, but your hunger isn't going to get you off the hook if you disobey me. Understand?"

Uri said, "I suppose you will want us to carry him off to Aelfrice and nursemaid him for you whenever he is in your way. Well, you can whistle for it."

"No shit?" I hitched my sword belt around so I could get

at Sword Breaker quick if I wanted her. "I guess you're not my slaves after all."

Baki tried to look humble. "We will do whatever you ask, Lord. We must. But I doubt that we could take him to Aelfrice with us. He is too big—"

Uri nodded, putting a lot of energy into it.

"Besides, he is too stupid. Once we had him there, we could not control him. We could not do it here even with Gylf helping."

I said okay.

"You have not asked my advice," Uri said, "but I will offer it just the same. I knew some of these creatures when they were common. They are stupid, lazy, and treacherous. But they are very good at hiding themselves and sneaking up on people, because they are of whatever color they wish to be. If you order this one to follow you without letting himself be seen, few would catch even a glimpse of him. I will not say no one would, because much would depend on where you went and how good the light was. Just the same, I think you might be surprised at how few did."

I shrugged, wishing I could ask Gylf's advice. "All right, we'll try it. But first, I want to take him back to the house and show him to Duns and Nukara, and find out what's become of Uns. After that I'll introduce him to Pouk, I suppose. Pouk will have to do most of the watching and feeding. I only hope Pouk doesn't become ogre-food himself."

Uri smiled. "He did not eat Uns."

"No, but it might be better if he had. Go back to Aelfr—"

"What is it?" Baki asked.

"Go back, and tell Queen Disiri, if you should see her—if you can find her, I mean—how much I'd like to be with her. How much I love her, and how grateful I am for all the favor she's shown me."

They said they would, and disappeared into the shadows.

I turned to Gylf. "If you're not an Aelfdog, and I have to admit you don't act like one, exactly what are you?"

Gylf only looked doleful, lying down and resting his muzzle between his paws.

"Can't you tell me? Come on, Gylf! Are you really one of the Valfather's dogs? That was what they said."

He looked at Org significantly.

"He counts. Is that what you're saying? You won't talk while he's around?"

Gylf nodded the way he had when I had first gotten him.

"Another disadvantage. Well, maybe there are advantages to having you, too, Org, but I haven't found out about them yet. I hope so." I started back to the house, motioning for them to follow me, and they both did.

Disiri was watching us then. I know that because of something that she gave me when we got here, not a drawing (although I thought it was a drawing at first) but a cutout of black paper glued to blue paper: a knight swaggering along with his hand on the hilt of a short sword; a monstrous thing behind him taller than he is, shambling on bowed legs with one scaly hand upon the knight's shoulder; and a big dog that looks small because it is following the monster. I have put it where I see it every day. It has not made me wish to go back to Mythgarthr, but I know it will someday.

The kitchen windows looked bright and cheerful when we caught sight of Nukara, Duns, and Pouk at last. I did not really feel like I was coming home, but it was like that. I would be able to eat—I had not eaten much before the fight—and to warm myself in front of the fire. Right then it seemed like everything that anybody could ever want.

All that counted, but it was not just that. I had been talking to Gylf and Uri and Baki, and even to Org, which was okay.

But the voices I heard through the greased skin in the kitchen windows were human, all of them. Sometimes that can make a big difference.

Pouk opened the door when I knocked. "There you are, sir. Missed you, I did. Knew you wasn't . . ."

He had seen the ogre behind me. I said, "This is Org, Pouk. You're not to harm him. If he misbehaves, tell me."

Pouk stood there frozen, with his mouth open. I do not believe he had heard a word I said.

"Org, this man is Pouk, another servant. He will see to it that you're fed and otherwise cared for. You must do what he says, exactly like you would do what I said."

Org grunted and looked at Pouk, and Pouk took a couple of steps backward. Maybe I ought to say here that Org did not snarl or anything, ever. He did not smile, and he did not frown. His eyes were like two black beads. They looked small in a big face that was mostly mouth. It was not a human face or anything close to that. A dog's face or a horse's face is a lot more human-looking than Org's.

I went on into the house, and Org came in behind me. Gylf went around us to lie in front of the fire. Duns and Nukara had been sitting at the table with Pouk, or that was how it seemed. They had stood up, probably, when Pouk went to the door. Now they looked every bit as out of it as he did. "Here's your ghost," I told them. "A solid one. Hear the floorboards creak? If you'd like to touch him, go right ahead."

Duns tried to talk three times before he could say, "You fought him?"

"I did, and I didn't like it, either. He beat me, and then he surrendered to me. It's kind of a long story, and I'd rather not get into the whole thing just now."

"Where's Uns?" Nukara asked. "Where is my son?"

"I don't know. He went with me and helped me, and I was

thinking of taking him on to work with Pouk for a while if he wanted. But when Org and I fought, he disappeared."

"Run off?" Pouk had recovered himself somewhat.

"I didn't see him go, so I don't know. If he did, I can't blame him. I felt like running too."

Gylf growled at Org, who seemed not to hear him.

"I'll have a word wit him," Duns was saying, "when he gits hum."

"You don't have to chew him out," I said. "He doesn't have it coming."

Pouk had drawn his knife. "We goin' to kill that now, sir?"

"Kill him after he gave up?" I shook my head. "If you'd been paying attention, you'd know what we're going to do. We're going to take him back to Sheerwall with us, and you're going to take care of him."

Pouk nodded. "We'll do for him there, sir, and have a hundred to help us."

"They'll do for him, you mean, if we don't stop them, and he'll kill ten or twenty of them first. We've got to find a way to keep that from happening."

Nukara gave me bread and cheese, and more soup. She found the carcass of a sheep for Org, and had me give it to him. He ate it bones and all, and seemed to be satisfied.

After that, we left. I kept thinking about my fight with Org and what I was going to do with him; Pouk probably asked questions, but I doubt that I answered them. Then we topped a hill and saw Sheerwall with the full moon behind it—the high, square towers crowned with battlements. Later I saw Utgard, which was a whole lot bigger (so big it scared you). And Thortower, which was taller and prettier. But Sheerwall was Sheerwall, and there was nothing else like it. Not for me.

I think it was a little after midnight by the time we got there. Master Agr had told me the password, even though I told him we should get back before sundown. Now I saw that he had been right. I yelled for the sentries and when they challenged me I gave it to them and they loosed the pawl. I had never seen the drawbridge let down before, and wished I could have seen more of it. As it was, about all I saw was the big chain moving and the stone counterweights going up. Sheerwall had a good wide moat and a narrow bridge without railings. I was a little scared and cantered across just to look like I was not.

When I got to the other side, I called the sentries over so I could talk to them. "In another minute something will come across your bridge that you won't believe," I told them. "I'm not going to ask you to promise not to tell anybody about it. If you think it's your duty to report it, you ought to do your duty. I will ask you not to gossip about it. Can I have your word on that?"

They say I could.

"Good. Like I said, you can report it if you think you should. But I'm ordering you not to fight it or try to stop it from crossing over. If you do, you'll have to fight me too. Just let it come across, and I'll be responsible for anything it does."

The older sentry said, "Good enough for us, sir."

I sort of grinned at him. "You haven't seen it yet." I was about to call to Pouk to tell Org that he could come across when I heard more horses on the bridge. It was Pouk, riding his and leading the rest, with Gylf trotting in back to make them keep up. I said, "I thought I told you to stay with Org until I yelled."

"Aye aye, sir." Pouk let go of the pommel long enough to touch his cap. "I'm tryin' to stay with him, sir. He's in here, sir. In this here bailey, sir."

"You mean he crossed without me seeing him?"

"No, sir. Not over this bridge here, sir. He swum th' moat." Pouk was staring around the dim courtyard beyond the portcullis. "Then he come around behind, like."

"I see. But I don't see him. Do you?"

Pouk hesitated, afraid of getting me angry. "No, sir. Not this minute I don't, sir. Only I think I know where he is, sir, an' if you want him I'll try to fetch him out."

"Not now." I turned back to the sentries. "I won't report this. You can do whatever you want to."

The older one cleared his throat. "We're with you, Sir—Sir . . ."

"Able of the High Heart."

"Sir Able, long as you're with us."

"I'm on your team, and I'm going to put that servant Pouk should have kept with him in the dungeon."

The younger said, "That's good, sir."

"I thought you'd like it." I was grinning again. "I'll have to find the head man there and talk to him, I guess, but it can wait 'til morning. He's probably in bed, and I'd like to be in bed myself. Who should I ask for?"

"Master Caspar, sir. He's under Master Agr, sir, and he's Chief Warder. You know where the Marshal's Tower is?"

"I'm staying there."

"Well, sir, you get on the stair in there like you would, only go down 'stead of up. First door you come to will be his taburna, sir."

"Thanks." It was not until I got off my horse that I knew how bone-tired I was. "Pouk, take them to the stable, all of them. Unsaddle them. Make sure they get water and oats, and clean stalls."

"Aye aye, sir."

"You know where my room is."

Pouk nodded. "Aye, sir."

"Good." I wanted to slump, but I knew I must not. I stood very straight instead, with my shoulders back and my chest out. "I'll be there as soon as I've seen about Org. Take our bags up there—everything we had on the boat and what we got off Sir Whatever-it-was. If the grooms give you a hard time, tell them it's my order."

"Aye aye, sir!"

The moat stunk, and the filth splashed by my boots was horse piss and droppings, but I did not care; I headed for the darkest corner of the bailey, knowing what I wanted to do, and knowing that after I got it done I could go to bed.

I was a woman in a dirty bed in a stuffy little room. An old woman sitting beside my bed kept telling me to push, and I pushed, although I was so tired I could not push hard, no matter how hard I tried. I knew my baby was trying to breathe, and could not breathe, and would soon die.

"Push!"

I had tried to save; now I was only trying to get away. He would not let go, climbing on me, pushing me underwater.

The moon shone through pouring rain as I made my way down the muddy track. At its end the ogre loomed black and huge. I was the boy who had gone into Disiri's cave, not the man who had come out. My sword was Disira's grave marker, the short stick tied to the long one with a thong. I pushed the point into the mud to mark my own grave, and went on. When the ogre threw me, it became such a sword as I wished for, with a golden pommel and a gleaming blade.

I floated off the ground and started back for it, but I could no longer breathe.

CHAPTER 42

I AM A HERO

I woke up sweating, threw off my blanket, and looked at the window. Gray light was in the sky. Sleeping, I decided, was worse than getting up; and I glued down my choice by pouring water in the cracked washbowl and scrubbing every part of me I could reach. When I lived with Bold Berthold we washed by swimming in the Griffin. That had been a lot better—in warm weather anyhow—and I wondered if the duke got baths half as good.

Pouk was snoring on the other side of the door. I could hear each snore clearly, and I thought sure the noise I made washing and getting dressed would wake him up, but it did not. For a minute I wanted to pour my wash-water on him, but I carried it to the window and threw it out instead, then I stuck my head out and looked around.

The castle might be called Sheerwall, but the wall was not really straight up and down. The big not-quite-square stones were rough, too, and were not set exactly even. I had done a good deal of climbing on the *Western Trader,* and now I stuck my boots in my belt, in back where they would be out of the way, and went over the sill.

In one way it was a tough climb, and in another it was not. I kept hitting places where I could not go down any further without sliding, and the wall was steep enough that a slide would not have been much different from a fall by the time I got to the ground. So I would have to give that spot up, and go sidewise or back up, and try someplace else. But it was good, hard exercise, and there was never a time when I really thought I was going to fall. Toug climbed around on the wall of Utgard once pretty much like I did that morning on the Marshal's Tower, and when he told me about it, it reminded me of this. Only there were vines, some kind of ivy, on Utgard. I will write about that when I get to it.

Once I was on the ground, the smell of bread baking steered me to the kitchen without a lot of side trips. I was good and hungry, and that helped. "You're not supposed to be in here, sir," a cook told me. "Breakfast in the hall when you hear the horn."

When I did not say anything, he added, "Fresh ham today, sir, and cheese with it."

"Bread and butter, and small beer." I knew because I had eaten there twice the day before. "How about eggs? Have you got any? What about apples?"

He shook his head. "No, sir. We do the best we can, sir."

"That's good." I patted his shoulder. "Since you do, you won't mind if I take this." It was hot loaf, good heavy bread with a lot of barley and spelt in it.

"A nice lady fixed a swell supper for me last night," I explained to the cook, "but I knew I was going to have to fight and I didn't want to eat a lot and slow myself down. You don't mind?"

"No, sir." His face showed he did. "Not at all, sir."

"Good. Come out into the hall for a minute."

"I have more bread to—" Seeing the way I was looking at him, he hurried out.

The hall was a lot bigger than the kitchen, maybe a hundred paces long and fifty wide. There was a dais for Duke Marder and his wife and special company. For the rest of us, long tables of bare wood, benches, and stools. Some servingwomen were setting places for breakfast: a greasy trencher and a flagon for everybody.

I said, "Master Caspar eats here, doesn't he? Where does he sit?"

"I work in the kitchen," the cook said. "I have no way of knowing, but Modguda could probably tell you."

I let him go. "I bet you're right. She will, too. We're old buddies."

She bowed woman-fashion. "I'm glad you're so much better, Sir Able."

"So am I." I turned to the cook. "You've got more bread to bake. Get to work!"

Modguda showed me where Master Caspar sat. He had a chair. That proved something, although I was not sure what. I sat down in it to eat my bread and told Modguda to fetch a flagon of beer.

"He—he'll be angry, Sir Able. Master Caspar will." She looked about ready to die.

"Not at you. And not at me, because I'll get up as soon as he comes and let him sit down. I just want to be sure I don't miss him." By that time a few people were straggling into the hall. I tried to guess which ones might be warders and work in the dungeon.

Modguda was short enough, and I was big enough, that she did not have to bend down to whisper in my ear. "Everybody's afraid of him, sir. Even you knights."

I had a mouthful, which gave me a good chance to think before I said anything. "Everybody can't be," I said when I had swallowed and had a sip of beer. "I'm not, so how could it be everybody?"

"He's the master of the dungeon, sir. You wouldn't want to go there, sir, but if you—"

I shook my head. "That's exactly what I do want. I was down there last night, but I had no flashlight—no torch, I mean—and couldn't see much. I'd like to go again and have Master Caspar show me around. That's one of the favors I'm going to ask him for."

Right then, somebody in back of me said, "Ask who for?"

It was a big guy who liked black. I asked if he was Caspar, and he nodded. Modguda had run while I was turning.

I got out of his chair and held out my hand. "I'm Sir Able of the High Heart."

He said, "Huh!"

"I just sat here so I wouldn't miss you when you came to breakfast. I've got something to talk to you about, and I thought it might be a good idea to do it while we ate."

"Say it now." He sat down hard. "I eat with my men, not with you."

There were half a dozen warders in black clothes around us by that time, some pulling out stools and sitting on them, and some just standing there to listen in. I began, "Okay, I'll go to your dungeon—"

"Most do."

The one sitting next to Caspar laughed, and it was not just some guy laughing at the boss's joke; everything he was planning to do to me some fine day was in that laugh of his. I knocked him off his stool, and when he started to get back up I picked it up and hit him with it.

The whole place got very quiet, fast. Somebody had set a

platter of fresh ham in front of Caspar. I pulled it over and took a piece, and got my bread and ate a little of that, too.

"You're the fellow that crippled all the other knights," Caspar said.

"Three or four. Maybe five. That's all." I picked up my flagon and took a drink.

He nodded. "Pass the pork."

I did. "It would be better if you were to say pass the pork, please, Sir Able. But I'll overlook it this time."

He grunted.

"I want us to be friends, Master Caspar. A servant of mine is staying with you, and I'd like you to take good care of him."

He turned to look at me, still chewing ham.

"So I thought—"

Woddet had come over while I was talking, and he broke in then. "Fighting in the Great Hall is forbidden. Master Agr wants to see you after breakfast."

"I'll be happy to talk to him," I said, "but we weren't fighting. We're talking about a private matter."

Woddet squatted to check out the warder on the floor, feel for a pulse and so on. "What about this?"

"Oh, him. I don't think he's hurt very much. If I'd hit him hard I would've killed him, but I didn't."

Woddet got up. "You'd better see Master Agr as soon as you leave here. Otherwise . . ." He shrugged.

Caspar said, "Otherwise, you're mine."

"I'd rather see the duke," I told Woddet, "but since Master Agr wants to see me, okay. Tell him it will be a pleasure."

"You want to come with me? I'll make a place for you at the table where we knights eat."

"I know where it is, but I've got to talk with Master Caspar just now and then Master Agr after that."

Woddet went back to the knights' table, and somebody a

couple of tables over started talking a little bit too loud, and pretty soon everybody was talking and eating like they always did. Modguda brought a round of cheese on a big trencher, and I got out my dagger and cut a slice. I have always liked ham and cheese, even if we had been getting it just about every meal.

"We brand our prisoners sometimes," Caspar said. "It depends on what the duke wants. Troublemakers. Thieves. You ever been branded?"

I was chewing, but I shook my head.

"I have." He pushed back his hood so I could see the brand on his forehead. "I didn't like it."

I swallowed. "Nobody likes a headache. We get them, just the same."

Caspar chuckled. He had a mean chuckle. "You say you've got a fresh prisoner for me?"

I thought about a friend of mine who had gone away to boarding school, and I said, "More of a boarder. You don't have to lock him up, but he'll be living with you until I go north to take a stand at some bridge or something."

"He'll be living with us."

"Yeah." I nodded. "I know you must feed your prisoners—they'd starve to death if you didn't, and they don't eat in here. All you've got to do is set out a plate of food for this servant of mine." I stopped to think about some things Uns had said. "Every other day might be enough. Just leave it out where he can find it, and if he hasn't eaten it in a couple of days, try someplace else."

"I ain't going to have people running around loose in my dungeon." Caspar sounded like his mind was made up.

"He's there already. All you've got to do is feed him."

Caspar's face got red, and his eyes got small.

"I put him in there last night, and I told him to stay there.

He promised he would, and as long as he gets enough to eat I think he will."

I had been hoping Caspar would relax a little after that, but he did not.

"You might find droppings, I guess. But in a dungeon that shouldn't matter."

Caspar wiped his dagger on his sleeve and stuck it back in the scabbard. "He's there right now."

"That's right." I was glad he was finally getting it. "I put him down there last night. You were asleep, and I didn't want to wake you up. A friend unbarred your door for me and barred it again after I left." I tried to remember whether I had really heard Uri put the bar back. I could not be certain, so I said, "Or anyway I told her to. I'm pretty sure she must have done it."

"This is a different friend," Caspar said slowly. "This isn't the one you left for me to wet-nurse."

"Right." The man I had knocked down was getting back on his feet and going for a big knife on his belt. I caught his wrist. "If you draw that, I'll have to take it away from you. You'd better sit down and eat something before all the cheese is gone."

Caspar stood up when the man was sitting down. "You might get to know Hob better before long."

"That's good," I said. "I'd like to patch things up, if I can. Meanwhile you'll take care of my servant, won't you? I know I'm asking a favor."

He turned and stalked out of the Great Hall.

Master Agr was standing with his back to the window when I came in. He nodded, cleared his throat, waited as though he were going to talk, then cleared it again. "Good morrow, Sir Able."

"Good morning, Master Agr. What is it?" They had told me to stand up straight the first time I had been there, and I was careful to do it again.

"Sir Able, I . . ."

I said, "Yes, Master Agr?"

Agr sighed. "I cannot conduct our conversation like this. Please sit down." He motioned toward a chair. "Bring that over here, please." He sat in his usual chair, behind stacks of reports and ledgers.

I carried the chair over, and sat.

"Fighting in the Great Hall is strictly contrary to His Grace's command. Did you know that?"

I nodded. "Yes, I do. I did."

"Yet you struck one of the warders with a stool. That is what has been reported to me. I didn't see it myself."

"With my fist first, Master Able. With the stool when he started to get up."

Agr nodded. I do not believe I ever saw him looking cheerful, and he certainly did not look cheerful then. "Why did you do that, Sir Able?"

"Because I had to talk to Master Caspar. I knew if I let that warder get up he would interrupt us. What I had to say was hard enough without having to tell him to put a cork in it all the time." I took a deep breath, feeling like I was going to make things worse but that I had to do it. "Let me say this, and then you can say anything you want. I'm not going to try to defend what I did, but I don't think it was wrong. Sometimes you've got to make an exception, no matter what the rule says. You're going to punish me for it. I know that, and it's okay with me. I'm not blaming you. I apologize for raising a ruckus and giving you trouble. But if the same thing happened again, I'd knock him down again just like I did."

Agr nodded. Nothing in his face had changed. "For those

of less than knightly rank, such as I am myself, the customary punishment is dismissal. For knights, it is banishment for a period of months or years."

"Fine. I've been wanting to go north anyway. How long should I stay gone?"

Agr rose and went to his window, where he stood looking out for so long that I began to think he was waiting for me to leave. When he finally sat back down he said, "There have been fights in the Great Hall before, but they were simple matters. This case is fraught with complexities. In the first place, Sir Able, a few of our knights still maintain that you are not one of them. You must be aware of that."

I said I was.

"They resent your eating at their table. If I punish you as a knight, they will resent that still more. Don't look like that, please. I'm not going to dismiss you like a servant."

"I feel that I've proved myself."

"So do I. So does His Grace. I'm simply saying that if I give you knightly punishment, the resentment will be that much greater."

"There will be none from me, Master Agr. You need not fear my resentment."

"I fear no man's resentment in any case," Agr told me, "but it is my duty to maintain order among you knights. To do that and a great many other things."

He sucked his teeth. "That is the first complication. The second is that when these fights have erupted in the past they have most often been between knight and knight. I can recall one in which two menials fought. That is the sole exception. I dismissed them both, but I've given my word that I will not dismiss you like a menial, Sir Able, and I won't. Yet if I banish you, the knights will be up in arms. Some because you received a knight's punishment. All the rest because a knight was banished for striking an insolent churl. They will protest to His Grace, at the very least."

"I will not," I said.

"No. I realize that. But there are seasoned knights here of whom His Grace thinks highly. Should they join the protest, and they may . . ." Agr shrugged.

"I'm very sorry this happened," I told him. "I really mean that."

"Thank you. Lastly, but by no means least, the warders are hated and feared. Not merely by all the knights but by everyone. I don't want to offend your evident modesty, but I feel quite certain that you are regarded as a hero by nine-tenths of those who know of what took place this morning."

"I am a hero," I told him. "I don't mean for knocking a warder down. That was nothing."

He smiled, a little bitterly. "Perhaps you're correct, Sir Able. In fact, I believe you are. But now that I've outlined the difficulties, I'd like to hear everything you have to say in your defense. If you've a speech in you, this is the time to give it."

"I don't." I thought about what had happened, and how nobody on the *Western Trader* would have cared. "I know you won't pay much attention to this, Master Agr, but it really wasn't fighting. I hit him with my fist, and afterward with the stool. But I wasn't really fighting him, because he never fought me."

"Go on."

"I hit him because he was going to threaten me, and keep on threatening me until I did. His Grace's ban on fighting is a good idea when everybody acts decently. Is it really worse to have a fight now and then, than to have people like him, people who like to hurt other people when they can't fight back, spitting in somebody's face while he's trying to talk to somebody else?"

"I take your point," Master Agr said. "Anything else?"

I shook my head.

"Then I have something else, Sir Able. Before I begin, let me say that I like you. I would be your friend, insofar as my office permits. I would like you to be mine."

"I am," I told him. "I know you've done a lot for me. I owe you."

"I locked away your weapons after the fight in the practice yard, your bow and quiver, and that—that false sword you're wearing now. I had to, or they would have been taken. His Grace told me to return them whenever you asked for them. You may recall it."

I waited, sure I knew what was coming.

"Yesterday it struck me that you had never asked, and I went to look for them, intending to have a page take them to you. They were gone. Today I see that you are wearing your sword belt. I take it you have your bow back as well? And the arrows? Because I no longer have them."

"They're up in my room." I winced a little, remembering the dreams my bowstring had given me the night before.

"Can you tell me how you got them?"

I shook my head. "We'd only fight, because you wouldn't believe me."

"Try me, Sir Able. I'd like to know how you got into my cupboards."

"Do you believe that I was knighted by Queen Disiri?"

Agr did not answer. Somebody was running outside, and we both heard him at once. He was heavy, and running pretty badly, because the footsteps were not regular. We heard him stop at the door and gasp for breath.

"The sentry will send him away, whoever he is," Agr said.

But the sentry did not. Before Agr had finished what he was saying the big oak door banged back and Caspar stumbled in and fell down at my feet.

CHAPTER 43

THE WAR WAY

Out of all our long trip north, the night I remember best was the one on which we separated. Svon took care of the horses, making Pouk do most of the actual work but watching to see that it was done right. Gylf had gone hunting, and I sat at our fire, looking into the flames and thinking of Sir Ravd, of Muspel, and of nights at our cabin in the woods—how you and I had gathered sticks, building a big fire in the little stone fireplace and roasting weenies and marshmallows.

And wondering, to tell you the truth, how the heck I had gotten from there to where I was now. Agr had told me that if I hurried and had good luck I could be in the mountains in six weeks. When he said it, it had not seemed possible that it was going to take that long.

We had met in a big, pleasant room in the duke's private quarters, we being Agr, Caspar, the duke himself, and me. I would have liked to have Hob there, too; and in a way he was, because he was what the rest of us were thinking about. Org had killed and eaten him.

"This pet of yours," Marder said to me, "this ogre you put

into my dungeon, is the least of our troubles. So let us deal with it first. Can you send it away?"

"To send him away would be to doom him, Your Grace." I had argued the whole thing out with Agr already, before we went in to see Marder. "You're going to say that he should be killed, and so is Master Agr. Master Caspar, too. All right, maybe the three of you are right. But I've accepted him into my service. I can't send him out to die."

Marder fingered his beard and Agr tried to pretend that none of this had anything to do with him. Finally Caspar said, "We got to get it out of there, Your Grace. Get it up in the bailey where the knights can get at it."

Marder shrugged; I had never seen him look so tired and old. "Sir Able will not order it out of the dungeon, knowing that he would be sending it to its death. I can send knights into the dungeon and have them kill it there."

Caspar shook his head. No way.

"But I could not guarantee their success. From what you say, they might not even be able to find it."

Agr repeated something he had said already, rephrasing it. "If this ogre is Sir Able's servant, Sir Able should have given it the strictest instructions, emphasizing that his protection would be lifted if it disobeyed."

"I ordered Org not to hurt anybody," I said, "and he promised he wouldn't. I think he must have heard that I'd hit Hob. He must have thought Hob was my enemy and it would be okay."

Marder nodded, I suppose mostly to himself.

"Hob would have been, if Hob had lived. Everyone in your castle is afraid of the warders, Your Grace, except me and you. I don't know what's behind all that, but it's got to be more than ugly faces and black clothes. If I go down in your dungeon, Master Caspar and his men will do everything they can think of to see I never come out. I know that. But if you want me to—"

"Your Grace!" Caspar had jumped up. "I swear—he—Sir Able don't—"

Marder shut him up by moving his hand about an inch.

I said, "I'll go anyway, if you tell me to. And I'll make it clear to Org that he shouldn't kill anybody else, not even Master Caspar."

Marder hid his mouth behind his hand, but I saw his mustache twitch.

"Only I've got a better plan, if I can just get you to agree to it. This will solve all the problems we've been talking about. It gets Org out of your dungeon. And it will be my punishment, too, one none of your knights can resent or argue about."

Marder sighed. "It will get you killed, you mean. The more I see and hear of you, Sir Able, the more reluctant I am to lose you."

"I hope not, Your Grace. You were going to send me out to make my stand. We talked about that outside my room."

He nodded. "I recall it."

"Then you remember you said you might send me to fight the Angrborn. Do it. Do it now. I don't know exactly how they go when they come into your duchy—"

Agr said, "I'll draw you a map of the War Way." (He did that, too, afterward.)

I nodded to show I had heard Agr. "But there can't be a lot of roads through the mountains. Let me take my stand someplace they have to go through. I'll take Org along, and I'll stay there until snow blocks the passes."

We talked about that for a while, Marder saying that as long as I did not come back before there was ice in the bay he would take my word that I had not left until the passes were closed. Agr sent Caspar for a page, then sent the page to that armorer back in Forcetti to tell him he had to hurry up with all my work.

Then Marder said, "There is another difficulty whose solution I see in this, Sir Able."

That was Svon. I remember looking up from the fire that night to get a good look at him, and seeing he was asleep and that Gylf had laid a dead hare pretty close to his head. I got it and skinned it, and stuck one haunch on a long stick the way you do, and held it over the fire.

It was getting brown when Svon sat up. "Are you going to eat all of that, Sir Able?"

I held up the rest. "There's more here. Take whatever you want."

"Good of you. We've been on short commons, eh?"

I reminded him that he had bought extra food for himself when we had stopped at inns or in villages. It was easy—too easy, to tell you the truth—to get mad at Svon. Maybe it was even as easy for us to be mad at him as it was for him to be mad at us. When I thought about it, I understood him well enough. He was still a squire, when there were a lot of knights younger than he was.

I was one of those myself.

He went off to cut a stick. When he came back, he put the other haunch over the fire too. "I could eat it raw, like your monster, Sir Able. But I'm a man, so I'll try to soften it up."

I stayed quiet, knowing he was trying to get me mad.

"Your ogre, I ought to have said. I don't like him."

I had another look at my meat, and turned the stick.

"I had a nice nap until I smelled this rabbit. Have you slept at all?"

I said no.

"Because you're afraid to sleep without your dog and your monster to guard you. Isn't that right? You're afraid I might stab you."

"I've been stabbed before," I told him.

His lips tightened. "Not by me."

"No."

"Allow me to tell you something, Sir Able. I know you won't credit it, but I'd like to say it whether you credit it or not. I won't stab you, not while you sleep at any rate. But your pet ogre will turn on you someday, asleep or awake."

"Would you defend me, if he did?"

"How am I to take that? Am I to say yes so you'll have something good to say of me when we return?"

I shook my head. "You're supposed to take it seriously, that's all. And answer it honestly—even if it's just to yourself." I was trying to get the meat I had been cooking off the stick without burning my fingers; when I did, I took a bite. It was hot enough to burn my tongue, and tough too. It tasted wonderful.

"You always tell the truth. Correct?"

My mouth was full, but I shook my head.

"You know you try to give that impression." He pointed his forefinger at me. "That impression itself is a lie."

I chewed some more and swallowed. "Sure. Since you're awake now, go see to the horses."

He ignored it. "You told His Grace that you had guided Sir Ravd and me in the forests above Irringsmouth. Another lie."

The scream of some animal made us both jump up.

Svon took a deep breath and grinned at me. "Your pet's killed somebody else."

I walked around the fire and knocked him sprawling.

He may have touched Pouk when he fell, because Pouk sat up. He stared at Svon, blinking and rubbing his eyes.

I picked up the stick Svon had dropped and passed it to him. "Here. The meat's got ashes on it, but they won't hurt you." After that, I went over to where our baggage was piled and got my bow and quiver.

Svon sat up. (Maybe he thought I had gone—I had found out already that I could be hard to see sometimes ever since Baki.) He fingered the back of his jaw and the side of his neck, which was where I hit him.

"Had it comin'," Pouk told him.

Svon said, "I ought to cut off his base-born head," and I stepped back a little farther. I did not want to kill him, and I knew that if he saw me I might have to.

Pouk had been looking at the meat I had given him. He decided it needed more cooking, and held it over the fire. "Wouldn't try, not if I was you, sir."

"I am a gentleman, and gentlemen avenge any wrongs they suffer," Svon said stiffly.

"Had it comin'," Pouk repeated, "so it ain't wrong."

"You couldn't know. You were asleep."

I turned to go. Behind me, I heard Pouk say, "I knows him, sir, an' I knows you."

"I'll kill him!"

Very faintly: "If I thought you meant it, sir, I'd kill you meself."

CHAPTER 44

MICHAEL

If I had known where I was going when I walked away from the fire, I would tell you. The truth is that I did not have any idea. I wanted to get away from Svon, and I wanted to get away from Org. That was all there was to it. I wanted to find a place where I could rest and get my head straight before I had to deal with them again. I could have built a fire where I stopped; but working in the dark it would have taken a long time, I was tired, and it was not really very cold at all then, even at night. I suppose it was about the end of June or early July, but I do not know.

Anyway, I just closed my cloak around me the way you do and lay down. I did not even take off my boots, something I heard about from Uri and Baki later. They found me while I was lying there asleep, and so did Gylf, who went back to our fire and tracked me by scent. All three stayed around to protect me, I am not sure from what.

When I woke up, the sun was high and bright. As soon as I was awake Gylf licked my face; he had been waiting his chance, and it was something he did only when he thought I needed bucking up. I kind of grinned and told him I was okay, and when he did not say anything back to me I knew somebody else was around.

Baki waved from a shadow when she saw I was looking her way, and Uri waved from under the same tree. "We feared that you might come to harm, Lord. All three of us were afraid for you."

"Thanks." I stood up and looked around for a stream, hoping I could get a drink and splash some water on my face, and maybe even take off my clothes and take a sponge bath after they had gone. There was not any, so I asked where I could find Pouk and Svon.

"I do not know where they are now, Lord," Uri said, "but Baki and I will search for them if you wish us to."

Baki said, "Gylf might know," but he shook his head.

Uri drifted toward me, a pretty girl about as slender as girls get, dark red but transparent in the sunshine. (Think of a naked coppery-red girl in a stained-glass window.) "Why did you go into this forest alone and by night? Surely that was foolish."

"It would have been foolish to stay where I was. Is there any water around here?"

"No," Uri told me, "not for a league or more." But Gylf nodded.

"You had water where you camped," Baki pointed out. "It was in your water bottles."

"If I had stayed there, Svon and I would have fought," I explained. "Besides, I knew Org had killed, and I wanted to see what it was."

Baki said, "Oh, we can tell you that."

"It was a mule," Uri said. "A woman came up the road on a mule, and Org rushed at it. I do not think he was going to kill her."

Baki added, "But she thought he was."

"The mule reared and threw her. Then Org got it. That was what you heard."

"He ate it, too. A lot of it, anyway."

I thought that over. "The woman escaped?"

"Yes."

A cloud passed between us and the sun just then, and Baki came forward, very real. "She had a sword, but she ran just the same. I cannot blame her for it. Who would want to fight Org in the dark?"

"I would," I said, "or at least, I did. Maybe I'll want to again someday. I don't suppose you know where he is right now?"

Both shook their heads.

"Then find him for me. Or find Svon and Pouk. When you've found somebody, come back and tell me."

They faded to nothing.

"You said you knew where to find water," I told Gylf. "Is it very far?"

He shook his head. "A nice pool."

"Please lead me to it."

He nodded and trotted away, looking over his shoulder the way dogs do to see if I was coming.

I had to trot too, to keep up. "Nobody else is around, are they? You can talk?"

"I did."

"Did Uri or Baki know about this water of yours, too?"

"Uh-huh."

"But they wouldn't tell me. It can't have been because they wanted me to die of thirst. This is a forest, not a desert, so it can't be very hard to find water. Why didn't they want me to know about this water of yours?"

"A god's there."

That stopped me dead for a minute. Parka was the first thing I thought of, then Thunor—he was one of the Overcyns that people talked about a lot. "Nobody calls the Overcyns gods," I told Gylf. "Nobody around here, anyhow. Was this Parka? Do you know who Parka is?"

He did not answer, and by that time he was almost out of

sight. I took off after him, running as hard as I could, but I never caught up until he got to the pool and stopped.

I looked for a god then, but I did not see one, so I knelt down and washed my hands and my face (I was sweating a lot) and had a good, long drink.

After that I splashed more water on my face, and spooned some up with my hands and poured it over my head; and while I was doing that, the sun came out again. Sunlight turned the drops that rained from my fingertips to diamonds and struck deep into the pool. At the bottom, way, way down, I could see Uri and Baki. They were in a room that seemed to be about the size of an airport. It had swords and spears and axes all over the walls and in stands and long racks, so that you saw the gleam of steel everywhere you looked. They were talking to something big and dark that writhed like a snake. Uri turned back into a Khimaira while I was watching.

Soon it faded out. The sun was still bright but was not shining straight down anymore. Or that is what I think. As soon as it was gone, a cloud came—or what seemed like one—and Gylf said, "The god's here." He got excited sometimes and he sounded excited then, but quiet and polite too.

I looked up, and there was no cloud. It was a wing, so white it glowed and a lot bigger than the *Western Trader*'s biggest sail; it was coming from the back of a man in armor sitting at the edge of the pool. I could not believe that the wings—there were four—really belonged to him. Just by looking at me, he knew that I could not; so he folded them around him. When he did it, you could not see his armor—he looked like he was wearing a long robe of white feathers. He said, "I too have been sent away."

"You too!" I was so surprised I really did not know what I was saying. "I've been banished from Duke Marder's court until there's ice in the bay."

"Thus I come to you."

He sounded like he knew all about it. My jaw dropped so far it almost hit the buckle of my sword belt.

"I do not. Yet I know you better than your mother ever could, because I hear your thought." He raised his right hand. (Later I got to know King Arnthor, and he would have loved to be able to raise his hand like that, but he could not. No human can.) "Your mother never knew you," he said. "I, who know so little, know that now. I make mistakes, you see. I am near perfection."

I was on my knees with my head down by then.

"You have my thanks," he said, "but you must stand. I have not come for your worship, but to your aid. I, too, am a knight in service to a lord. My name is Michael."

All I could think of when he said that was that it was a name from our world. It seemed like a miracle then. It still does. He had a name from Earth, and he had come to Mythgarthr to help me.

"By putting my knowledge at your disposal."

I was so happy I could not think of anything to say. I stood up, remembering that he had told me to, and stared at him while he looked at me. There was no white to his eyes, and no black dot in the middle. It was like I was looking right through his head at Skai.

"You think of Skai, of the third world. You believe I have been dispatched from the castle you see there."

It was not easy to nod, but I did. "I—I hope so."

"I have not. I am of the second world, called Kleos, the World of Fair Report."

"I didn't even know the name of it, My Lord." I just about choked, realizing that I was talking to him the way I had to Thunrolf. "I . . . I'd like to get to that castle, if I could. Is that wrong?"

"It is a higher ambition than most."

"Can you . . ." I remembered Ravd and knew I was putting my foot in it. "Will you tell me how?"

Michael studied me again; it seemed to take a long time. Finally he said, "You know the rudiments of the lance."

I nodded, too scared to speak.

"You have been taught by one skilled with it." Michael snapped his fingers, and Gylf came over and lay down at his feet, looking very proud.

"Yes," I said. "By Master Thope. He was wounded too badly to practice with me, but he could tell me things, and one of his helpers would joust with me."

That made Michael smile. It was such a little smile that I could hardly see it, but it seemed like it made the sun brighter. "It does not trouble you that your dog prefers me to you?"

"No," I said, "I prefer you to me, too."

"I understand. Master Thope is skillful with the lance, but he will never reach the castle of which we are speaking. What lies beyond skill?"

I started to say something dumb, then I stopped. I do not even remember what it was.

"When you know, you will go there. Not before. Have you more questions? Ask now. I must soon depart."

"How can I find Queen Disiri?"

There was no smile at that. "Pray, rather, that she does not find you."

I felt like I had been kicked.

"Very well. I myself am less than perfect, as I have learned at cost. Learn to summon her, or any of them, and she must come to you."

"Uri and Baki come sometimes when I call them," I told him. "Is that what you mean?"

"No." Michael stroked Gylf's head. "You must call her, or any of them, as those you call Overcyns would call you."

"Will you teach me?"

Michael shook his head. "I cannot. No one can. Teach yourself. So it is with everything." He closed his eyes, and a one-eyed man with a spear came out of the trees, knelt, and laid his spear on the ground at Michael's feet. Gylf fawned on this one-eyed man.

Then he was gone, and the spear, too.

"You see? How could I, or anyone, teach that?"

I looked around at the bright pool and the sunlit glade. I was really looking for the one-eyed man—okay, for the Valfather, because that is who it was—but even then I knew I never could forget them. That was right enough. Later when I forgot about everything, even Disiri for a while, I still remembered them.

"If you have no more questions, Sir Able, I will go."

"I have more, Sir Michael." It was terribly hard to say that. "May I ask them? Three more, if . . ."

"If that is not too many. Ask."

"One time I was on—on a certain island, the island where Bluestone Castle used to be."

He nodded.

"And I saw a knight there, for just a moment. A knight with a black dragon on his shield. Did I call him, the way you called the Valfather?"

"He called you." Michael stood.

His wings opened a little, and I could see the gleam under the white glow. I said, "Can you fly in mail?"

Something that was not very far from a laugh showed in his sky-colored eyes. "That was not your second question."

"No. I was going to ask who the knight I saw was."

"Yes, I can. But I have come here to descend, not to fly. As for the knight you saw, I tell you that there was no one on that island save yourself."

"I don't understand that at all."

"Your third question is the wisest. Things always fall out so. Ask it."

"It was what question I should ask."

The smile returned. "You should ask whence came the tongs that grasped Eterne. Notice, please, that I did not say I would answer you. Farewell. I go to Aelfrice to seek that far-famed knight, Sir Able of the High Heart."

With that, Michael walked over the water to the middle of the pool and sank out of sight.

CHAPTER 45

THE COTTAGE IN THE FOREST

I spent the rest of that day doing something I had never done before, something I would have sworn on a stack of bibles that I would never do. I had seen a stone table at Sheerwall where they sacrificed before a war or battle, and I built one as much like it as I could beside that pool, carrying stones all day while Gylf hunted, and fitting them together sort of like a puzzle. I got it finished just before dark.

Next morning I collected a lot of deadwood, enough for a really big fire—that was a lot easier than the stones had been. I could break most of the pieces I found over my knee, and if I could not I laid them down so that they could not move when I hit them, and whacked them with Sword Breaker. Then Gylf and I went hunting together. He had brought in a partridge and a marmot the day before, but we were after something big for the sacrifice. Just about the time the sun touched the treetops we got a real nice elk. No antlers, of course, at that time of year; but it was a big bull just the same. If it had been in antler, they would have been good ones. I saw it on a ridge about two hundred yards away. My bowstring had about driven me crazy the night before, giving me other people's dreams; and I had been thinking of throwing it away. When I saw the elk I got glad I had it very fast. My arrow flew like lightning, catching the elk in back of the shoulder about halfway down. It ran like the wind at first, but Gylf got out in front and turned it, heading it back toward our table until it fell the last time.

I am big, thanks to Disiri, and lots of people have told me how strong I am; but I was not strong enough to carry that elk. I had to drag it, with Gylf pulling with his teeth over the tough parts. Finally I gave up. I told Gylf we couldn't do it, and we would have to take part to eat and leave the rest. Then he got big and black, and picked up the elk like a rabbit, and carried it for me. The funny thing was that I could tell even when he was big like that, that he was afraid I would be mad. I was not. Scared, sure. But not mad.

We got the elk up on the wood on the table, and covered it with more wood. Then we praised the gods of Kleos, both of us, and I set the wood on fire. It was only Gylf and me, but I had never felt as good about anything as I did that night.

When I finally got to sleep, it was the same thing it had been the night before. I was somebody, then somebody different, and then somebody new. Sometime I was back with you and Geri, only all of us were older. To tell the truth, I was glad when Uri woke me up. I knew I should be mad, but

I could not hack it. She said, "You spoke while you slept, Lord. I thought this best."

I told her yes, I had been a little girl that they were going to operate on, only I knew the anesthetic would not work on me and I would feel everything. "Okay, what is it?"

Baki bowed. "We have done as you bid us, Lord."

Uri nodded. "I have found your servant Svon, and Baki your servant Pouk."

I said that was swell, and I would go in the morning.

"To your servant Svon, Lord? Or to your servant Pouk?"

"They're separated?"

"Even so." Baki pointed. "Your servant Pouk is two days' ride north along the road we followed until you went alone into this forest, Lord."

I knew I was going to have to leave the pool—I had known that all along—but I did not like it. "Where's Org?" I asked.

Uri said, "Your servant Org is with Svon, Lord."

"I see. Master Agr gave me a charger, a chestnut stallion called Magneis. Where is he?"

Baki said, "I know him well, Lord. He is with your servant Pouk, Lord. All the horses are."

"Then I had better go to Pouk first. Which way to the road? Will I find him if I follow it north?"

"I cannot say, Lord. He will travel the faster, I believe. But no doubt he will halt when he reaches the mountains."

"He'll halt a lot sooner than that," I said, "if you tell him to. Find him again, and tell him I said for him to turn back south."

Both shook their heads. "He will not believe us," Uri declared. "He has not seen us, and will in no way trust us."

Baki said, "He will chant spells against us that may well destroy us, Lord. Will you send us to our deaths?"

I laughed. "Are you telling me that Pouk—Pouk, of all people—knows spells that will work against you Aelf?"

Uri looked around to make certain no one was listening, and spoke in a guilty whisper. "He is ignorant, Lord, and ignorant people are dangerous. They credit their spells."

Baki added, "He is of the old gods, Lord, even as you. His kind has not forgotten."

"You've got to obey us." It was a new thought for me.

"Yes, Lord. Even if we have fed you, we must. As you obey the Overcyns, Lord."

That was a barbed remark if there ever was one. We obeyed the Overcyns, mostly, only when we were afraid we could not get away with not obeying. I had been here long enough to see quite a lot of that.

The upshot was that I told them to go south and stay in Mythgarthr with Svon and Org while Gylf and I went after Pouk and the horses. Then I went back to sleep and slept like a baby.

While we were tramping through the woods next morning, Gylf wanted to know how it was that Pouk got all the horses.

"He and Svon fought," I said, "and Pouk won. He let Svon keep his money and his weapons, but he took the horses, Svon's included, and the camping gear."

"No sword."

I shook my head. "Right, Pouk doesn't have one. But there's a woman with him, that's what Uri and Baki said, and she's got a sword. She had the point at Svon's neck after Pouk knocked him down. That's what they said."

I stopped for a minute to think about that, and then I said, "I believe she must be the woman who had the mule that Org ate."

Gylf grunted. "Why's she here?"

"Uri and Baki didn't know. Or if they did, they weren't telling."

Gylf did not ask about the things I had seen when I had looked into the pool. I do not believe he had seen them, and I had not told him about them. I asked Uri and Baki though, and they had admitted the dark thing I had seen was Setr, calling him Garsecg to make him sound less threatening. He was a new god, they said, and they had to obey.

We reached the War Way a little after noon, and walked up it all afternoon without seeing anybody, and camped beside it that night.

About the time sunrise should have come, it started to rain, and the rain woke me up fast. I was cold—it was the first time I had been cold in quite a while—and wet and shaking. And hungry, with nothing to eat and Gylf gone. I piled sticks on our fire and cussed the smoke, and tried to get as warm and dry as I could for quite a while.

Finally it got lighter. I put out the fire and went off down the road in the rain, knowing Gylf would catch up.

Which he did after two or three hours. But the weather got worse and worse. It rained all the time, sometimes a little and sometimes a lot. The rain washed away the smells of the animals, so Gylf could not catch anything. After days of that, I stopped being hungry and started getting weak, and I knew we had to hold up and hunt—and get something, too, or we would die.

The next day we did, a young aurochs, the first I had ever seen. Gylf pinned him, and I ran up and stabbed him in the neck with my dagger. They look a little like a bull and a little like a buffalo. The place where he died was about as bad as it could possibly be, a thicket at the bottom of a steep little hollow. I could have asked Gylf to carry the aurochs like he had the elk, but I did not. I hacked off a haunch, and carried it to a place where it might be possible for us to build a fire if we were really, really lucky. That haunch probably weighed about a hundred pounds or maybe a hundred and fifty, but it felt like two tons by the time we found the place and I finally set it down. We built our fire and ate as much as we could hold, and listened to the wolves fighting over the rest.

A storm got me up the next morning, a real howler with driving rain and thunder walking from hill to hill. Trying to make a joke, I told Gylf I was afraid Mythgarthr was going to be dismasted.

"Like home," he said; our fire was out, but his eyes glowed crimson every time the lightning flashed.

I said, "What do you mean, home? We never lived any place with weather as bad as this."

"My mother. My brothers. My sisters, too."

I wanted to know where it was, but he stopped talking. All right, I knew he meant Skai; but I wanted him to talk about it. He never would say much about Skai.

We sat out the whole day, waiting for the rain to stop, and when it got dark I heard them. I think that was the only time I ever did until I got to Skai myself. I heard the baying of a thousand hounds like Gylf, and the drumming of the hooves as the Valfather's Wild Hunt swept across the sky. Gylf wanted to follow them, but I would not let him.

The weather was a little better the next day, but we could not find the War Way again. I knew we had turned west when we had left it to hunt, so we tried to walk east or northeast; but you could not see the sun so a lot of it was guesswork. Then too, there were about a hundred things in that forest to make us go south instead. Or north, or even west—thickets, tangles of briars, creeks high and fast with rainwater, and gulches.

Finally we hit a pretty good path and decided to follow it as long as it was not clearly going wrong. It ended at the door of a stone cottage that looked like it had been empty for years. Half the roof had fallen in. The shutters had fallen off or been blown off and were rotting in the grass and weeds. The door was open, hanging by one hinge.

"Nobody lives here," I told Gylf. "Let's stop and build a fire and hunt around for something to eat. Maybe we can get dry tonight."

"Path," he said.

"You're right, somebody made the path. But he doesn't live here. He couldn't. Probably he just comes around sometimes to look at it." I had no idea what for, but Gylf did not ask me.

"Knock," he told me when I got to the doorway.

It seemed silly, but I did, tapping on the ruined door with the pommel of my dagger. There was no welcome and no challenge from inside. I knocked harder to show my heart was in it, and called, "Hello? Hello?"

Gylf had been sniffing. He said, "Cat."

I looked around, surprised. "What?"

"Stinks. Cat's in there."

I stepped inside and said, "So am I."

Gylf came in after me, and a big black cat at the far end of the room hissed loud enough to scare you and ran up the wall into the loft.

The fireplace was full of dead ashes, but there were a couple of dry logs beside it, and some dry leaves and sticks in the kindling box. I stood one log on end and hit it with Sword Breaker hard enough to split it.

"Good one!" Gylf growled; and right when he said it, it seemed like somebody else said, "Food . . ." I looked around, but I did not see anyone.

I arranged the wood and the kindling, and got everything to burning good with my flint and firesteel. We had a little meat left from the aurochs. I got it all out and laid it on the hearth. "Take whatever you want," I told Gylf, "as long as you leave a couple pieces for me."

After that I went out into the rain again to cut a green stick.

CHAPTER 46

MANI

Cutting a stick probably did not take me very long, but standing out there in the rain and the cold, when I knew there was a fire in the cottage, it seemed like forever. I got one and ran back in, and it seemed to me I could hear somebody talking that shut up as soon as I came through the door.

Two of the pieces of meat I had laid on the hearth were gone. I picked up one of the others and put it on my stick and held it over the fire, trying to dry myself at the same time. Gylf came over and lay down, and I said, "Who were you talking to?"

He shook his head and went over to the dry corner and lay down there.

"You know," I said, "sometimes I wish you were just a regular dog that couldn't talk. If you were, I'd never be mad at you for not talking. Like now. You know there's somebody else in here with us, and I know it too. Only you won't tell me."

He did not say anything; I would have been surprised if he had.

When my meat was about done, I said, "I know there's somebody in here. I'm a knight, and my word means a lot to me. Whoever you are, I don't want to hurt you. If you'd like this nice piece I barbecued, just come out and say hello, and I'll give it to you."

Nothing.

I looked around carefully after that, the room being lit up by the fire and a whole lot brighter than it had been when we came in. There was nobody there but Gylf and me, and no furniture or anything that somebody might be hiding behind.

I bit off a piece of meat, chewed, looked around some more, and thought. Nobody was out on the path. I put my head out the one little window and looked around, and there was nobody there either. A dark doorway led to a little back room. There was an old string bed in there falling apart, with nothing on it but a bundle of dirty rags. "If there wasn't anybody here," I said out loud, "my dog would talk to me. But since you want to hide, I'm not going to look for you. I'd like to eat and dry my clothes. Is that okay? As soon as the rain lets up, we'll go. No hard feelings."

Nobody said anything, but Gylf went to the door and wagged his tail, which meant that he would like to leave right now. I said, "You're not tied up, are you? If you want to go I'm not about to stop you."

He went back to his corner.

"Is this somebody who might hurt us?" I asked him.

He shut his eyes.

"Up to you." I put the last piece of meat on my stick. "You won't talk to me? All right, I'll stop talking to you."

That meat was just about done when somebody whispered, "*Please . . . ?*"

I looked around. "If you'd like some of this, come and get it." (You used to say that when you were dishing up, remember?)

"Please . . . ?"

That time I knew where the whisper was coming from. There was somebody in that back room after all. I took the meat in there. "Are you too sick to walk?"

Nobody answered, but the bundle of rag on the bed moved. I held out the meat, and all of a sudden I was as scared as I had ever been in my life.

"I . . . Thank you. You . . . kind to an old woman." Here there is something I know you will never believe. It was the rain outside talking. The way the drops hit made the words. They said, "Her blessing . . . wherever . . ."

I crouched down beside the bed thinking I was letting the whole thing spook me, that there was somebody there—that there had to be—who needed help.

"I . . . bless. Curse."

I said, "How about if I pull off a little piece for you?"

"Never die . . ."

I thought that might be a yes, so I pulled off a little bit of the meat.

A mouth—a hole, really—opened in the rags. I put that little piece of meat into it. Her head came out of the rags after that. Only her head. It rolled to a place where the strings were broken and fell through onto the floor, and that piece of meat I had pulled off fell out of the mouth.

I will never forget that. I wish I could. I have tried to, but no go. It is always there.

Picking up that head was as hard as anything I have ever done, or almost. I did it just the same. The skin was like old leather; it did not feel dirty, or anything like that. I carried it back into the other room to show Gylf, and because of the firelight I had a better look at it in there. There were still a few dirty gray hairs on it, but the eyes were gone.

"This was talking to me, too," I told him. "I don't think it's going to talk any more, though. When I put some meat in its mouth it found out it was dead, or anyhow that's what it seems like. So it's gone, and you can talk now."

I really thought he was going to. That was why I said it. But what he really did was get up and go out into the rain.

I had been going to throw the head into the fire. That had been in the back of my mind all the time, but I did not do it. I set it down on the hearth and went to the door so I could wash my hands with rain, and I just kept going—out into the rain with Gylf.

It finally stopped a little before sundown. I took off my clothes and wrung them out. They had been pretty dirty, but the rain had given them a good washing and washed me too. "My armor's going to rust," I told Gylf, "but there's nothing I can do about that. Sand will take the rust off, if we ever find any. And oil will keep it from rusting more. Oil or grease, if we can't find oil." I was shivering.

"Fire?" That was the first time Gylf had talked since he had clammed up in the cottage.

"If I can find stuff dry enough to burn. I'll look."

"I'll hunt," Gylf told me.

I said go ahead, but keep an eye out for the road.

He started to leave, and an idea hit me. "Wait. You weren't talking to that dead person, were you? Because if you had been, you'd have told me when I brought in the head. So who was it?"

He would not look at me.

"I thought that's who it had been. But the voice you talked

to was inside. When she talked the voice was outside, the raindrops talking for her somehow. Besides, the voices weren't the same. Okay, if you weren't talking to the dead person, who was it?"

Gylf had left before I finished. I cussed a little, calling him a stiff-necked fool dog and so on; and when I finally shut up, somebody who sounded scared sort of whined, "It was I."

I grabbed for Sword Breaker, but there was nobody around.

"You have wonderful muscles," the new voice said. "Do you stretch a lot?"

I nodded, still looking around and not seeing anybody.

"So do I. I can show you a kind of tree that will burn when it's wet. Would you like to see it?"

I had been trying to decide whether it was a woman or a man; but the voice could have been either one, and there were tones in it that did not sound like a real person at all. I said, "Yes, we could really use wood like that. Please show me where it is."

"It's not much farther than you could roll a ball." The soft voice had gotten fretful, like a tired little kid. "Do you think we could dry ourselves in front of the fire?"

I said, "Sure. I'm going to put my boots on, but I'll leave my armor and clothes here. Is that okay?"

He did not say anything, so I said, "Listen, you don't have to do this if you don't want to, but could you maybe let me in on what you and Gylf were talking about back there?"

"He doesn't like me."

I was pulling on my boots. That is never much fun, but now my feet were wet and so were they, and it was flat mean. When I got the left one on, I said, "I'm sorry to hear that."

"How do you feel? About me, I mean." It was a purling,

puling, mewling sort of a voice, and sometimes it reminded me of seagulls.

I did not like it much, but I had the feeling I would get used to it pretty soon. Besides, it was going to show me that wood, so I said, "Really friendly. If you're right and this kind of tree you're talking about will burn for us, hey, I'll be your friend for as long as you want me."

"Do you mean it?" It was a little closer now.

"Absolutely." I was getting my other boot on.

"You were kind to the witch, but I'm not dead."

"I didn't know she was dead 'til afterward," I said. "I didn't know she was a witch, either. Gylf and I thought she was still alive, because of the path."

"Oh, she got up and went out sometimes."

That shook me, and he saw it. He laughed. It was not a nice laugh, and was not like any other laugh I ever heard in my life.

When I stood up, he said, "It's called pitch pine. Did you mean that? About being friends? You'll have to whittle some shavings first. I never promised you wouldn't have to do that, you know."

"No problem."

"About being friends," he asked, "was that serious?"

"You bet," I said. "You and me are pals for life."

"Well, I need a new owner, and a knight might be nice, but you've got that big bow. Did the string get wet?"

"The string's in my pouch here." I picked it up and showed him. "It's probably still pretty dry, but I'm not about to take it out to see."

"You wouldn't like me."

I said, "I *do* like you. Honest."

"To eat. Possibly you hate us. Many men do, and your dog does."

I tried then to think of something I really hated. When I had been where they kept the ropes on the ship I had hated the rats, but after a while it came to me that it was crazy. They were just animals. I tried to kill them, sure, because once or twice they bit me when I was asleep. But there was no point in hating them, and I quit. Finally I said, "I try not to hate anything, even rats."

"I am *not* a *rat.*"

"I never said you were."

The limbs of a bush over to my right trembled a little, spilling a few drops of water. When I saw that, I figured he was pretty small. In a way, that was right. But it was wrong too.

I said, "Are you invisible?"

"Only at night. Follow me."

"I can't see you."

"Follow my voice."

I did the best I could, leaving the glade where I hoped to build a fire and tramping though the wet forest. I felt like I was going to freeze solid.

"Over here."

That was the first time I saw him (except it was really the second). There had been something black on a fallen log, but it was gone before I got a good look.

"Right here. See the little tree?"

I said, "I think so."

"Break a twig and smell it. Remember the smell. The sap will get on your hands and make them sticky."

The little knife I had carved my bow with was in the pouch with my bowstring. After I had broken a twig like he said, I got it out and cut off eight or nine branches.

"See how the sap runs wherever the tree is hurt?"

"Sure," I said. "Will it burn?"

"Yes, it will. So will the needles."

I carried everything back to where I had left my sword belt and so on, and whittled away at the branches until I had a big pile of shaving and pine needles, with everything soggy with sap. By the time I finished, my knife was black. So were my hands.

"I don't like it either," his soft voice told me, "but it's a nice color."

"The sap color you mean. It only looks black because dirt sticks to it." I was rubbing my hands with wet leaves, which hardly helped at all.

"Black is the boldest color and the best. The most dramatic."

I said, "Okay, if this stuff burns good I'll love it no matter what color it is." I quit rubbing and got out my flint and firesteel. The first good shower of sparks got me a hissing, popping yellow flame.

"See?"

"I sure do." I was picking up dead wood to throw on my fire. "You know, you're a really nice cat."

"You saw me?"

"Yeah, when you ran up into the loft. That was you."

"You don't hate us? Many men do." The cat popped up out of some wildflowers on the other side of the glade. It was awfully small for a person, and it was a darned big cat, maybe the biggest I ever saw.

"I like you," I said. "I'd like to pet you. I mean, when I get my hands clean."

"You could lick them, couldn't you?" The cat did not seem very sure about that but was willing to try it on me. "My name's Mani, by the way."

"I'm Sir Able of the High Heart," I said. "Pleased to meet you, Mani."

By the time I had a good big fire going, Mani was rubbing up against my legs.

CHAPTER 47

GOOD MASTER CROL

"Rabbits. Best I could do." Gylf dropped them near my head. "But I found it."

I sat up, rubbing my eyes. "You found the War Way?"

"Yep."

"That's wonderful!"

Gylf grunted and lay down. I could tell he was tired. "People, too."

I was cutting off the head and paws of the biggest rabbit so I could skin it. "Nice people?"

"Tried to tie me up."

"I see. Were they woodcutters or something?"

He took his time with that one. Finally he said, "Don't know."

I was busy pulling off the skin.

"Cook for me?"

"Sure. The whole rabbit if you want it. You caught it, after all."

From a limb about ten feet up, Mani said, "You might pass that head, if there's no call for it down there."

Gylf growled.

I picked the head up by the ears and tossed it into the leaves where Mani could grab it. "Mani's our friend," I told Gylf.

He just shook his head.

"I think you'd better get over this business of not talking while he's around. It's not like he's a man or a woman or even one of the Aelf. He's an animal like you, and he's heard you already. In fact, you talked to *him* when I wasn't there."

"Right."

"Thanks." I rubbed his ears. "You're the best dog in the world, you know that? You're my best friend, too."

From up on the limb, Mani said, "Do you know some Aelf? That sounded like it."

"Yes, and when we met I thought you might be one. But there was a little sunshine while we were building the fire, and you didn't dodge it."

"I'm a cat," Mani explained.

Gylf curled his lip.

"I get it. Gylf, how about if you tell me what you and Mani were talking about when I came into the cottage? Is it something I ought to know?"

He shook his head until his ears flapped. "Nope!"

"Are you ashamed of what you said? We all say stuff when we're mad that we're ashamed of afterward."

He was quiet.

"We say it," I said, "but it takes a big dog to admit it." I felt kind of silly then, but to tell you the truth I would a lot sooner talk to animals than to most people.

"He's ashamed of having spoken to me," Mani explained, "exactly as I am ashamed of having spoken to a dog. You will recall the meat you left in front of our fire."

That reminded me of the rabbits, and I got back to work.

"He was gobbling it," Mani continued, "when I, being famished, skillfully snatched a piece from under his greedy nose."

"I see." I got up to cut a green stick.

"He called me names, dog fashion. Vile epithets. I pointed out that he himself was a mere vagabond who had entered my mistress's home without the least invitation or exculpation in law. He informed me—I omit his insults—that he was the dog of a noble knight, giving your name."

I put the rabbit I was going to cook for Gylf on my stick. "I notice that you didn't try to steal any meat while I was cleaning this."

"I hope to persuade you to cook some fraction of one of your remaining rabbits for me," Mani said politely.

"But you're still eating the head," I said, positioning the rest of the rabbit over the fire.

"True. I thank you for that."

"So Gylf gets the first piece. After that, I get a piece, because I've never had any yet. But I'll give you another piece when we've gotten ours."

"I am confident of your generosity."

"Will you talk when there are other people around? Gylf won't."

"Good news! Let them come and silence him." Mani let the rabbit's skull fall. "As for me, it will depend on who they are, I suppose. How they feel about cats and so forth. I'll have to see." He began to wash his paws.

"So will I. Do you object to a test?"

He did not reply, and I took his silence for agreement. I called, "Uri! Baki! I need you."

I was expecting one or both to step out of the darkness of the surrounding trees, but neither did.

"Uri! Baki!"

Mani coughed politely. "Yelling like that could bring us unwelcome guests, if I may say it without offense."

"They're mad at me for making them stay up here when the sun is out," I explained. "Sunshine doesn't really hurt them much unless they stand in it, but they don't like it."

"Uri and Baki are of the Aelf, I take it. Watch that meat of ours, please."

I did.

"Do you really know Aelf? I mean, are you on friendly terms with them? Normally?"

"I'm not as friendly as I'd like to be with one of them," I said.

Mani wanted me to explain, and I did, a little; but I did not like it, and when he saw I did not he shut up. We cooked the rest of the rabbits, sharing them between the three of us, but there was not a lot said after that.

There was still rain on the grass when we struck the War Way next morning. Gylf ran in front to show me the way; when Mani was not riding on my shoulder, he trailed behind to stay away from Gylf. Half an hour's fast walking got us in sight of some pavilions where sleepy servants were tidying up and seeing to a hundred or more horses and mules. A man-at-arms with a partisan stepped into the road to make us stop.

"I'm Sir Able of the High Heart," I said, "a knight of Sheerwall Castle who's been lost in this forest. If you'll lend me a horse, I'll be very grateful, and I'll return it as soon as I rejoin my servant, who has my own horses."

The man-at-arms bawled for his sergeant, a somewhat older man-at-arms who had a steel cap and a hard leather shirt. I explained all over again, and the sergeant said, "You'll have to ask Master Crol, sir. That your hound?"

"Yes. His name's Gylf."

"We seen him last night and tried to catch him, but he give us the slip. Good huntin' dog?"

"The best."

"Well, you come along with me, sir." The sergeant patted Gylf's head, which Gylf tolerated to show there were no hard feelings. "Had any breakfast?"

I shook my head. "We ate a couple of rabbits last night, and to tell the truth I was really glad to get them. But that was supper for Gylf and me, and for my cat. I didn't get as much as I wanted, and they didn't either."

"You got a cat, sir?" The sergeant looked around without seeing Mani.

"Somewhere." I could not help smiling. "He's only invisible at night, so I suppose he's hiding 'til he finds out if you're friendly."

"I ain't, sir. I'm a dog man, myself. What's a cat good for anyhow?"

Gylf barked softly.

"Well," I said, "I talk to mine. You can learn a lot from a cat."

A servant carried a big tray loaded with steaming food into the nearest pavilion. The sergeant said, "That'll be breakfast for Master Crol, and them other upper servants, sir. Let's see if Master Crol wants to talk while eatin'. If he does, maybe you'd get a bite too."

I said I hoped so.

"Master Crol's a cat man, I guess. He's got a dozen back at the castle, anyhow. Might be best if you left the hound with me, sir. I won't hurt him."

"I know you wouldn't," I told him, "but I'm going to take him with me just the same. If Master Crol objects to him, I'll walk."

The sergeant grinned and touched his steel cap. "Wait here, sir. Shouldn't take long."

It took quite a bit longer than I hoped, but that gave me a chance to rub Gylf's ears and look around at the camp, which was big. There had to be close to fifty servants of one kind or another, and a bunch of archers and men-at-arms.

"He'll see you now, sir," the sergeant said when he came

out. When he was closer, he lowered his voice. "I told him about your dog. He said it was all right."

The inside of the pavilion was dark after the sunshine outside, but I could see three men eating at a small table. "Good Master Crol?"

The man facing me motioned me to come closer. "You are Sir Able, one of Duke Marder's knights?"

I said I was.

"Lost? And you'd like something to eat?"

"Most of all, I'd like you to lend me a decent horse," I said, "but I'd like a bite to eat, too, if it's not too much trouble."

"What if it is?"

I could not tell whether he was looking for a fight or making a joke. I said, "Then let me borrow a horse, please, and I'll be gone."

He clapped his hands. "We must get you something to sit on, Sir Able. Does that hound eat as much as I think?"

Gylf wagged his tail, so I said, "More."

"I'll have them bring something for him."

One of the other men got up. "I've had enough, and had better see to business. You may have my seat, Sir Able, if you want it."

I said thanks and sat. "I've got a cat, too. He seems to be hiding just now."

"I understand."

"I'd like a little food for him, too, when I find him."

A servingman came in, and Crol told him to take away the dirty trencher the other man had been eating from and bring me a clean one. "And bones. With meat on them."

"I'm Master Papounce," the man across the table said. "The servants are my charge. Master Egr, who just left, has the baggage train and the muleteers. Sir Garvaon has our men-at-arms and archers."

Crol added. "They're in the big pavilion. Can you use that bow?"

It was what Master Agr had asked me once. "I can shoot as well as most men," I said.

"We might have a match tonight," Papounce suggested. "Sir Garvaon's a fine bowman."

"I'll be far ahead of you," I said, "if I can get a horse."

"That's up to Master Crol. He's Lord Beel's herald, and he's in charge of everything save Sir Garvaon's men."

Crol shook his head. "His Lordship must see him. I—"

Two servingmen came in, one with a clean trencher for me, butter, and a basket of rolls, the other with a big bowl of scraps and bones for Gylf.

When they had gone and Gylf was cracking bones, Crol tugged at his beard. It was a black spade beard, as I could see by then. The face above it looked old enough to make me wonder whether that black was not a dye job. He said, "You are not of noble lineage, Sir Able?"

I shook my head, and tried to explain that our father had run a hardware store; when I saw that was going to get me into more trouble, I said that my brother Bold Berthold had raised me and he had been a peasant.

Papounce asked, "But aren't you a knight? That's what we were told."

"I am," I said. "I'm a knight in the service of Duke Marder of Sheerwall."

"My own parents were peasants," Crol said. "I became a man-at-arms. My father was proud of me, but my brothers were jealous."

"Bold Berthold would have been proud of me, I know," I said, "and if he were well, and young again, I would have him in a mail shirt and a steel cap as quick as I could work it.

I've never known anyone as brave as he was, and he was strong enough to wrestle bulls."

"You're strong yourself?" Crol's teeth gleamed between the black beard and his black mustache.

I shrugged.

He reached across the table. "Let's see you squeeze my hand while I squeeze yours."

I missed my grip, and Crol's hand (bigger even than mine) closed on mine like a vise. I kicked the pain out of my head, if you know what I mean, and I became the storm pounding the cliff Garsecg and I had stood on, wave after wave, with boulders flying in them like Ping-Pong balls.

"Enough."

I let go.

"If I were Duke Marder, I'd have knighted you myself. What Lord Beel may make of you, I don't know. Have you had enough to eat? We can go over and see if he and his daughter are up."

Papounce leaned toward Crol and whispered long enough for me to grab another bite of ham.

"I won't mention your father or your brother," Crol told me. "If you didn't mention them either, that might be wise."

"I won't, unless Lord Beel—"

Something big, heavy, and soft hit my lap, and Mani's head, bigger than my fist, came up over the edge of the table to look at my trencher. I could not help grinning at him, and Crol and Papounce laughed; and then a big black paw put out claws big enough to hook salmon and latched on to the rest of my ham.

Crol said, "We'll stay a minute or two longer. No harm done."

"Thanks. I wanted to say that I'm not ashamed of my family. It may hurt me here, like it did in Sheerwall, but nothing anybody says will make me ashamed of them. As for Bold Berthold, I told you about him. I told Sir Ravd once, and his opinion was pretty close to mine."

Papounce said, "He's a doughty knight, from what we hear."

"He's dead," I told them. "He died four years ago." I pushed my little stool back and stood up.

CHAPTER 48

TOO MUCH HONOR

Beel's pavilion was the richest. The walls and roof were crimson silk, and the ropes were braided silk cords. The poles were turner's work, of some dark wood that looked purple when the sun hit it. The men-at-arms guarding it saluted Crol as three maids came fluttering out like a little flock of sparrows; the first one was carrying a basin of steaming water, the second one towels, and the third one soap, sponges, and what may have been a bundle of laundry.

"We'll have to wait a bit," Crol remarked as one of the men-at-arms rapped a pole; but a servingman with the face of a sly mouse popped out of the door to tell us to come in.

Beel sat at a folding table on which a platter of quail smoked and sputtered; his daughter, a doe-eyed girl about sixteen, sat beside him on a folding chair. She was picking bits from one of the quail.

Beel himself, a middle-aged man so short you noticed it even when he was sitting down, studied Mani, Gylf, and me, smiled just a little, and said, "You bring me a witch knight, I see, Master Crol. Or a wild knight, perhaps. Which is it?"

Crol cleared his throat. "Good morrow, Your Lordship. I trust you slept well."

Beel nodded.

"I thought it would be better for Sir Able to fetch along his dog and cat, Your Lordship, because Your Lordship was bound to hear about them. Then Your Lordship would have wanted to know why I hadn't let Your Lordship see them for yourself, and quite right too. If they offend, we can take them away, Your Lordship."

The thin smile returned as Beel spoke to me. "I usually see no one but my herald with a cat upon his shoulder. It's a novelty to see somebody else wearing one. Are you as fond of them as Crol is?"

I said, "Of this one, My Lord."

"Sanity at last. He has a score, I swear. His favorite is white, though, and nothing like the size of that monster. Would he like a bird, do you think?"

Beel held up a quail; and Mani jumped from my shoulder to the tabletop, accepted it with both front paws, made Beel a dignified little bow, leaped from the table to the ground and disappeared behind the tablecloth.

"Witch, wizard, or warlock," Beel muttered. "Leave us, Master Crol."

"But, Your Lordship—"

Beel silenced him with a gesture; another sent him hurrying away.

"Is that a glamour, Sir Knight? Are you in fact an aged crone? What form would you show if I were to lash your face with a witch-hazel wand?"

I said, "I don't know, My Lord. I'm really a boy about

your daughter's age. Maybe you'd see, if you did that. I can't be sure."

The smile flickered and died. "I know the feeling. Sir Able, is it? You are a knight? That's what everyone tells me."

"Yes, My Lord. I'm Sir Able of the High Heart."

"Do you wish to travel with us to Jotunland? That's what I gathered from the man I talked to."

"No, My Lord. I only want to borrow a horse so I can catch up with my servant." Just then it struck me that Pouk might have passed them on the road; and I said, "Have you seen him? A young man with a big nose and one eye?"

Beel shook his head. "Suppose I give you a horse, a good one. Will you leave us?"

"At once, My Lord, if you're willing I should. And I'll return it as soon as I can."

"We're traveling north, and won't halt until we reach Utgard. Will you follow us there? To return my horse?"

"I'm going to ride ahead of you," I explained. "I'm supposed to take my stand at a mountain pass and challenge all comers. Before we engage, I'll return your horse and thank you."

Beel's daughter giggled.

Her father gave her a look that would have shut up almost anybody. "I am on the king's business, Sir Able."

I said, "A great honor, My Lord. I envy you."

"But you'll fight me just the same?"

"I'm honor bound to do it, My Lord. Or to fight your champion, if you designate one."

Beel nodded. "I have Sir Garvaon with me, the bravest of my knights and the most skilled. Will he do?"

"No problem, My Lord."

"When he breaks your head and a few other bones, will you expect us to stay our errand to nurse you?"

I said, "Of course not."

"You don't fancy yourself invincible? I ask because I was told you were."

"No, My Lord. I've never said that, and I never would."

"I didn't say you said it, only that I had been told you thought it. Yesterday, Sir Garvaon mentioned that one of his men had driven off a crippled beggar."

He waited for me to talk after he said that, so I said, "I hope he gave him something first."

"I doubt it. I had Sir Garvaon's man brought to me. I expect beggars in Kingsdoom, not in the wild, and I asked him what the beggar was doing out here. He'd told Sir Garvaon's man that he was searching for a most noble knight, Sir Able by name, who had promised to take him into his service. You look surprised."

I was, and I admitted it.

"Who was this beggar, Sir Able? Have you any notion?"

I shook my head.

Beel's daughter said, "You must have given him a few coins and a kind word once." Her voice was soft, and it made me think of a guitar that some girl was playing alone in a garden at night.

I waited for her to go on, because I wanted to hear more if it, but she did not. Finally I said, "If I did, My Lady, I've forgotten it completely."

"A noble knight," Beel said it as if he were talking to himself, although I knew he was not. "My grandfather was His Majesty's grandfather as well, Sir Able."

I bowed, not really knowing whether I should or not. "It's an honor to me just to talk to you, My Lord."

"My father was a prince, the younger brother of His Majesty's father. It is no small distinction."

"I know that," I said.

"I myself am a mere baron, but my older brother is a duke. If he and his son were to perish, I would be duke in my turn, Sir Able."

I did not know what to say, so I just nodded.

"A mere baron. And yet I have my cousin's confidence. Thus I am sent to the King of the Angrborn bearing rich gifts, in the hope that my protestations will terminate his incursions. I do not tell you all this to boast, Sir Able. I have no need to boast, or even to impress you. I tell you so that you will understand that I know whereof I speak."

I nodded again. "I don't doubt it, My Lord."

"I could name to you every knight of noble birth—and not the names merely, but the family connections and deeds of valor as well. Not of some. Not of most. Of all."

"I understand, My Lord."

"I am equally familiar with every young man of noble lineage who would be a knight. There is no nobly born knight in all Celidon named Able. Nor is there any nobly born youth of that name, whether aspirant to knighthood or not."

I should have caught on before that, but I had not. Now I finally got it. I said, "I'm not of noble birth, My Lord. I guess that beggar said I was? But he probably doesn't know anything about me."

"Crol thought you noble. Did you sense it?"

I shook my head. "I told him I wasn't."

"He did. It was apparent in his behavior. Your lofty stature, your physique, and your face—your face most of all—might support a claim to nobility."

"Well, I won't make one." I felt like I did sometimes in school then, and it was hard not to fidget.

"I was tempted to invite you to sit when Crol brought you in. I am tempted still."

That got me a nice smile from the daughter that meant she would not have minded.

Beel coughed. "I will not, however, Sir Able. I ought to inform that as a matter of policy I almost never sit with my inferiors."

"It's your table," I said.

"So it is. Sitting encourages familiarity, and I am forced to punish men whom I myself have corrupted." Beel shook his head. "I have done that once or twice. I did not find it pleasant."

I said, "I bet they didn't, either."

"True. But—"

The daughter interrupted us. "May I pet your cat?" As soon as she said that, Mani came out from under the table and jumped into her lap.

"I asked the man I questioned whether the noble knight of whom the beggar had spoken thought himself invincible." I would have expected Beel to be angry then, but he was smiling while he waited for my answer.

"It seems like a funny question," I said. "I doubt if there's any such knight, anywhere."

Here I have to stop to say that Beel's pavilion was divided into halves by a curtain—more scarlet silk, but not as heavy as the outside stuff. I have to say it because Baki peeked around it and grinned at me.

"I agree," Beel was saying. "But my question only seems odd. I asked it because of something one of the sons of my kinsman Lord Obr had told me the day before."

I can be pretty stupid sometimes, but I got that one. "Squire Svon?"

"Yes. I think you know him."

"He's my squire, My Lord."

Beel shook his head. "Not if he has deserted you. He said that he had not, but it seemed to me otherwise."

"He didn't." I suppose that should have been hard to say, but it was not; I knew it was the truth and I wanted to get it out.

"I am delighted to hear it. You are going to the Northern Mountains to take your stand in a pass. For how long, Sir Able?"

"'Til there's ice in the sea, My Lord. Ice in the Bay of Forcetti."

"Midwinter, in other words." Beel sighed. "I would not have been astonished if you had told me Svon deserted you."

I shook my head. "He didn't."

Beel sighed again and turned to his daughter. "He is a connection of your grandmother's, a younger son of Lord Obr's. Obr is your great-aunt's nephew."

She nodded.

"Young Svon told me certain things. It is unpleasant to question the veracity of those nobly born, but his—he . . ."

I waved it away. "I get it."

"So does Idnn, I'm sure," Beel said, and turned back to her. "He was squire to a certain Sir Ravd, a knight of high repute. He is said to have deserted him on the field of battle. I am not saying he did so—I doubt that he did. But his character is such that the lie could be believed. You understand?"

The daughter (that was Idnn) said, "You must have known him better than my father, Sir Able. Do you believe it?"

I said, "No, My Lady. I don't believe things like that unless I see proof, and nobody seems to have any."

Beel's thin smile was back. "I asked him what he was doing among these unpeopled hills, as anyone would. He told me a great deal, not all of which I credited. For one thing, he told me he had been made squire to a peasant now called a knight."

He waited for me, but I stayed quiet.

"You are, of course, of gentle birth, Sir Able?"

"I'm not. I won't go into my family—you wouldn't believe me if I did. But basically, Svon's right."

Beel's eyes got just a little bit wider.

"I want to say this, though. Please listen. I really am a knight, and I haven't told you a single lie. I didn't lie to your herald either. Or to the sergeant that brought me to him."

Gylf pushed against my leg then to show that he was on my side.

"This puts things in a new light." Beel clapped, and the mousy-looking servingman scampered in right away.

"We've kept Sir Able standing much too long, Swert. Fetch another chair."

The servingman nodded and ran off to get one.

Beel said, "I want to make certain there is no mistake. Your father was a peasant."

"My father sold hammers and nails. Things like that. He died while I was young, so I have to say I never really knew him. But I know what my brother said, and what other people have said. If we were back home, I could show you where his store was."

"Good. Good! And how did you learn the secret arts? May I ask that? Who taught you?"

I said, "Nobody, My Lord. I don't know anything about magic."

Idnn giggled.

"I understand. One takes certain oaths, Idnn. Oaths one dares not break." Beel smiled at me. "I am an adept myself, Sir Able. I will question you no more, if you do not question me. I might say, however, that young Svon himself had noticed certain—irregularities is too strong a word, perhaps. Certain phenomena, while in your company."

The servingman came back with a folding chair, very

pretty, with silver fittings. He opened it up and set it at the table where I would be across from Idnn. Beel nodded and I sat down, taking it easy because I was not sure the chair would hold me. Gylf lay down next to me.

"I spent much of my boyhood in a peasant's house," Beel told me. "It was my nurse's, outside my father's castle of Coldcliff. When my older brothers were at their lessons in the nursery, my nurse would take me home so that I might play with her own children. We had great games, and ran through the wood. And fished, and swam. Doubtless it was much the same for you."

I nodded, remembering. "Yeah, I did all that, and I lay on my back in the grass, sometimes, to watch the clouds. I don't think I've done that since I came here."

Beel turned to Idnn. "It's good for you to hear all this, though you may not think so now."

She said, "I'm sure it is, Father."

"You see our peasants plowing and sowing, and their women spinning and so forth, hard work that lasts from the rising of the sun until its setting in many cases. But you need to understand that they have their own prides and their own pleasures. Speak kindly to them, protect them, and deal fairly with them, and they will never turn against you."

"I'll try, Father."

He turned back to me. "I must explain to you what has been running through my mind. This hill country is by no means safe, and the mountains will be worse. We have Sir Garvaon and his archers and men-at-arms to protect us. But when I saw you, I was minded to keep you with me. A young knight—and more than a knight—brave and strong, would be a welcome augment to our force."

"It's really nice for you to say that," I began, "but—"

"Examining you more closely, however, I feared you might prove overly attractive to Idnn."

I felt my face get hot. "My Lord, you do me too much honor."

His thin smile came again. "Of course I do. But so might she." He glanced sidelong at her. "Idnn's blood was royal, not so long ago. Now it represents the cream of the nobility. Soon she will be a child no more."

Thinking how it had been with me I said, "For her sake, I hope she stays right where she is a while longer."

"As do I, Sir Able. When I had considered those things, I thought to give you the horse you asked of me and hurry you on your way."

"That's—"

"But a peasant!" Beel's smile was wider than it had been. "A peasant lad could not hold the smallest attraction for the great-granddaughter of King Pholsung."

Idnn's left eyelid sort of drooped when he said that. He did not see it because he was looking at me, but I did.

"Therefore, Sir Able, you are to remain with us for as long as we have need of you. Sir Garvaon's pavilion will hold one more cot. It must, and Garvaon himself will welcome a companion of his own rank, I know."

"My Lord, I can't."

"Can't ride with us, and eat good food, and sleep like a human being?"

Idnn added her acoustic guitar to her father's gargly tenor. "For me, Sir Able? What if I'm killed because you weren't with me?"

That made it rough. "My Lord, My Lady, I promised—no, I swore—that I'd go straight to the mountains to take my stand, as His Grace Duke Marder and I had agreed."

"And stay there," Beel said, "until midwinter. Nearly half a year, in other words. Tell me something, Sir Able. Were you riding swiftly when you came to us? Did you gallop up to this pavilion and leap from the saddle to stand before me with Master Crol?"

"My Lord—"

"You had no horse. Isn't that the fact? You came to me to borrow one."

Not knowing what to say, I nodded.

"I am offering to give you one. Not a loan, a gift. I will give it on the condition that you will travel with my daughter and me until we reach the pass you intend to hold. I ask you this single question. Will you travel faster by riding with us, or by walking alone? Because you must do one or the other."

Mani poked his head above the table to grin at me, and I wanted to kick him.

CHAPTER 49

THE SONS OF THE ANGRBORN

Upward, always upward sloped the land that day and the next, and as day followed day I came to understand that we were among the towering, rocky hills which I had glimpsed a time or two from the downs north of the forest in which I had lived like an outlaw with Bold Berthold, and that the true mountains, those mountains of which we had scarcely heard rumors, the mountains that lifted snow-covered peaks into Skai, were still before us, and still remote.

Then I left the War Way and Beel's lumbering train of pack horses and mules, and rode up one of those hills as far as the white stallion he had given me could carry me, and dismounted when my stallion could go no farther, and tied him to a boulder and scrambled up to the summit. From there I could see the downs, and the dark forest beyond them, and even glimpse bits of the silver thread that was the Griffin. "Tomorrow I'll find the spring it rises from," I promised myself, "and drink from the Griffin in honor of Bold Berthold and Griffinsford." I did not say that to Gylf, because Gylf had stayed behind to guard my stallion. Or to Mani, because Mani was riding with Idnn, tucked into a black velvet bag, generally with his head and forelegs sticking out. I would have said it to Uri and Baki if I could, but I had not seen either of them since Baki had peeked around Idnn's curtain.

I said it to myself, as I said, and even though I knew how foolish it was, I did not laugh.

The wind was cold enough up there to make me wrap myself in the gray boat cloak Kerl had kept for me and pull up the hood, and blowing hard enough to make me wish the thick wool was thicker, too; but I stayed up there for more than an hour looking, and thinking about the kid I used to be, and what I was now. I was all alone, the way I used to be when I told Bold Berthold I was going hunting and wandered off hunting memories through the forest and sometimes out to the edge of the forest and onto the downs, where I always sighted elk but the elk were always too far.

All right, I was not going to write this, but I will. When I had been up there a long time and settled everything in my mind, I remembered Michael; and I tried to call Disiri to me the way he had called the Valfather. It did not work, and I cried.

The sun was low in the west by the time I got back to Gylf and the stallion. "They went on," Gylf said, and I knew he meant that the last mule and the rear guard—I was supposed to be bossing the rear guard—had passed him on the road below a long time ago.

I said I knew it, but that we would catch up to them pretty quick.

"Want me to scout?"

I thought about that while I rode down the hill. I had been alone for quite a while and had enough of it. I wanted company and somebody to talk to. But I knew Gylf pretty well by that time, and I knew he did not volunteer to go hunting or protect something, or anything else, unless he was pretty sure it ought to be done. So he had heard something or seen something or most likely smelled something that worried him. Naturally I started listening, and sniffing the wind, and all that, even though I knew perfectly well that his ears were sharper than mine and I might as well not have had a nose.

"Want me to?"

So he was really worried. "Yeah," I said, "go right ahead. I'd appreciate it."

As soon as I said that, he was off like an arrow. It was a brown arrow at first, but a black arrow before it had gone very far. Then I heard him baying as he ran, that deep bay you hear from clear up in Skai, when the lead hound is all alone out in front of the pack and even the Valfather on his eight-legged hunter cannot keep up.

He woke the thunder. You will say no way, but he did. It boomed way off among the real mountains; but it was there, and getting closer. I wanted to spur my stallion then, but he was still picking his way among the rocks. Finally, just to make myself feel better, I told him, "Go as fast as you can without breaking your legs or mine. I don't think a broken leg's going to be much help out here."

He nodded like he understood. I knew he did not, but it

was nice just the same. Mani liked to brag and he liked to argue, and right then I liked my white horse a lot better.

"Hey," I said, "I get to do all the talking. Cool!"

His ears turned to me. I think it was his way of saying that he was a good listener.

As soon as he had grass under his hooves, I gave him the spurs (gilded iron spurs that Master Crol had found somewhere for me) and he galloped hard until we got to the War Way, and harder after that, up and up through a cleft that seemed just about as high as that hilltop I had been on, and then along a narrow gorge until I caught the rumble of stones. I pulled up sharp when I heard that, because I already had a pretty fair idea what it might be.

The side of the gorge was a shorter climb than the hill had been, but I was tired already, it was cold, and the first stars were coming out. I could not see handholds, and when I did they were usually just shadows or something. I had to feel my way up, and it seemed like it was taking hours.

The stones rumbled again when I was about halfway up. Then it got quiet. Somebody gave a wild yell. That must have been quite a way off, but it seemed closer because of the way it bounced from rock to rock. The moon rose. For some crazy reason I looked at it; and when I did the flying castle passed in front of it, black against the white face of the moon and looking like a toy. Back then I was not even sure it was the Valfather's (which it is), but seeing it like that helped a lot. I know you will say there is no sense to it, but it did. I was the sea, and I was looking up at the moon and that six-faced castle and reaching for it with big foaming waves like white hands. And bang! I was at the top with my fingers all torn up and the blood running off them a little and there was war in the wind and it was too dark to shoot a bow. I sprinted down that way, jumping over cracks and down little cliffs and nothing in the world was going to stop me.

Then a hairy hand about as big as the blade of a spade did it. Two hands picked me up, but my left arm was free and I stuck my dagger into that big man's neck before he could throw me over the cliff. When he fell it was like a tree falling, and we both ended up too close to the edge, with him bleeding and thrashing around and trying to get up. I got up first and hit him in the head with Sword Breaker, and heard the bone break under the blow. He fell back down after that, and he never moved again.

Down below someone was shouting, *"Finefield! Finefield!"* I guess I recognized Garvaon's voice, because I knew it was him and figured it must be the name of his manor. I did not have one, so I yelled, *"Disiri! Disiri!"* so Garvaon would know I was up there helping.

After that *Disiri!* was always what I yelled whenever I fought. I may not remember to write that down every time I talk about fighting, but that was the way it was. When I got to Skai (let me say this before I forget) I did it there too. Finally Alvit asked what it meant and I could not remember. After that I tried and tried. It hurt, way down deep.

Naturally when I was running along the top of the cliff I did not know any of that. Pretty soon I came up to three of the biggest men I had ever seen. They were rolling a boulder to the edge. Sword Breaker got the first one in the forehead—that was about as high as I could reach—when he turned to look at me. A rock hit my steel cap and knocked it off. I think I sort of stumbled around a little after that. Somebody grabbed my wrist and I cut with my dagger and he let go. I remember seeing his knee as high as my crotch, and hitting it with Sword Breaker for all I was worth.

Somebody else threw a spear. It did not go through my

hauberk but knocked me down. We both grabbed for it, and he lifted it up and lifted me too because I was holding on to the shaft. I kicked him in the face and he dropped it. I jumped up and hit him pretty much like I was playing football and knocked him over the edge, and just about went over myself. When I got my balance I looked down, and he was still bouncing off rocks. He bounced out of the moonlight, and right after that I heard him hit bottom.

I had dropped Sword Breaker and my dagger. The dagger's blade was polished bright and shone in the moonlight, but I had to grope around for Sword Breaker.

I straightened up, and there was a great big man, more than tall enough for the NBA, coming at me with a club. I crouched—I guess I was going to rush him as soon as the club came up—but something black and a lot bigger than he was grabbed him. All of a sudden he was not a big man at all, only another little man that had walked around awhile and was going to die now. He screamed when the jaws closed on him. (I could hear his bones breaking—it always sounds terrible.) Gylf shook him like a rat and dropped him.

"You better clear out of here, Lord." It was Uri and she was right at my elbow with a long, slender blade; I had never seen her come, or heard her either, but there she was.

On my left Baki whispered, "You will be killed, Lord, if this goes on much longer."

"You can see in the dark better than I can," I said, "are there any more around here?"

"Hundreds, Lord, the way you're going."

I told them to follow me.

When the fight was over, the dead horses and mules had to be unloaded and their loads put on the ones we had left. Then we had to put the dead people on top of the loads. We got going again around midnight, and we traveled until it was light, with

Garvaon out in front and Gylf and me out in front of Garvaon maybe a hundred or a hundred and fifty paces. The sun came up right about when we came out of the gorge and onto a mountain meadow that had thick green grass and even wildflowers. It slanted like the deck of a ship with the wind hard abeam, but it looked really good to us by then anyway. We stopped and unloaded the animals and put up the pavilions. Most of us went to sleep then, but Garvaon and a dozen men-at-arms stood guard, and Gylf and I went back to where the battle had been. Mani went with us, riding on my saddlebags.

We stayed in that meadow all day and all night. The next morning Beel sent for me. The table was up, just like before, and there were two folding chairs. "Sit down," he told me. "Breakfast should be here in a moment or two."

I said thank you.

"You climbed the cliffs to fight the Mountain Men. So I've been told, and once I caught a glimpse of you up there myself. Or so I believe."

I nodded. "I'm gratified, My Lord."

"Great stones fell among us." Beel sounded like he was talking to himself. "And bodies, too. The corpses of our foes. While the mules were being reloaded I amused myself, and Sir Garvaon as well, by examining them by lantern light. Perhaps you did the same, Sir Able?"

"No, My Lord. I had to go back for my horse." I would have passed on breakfast just then if I could have gotten up and gone out of that pavilion.

"I see. Normally I breakfast each day with my daughter, Sir Able. She is not here today. You will have observed it, I feel sure."

I nodded. "I hope she's not sick."

"She is well and uninjured. Thanks to you, in large part, I believe."

"I'd like to believe that too."

Beel made a steeple of his fingers and sat looking at me until the food came. "Help yourself, Sir Able. You need not wait on me."

I said I would rather wait, and he took a smoked fish, and some bread and cheese. "I like to breakfast with my daughter."

I nodded like before. "She must be good company, My Lord."

"It gives me an hour or so in which to speak with her. I am busy, often, all day."

I said, "I'm sure you are, My Lord."

"There are many of my rank, and of higher rank than I, who do little work, Sir Able. Little if any. They lounge about at court, and lounge equally on their estates. Their stewards manage their estates on their behalf, just as mine does for me. Should the king try to persuade them to fill some office, which as a sensible man he seldom does, they beg off on one excuse or another. I have endeavored to be a man of a different stamp. I will not trouble you with all the offices I have held under our present Majesty and his royal father. They have been varied, and some have been onerous. I was First Lord of the Exchequer for near to seven years, for example."

"I know it must have been a hard job," I said.

Beel shook his head. "You may think you do, Sir Able, but you really have no idea. It was a nightmare that seemed it would never end. And now this."

I nodded, trying to look sympathetic.

"Breakfast gives me one hour a day in my daughter's company. I have tried to be mother and father to her, Sir Able. I will not say I have succeeded. But I have tried."

Beel sat up, straightening his shoulders. He had not eaten

a bite. "I sent her off this morning to breakfast with her maids. She was surprised and pleased."

I said, "She can't really have been pleased." I had not eaten either up to then, and I decided I might as well start.

"Thank you, Sir Able. She was, however. I sent her away because I wanted to speak with you. Not as a knight, but as a son, for I wish with all my heart that the Overcyns had vouchsafed me such a son as you."

I did not know what to say. Finally I said, "That's a great honor, My Lord."

"I am not trying to honor you, but to speak the truth." Beel paused; I think to see how I felt about what he had said. "Men like me, noblemen high in His Majesty's councils, have no great reputation for truth. We are careful about what we say and how we say it. We must be. I have lied when my duty demanded it. I did not enjoy it, but I did it to the best of my ability."

I said, "I've got it."

"Now I am going to tell you the truth, and only the truth. I ask to be believed. But I ask more. I ask you to be as honest with me as I am with you. Will you do it?"

"Of course, My Lord."

Beel got up and went to a chest, opened it, and took out a roll of parchment. "You have a manor, Sir Able? Where is it?"

"No, My Lord."

"None?"

I said, "No, My Lord," again.

He sat back down, still holding the parchment. "Your liege sends you to take your stand in the Mountains of the Mice. For half a year."

"I hadn't heard them called that. But yes, he does."

"It is the designation the Angrborn use. We name them the Northern Mountains for the most part, or merely instance some individual range. Why do you think the Angrborn speak of them as they do?"

I put down the slice of bread I had been about to eat. "I can't imagine, My Lord, unless it's because there are many mice here."

"There are no more than in most places, and fewer than in many. They name it as they do because of the men that you fought last night. They are the sons of the Angrborn—sons that the Angrborn have fathered upon our women. I see that I have surprised you."

CHAPTER 50

WHO TOLD MY DAUGHTER?

I took a bite of bread, chewed it, and swallowed. "I hadn't known such a thing was possible, My Lord."

"It is." Beel paused, his fingers drumming the table. "I suppose it must be painful for the women, at first at any rate."

I nodded.

"The Angrborn raid our country for women as well as wealth. It is my task to stop those raids if I can. If I cannot, to diminish their size and frequency. King Gilling is not always obeyed, and the more remote his people are from Utgard the freer they think themselves. But if it is seen that he disapproves of their incursions, we will be subject to fewer, and they are apt to bring less strength."

"I wish you luck," I said, "and I mean that."

"King Gilling has indicated that he will accept me as His

Majesty's ambassador, at least. But I was speaking of the Mice, as the Angrborn call them—of the huge men who attacked us. They are born into the households of the Angrborn, the sons of their masters by their slave women. Often they try to remain in Jotunland after the deaths of their fathers. They may offer to serve his legitimate sons, for example."

I nodded to show that I understood.

"Sometimes they succeed for a while. They are then slaves like their mothers, swineherds or plowmen. The pigs and cattle of the Angrborn are no larger than our own, as I understand it."

"For a time, you said."

"Eventually they are driven out. Or killed. A king's son, the son of a free woman, would not be treated so; but these are. Those who live pass from place to place, hunted like rats, or like the mice whose name they bear, until they reach these mountains, where the Angrborn themselves do not dwell. There are many caves—the Angrborn call them Mouseholes. The Mice live in them like beasts, and are less than beasts. What do you intend to do today, Sir Able?"

I was taken aback. "Travel north with your party, I suppose, My Lord."

Beel shook his head. "We will not travel today. We're all tired, and we must discard some supplies so the mules will not be overburdened. The responsibilities of men who died must be assigned to others, and we must find a way to carry our wounded that will not give them too much pain."

"Then I'll sleep this morning, and go looking for the source of the Griffin this afternoon."

"You got little sleep last night, I imagine. Few of us got much."

I had slept, but by the time I turned in it had been a day, a night, and a day. I was still groggy and I said so.

"I see. Would you be willing to do me a favor, Sir Able?"

"Of course, My Lord. Anything."

"Then sleep this morning as you had planned, but give up your hunt for the source of the Griffin for one day at least. It would be a hazardous undertaking in any event. Have you given thought to the dangers you might encounter, wandering alone through these mountains?"

"I have, My Lord." I smiled. "Also to the fact that they would encounter me."

"That is well said. Nevertheless, I ask you to abandon your hunt for my sake. Will you do it?"

"Of course, My Lord. Gladly."

"You are a good bowman?"

"Yes, My Lord."

"No beating around the bush. I like that." For the first time that morning, one of his thin-lipped smiles tugged at the corners of Beel's mouth. "Master Papounce has been after me to stage a match between you and Sir Garvaon. Garvaon is a famous bowman."

"Everybody says so, My Lord."

"He is seconded by Idnn, who hunts. She shoots well for a woman." The thin smile turned bitter. "I refused because I felt our time might be better spent in travel. But we will not move on until tomorrow, and such a match might lift our spirits. The men who attacked us—it may suit giants to call them mice, but would seem ill from me—were high above us on the mountain. They hurled great stones down on us, and we shot arrow after arrow up at them, often seeing no more than a moving shadow. The need for expert archery can rarely have been made plainer."

I drained my flagon and refilled it from the pitcher.

"You will do it?"

"Of course, My Lord. I said I would."

"If you lose by but a narrow margin, no harm will be done. But should you lose badly, you may be ridiculed. It might be well for you to prepare yourself for that."

"It might be well, My Lord, for those who would ridicule me to prepare themselves for me."

"We cannot afford the loss of a single man, Sir Able. Please bear that in mind."

"I will, My Lord, provided they do."

"I see. Well, I've told Papounce and Garvaon that I would do this, so I suppose I'll have to go through with it. Try to restrain yourself."

"I will, My Lord."

Beel gnawed his lips while I finished a piece of smoked sturgeon. When I wiped my mouth, he said, "You may depart, Sir Able, if you've had enough to eat."

I shook my head. "You didn't send Lady Idnn away so we could talk about shooting at a mark, My Lord. What is it?"

Beel hesitated. "I nearly raised this topic when we first met. When Crol brought you in. You remember that day, I'm sure."

"Sure."

Beel sighed. "I spoke of Svon then. He is a distant cousin of mine, as I said."

I nodded, wondering what was coming.

"He seeks to become a knight. No higher distinction lies open to him." Beel left his seat to go to the doorway of his pavilion and look out at the rocks and snow-mantled peaks. He was still holding that roll of parchment.

When he turned back, I said, "I have never stood in his way, My Lord."

"He quarreled with your servant. He told me so. Your servant beat him and drove him off. Did I tell you that?"

"I knew it, Your Lordship. I don't believe I learned it from you."

"Perhaps you learned it from Svon himself?"

I shook my head.

"You learned of it from another traveler, then."

"Yes, My Lord."

"This is awkward, and I am by no means certain I can do justice to it. You have seen my daughter Idnn."

"Yes, Your Lordship. A beautiful young lady."

"Precisely. She is very young, and delicate of form as of feature. Could your servant beat her? If he chose?"

I had to think about that one—not about the answer, but about where he was going with it. Finally I said, "I hope he would never do such a thing, My Lord. I know Pouk well and he's got his faults, but he's not cruel or brutal."

"He could do it if he chose?"

"Of course, My Lord, if I were not there to prevent him. Pouk is twenty or so, and strong and active."

"Just so. Let us suppose it has occurred. My daughter would feel deeply shamed at having been beaten by a churl. But she would feel no shame at all because the churl had been able to defeat her. No sensible person would suppose that a delicate girl like Idnn could enter the lists with an active man of twenty."

I nodded.

"When Svon was a boy of ten, he might have felt the same way and been justified in his feelings. What troubles me . . . One thing that troubles me is that Svon appeared to feel so now. He would be a knight. If Duke Marder were to offer him the accolade, the golden spurs and the rest of it, he would accept at once. How would you feel if this servant of yours were to beat you?"

I tried to talk. It seemed like I was choking.

"Exactly. I am no warlike man, Sir Able. While you were learning the craft of knighthood, I was learning to read and to write, history, languages, and the rest of it. If Sir Garvaon, let us say, and I were to come to blows, I should feel no shame about being beaten. But a servant? I would whet my sword and seek a second encounter."

"I'm glad Svon didn't, My Lord."

"Are you? For Svon's sake?"

"You shame me, My Lord. He was—he is—my squire. I've got a duty to him."

Beel nodded, making a steeple of his fingers. "I have told you this because I feel you are a man of honor. It may be that Svon will return to you. If so, you may be able to do something. I hope so."

"I'll try, My Lord. Just how it might be done . . . Well, I don't know. I'll have to think about it." I got up.

Beel indicated the folding chair. "Since you chose to remain, we have other matters to discuss. I will try not to keep you from your bed too long."

I sat down again.

"Svon told me that you had set a demon on his track. Are you surprised?"

"I am, My Lord. I—I believe I know what he means by that, but I did no such thing. May I explain?"

"I invite it."

"I have another servant, My Lord. His name is Org. He is no demon."

The thin smile returned. "One meets neither demons nor dragons in the worlds above Aelfrice, Sir Able. That's one of the things I learned while you were being taught to manage a shield. I did not say Svon was pursued here by a demon, only that he had said he was, and said you had done it."

"I didn't, My Lord. But I have reason to believe that when Svon left, Org went with him. He might be an unpleasant traveling companion, My Lord."

"Is this Org a large, strong man? Big shoulders?"

I sort of picked my way among words. "He's big and very strong, My Lord. He's bigger than I am and his shoulders are wider than mine."

"You did not set him on Svon?"

"No, My Lord. I wasn't there when Svon and Pouk fought and separated. May I try to guess?"

"Please do."

"Maybe Org is afraid Svon will try to hurt me somehow, and he's following him to stop him."

Beel nodded. "That seems likely enough. Svon was going back to Sheerwall, so he told me. He dined with us, bought a mount, and stayed the night. It would have been a fortnight ago. Something like that."

I nodded.

"That night one of our sentries reported seeing a very large man in the moonlight, some distance away. He called him a giant—an Angrborn. You know how those fellows are."

It seemed a bad time to say anything.

"When he told his sergeant, the sergeant went to the place and looked around. He said he found a footprint in mud. A very large foot, he said, bare, with long toes. He said there appeared to be claws on the ends of the toes. You can see why I'm curious."

"I sure do, My Lord."

"Is that all you have to say?"

I nodded. "All I'll say willingly, My Lord."

"Very well. Svon has my sympathy. Don't stand up again, please, Sir Able. I see you making ready to do it, but we are only just come to the matter I most wished to discuss."

The steeple vanished. Beel leaned forward, anxious and thoughtful. "My daughter and I were both in that accursed declivity when we were attacked. I remained with her every moment. There wasn't much I could do, but I was determined to protect her if I could."

"Naturally, My Lord."

Beel's voice sank to a whisper. "She shall wed a king before all is said and done. She shall wed a king, and our blood will be royal again."

"I understand, My Lord."

"She is precious to me, and so I kept her under my eye. At no time was she up on the cliffs where our enemies were."

"Naturally not, My Lord."

"And yet, Sir Able, she talks almost as though she were. Those cliffs, she has told me, are littered with dead, hairy men of monstrous stature slain by you and your dog. I find it difficult to credit a dog's slaying even one such man, let alone dozens, but that is what she says. You have boasted of your honesty in the past."

Seeing how I looked, Beel changed it. "*Boasted* is too strong a word perhaps, but you've laid claim to truthfulness. You told me that you had not lied to me or to Master Crol. Do you deny it?"

"No, My Lord."

"Can you make the same claim today?"

"I can, My Lord. I do."

"Then I would appreciate straightforward answers to a few questions." Beel fell silent, studying my face, then his own hands. He had eaten nothing and drunk nothing.

"I like you, Sir Able. I like you more than any man I have met since I met His Majesty. I hope that you are aware of it."

"I was not, My Lord, but I'm very flattered. May I say I know you're a really good man, a loyal servant of the king, and the loving father of your daughter?"

Beel nodded. "It's my daughter who concerns me now."

"I know it, My Lord. I haven't hurt her, or tried to."

"You see the curtain that divides our pavilion. She sleeps behind it, and I before it. I wash and dress here, she there."

"I've got it."

"Thus we cannot see one another. But we can hear one another perfectly. The curtain is of silk, which has small weight and occupies but a little space. It blinds us, if you will permit the expression. But it offers no resistance to sound."

I nodded.

"Thus we often speak to each other when we lie abed. In the morning too, while her maid dresses her and Swert dresses me."

"Okay."

"This morning she spoke of the battle, and she spoke as one who had been on the cliff tops—of broken heads, and broken arms and legs, of men crushed and torn, too, as though by a lion's jaws. She said that you had killed many of these men, Sir Able. Is that true?"

"Yes, My Lord."

"May I ask what weapons you employed?"

I got out my dagger and laid it on the table, and drew Sword Breaker and laid it beside the dagger. Beel picked up Sword Breaker to look at it, and I said, "That's not a sword, My Lord. I know it looks like one, but it's a mace."

He felt the corners of Sword Breaker's blade, tried to flex it, and laid Sword Breaker down again. "You are of low birth, I realize. But you are a knight, not a peasant, and a knight is entitled to wear a sword."

"When I've got the one I want, I will, My Lord."

"What sword is that?"

"Eterne, My Lord."

Softly he said, "The perfect blade is a legend, Sir Able. Nothing more."

"I don't think so, My Lord."

"Wizard, witch, or warlock." He sighed. "Which is it? I have some knowledge of the art myself, although I boast no great power."

I did not say anything.

"I confess it in order that you may know I am not your foe. You may confide in me as a fellow adept."

"All I can confide is that I don't know a thing about magic, My Lord."

"Wizards never tell. It was a saying of my nurse's, but I didn't know there was so much truth in it. You've been on those cliffs, Sir Able? It was you who slew our foes there?"

"Yes, My Lord. Some of them. Most of them were killed by my dog. The arrows of your archers killed some too."

"Did you take my daughter up there? After the battle?"

"No, My Lord."

"Did you see her there when you were there yourself?"

"No. If she's been up there, I know nothing about it."

"This is the deed to the manor of Swiftbrook, Sir Able." Beel held up the parchment. "Did you speak to her without my knowledge, telling her of the battle?"

"No, My Lord."

"Who was with you on the cliffs? Anyone?"

"My dog and my cat, My Lord. You've seen them."

"Who was it who told my daughter of the scene there? The men you slew, and the way they died?"

"It wasn't me, My Lord. Don't you think you ought to ask her?"

He got quiet, and I knew there was not a lot I could say then without making it worse. Besides, I had things to think about myself. I buttered bread, laid smoked sturgeon on it, and folded it over.

At last Beel said, "You're hoping that I will send you off to find your servant."

"That's right, My Lord."

"I won't. You had better get some rest, if you're to shoot against Sir Garvaon."

I nodded, stood up, and returned Sword Breaker and my dagger to their scabbards.

"You're still willing to contest with him?"

"Any time, My Lord." I did not say it, but my bowstring was putting me through hell every night. It seemed to me then that it was high time I got something for it.

"I will judge your contest."

I nodded. "Sure, My Lord."

"I will do my utmost to judge fairly, Sir Able. My honor is at stake in that."

"I understand, My Lord."

"You may go." Beel sighed. As I was stepping out of his pavilion he added softly, "Yet I hope Sir Garvaon has the victory."

CHAPTER 51

ARCHERY

In the dream I had that morning, I was myself for a change, but very young, much younger than I had been when I came out of Parka's cave. I was sitting in a little boat and paddling up the Griffin. Bold Berthold stood watching from the bank, and Setr swam beside me, spouting water and steam like a whale. Up the river, Mother was waiting for me. Pretty soon Bold Berthold was left behind. I saw Mother's face among the leaves of a willow and in a hawthorn, beautiful and smiling, and crowned with hawthorn blossoms; but the Griffin wound on, and when the hawthorn was past I saw her no more. From time to time I glimpsed a griffin of stone from whose mouth the river issued. I tried to reach it, but came instead to an opening in a tube of thick green glass.

And emerged at once, mounted on a gray warhorse and gripping a short lance from which a pennant fluttered. The stone griffin stood before me, tall as a mountain and more stern. I couched the lance and charged, and was swallowed up at once.

It was past noon when I woke. I yawned and stretched, thinking about Mother's face in the willow leaves and in the hawthorn blossoms. She was only a girl, and although there was a lot of sleep in the thought, there was more sorrow than sleep.

She was still a young girl, not a great deal older than Sha, when she went away.

"You're awake just in time. I trust you slept well?" Mani was sitting at the foot of my cot, washing his face with his paws.

I yawned again. "I thought you'd be with Idnn."

"Your dog wanted to cadge food. Since I'd had more than enough from Her Ladyship, he enlisted me to stand his watch."

I put my feet over the edge of the cot. "I'm glad you two are speaking now."

"Oh, we understand each other perfectly," Mani said. "He thinks I'm detestable, and I think he is. Doubtless we're both right."

"You've been talking to Idnn."

Mani's eyes (very beautiful green eyes that seemed to glow) opened wider. "How did you find that out?"

"Was it supposed to be a secret?"

"Well, *she* wasn't to tell anybody. I made her promise."

I had found my clothes. I laid them out on the cot and looked into the corners of Garvaon's pavilion to make sure there was nobody around except Mani and me.

"She told her father, and he reported me to you. Isn't that it?"

"No." I tied my underwear and straightened out a fresh pair of socks. "She told her father things she'd heard from you, and he's been trying to find out how she learned them."

"Oh." Mani stretched, throwing his tail into S curves. "Did you tell him?"

"No."

"Probably for the best. You don't mind if I tug your blanket a little?"

"Try not to tear it." I pulled on my socks.

"All right." Mani tugged; his claws were big, sharp, and black.

"This is going to sound pretty silly, but I didn't know you were going to talk to anybody except me."

"Because your dog doesn't?" Mani yawned. "He could talk to some other people, too. He just doesn't want to. Are you mad because I talked to Her Ladyship? You didn't tell me not to."

"I—no."

"I told her you were my owner." He grinned. "And I said a great many other complimentary things about you. She was quite taken with you already, and she lapped it up."

"I suppose I should thank you."

"Not necessarily. Ingratitude is my lot in life, and I became reconciled to it long ago."

I had buckled my belt. Before I spoke again, I worked my

feet into my boots. "I'll try to make my gratitude a lot more tangible, but it may take a while."

"Well, you could let me keep talking to Idnn. If you don't, I'll have to avoid her, and that's bound to be awkward at times."

I pointed my finger at Mani's neat black nose. "You know perfectly well that you'd talk to her even if I told you not to."

"I'd have to, wouldn't I? I mean if she cornered me. She'd say, 'I know perfectly well you can talk, Mani, and if you won't talk to me I'll have my father's archers use you for practice.' Then I'd say, 'Oh, My Lady, please!' And the fat would be in the fire."

"Okay," I decided, "you may talk to her when there's no one else around. Except for me. You may talk to her when I'm there, or Gylf."

Mani made me a mock bow. "My Lord."

"Don't do that. It reminds me of Uri and Baki, and I don't like it when they do it."

"Your wish is mine, Great Owner."

I knew Mani was trying to get my goat, but it was hard not to laugh. I said, "In return for being so nice to you, I'd like you to answer a few questions. Will you?"

"Anything, More Than Divine Master."

"You told me once you weren't from Aelfrice. Do you stand by that?"

"Correct."

"Are you from Skai, then?"

"I'm afraid not." Mani began to wash his right front paw, a small and surprisingly neat pink tongue darting in and out of his large, scarred face. "Wouldn't it be simpler to ask what world I was born in?"

"Then I do." I picked up my hauberk and wiggled into it.

"Just out of curiosity, do you intend to wear that when you shoot against Sir Garvaon?"

"Yes. I do."

"What in the world do—well, all right. Back to the subject, Mani. I was born right here in Mythgarthr, although I've been to Aelfrice a couple of times. Next you'll want to know how it is that I can talk. I don't know. Some of us can, though not very many. Some dogs can, even, but not all of you can understand us. My late mistress knew how to give a talking spirit, and she gave one to me."

"You're saying Gylf was born here, too."

A man-at-arms thrust his head into the tent. "They're about ready for you, Sir Able."

"I'll be out in a moment," I told him.

"I'm not saying that," Mani said when the man-at-arms had gone, "and I don't think it's true. I've never seen him eat his own droppings, for one thing."

I put on Sword Breaker. "I was once told that no one could travel more than one world from the one that he—or she—was born in."

Mani nodded. "One hears all sorts of things."

"I've learned since that it isn't true. You were a witch's cat, so you ought to know all about it. Will you tell me? The truth?"

"If you insist. First I ought to say that you shouldn't be mad at the person who told you that. He was just trying to keep you from getting in over your head." Mani smirked. "Here are the facts. You can believe me or not, whatever you choose."

I found my bow and strung it. "Go on."

"In theory," Mani said smugly, "anybody can travel to any of the seven worlds. You can't go lower than the first, though, or higher than the last, because there's nothing below or above to go to."

"I understand."

"In practice, it's hard to go up but easy to go down, just like climbing a hill. Do you have much trouble getting to Aelfrice?"

"My problem is staying out of it," I said.

"Exactly. You wouldn't have much trouble going from Aelfrice all the way down, either. But you might never get back."

Nodding, I picked up my quiver and left the pavilion.

Garvaon met me. "We've all shot except you," he said. "You and I are to have five arrows each. Did Lord Beel tell you what the prize was?"

I shook my head.

"It's a helmet, a particularly nice one with a lot of gold trim. Not gilt, gold."

"That's good, I've lost mine."

"I know. When we fought the big men."

I nodded again.

"So His Lordship thinks you're going to win, and has put up this helmet for you."

We had been striding along, and had reached the crowd that had collected to watch us shoot, archers and men-at-arms, servants, and muleteers. Beyond their milling ranks, I saw the prize helmet atop a pole, and Beel himself.

"So I propose a side bet between you and me," Garvaon was saying. "A boon. If you win, I'll be honor bound to do you whatever favor you ask. When I win—and I warn you I will—you'll owe me a favor in the same way."

"Done," I said.

We shook hands, smiling, and walked through the crowd shoulder-to-shoulder.

There was an embroidered banner hanging from the trumpet Master Crol blew, turning north, east, south, and west, and holding the notes so the silvery challenge of civilized war filled the mountain valley and echoed from rock to rock. When he finally took the trumpet from his lips, he shouted, "Sir Garvaon of Finefield! Sir Able of the High Heart!"

At this last, the string of my bow seemed to catch the sound, humming as the strings of a lute do when the orchestra speaks without her.

I'm a knight, I thought. I am a real knight at last, and there's no one here who wouldn't swear to that.

I stood a little straighter then, looked up, and squared my shoulders; and for the first time really realized that I overtopped Garvaon by a good three fingers, though Garvaon's conical steel cap made him look taller than I was.

"There is the target, my good knights," Beel was saying. He pointed as he spoke. It was a round shield with an iron boss at the center. It hung from a scrubby tree at the end of the valley, at least two hundred yards away.

"You will shoot alternately, until each has shot five arrows. Sir Garvaon, Sir Able, and Sir Garvaon again until ten arrows have flown. Is that clear?"

Garvaon said, "Yes, Your Lordship."

"Those arrows that fall short will count for nothing. Those that reach the target, but do not strike it, will count for one. Those which strike it, two." Beel paused, looking from face to face. "And those which strike the iron center, if any do, will count as three. Do you both understand?"

We did.

"Master Papounce stands ready to ride."

Looking around, I saw him at the fringe of the crowd, on foot but holding the reins of a nervous roan.

"If there is a question as to whether a shot reached the target, Master Papounce's testimony will settle the matter."

A murmur of excitement swept the crowd.

"Sir Garvaon! You are the senior. Step to the line."

Garvaon did, taking from his quiver a shaft fletched with gray goose and tipped with a war point. When he drew, he drew and let fly in a single, smooth motion, the nock pulled back to his ear—the arrow disappearing like magic. His bowstring sang.

All of us tried to follow the high arc of the arrow as its faint whistle faded to silence. Down on the brown target it plunged, like a falcon on a rabbit.

We all gasped. Garvaon's first arrow had hit the target midway between the edge and the iron boss. It stayed there, sticking in the target.

"Sir Garvaon has two," Beel announced. "Sir Able? Will you shoot?"

As I stepped to the line, Idnn appeared with Mani on her shoulder; she held out a green silk scarf. "Will you wear my favor, Sir Able?"

It surprised me so much I could not say a word. I took her scarf and knotted it around my head the way I had seen scarves—red, blue, pink, yellow, and white—tied around the helms of knights at Sheerwall.

Someone raised a cheer for Lady Idnn, caps were thrown into the air, and for half a minute or more I thought about the way I would feel if my shot did not match Garvaon's.

It's up to me, I told myself. I direct the arrow, and it's not a matter of chance.

There was a slight breeze, just enough to stir Idnn's scarf. It was close to squarely at my back, but over so long a course it was bound to drift the arrow just a trifle to the left.

I chose a long, pale shaft of spiny orange, one I had shaped myself and knew to be as straight as my eye and hand could make it. Seeing it, I remembered the wild swan whose feathers had fletched it. How proud I had been of it! And how good it had tasted when Bold Berthold and I had roasted it over the fire that night!

The arrow was at the nock already, as if the string had gone looking for it.

Forget the people, forget the girl with the cat. Think only about the target.

They gasped, and I lowered my bow and took a good, deep breath. That flat-flying arrow could never reach so far. I shut my eyes, knowing that in a second or two I would have to smile and shrug, and get myself set for my next shot.

A faint noise, like the noise that a pebble might make if it were dropped into a tin cup, reached us from far away.

CHAPTER 52

TO POUK

"Missed!" somebody shouted.

"Hit!"

"Hit the center!"

That too was contradicted, and I opened my eyes.

Frowning, Beel had raised both hands for silence. "If Sir Able's shot struck the iron boss of the target, his arrow will have rebounded, and there will be damage to the point. The iron may be scarred as well. Master Papounce? Will you investigate for us?"

Papounce was in the saddle already. At Beel's nod he galloped away.

Someone near me said, "If it hit the middle it would've bounced off and I'd have seen it."

"The distance was only a hundred paces when my archers and I were shooting against each other," Garvaon whispered. "His Lordship had it moved way back for you and me, but he wouldn't hear of Papounce standing near it and signaling any more. Armor and a few steps away, and he'd have been safe enough."

I did not think so, but I nodded out of politeness; I was watching Papounce, who had reined up at the target and dismounted, seemingly to look at its boss. While I watched him, he walked behind it, and seemed to look at the trunk of the tree from which the target hung.

"Going to win that steel cap, Sir Able?" It was Crol, still carrying his trumpet.

I tried not to smile. "I doubt it. To tell the truth, I'll be happy if I don't disgrace myself."

"The king had one like it made for King Gilling," Crol explained. "Bigger than my washbasin. His Lordship liked it so much he had one made for himself." Crol gestured toward the helmet on the pole. "That's it up there. King Gilling's is on one of the mules."

"It will look good on you," Garvaon told me, "but you'll have to beat me first."

Papounce had mounted again and was trotting back to the camp. Idnn caught my sleeve and pointed.

"Yes," I said. "We'll know soon, My Lady."

She got up on tiptoe; I saw she wanted to whisper and bent so she could talk into my ear. *"Something's happened! He's not galloping. He needs time to think."*

I stared, then bent again.

"Your cat told me, and he's right! Trotting, with Father's eyes on him? Something's afoot!"

Papounce dismounted and drew Beel aside. For at least two minutes they conferred, and I (I had been trying to edge nearer) caught Beel's incredulous, "Split the rock?"

Then he raised his hands for silence. "Sir Able has three."

There were murmurs and shouted questions, all of which he ignored. "Sir Garvaon has the next shot. Clear the way for him!"

It missed the target, falling to the right.

This time Beel spoke to Crol, who bawled, "Sir Garvaon has three!"

I had shot my best arrow first. I picked a good one from those I had left and nocked it, telling myself firmly that I did not need to hit the middle again. If I hit the target at all, that would be enough.

I shot, and Papounce was sent off exactly as he had been before, and there was another wait while he galloped to the target and looked it over. I unstrung my bow and made myself relax, trying to keep from catching the eye of anybody who might want to talk to me.

I got another three. That made my score six.

Garvaon shot again. His third arrow hit near his first.

I was starting to feel like I was cheating, and I did not like that. Instead of shooting at the target, I aimed for the top leaves of the scrubby little tree they had hung it on. I shot, and watched my arrow fly true to aim. It passed through the leaves and hit the cliff-face behind them. A few pebbles fell, then a few more.

All at once the cliff face gave way, collapsing with a grinding roar.

* * *

Gylf found me about a mile away from our camp, and woke me by licking my face. I sputtered and sat up, thinking for a minute that I saw the old woman from my dream, the one who had owned the cottage, behind him. It was very dark.

"Why here?" Gylf demanded.

"Because it's sheltered, and I hoped it wouldn't be quite so cold."

"It" was a crevice in the rocks.

"Hard here," Gylf explained. "Tracking."

"Hard sleeping, too. I'm p-pretty stiff." The fact was that my teeth were chattering.

"Fires back there. Food."

I said sure. "But I wouldn't have gotten anything much to eat before. Everybody wanted to talk to me. I told Lord Beel I'd meet him in his pavilion later—"

"Give it to you?"

"The pretty helmet?" I stood up and stretched, and wrapped myself in my cloak, adding the blanket I had taken from camp. "I don't know. Or care, either."

"All asleep." Gylf wagged his tail, and looked up at me hopefully.

"You want me to go back, don't you? It's nice of you to worry about me."

Gylf nodded.

"But if I stay here . . ."

"Me, too."

"You'd keep me warm, anyhow. I wish I'd had you here earlier."

He trotted ahead to show the way; and I followed more slowly, still cold and tired. I had hoped to find one of the caves the Angrborn called Mouseholes, and was mad at myself for having failed. Gylf would have found one for me, and I knew it. Or Uri and Baki probably could have, if I had called them and they had come. But that would have been Gylf finding it or them finding it. I had wanted to do it myself.

The moon had not yet risen, and the camp looked ghostly—Beel's scarlet pavilion dead black, Garvaon's and Crol's canvas pavilions as pale as ghosts, the bodies of sleeping servants and muleteers like new graves, and the few tortured cedars like Osterlings come to eat the bodies.

A picketed mule brayed in the distance.

"I'm going to send you to Pouk," I told Gylf. I had not decided until then. "Not right now, because you deserve food and a good rest before you leave. In the morning. I want you to find him and show yourself to him, so that he'll know I'm nearby. Then you can come back here and tell me where he is and whether he's all right."

Gylf looked back and whined, and a sleepy sentry called, "Sir Able? Is that you, sir?"

When I finally got to my cot in Garvaon's pavilion, I found the gold-trimmed helmet on it. After I had adjusted the straps inside, it fit like it had been made for me.

CHAPTER 53

BOONS

Next morning at breakfast, eating off by ourselves because Garvaon had told some of his archers and men-at-arms to keep everybody away, he and Gylf and I were joined by Mani, who got in my lap and ate whatever I passed to him, just like a regular cat.

"Lady Idnn's just about adopted that tomcat of yours," Garvaon told me.

"She may have him if he wants her."

Garvaon stared, then laughed. "You're quite a fellow." The point of his dagger carried a sizable chunk of summer sausage to his mouth, and he chewed in a way that showed he was thinking about something. "Can we talk man-to-man?"

"May," I said. "Sure. Of course."

"I said man-to-man, but that's not exactly it." Garvaon could not quite meet my eyes. "I'm a pretty fair knight. I can outshoot and outfight any man under me. I've won a few tournaments, and taken part in seven pitched battles."

He waited as if he expected me to challenge the number.

"Seven pitched battles, and I've lost count of how many skirmishes like that scuffle in the defile. But you're something else."

"I'm a lot younger than you are," I said, "and a lot less experienced. I know that."

"You're a hero." Garvaon almost whispered it. "You're the kind of knight they write songs and poems about, the kind that gets taken up to Castle Skai."

I froze when he said that.

"You didn't know about the castle up there? It's where the Valfather lives."

"I did," I said slowly, "but I didn't know anybody else knew."

"A few do."

"And they take . . . take us up there? Sometimes?"

Garvaon shrugged. "What they say."

"Have you ever known anybody who—who they took?"

"Whom," Garvaon told me. "Not 'til now. But I know you, and they'll take you."

We were pretty quiet after that, I passing more food down to Gylf and Mani than I ate myself.

Finally Garvaon said, "You've got a boon coming, you know. I have to give you anything you want. Remember our side bet?"

I shook my head. "I didn't win."

"Bah! You know you did."

"We were supposed to shoot five arrows apiece. We only shot three."

"And you missed on purpose with the last one."

He was right, and I could not think of anything I could say that would not be a lie.

"You didn't want to show me up in front of my men. You think I don't know?"

I got busy eating.

"Maybe you think I left the helmet on your bed. It was Master Crol. Lord Beel told him to."

"I should give it back. Sir Garvaon . . . ?"

"Keep it. You need it."

I wiped my dagger on my sleeve and put it away. "I'd like to offer you a deal. You want to give me a boon."

Garvaon shook his head. "I don't want to, I owe it. I'm ready to pay, any time."

"Your honor makes you, you mean."

Garvaon nodded.

"I have honor, too."

"I know. I never said you didn't."

"Then let's take care of mine and yours together. I'll grant you a boon, whatever you want. And you can grant mine. How's that?"

"May. Name it."

I took a good, deep breath. "I want you to teach me swordcraft. I'm flunking there, and I know it."

"Is that all?"

"I think it's a lot. Will you? We could start tonight, once we've made camp."

Gylf got up, laid a paw in my lap for a second, and trotted away.

"Now I'm supposed to ask a boon, too," Garvaon said. "Only I don't really need it anymore. All right if I tell you what it was going to be?"

"Sure. I'd like to know."

"I was going to ask what made Lord Beel so sure you were going to win. Only I know now. Can I reserve mine?"

"Absolutely."

"He wants to see you before we go, by the way. I was supposed to tell you."

Beel and Idnn were still eating when I came in. Mani jumped off my shoulder to reclaim Idnn's lap.

I bowed. "You wanted to see me, My Lord?"

Beel inclined his head. "Yesterday you promised you would speak with me later."

"I tried to, My Lord."

"You left the camp."

I nodded. "So I could come back without being seen, My Lord. I waited too long, and you had gone to bed. I thought I'd better not disturb you."

Idnn asked, "Did you come into our pavilion?"

"Not into your half of it, My Lady. I would never do such a thing."

She smiled. "What? Never?"

Beel jumped in. "This was after dark, I take it."

"Just at moonrise, My Lord."

Idnn said, "I didn't hear you, and I slept badly last night. Do you know what I was doing at moonrise?"

"He does," Beel told her. "Look at his face. You went outside in your nightdress, didn't you?"

It was hard to talk after that, but I did it. "You were looking at the moon, My Lady. I thought it would be better if I didn't interrupt you."

Mani grinned from Idnn's lap as she asked, "Did the sentries challenge you, Sir Able? I didn't hear them."

"No, My Lady."

Beel frowned. "You crept past them?"

"Yes, My Lord. Past the sentries at this pavilion anyway. I knew they'd delay me."

"It should not be possible."

I said, "It isn't too hard for one man, My Lord."

"In armor."

I tried to change the subject. "Yes, My Lord. But without a helmet, because I had none—I have one now, thanks to your generosity."

Beel ate a coddled egg without saying another word, while Idnn smiled at me.

When his egg was gone, Beel said, "The black cat suits you. Your dog would suit me better, I think. Where is he?"

"I sent him to Pouk, My Lord."

"Refresh my memory, please. Who is Pouk?"

"My servant, My Lord. He went north to wait for me in the mountain passes."

"The servant who beat Svon."

"Yes, My Lord."

"Will your dog do that? Go to someone whole leagues away, just because you told him to?"

"I don't know, My Lord, but I think so."

Idnn was looking down at Mani. "Your cat thinks this is very funny."

"I know, My Lady. He probably hopes Gylf will get into trouble. I hope he doesn't."

"Will you ride with me today, Sir Able? I should be delighted to have your company."

I shook my head. "I'm deeply honored, My Lady. But I have to ride ahead to make sure we don't get dry-gulched by the Mountain Men again."

"Please, Sir Able? As a favor to me?"

Beel cleared his throat. "I want to ask you about your bowmanship. Yesterday . . ."

I nodded. "I understand. But I could explain how I got past your sentries a lot easier than I could explain how I missed the target as badly as I did with my third shot."

Idnn smiled at Beel. "Wizards never tell, Father. Remember?"

CHAPTER 54

IDNN

The morning sun had driven off the last chill of the night long before we broke camp. The mountains in which we had been ambushed gave way to a considerable valley, mostly wooded, through which a swift river flowed. Beyond it the War Way rose and rose as far as my eyes could trace its winding curves, which vanished at last among peaks whose summits were lost in cloud.

"Pouk will be there," I whispered to the white stallion Beel had given me, "and Gylf with him." I wanted to gallop then, but I was forced to settle for a quick trot. Tomorrow, I thought. Tomorrow we will be at the first of the high passes; but tonight, almost certainly, we will camp in the valley, where there is open ground and water.

Had Gylf crossed the river already? It seemed likely.

The trees, which had appeared a solid forest when I had looked down on them from the heights, were scattered groves when I reached them, too open at first for anyone to mount an ambush. I halted at the first such grove and waited until I saw the sun glint on Garvaon's helmet, then turned and rode again, trotting for a long bowshot before I reined up and paused to listen.

A score such pauses got me nothing more notable than the wind's sigh and the rustle of leaves, with a birdcall or two; but at the next my ears caught the steady tattoo of galloping hooves. Thinking someone was hurrying forward to speak to me, I remained where I was. Instead of growing stronger, the sound faded away altogether.

I thought then of stringing my bow; but I shrugged, loosened Sword Breaker in her scabbard, and rode on.

The road wound about a huge gray boulder topped with stunted trees, the moldy skull of a hill, with more trees huddled around it. Beyond, the War Way ran nearly straight for a league and more; and there, in the middle distance, a rider waited.

It was an excuse to gallop, and I took it.

Idnn smiled when I reined up, and Mani sprang from her saddle to mine.

"You shouldn't risk yourself like this, My Lady."

Idnn's smile widened. "How is it best to do it?"

I took a deep breath, half minded to offend her for her own good. "By—by . . . Oh, never mind."

"You wouldn't ride with me, so I decided to ride with you."

I nodded.

"I lagged behind, back among the mules where I belong, and then when we got into the trees I went off to the left far enough that they wouldn't see me when I passed. This is a lovely wood to gallop through. You knew who I was as soon as you saw me, didn't you?"

I nodded again.

"Because you didn't draw that sword thing. You just hurried to me. Now you're going to send me back."

"Take you back, My Lady." It was hard to say, although not as difficult as the thing I had not said.

"Because you don't trust me to obey your orders." There was something heartbreaking in her smile.

"I'm a lowborn boy, My Lady. My father was in trade, and my grandfather was a farmer, what you'd call a peasant. People keep reminding me. Your great-grandfather was a king. I've no right to give you orders."

"Suppose we were married? A husband has the right to give his wife orders, no matter who her great-grandfather was."

"We'll never be married, My Lady."

"I didn't say I'd obey, you'll notice." She stretched out her hand; and when I ignored it, she caught the strap that held my quiver. "Are you really going to take me back?"

"I've got to."

Mani said, "But you don't want to, do you? Doing things you don't want to do always ends in trouble."

Idnn laughed, the sad something that had crept into her smile forgotten. "I'd been wondering whether he'd talk to us when we were alone together."

"He's right," I told her, "doing what you don't want to do generally brings trouble. But there are times when you've got to, and face the trouble."

Idnn nodded her agreement. "That's why I won't separate myself again and ride south instead of north. Go back to Kingsdoom." As if she felt some explanation was needed, she added, "We have a house there."

I tried to pull free, but she kept her sweating gelding beside my charger.

"That was what you were going to tell me to do, wasn't it? Go home to Kingsdoom. Just a minute ago, before you lost your nerve."

"You would be a fool to take my advice, My Lady, and worse to take your own."

"Or I could go to Thortower, and tell the king some cock-and-cow story. You stopped My Ladying me there for a moment. I wish the moment had been longer."

Summoning all my resolve, I said, "I've got to take you back to your father, My Lady."

Her laughter had gone. "Sir Able?"

"Yes, My Lady?"

"Let me ride with you for an hour, and talk to you whil we ride, and I'll go back to my father without any argument.

"I can't permit that, My Lady. You have to return to hi now."

"Half that."

I shook my head.

"I have a fast horse, Sir Able. Suppose he falls and I' hurt."

I caught the wrist of the hand that held the strap.

"I'll tell my father you laid hands on me!"

I nodded. "It's the truth, My Lady. Why shouldn't yo say it?"

"Don't you care for me at all?"

Mani intervened. "Let me judge. I like both of you. I you'll promise to do what I decide, you won't have to figh Wouldn't that be better?"

Idnn nodded. "You're his cat, so that gives him the advan tage. But I'll agree to do whatever you say, even if I have t go back right now."

"Master?"

"I shouldn't. But all right."

"Good." Mani licked his lips. "Hear my judgment. You tw have to stay together talking until you get to that big tree dow there, the one that's lost its top. Then Idnn has to ride straigh back to her father, and she can't say you touched her, or any thing else to hurt you. Now you have to do it. You promised."

I shrugged. "That ride will take half the morning, I'n afraid. But I gave my word, and I'll keep it."

"No longer than a dance," Idnn declared, "but before we ge there, the Mountain Men will attack. We'll be taken prisone all three of us, and spend the next ten years huddled in a froze dungeon. By the time we're released I'll be ugly and no one will want me, but Mani and I will make you marry me."

I snorted.

"When we're both old, bent, and gray, and have thirty-three children, we'll come riding down this road once more. When we reach that tree you'll ride up into the air or down into the ground, and never be seen again."

"Mee-yow!" said Mani.

"Oh, yes, I get to keep you."

I said, "Is this what you wanted to talk to me about?"

"No. Not really. It's just that I've gotten so used to making up stories like that to get my mind off things that I can't help it. I've made up about a thousand, but Mani and my old nurse back home are the only ones who've heard any of them. And now you. Have you ever seen one of the Angrborn, Sir Able?"

Coming as it did, the question took me off guard. I scanned the glades to either side of the War Way, suddenly conscious that I should have been doing it—and had not been—ever since I had caught sight of Idnn.

"I don't mean I see one, I never have. Have you?"

"Yes, My Lady. Not for long."

"The Mountain Men were huge. That's what Mani said. As big as you?"

"Much bigger than I am, My Lady."

"And the Angrborn?"

"As large as I'd be to a little child."

Idnn shuddered, and after that we rode on in silence. At last she said, "Do you remember what I told you when we met just now? I said I ought to be in back with the mules. You didn't argue about it at all. Were you trying to be insulting, or did you really understand what I meant?"

"I believe I understood, My Lady."

"But that doesn't move you? Not at all?"

Feeling about as miserable as I had ever been in my life, I said nothing.

"Our supplies are on those mules. The food we eat every day, and the pavilions. But most of them are carrying gifts for King Gilling of Jotunland."

"I know."

"There's a big helmet in there, one just like the one you're wearing now. A helmet the size of a punch bowl, all brave with gold."

Mani said, "And silks and velvets. Jewels."

Idnn nodded. "We're trying to buy peace. Peace from King Gilling and his Angrborn. There's a war in the east and the Osterlings are creeping into the south, as if the nomads weren't bad enough. Do you know about that?"

I said, "Someone mentioned troubles in the south when I was at Sheerwall, My Lady. Sir Woddet, perhaps. I didn't pay a lot of attention. I thought they couldn't be serious, since the south had been pretty peaceful when I was there. I thought that if things were really bad to the east, we'd be sent there to fight."

"If Marder's knights were sent away, the whole of the north country would lie open to King Gilling." Bitterly she added, "We'd probably give it to him if he'd pledge to keep his people out of the rest of the king's lands."

"If he will not agree to peace, we should go into his lands and fight him and his people there."

"Bravely spoken. They're not supposed to have much to steal, though. Have you any idea how much one of those Frost Giants *eats*?"

"No, My Lady."

"Neither do I. I only hope I don't have to cook for mine."

I did not know what to say to that.

"You've known all along. Isn't that right?"

I shook my head. "Not all along, My Lady. Only since I learned that the Mountain Men, those big men the Angrborn call Mice, were really their children by our women. But—but . . ."

"But you couldn't imagine how such a thing could happen, like the mating of a knight's charger with a child's pony."

"Yes, My Lady."

"Nor can I. No, I can, it's just that I can't talk about what he'd do to her, and how she'd feel afterward."

Idnn squared her shoulders, tossing back her mane of long, dark hair. "It happened at Coldcliff when I was small, Sir Able. It really did. Coldcliff's my uncle's, but we went there to visit. I had a little pony then, and I was wild about her. My father let me ride her. When we got home and her time came, the grooms had to cut her foal out. They found a mare to be wet-nurse to it. They had to, because she died. Do you think I'm making this up?"

"No, My Lady."

"I wish I were, because it would have a nicer ending. My father wanted me to ride him, because by the time he was big enough to ride I was bigger, too. But I never would, and eventually we sold him."

Idnn had begun to cry, and I urged my mount ahead of hers.

When I reached the tree, I wheeled my stallion to look back at her. "You're to go to Lord Beel now, My Lady. That was our agreement."

She reined up. "I have not reached it, Sir Able. Not yet. When you came, I thought my rescuer had arrived."

"My Lady, I've listened to you, and learned more than I ever wished to know. I beg you listen to reason, if only for a minute or two."

"I owe a duty to my father." She spat out the words. "That's what you're going to say. My father's the younger son of a younger son. Do you have any notion what that means?"

"Very little, my lady."

Her lovely voice fell to a whisper. "We were royal, not so long ago. Almost within living memory. My grandfather was a duke, as my uncle is now. My big brother will inherit the barony. My little brother will be a knight. A knight at best, with a poky manor house a week's ride from any place that matters and a couple of villages."

Dropping her reins to her gelding's neck, she wiped her eyes with her fingers. "It devours my father. It's as if he had swallowed a rat, and it were gnawing his heart. Hear me, Sir Able."

I nodded.

"He's served the throne faithfully for twenty-five years, knowing all the while that if only things had fallen out differently, differently by the merest trifle, he'd be sitting on it. But the king has not been ungrateful. Oh, no! Far from it. Do you know what his reward is?"

"Tell me, My Lady."

"Why, *I* am. His daughter, the daughter of a mere baron, is to be a queen, the Queen of Jotunland. I will be given to King Gilling like a cup, a silver goblet into which he may pour his sperm. So that when my father returns to Thortower he can say, 'Her Majesty, my daughter.' "

I nodded. "I understand, My Lady. But I wasn't going to speak of your duty to Lord Beel. I asked you to listen to reason. Duty's like honor. It lies outside it. You want me to rescue you, you say. By rescue you mean I'm supposed to carry you off to Candyland, where your every wish will be granted. I know no such place, and I wouldn't know how to get there if I did."

Idnn had begun to cry again, sobbing like the little girl she had been only a year or two ago.

"You don't think much of knights. Most of the knights at Sheerwall didn't think much of me. Look at me. My armor is still rusty from tramping through the forest in the rain and sleeping wherever I could. Wistan's been instructing me in the best ways to get it bright. My own squire left me in disgust. Half my clothes have been borrowed from Sir Garvaon and his men. Your father gave me this horse. I have no land and no money, and if I were to get one of those manors you think are miles beneath you, I'd be as happy as your father could ever be to see you a queen."

Idnn only cried; and I rode back to her, took hold of her bridle, and turned her gelding around, then gave its rump a good hard slap.

It trotted off, with Idnn still crying on its back; before they had gone far, Mani sprang from my saddlebow and slunk into the tall, coarse grass beside the War Way.

CHAPTER 55

SWORD AND SHIELD

"See how I'm holding my sword," Garvaon said, "with my thumb on top? I want you to hold yours the same way."

What Garvaon was really holding was a green stick that he had cut, and the sword I held was another stick.

"With an ax or a mace, what you want is power. You want to hit as hard as you can with it, because it won't do much damage unless you do. A good sword will do a lot of damage with just a light stroke, so what you want is finesse. You're not going to try to split the other man's shield. That's not what a sword's for."

He paused to study my grip. "A little farther forward. You want your hand up against the guard, not up against the pommel."

I inched my hand forward.

"That's better. Sometimes you want to drop your shield and hold with both hands for a stronger blow."

"Like an ax?"

"No. You still don't chop. You slash." Garvaon took a step backward, looking thoughtful. "I had a lot of trouble with that as a boy. With slashing instead of chopping, I mean. I used to get beaten for it. So here's what did it for me. When you chop, you expect your ax to stay there. Think about chopping wood. But when you slash, you expect your blade to go on by. The edge of your blade is going to hit the other man's neck, maybe a hand back from the point. Then the rest of the edge between that place and point is going to slide along the cut. After that, the point. The whole blade's going to come free, and you can slash again, backhand or forehand."

I nodded, although I was not sure I understood.

"You try to put the weight of your arm behind the weight of your blade, but if you lock your wrist you'll chop. Now that tree right there's the other man. I want to see you go at him, and I want to see you slash."

I tried.

"Faster!"

"I wanted you to see what I was doing," I explained.

"I'll see it. Listen here." Garvaon caught me by the shoulders. "Speed isn't the main thing. It isn't the most important thing. It's *everything.* If you haven't got it, it doesn't matter whether you hold your sword right, or how brave you are, or whether you know a couple of dozen tricks."

I nodded, trying to look surer than I felt.

"Have you ever seen how a bull fights? A couple of really good bulls?"

I shook my head.

"They're fast. It takes your breath, how fast they are. They stand off and paw the ground, testing it so they won't lose their footing. As soon as one starts, they come together like lightning. I said good bulls, understand? If they're good they're fast, because if they're not fast it doesn't matter how strong they are. If one's a little slow, the other will catch him in the side, and then it's all over. Now do it again. Fast."

I did, blocking imagined blows with the shield I had borrowed from a man-at-arms and whipping the tree with my stick until I was panting and dripping sweat.

"That was a lot better," Garvaon told me. "Now let's see you come at me."

I rushed him, but found his shield wherever my stick hit, while Garvaon's stick tapped my knees and calves.

When he had smacked both my ears with it, he stepped back and dropped his point. "You're fast, but you're making a couple of bad mistakes. Every cut you make's a separate operation."

I nodded.

"That's not how it's supposed to be. The next cut has to flow out of the last one." He showed me, his stick flying and fluid. "This is easy, because the sword's so light. When I practice back home, I use a practice sword that's heavier than Battle Witch."

Reflecting that Sword Breaker was heavier than any actual sword I had handled, I nodded again.

"Now let's see you do it. Down then back up. Left, then right. Up and across. Keep your arm behind it. You're not waving a stick, you're cutting with a sword. He's wearing mail and there's a leather jerkin under it. . . .

"You're slowing down. Don't! If you get tired you'll die. That's better."

The cuts became the surges of the clear sea of Aelfrice, the green stick that was the Green Sword, that was Eterne, curling like a wave and breaking like an avalanche, only to return to the sea and rush ashore again.

"That's it! That's it!

"All right. Enough."

Gasping, I stopped.

"That was good. If you can do that every time with a real sword, you're a swordsman." Garvaon paused, and for a moment his hard, narrow eyes grew vague. "Master Tung used to say a true swordsman was a lily blooming in the fire."

He coughed. "Master Tung taught me when I wasn't any higher than your stick. Do you understand what he meant?"

Recalling the fight on the Osterlings' ship, I said, "Maybe I do, a little."

"Every Overcyn in Skai knows I never did." Garvaon laughed self-consciously. "But he said it over and over, so it must have meant a lot to him, and he was a wonderful swordsman."

"And a good man. He must have been. If he hadn't been, you wouldn't talk about him the way you do."

"You're not a wonderful swordsman," Garvaon told me, "but you're coming along. Maybe if you can get to the bottom of that business about the lily in the fire you will be."

With his stick, he tapped my shield. "I said you were doing two things wrong. Remember that? What were they?"

"You said—you said my sword wasn't like the sea. Not like it enough, anyway." I groped for another idea. "And you said that . . ."

"I didn't say it. I'm not asking what I said. I'm asking what you were doing wrong. You got the first one. You've got to make your sword flow. Now what was the other one?"

"I don't know."

"Think about it. Think back on our fight and the way you were fighting me."

I tried.

Garvaon said, "While you're thinking, I'll tell you a little secret. If you want to be good, you've got to think about your fights after they're over. It doesn't matter if they're real or practice, or what the weapons were. You've got to go back inside your mind and look at it. What did he do, and what did you? How did it work?"

"You kept hitting my legs," I said, "and then you got my head. I was hitting your shield all the time. I didn't want to and I tried not to, but that's how it always was."

"Good enough. When you came at me, you came sword-side first, like this."

Garvaon demonstrated.

"That was because you were thinking sword, sword, sword when you ought to have been thinking shield, sword, shield, sword, shield. Your shield is every bit as important as your sword. Never forget that."

He paused to look at his own. "Sometimes I've fought men who had never really learned it, and I've always known after the second breath. They go down fast."

I swallowed. "Like I would have, if you'd had a real sword. That first cut to my ankle."

"Right. Now we're going to try something different.

Switch your shield over to your right hand, and hold the sword in your left. I want you to think shield, sword, shield, sword. Understand?"

So I learned to fight left-handed. It sounds dumb, I know, but it was a good lesson. When the shield is on your right arm and the sword is in your left hand, you use the shield as much as the sword, and that is the way to win. Beginners are always thinking about how they are going to stab or cut. Seasoned fighters think about staying in one piece while they do it. What's more, they know you can make the shield your weapon and the sword your defense.

But first of all speed. Which is what Garvaon stressed over and over. If you cannot do it fast, you cannot do it. A young knight—as I was—has it in him to be faster than an older one like Garvaon. I knew that, and so did he. But he kept on being faster just the same, because he had fought and practiced so much that it was second nature to him. I did not get a lot of lessons from him. I rode ahead into Jotunland before we had gone much farther. But I learned enough that when I got to Skai some of the knights there, knights who were still famous in Mythgarthr, said I was a better swordsman than most newcomers.

Garvaon was a simple man, and it was that simplicity that made him hard to understand, although I am a simple man myself. He practiced with his men whenever he could, and he taught them to the best of his ability, which was great. He told me once that he was always afraid before the battle, but never afraid once battle was joined. That is the thing that makes men attack too soon, sometimes; but if it ever made Garvaon attack too soon, I never heard the story. When it was time to fight, he told them to follow him and waded into the thick of it. He took pride in his appearance, and in the appearance of his men. He did his duty as he saw it, saw that most men did not, and was a little contemptuous of them because of it. He was the kind of fighting man who sees to it that none of the horses has a loose shoe.

CHAPTER 56

ASHES IN THE PASS

For an hour I had been in sight of the pass as we toiled up the War Way. Now, abruptly, there was someone—no, two people—standing in the road there, crimson against the cloudy sky. I wanted to spur the stallion, but he had been working hard all morning, and whatever reserves he had might be needed that afternoon.

One of the figures was waving and pointing, hips thrown to counterbalance the graceful body; as it pointed I realized it was not that they were sunlit against the lowering clouds; but that they were in fact red.

And women.

"Uri! Baki! Is that you?" .

Something bent and so dirty that it seemed to have been molded from the mud of the road rose from the ditch to catch my stirrup. "Master? Sar Able? Master?"

Startled, I pulled up.

"Master! I found ya!"

I could only stare at the starved, grimy face.

"Ya was goin' to take me. Ta give me a place, Master. Ya tolt Ma."

"I'm sorry," I said as gently as I could. "Do I know you?"

"Uns, Master. I'se Uns, 'n I fought Org fer ya after he t'rue ya inna barley."

"The farmwife's son." I was thinking out loud. "The younger son."

"Yessar. Yes, Master. Org'd a' killed ya if it hadn't been fer me." His watery eyes were exactly like those of a wounded animal.

"He hurt you," I said. "I thought you'd run."

Uns nodded frantically. "Ma said. She said you was goin' ta take me on on'y ya t'ought I'd run off. So I gone lookin' fer ya. I can't stand up straight, but I can walk pretty fast." Something like pride crept into Uns' soiled face. "Dey tolt me inna castle where ya'd went. A scullion done, Master, 'n give me somethin' too. How far 'twas, 'n how bad, but I come anyways. I knew I'd find ya, Master, 'n it'd be awright."

From the white stallion's other side, Uri reached up to tap my thigh. "When you are through talking to that beggar, Lord, Baki and I have something of importance to show you."

I looked around at her. "Is it urgent?"

"We think so."

"I'm going up there, Uns." I pointed as I spoke. "Meet me there. Or if I've gone before you arrive, follow me just as you've been doing. I'll get you a horse as soon as I can manage it."

Uri said, "May I sit behind, Lord? I ran down to you."

I thought about how it would feel. "No, you can't." I dismounted. "But you may have the saddle to yourself. I'll lead him."

"I cannot ride while you walk!" She sounded indignant.

"Then you must walk with Uns and me."

"I will climb the rocks," she decided, "there is shade there." For a time we saw her slipping into crevices like a shadow or springing from point to point like a goat, dodging the sunlight whenever the sun broke through the clouds; soon it seemed that she had faded into the wind.

"Dat's a Aelf, Master," Uns declared. "Her 'n her sister come snoopin' round couple times wilst I'se on da road, on'y I woun't tell 'em nothin'."

"It would have done no harm," I said. "I'm glad they didn't hurt you."

Uns chortled. "Oh, dey done wat dey might, Master, on'y 'twasn't much."

"It's good that you can make merry about it, Uns. I don't think most people could."

He grinned; he had crooked, yellowed teeth. "Found ya, dint I, Sar? So aw's fine, watever 'tis. Wat do I care fer dem Aelfs?"

"If you're going with us," I said slowly, "things are sure to be far from all right with you. We are already on the marches of Jotunland."

Uns looked frightened.

That evening we camped in the valley on the other side of the pass, in a place nearly level, where a tortuous path wound down a gorge to a foaming stream. I came to Beel's pavilion there and found him conferring with Garvaon while Idnn looked on.

"Sit down," Beel said when his servingman had fetched a folding stool. "Sir Garvaon and I have been discussing the dangers we face from this time forward. I was on the point of sending the sentry for you when he said you were waiting outside. You're our best bowman, and that may mean a great deal."

"But a poor swordsman." I smiled wryly; I was tired, so tired that I was very grateful for the stool on which I sat and wished it had a back.

Garvaon shook his head. "Don't you believe him, You Lordship. He's better with a sword than most, and improving every day. What about a little practice when we're through here, Sir Able?"

"I'll do my best."

Idnn said, "Shame on you, Sir Garvaon. Look at him He's drooping like a lily."

"Needs the fire to wake him up. Then he'll be at me like lion."

I cleared my throat. "I'm tired, I admit. But I've had ba news today."

Beel asked what it had been.

"I told you I'd leave you when we reached the pass whe my servant waited, Your Lordship. I'm sure you remember

Idnn said, "I do."

"Yet we've come beyond it, and I'm still here. I think also told you that I'd sent Gylf ahead to let Pouk know I wa coming."

"Gylf's your dog?" Beel inquired.

"Yes, My Lord."

Idnn said, "May I borrow your cat again, Sir Able? I mi him."

I spread my hands. "I'd gladly lend him if I had him, M Lady. Though he left you, he hasn't returned to me."

Beel said, "And your dog?"

"My Lord has run ahead of me. Gylf hasn't returned."

Garvaon said, "You'd better tell us."

"I'll be as brief as I can. My man Pouk seems to hav thought the pass back there a suitable place for me to tak my stand as I had pledged myself to do. He camped ther apparently for several days. We found the remains of tw fires, and even the spot where he'd pastured the horses."

Garvaon raised an eyebrow. "We?"

It was surely not the time to introduce Uri and Baki. I said, "My servant Uns and I. Uns was the crippled beggar one of your men-at-arms questioned. Separated from me, he's been forced to beg."

I waited for someone else to speak, but nobody did.

"Now I'm forced to beg for him, My Lord. He has no horse, and that's what I came to see you about. Can you spare one? Or a mule—anything."

"You found your servant's camp," Beel said. "Go on from there, please."

"I found it, but they weren't there. Neither my servant nor the woman I'd been told was traveling with him. Neither was Gylf. Or Mani, my cat, for that matter."

"They had gone north?" Beel inquired.

"Yes, My Lord. They must have. There is only this one road, this War Way. If they'd gone south we'd have met them on the road. So they went north."

Garvaon said, "Into Jotunland."

Beel shrugged. "We ourselves are in Jotunland now. We entered it as soon as we left the pass and started down. No doubt we're in more danger now than we were yesterday, but I can't honestly say that it feels much different."

Idnn said, "Do you think your servant—and this woman you say is such a mystery to you—would have gone north on their own?"

"Pouk certainly wouldn't. What the woman might do, or might force or persuade him to do, I can't even guess at."

Garvaon grunted agreement. "Who knows what a woman will do?"

Idnn shot him a glance. "Why, women do. Sometimes, at least."

Beel muttered, "This is no time to begin quarreling."

"I'm not quarreling, Father. I'm explaining something Sir

Garvaon ought to have learned for himself. But I'd rather S
Able explained a few things to me. Can I ask you question
Sir Able?"

I sighed, sagging on my folding stool. "Yes, My Lad
You may."

"Then I'll ask a very obvious one. This man of your
Pouk? Would he have fought if the Frost Giants had tried
seize him and your horses?"

"I doubt it very much, My Lady."

"What about the woman you said was with him? Woul
she have fought?"

I smiled. "I was told she had a sword, My Lady. So poss
bly she would. You must tell Sir Garvaon and me."

Garvaon said somberly, "Some women would."

"Because there was blood," Idnn continued. "You four
the ashes, didn't you see the blood? Sir Garvaon did, and h
showed it to me."

Beel sighed. "I've told my daughter not to ride with th
vanguard. Apparently I must also tell the vanguard not
ride with my daughter."

Garvaon said, "My Lady rode up while I was examinir
the campsite, Your Lordship. I'd dismounted, and no dou
she'd seen I'd found something. Naturally she was curious

Idnn smiled as if to say, "You see how Sir Garvaon de
fends me?"

Beel's attention was on me. "I saw the blood, of cours
And the ashes and the rest. I found a foot-mark in tho
ashes, off to one side of the younger fire where it was som
what hidden by the shadow of a stone. Did you see it?"

I shook my head, too discouraged to speak.

"The paw-mark of a very large wolf or dog. As for th
blood, your servant may have resisted. It's possible you mi

judged him. Or the woman may have, as Idnn suggests. Or they both may have."

I said, "I suppose so."

"It's also possible, unfortunately, that one or both may have been injured, although they did not resist. Or that the woman beat your servant, or that he beat her. We have no way of knowing."

"My Lord . . ."

"Yes? What is it?"

"This isn't what I came for. I came hoping to get a horse for Uns. But you know something about magic. Would it be possible for you, somehow, to find out what happened to them?"

For a moment there was no sound in Beel's silk pavilion except Idnn's sharply indrawn breath.

At last Beel said, "Perhaps I should have thought of that. It may tell us nothing. Let me be quite frank with you, Sir Able. I fail more often than I succeed."

"But if you succeeded, My Lord—"

"We might learn something of value. Perfectly true."

His daughter smiled and leaned toward him, and he said, "You want the excitement. Mountebanks feign magic as a show, Idnn, pretending to swallow swords and toads. But magic, real magic, is not entertainment. Do you know how the Aelf came to be?"

She shook her head. "No, Father. But I'd like to, even if there aren't any."

"There are. What about you, Sir Garvaon? Sir Able? Do either of you know?"

Garvaon shook his head. I nodded.

"Then tell us."

"There's someone called Kulili in Aelfrice, My Lord. Maybe I should have said in the world we call Aelfrice, because it doesn't really belong to the Aelf, it belongs to Kulili." I paused. "I'm only telling you what I've been told, though I believe it's true."

"Go on."

"All right. There were disembodied spirits in Aelfrice then, creatures something like ghosts, although they'd never been alive. Kulili made magic bodies of mud and leaves and moss and ashes and so forth, and put the disembodied spirits into them. If she used fire, mostly, they became Fire Aelf, Salamanders. If she used mostly seawater, they're Sea Aelf, Kelpies."

"Correct." Beel looked from me to Garvaon, and from Garvaon to Idnn. "We're not like the Aelf. We're much more like Kulili, having been created, as she was, by the Father of the fathers of the Overcyns, the God of the highest world. Here, as there, he also created elemental spirits. As Sir Able says, they're rather like ghosts. They are creatures both ancient and knowing, having the accumulated wisdom of centuries of centuries."

Garvaon coughed and looked uncomfortable.

"They hope that we will someday do for them what Kulili did for the Aelf. Or at least that is how it seems to me. Then they may try to take Mythgarthr from us as the Aelf have wrested Aelfrice from Kulili. I don't know. But in our own time, what is called magic consists of making contact with them and persuading them to help the magician, either for a reward, or out of pity—as the Overcyns help us at times—or simply to earn our trust."

Garvaon said, "It can be dangerous. So I've heard, Your Lordship."

Beel nodded. "It can be, but I'm going to attempt it tonight, if Sir Able will assist me. Will you, Sir Able?"

"Of course, My Lord."

"We may find your dog, your servant, and even this mysterious swordswoman. If we do, we may learn things that will stand us in good stead in Jotunland. But the most likely outcome is that we'll learn nothing at all. I want you to understand that."

"I do, My Lord."

"Sir Garvaon may attend me or not, as he chooses."

Idnn declared, "*I'll* attend you, Father. You can count on me."

"I feared it."

Garvaon said, "I'll be at your side, Your Lordship. You may rely on me, always."

"I know it." Beel turned back to me. "I'll talk to Master Egr about getting a horse for your beggar. Meet me here when the moon is high. Until then you're dismissed."

Garvaon rose too. "Get some rest. Maybe we can have a little practice before it gets too dark."

CHAPTER 57

GARVAON'S BOON

Outside, the other pavilions had been erected as well. The kitchen fires were burning, although a dozen men were still fetching wood, and the ring of axes sounded from the mountain slopes. Muleteers led strings of braying, weary mules over the edge of the gorge and presumably down the precipitous path to the stream.

In Garvaon's pavilion, three men-at-arms were setting up cots. Mine was up already; the blanket Garvaon had found for me had been laid on it, and Mani was seated on that. "Well, well," I said, "where have you been?"

Mani gave the three men-at-arms a significant look.

"All right, you spoiled cat." I sat down and pulled off my boots. "You don't have to talk to me if you don't want to. Just let me lie down."

Mani did, and laid himself so his head was at my ear. After that, I dozed off for a few minutes.

When I woke up again, Mani said, "I have news. Those Aelf girls found your dog. One of the giants has chained him up."

I yawned and whispered, "Can't they free him?"

"They're trying. *I* wouldn't, but apparently they think you'd want them to. At any rate, that's what one told me, and she made me promise to tell you. She wanted to get back to getting the chain off your dog—or whatever the brute actually is."

To give myself time in which to think, I asked, "Which one was it?"

"The ugly one," Mani whispered.

I turned my head to look at him, and opened my eyes. "They're both quite pretty."

"*You* at least wear fur."

"Clothes, you mean. They could wear clothes too, if they wanted to. But it's warm in Aelfrice, so most of the Aelf don't. Clothes there are for . . ." I groped for a word. "For dignity. For kings and queens."

"Every cat is royal," Mani declared in a tone that said he would be mad if you argued. "I am myself."

The last of the men-at-arms was leaving the pavilion as he spoke, and I noticed he was holding two fingers pointed at the ground.

"You were overheard, Your Most High and Catty Majesty," I told Mani.

"Don't mock me. I won't tolerate it." Mani sat up and spoke a little louder.

"I apologize. It was rude of me, and I'm sorry."

"Then the incident is forgotten. And don't worry about those fellows, nobody believes them anyhow. As for your Aelf girls, I admit the fire color is attractive, and they have fur here and there. When I say the ugly one, I mean the one who looks least like a cat."

"That would be Baki, I suppose."

"I'll not dispute it." Mani began to clean his private parts by licking them.

"Mani, I just had an idea."

"Really, Sir Able?" Amused, he looked up. "You?"

"Maybe not, but I thought of something. You must have seen a lot of spells cast, a lot of fortunes told and so on."

"I've watched my share," Mani admitted.

"So you probably know a good deal about magic yourself. Tonight Lord Beel's going to try to find Pouk by magic."

Mani purred softly.

"I'll be there, and so will Lady Idnn. I doubt that anyone will object if I bring you along. Will you come?"

He licked a large black paw, studied it, and licked it again. "I'll consider it."

"Good. That's all I can ask. Watch what goes on, and if anything occurs to you, tell me."

"I don't know Pouk," Mani said thoughtfully. "Does he like cats?"

"Absolutely. There was a cat on the *Western Trader,* and Pouk was very fond of it."

"Really?"

"Really, I wouldn't lie to you about something like that."

"In that case, what was this cat's name?"

"I don't know, but Pouk—"

I broke off as Garvaon entered the pavilion. "Ready for your next lesson, Sir Able?"

"Absolutely." I sat up.

"It's nearly dark already." Garvaon sat down on his own cot. "So I'd just like to talk about foining tonight. We won't have a lot of time anyway. You can see the moon above the mountaintops."

"What's foining?"

"Stabbing with your sword. Pushing the point." Garvaon gestured. "I have the feeling we may be fighting again soon. I could be wrong, but that's the feeling I have."

"I think so too."

"Foining's one of the best ways of taking down your man in a real fight. People don't like to talk about it."

I waited.

"I don't myself, because quite a few of us consider it unfair. But when it's you or him . . ."

"I understand."

"It's not lawful in tournaments, not even in the melee. That's where the business of unfairness comes from. But it's not lawful because it's so dangerous. Even if you grind the point off the sword, you can hurt somebody pretty badly by foining."

I got up. "Can I show you my mace?"

"That thing that looks like a sword? Sure."

I drew Sword Breaker and handed it to Garvaon. "The end is squared off. See?"

Garvaon nodded. "I do, and I think I know what you're going to say."

"I hit another knight in the face once with the end."

"How'd it work?"

I had to think about that. "He was as tall as I am, as I remember. But he fell down, and I had no more trouble with him. He kept his hands on his face after that."

Garvaon nodded and smiled. "You gave yourself a better lesson then than I could ever give you. You probably knocked some teeth out, and you may have broken bone, too. But if you'd had a real sword with a sharp point, you'd have killed him. And that's better."

He drew his sword. "This's the best kind for foining. A little taper to the blade, and a good sharp point. You want a light point for finesse, but you want some weight to your blade, too, so it foins hard. Foining's the best way to get through mail. Did you know that?"

I shook my head.

"It is, and it's the best way to give him a deep wound, whether he's got mail or not. The Angrborn don't wear mail very much."

"I didn't know that, either."

"I think they think they don't need it with us. Have you ever fought one?"

"No, I saw one once, but I didn't fight him. I was scared stiff."

"You'll be scared next time, too. Everybody is. You see one, and you think you need a whole army."

"Have you fought them?"

Garvaon nodded. "One. Once."

"You killed him?"

Garvaon nodded again. "I had a couple of archers with me, and one put an arrow in his chin. He threw his hands up, the same way your man did when you got him in the face. I ran in and cut him right over the knee." Garvaon's finger indicated the place. "Right here. He fell, and I foined all the way through his neck. We brought his head back to show Lord Beel, pulling it behind two horses." Garvaon smiled at the memory. "It was about as big as a barrel."

"They're as big as people say, then. I know the one I saw looked terribly big."

"Depends on who the people are, like always. But they're big, all right. It's a jolt anytime you see one. They aren't made quite like us, either. Their legs are thicker than they should be. They're wide all over, and their heads ought to be smaller. When you cut one off like I did, it's so big it scares you."

For perhaps the hundredth time, I tried to visualize a whole raiding party of Angrborn. Not one alone, but a score or a hundred marching down the War Way. "I understand now why this road's so wide."

"The thing is, they're slow. I don't mean slow walkers. They'll get someplace a lot faster than you will, because their steps are so long. But slow at turning and things like that. If they weren't, we wouldn't stand a chance."

"Speed is everything," I said.

"Right. I've fought you. With those practice swords we use, I mean. You're strong, one of the strongest men I ever came up against. But you're not stronger than one of them, so you've got to be faster. And smarter. Don't think it's going to be easy."

"I never have," I said. "I knew a man who fought them."

"Did he win?"

I shook my head. "I want to ask you more about foining. But first, what do you think about what Lord Beel's going to do tonight?"

"My honest opinion? Between the two of us?"

"Between the three of us." I smiled as I stroked Mani's head.

"All right. I doubt anything will happen, and probably we won't find out anything."

"I thought you were worried about it," I said, "when we were in his pavilion, I mean."

"I was." Garvaon hesitated, and looked around. "I've been with him before when he's tried to do something like this. Usually nothing happens, but sometimes something does. I don't like things I can't understand."

"May I ask what happened?"

Garvaon shook his head. His face was grim.

I let out my breath. "All right. I'll see for myself tonight. Do you think we ought to have a look at the moon?"

"Not yet. I want to talk to you a little bit more, and it hasn't been long enough anyhow. We haven't been together very long, but I've been doing my best to teach you, like I said I would. You'll allow that?"

"Of course."

"We fought the Mountain Men together, too."

I nodded. "Yes. We did."

"So we're friends, and you owe me a boon."

Mani, who had been ignoring us since it became apparent that there would be no more talk of magic, regarded Garvaon with interest.

"You'll admit that, Sir Able?"

"Sure. I never denied it."

"I reserved my boon, and I wasn't going to ask it, since you won. We both know it."

"I owe you a boon," I said, "you only have to tell me what you want."

For a second or two Garvaon sat studying me. "I'm a widower. Did you know that?"

I shook my head.

"I am. It will be two years this fall. My son died too. Volla was trying to bear me a son."

"I'm sorry. Darned sorry."

Garvaon cleared his throat. "Lady Idnn has never showed any interest in me."

I waited, feeling Mani's claws through the thick wool of my trousers.

"Not until today. Today she smiled at me, and we talked like friends."

"I've got it," I said.

"She's young. Twenty-two years younger than I am. But we're going to be living in this Frost Giant king's stronghold. There won't be many real men around."

"You and her father," I said. "Your archers and men-at-arms, and her father's servants."

"Not you?"

"Right. I won't be there. I'm going to find Pouk and get back my horses and the rest of my stuff. When I've done it, I'll take my stand someplace in these mountains. That's what I promised Duke Marder I'd do, and it's what I'm going to do."

"You aren't going to stay?"

"I'm not even going as far as King Gilling's stronghold, if I find Pouk before we get there. Do you still want your boon? What is it?"

"You're younger than I am."

"Sure. A lot."

"You're bigger, too, and you're better-looking. I know all that."

"I'm a knight with no reputation at all," I reminded him. "Don't leave that out. If you've wondered why I'm so hot to find Pouk, one reason is that he's got everything I own with him. You've got a manor called Finefield, don't you?"

"Yes."

"A big house with a wall around it."

"And a tower," Garvaon said.

"Fields, too, and peasants to plow and plant and herd your

cows. I don't have anything like that." All the time we were talking, I was thinking about what Idnn had said about Beel giving her to King Gilling, but I could not tell Garvaon and I would have been afraid of what he might do if I did. And underneath those things I kept thinking over and over that if Idnn really wanted to be rescued, here he was.

Garvaon said, "You wish me to name my boon. This isn't easy for me."

"I think I can guess it, so you don't have to."

"I want you to give me your word, your word of honor, that you'll do nothing else to lessen me in her eyes. You're a better bowman than I, and everyone knows it. Let it be enough."

"I will."

"If she rejects me, I'll tell you. But until she does, and I tell you so, I want you to promise you won't try to win her for yourself."

CHAPTER 58

BACK TO THE ASHES

"You've got my word." I offered Garvaon my hand.

He took it; his own was like he was, no bigger than most but hard and strong. "You want her, naturally."

"I don't."

"She's beautiful."

"She sure is." I nodded. "But she's not the one I'm in love with."

"She's the daughter of a baron, too." For a moment Garvaon looked ready to give up. "His only daughter."

"You're right. Beel won't make it easy."

Garvaon squared his shoulders. "I have your word, Sir Able. What was it you wanted to ask about foining?"

"What should I do when the other man foins? How can I guard against it?"

"Ah." Garvaon stood and picked up his shield. "That's a good one. First you need to know that it's hard to guard against. If he likes it, you've got to take that very, very seriously."

"I will."

"Second, you need to know when he's most likely to do it. Do you still have that shield you used last night?"

I shook my head. "I gave it back to Beaw."

"Then take mine." Garvaon got out the sticks that were our practice swords.

"Don't we need more light?" I put Mani down.

"We're not going to fight. I just want to show you a couple of things. You remember what I said about not coming at your man right leg first? Another reason is that if he knows much about foining, he can stick his sword in it.

"That's right, square up. Now I'm not going to put my point in your face or your leg, which is what I might do in a real fight. I'm just going to foin your shield. I want you to stay squared up, but back away until I can't foin your shield without taking three or four steps toward you."

I took a couple of short steps backward, still on my guard.

"That it? Get set." Before Garvaon finished the last word, the tip of his stick hit the shield.

He sprang back. "Did you see what I did? I was leading with my left leg a trifle. I took a long step with my right. Add the length of my arm to the length of my blade and it's as tall as I am."

"It was like magic," I said.

"Maybe, but it wasn't. You've got to practice that long step. It isn't as easy as it looks. Also you've got to hold your shield up over your head when you take it. You're wide open to an overhand cut, if your man's fast enough."

"I'd like to see that," I said.

Garvaon glanced at the doorway. "It's brighter out there. I'll teach you how to make anybody back off, then we'd better call on His Lordship."

With his shield on his arm, he demonstrated the thrust and had me do it. At the third, I felt Mani tugging my leg.

"Ready to go?" Garvaon asked.

"I should go back and dig out my helmet," I told him. "Lord Beel will want to see me wearing it. Tell him I'll be along in a minute or two."

Back in the pavilion, I stooped to talk to Mani. "What is it?"

"I ran over to Idnn's to watch the preparations," Mani explained, "and he's going to do it right there. He ought to go back to where the ashes were. Tell him to put some ashes in the bowl, too."

The front of Beel's pavilion was lit with a dozen candles. The stony ground had been smoothed, and a carpet laid over it. Beel sat cross-legged on the carpet with a wineskin, a gold bowl, and a gold cup before him. Idnn was in a folding chair in front of the silk curtain, with Garvaon standing beside her.

"There you are," Beel said. "Now we can begin."

I bowed. "Would it be possible for me to speak in private with My Lord for a moment?"

Beel hesitated. "Is this important?"

"I think so, My Lord. I dare hope you'll think so too."

Idnn said, "Sir Garvaon and I will wait outside, Father. Call us when you're ready."

"I will not order my daughter out into the night." Beel turned to me. "If we go a short distance from the camp, will that be sufficient?"

We walked a hundred yards up the valley. Beel stopped there, and turned to face me. "You might begin by explaining why you would not speak in the presence of my daughter and my trusted retainer."

"Because I needed to advise you," I explained. "As a mere knight—"

"I understand. What is it?"

"You called me a wizard. I'm not, but I've got a friend who knows a little about magic."

"And he—or she—has taught you a few simple things, I suppose. Your modesty becomes you."

"Thank you, My Lord. Thank you very much." I looked around for Mani, but Mani was nowhere in sight.

"I've a question, Sir Able. In the past, you have not been entirely disingenuous in answering my questions."

"Maybe not. I apologize."

"If I listen to your advice—this friend's advice, though I supposed that you came to me alone when you first sought the loan of a horse—will you answer one question fully and forthrightly? Upon your honor? Because I will not hear your advice otherwise."

I shook my head. "This is very important to me, My Lord."

"All the more reason for you to pledge yourself."

"All right, I'll promise. But only if you take my advice as well as listen to it."

"You would command me?"

"Never, My Lord. But . . . Well, I've got to find Pouk. Won't you do as I advise? I'm begging."

"The choice is mine? Save that you will not pledge yourself unless I do as you wish?"

"Yes, Your Lordship."

"Then let me hear you."

When we returned to Beel's pavilion, he ordered horses brought for all of us. Another horse carried the carpet, the wineskin, and other things; and a sixth, his servingman.

"We are going back up to the pass," Beel told Garvaon. "You should ride before us, I think. Sir Able can bring up the rear, which may be the more dangerous post."

What it really was, I thought as I rode rear guard, was the loneliest. If that were not bad enough, I had to rein in my stallion every minute to keep him behind the sumpter that carried the baggage.

The rocks, and the occasional tree and bush to either side of the War Way, concealed no enemies that I could see; and although I listened hard, I could hear only the cold, lonely song of the wind, and the *clop-clop* of hooves. The moon shone bright, and the cold stars kept their secrets.

When I rode out on a rocky spur far up the mountainside and looked down on the camp, its dark pavilions and dying fires seemed every bit as far away as those stars. . . .

CHAPTER 59

IN JOTUNLAND

Beel ordered the carpet spread between the ashes and asked everyone why there had been two fires. I shook my head; but Idnn said, "Sir Garvaon will know. Wilt tell us, sir knight?"

"They built their first fire here." Garvaon pointed. "That was because it offered the best shelter from the wind, which is generally in the west. The next night, or it could have been the night after that, one of them saw it could be seen from the north."

"And it was seen," Beel muttered. "Now we will see what I will see myself, if I see anything. I must caution all of you again that this may not prove effectual."

He glanced down at the bowl his servingman held. "Why that's silver! Where's my gold bowl, Swert?"

"I told him to bring this one, Father," Idnn said. "You charm by moonlight, and not by day. This is my fruit bowl. I think it may bring you good fortune tonight."

Beel smiled. "Have you become a witch?"

"No, Father. I know no magic, but I had the advice of a friend who does."

"Sir Able?"

She shook her head. "I had to promise I wouldn't tell you who it is."

"One of your maids, I suppose."

Idnn said nothing.

"Not that it matters." Beel knelt upon the carpet. The servingman handed him a silver goblet and a skin of wine, and he filled both bowl and goblet.

Mani had crept up to watch; to get a better view, he sprang onto my shoulder.

"I ask all of you to keep silent," Beel said. Reaching into his coat, he produced a small leather bag from which he took a thick pinch of dried herbs. Half he dropped into the bowl, the rest into the goblet. Closing his eyes, he recited an invocation.

In the hush that followed, it seemed to me that the song of the wind had altered, humming with words in a tongue I did not know.

"Mongan!" Beel exclaimed. "Dirmaid! Sirona!" He drained the silver goblet at a single draught and bent to look into the silver bowl.

So did I, crouching beside him. After a moment I was joined by Idnn, and she by Garvaon.

As through the mouth of a dark cave, I beheld a forest of unearthly beauty. Disiri the Moss Queen stood in a glade where strange flowers blossomed, naked, more graceful than mortal women and more fair; her green hair rose twice the height of her head, nodding and flowing in the breeze that stirred the flowers. The younger Toug cowered before her, and I waited on my knees. With a slender silver sword, she touched both my shoulders.

"This is of the past," I murmured to Beel. "Drop ashes into the wine."

Beel regarded me with empty eyes; but Idnn brought a pinch of ash and dropped it into the bowl, where it seemed to dull the luster of the surface.

It became the gray coat of a thickset man who walked a long and muddy road across a plain veiled by cloud. Towers, squat and huge, rose in the distance. With his staff, this man struck down a woman no larger than a child. A ragged figure who had been driving before them horses no bigger than dogs threw himself over her, offering his back for hers. The man in the gray coat struck him contemptuously, then nudged both with the toe of his boot.

The toe of the black boot nudging Ulfa grew until it filled the bowl, which held only ashes floating on wine.

"Listen!" Garvaon rose.

I rose, too, and listened; but I heard nothing except the moaning of the wind—an empty moan, as if the thing that had come into it was gone.

Idnn and the servingman were helping Beel to his feet. In another moment Garvaon was in the saddle and clattering away.

"Our camp is being attacked," I told Idnn; I got Mani off my shoulder and handed him to her. "I have to go. Stay here 'til I come for you."

She shouted something as I rode away, but whether she had pleaded for me to stay, or wished me good luck, or begged me to keep Garvaon safe, I had no idea. I wondered about it, and other things, as I spurred the stallion down the steep mountain road.

For a minute it seemed trees were walking where the camp had been. No fires remained, and no pavilions. My stallion shied as something large and loud hit the ground beside it.

I got my bow and quiver from behind the saddle and slid off the stallion's back. Somewhere in the darkness, another bow sang.

A second stone flew, hitting the white stallion. He screamed with pain and galloped away. Bracing the foot of my bow against my own, I leaned my weight on the supple wood and fitted the looped bowstring into the notches at the bowhead.

I pulled an arrow to my ear and let fly. A hundred paces off, the giant who had been stoning the white stallion bellowed, a noise like thunder.

I sent a second arrow after the first, and a third after the second, guessing at eyes I could not see.

The giant crumpled.

Dawn found two weary knights making their way back up to the pass. My white stallion was lame, and I walked more than I rode, giving my saddle (a big armored one that weighed as much as some men) to Uns to carry.

Garvaon could have outdistanced us easily, but he seemed too tired even to urge his horse forward. The scabbard that had held Battle Witch hung empty. Then Idnn waved to us from a point of rock not far below the snow line, and he drove his heels into his horse's sides and disappeared around the next bend.

"Ah, love!" sighed an insolent voice not far from my ear; I looked around, surprised, and saw Uri on my stallion. "You're back!"

She grinned at me. "No, that is my sister."

"Aren't you afraid Uns will see you up there? He's not very far behind us."

"I care not a whit if he does, and I will leave anyway as soon as you are out of this shadow."

I stopped, biting my lip while I stroked the stallion's muzzle. "I told Lord Beel about you and your sister. I had to."

"She is not really my sister. We just say that."

"Aren't you angry?"

Uri grinned again. "It will make a lot more trouble for you and for him than for us. Did you explain that my sister and I are your slaves?"

I shook my head. "I called you my friends. I wanted him to come up here when he tried to see where Pouk was for me, and he promised to if I'd answer one question, a complete answer. I've forgotten the words he used, but that was what he meant."

"And did you?"

"Yes. I kept my promise, and he kept his. He wanted to know why I couldn't use my own powers to look for Pouk, and I had to explain that the only way I had to look for him was to send you two after him." I paused. "I didn't tell him your names."

"That is well." Uri smiled.

"I said I'd sent Gylf after Pouk and now you two were trying to find out what happened to Gylf."

"Nothing complicated. A giant had caught him and had his slaves chain him up. We know all about chains, but we had to go back to Aelfrice for tools, and then come back up here, and then find him again because they had moved him. Where's your cat, by the way? Have you lost that, too?"

"He's with Lady Idnn."

"He isn't." Mani jumped to the top of a boulder. "He was with Idnn when she waved, but that other knight came running, and I thought the least I could do was come down here to meet you. She didn't want me around right then anyway."

Uri said, "I am surprised you knew it."

"Meaning I'm intruding on a tête-à-tête between you and my own dear much admired master, the renowned knight Sir Able of the High Heart. He has only to ask me to leave, and

I'll vanish in a flash of black far lovelier than your own dingy whatever-it-is color. Master?"

"You may remain if you choose."

"A lawful decision." It was Mani's turn to grin. "The law being that the cat may do whatever he wants. You are his slave, young woman? I believe I overheard you say that."

"Yes."

"Well, I'm his cat, a much higher post."

I motioned to Uri. "Uns is coming around that last bend, so unless you really don't care if he sees you—"

She slipped off the stallion and stood under its head. "Baki is returning our tools, and I came to tell you your dog is free."

"Is he coming back here?"

"No thanks for a hard task well done? I told her you'd be ungrateful."

"I'm grateful. Very grateful. But I'd hoped to thank you both together, and we haven't much time."

"I'll run down and see to it that Uns falls over me," Mani suggested.

Uri sneered. "He cannot see two strides ahead. Just look at him."

I did, and he was bent nearly to the ground. "I'll put the saddle back on the horse when he gets here."

"He is a true man, at least, just as I am a true Aelf."

Mani made a cat-noise of contempt.

"But your dog is something more, Lord, and this cat is less natural than I."

"The Bodachan gave Gylf to me," I said, "he says they raised him from a puppy."

"But was he theirs to give? They fear cold iron."

A hundred steep strides down the War Way Uns called, "Master! Sar Able! Wait up!"

CHAPTER 60

WHAT DID YOU SEE?

He had sounded out of breath, and it occurred to me that he might have been calling like that without my hearing him for an hour or more. "I'm waiting," I yelled, "and we'll put that saddle back on him when you get here." I looked around for Uri.

"She skedaddled," Mani told me, "though I wouldn't be surprised if she's hanging around to spy on us."

"I wanted to ask her whether Gylf was coming back," I explained. "As a matter of fact, I did ask her. She just didn't answer."

"I can," Mani declared. "Ask me."

"You can't possibly—" I looked down the road again, but saw only Uns. "All right, I will. Is Gylf coming back here?"

"Of course not. I know you won't take my information seriously, but no, he isn't."

I just stared at him.

"You want to know how I know," Mani continued. "Well, I know the same way you ought to yourself. I know because I know your dog. Better than you do, obviously. You sent him to find this Pouk?"

"Yes. You were there."

"So was Sir Garvaon, so you two didn't talk. But if you sent that dog to hunt Pouk, he'll hunt Pouk 'til you tell him not to. Or until he loses the trail completely and has to slink back and report his failure."

Uns caught up with us soon after that; and I took the saddle from him, put it on the lame stallion, and mounted. Mani had jumped onto the saddlebow while I was tightening the cinch.

"You need a rest," I told Uns. "I'm going to join Lord Beel and his daughter, and Sir Garvaon, in the pass. After that, we'll come back down. I want you to wait for us right here."

Uns shook his head stubbornly. "My place's wid you, Sar Able. Be 'long quick's I kin."

"As you like," I told him, and touched my heels to the stallion's sides.

He made off at a limping trot; and when Uns was no longer in sight, I said, "I suppose you think I'm mean."

"Well, he *is* crippled," Mani conceded, "but I have a firm policy. Never feel sorry for birds, mice, or squirrels. Or for men, women, or children save for a few close friends."

"It's because he's crippled that I treat him as harshly as I do," I explained. "He could have gone on living with his mother, and done little or no work, and his brother would have continued to take care of him when she was gone. That was why he left."

"I know the feeling," Mani said. "Every so often you want to get outside and hunt for yourself."

"Exactly." We were nearly at the pass, and I slowed the stallion to a walk. "He wants to be useful—to do real work, and sweat and strain and share his master's fortunes."

Mani remained silent.

"I've made myself a knight. That's high up for a poor kid that lost his folks early. Uns is scared he may never have a spot at all. I'm trying to show him that he's got one—that somebody wants him around for what he can do, and not just because they feel sorry for him."

"Over here, Sir Able!" It was Beel's servingman. "His Lordship is waiting for you."

I neck-reined the limping white stallion, who picked his way reluctantly among the rocks.

"Were you speaking to me before I hailed you, Sir Able? If so, I couldn't hear you. I apologize for it most humbly, Sir Able."

"No. I was talking to my cat. You have nothing to apologize for as far as I know."

"Thank you, Sir Able. That is most gracious of you. They're over there, Sir Able, by the rill. Perhaps you see the horses."

I nodded. "His Lordship didn't want to camp where Pouk had, I take it."

"Pouk is the gentleman—?"

"He's my servant." I had to touch the white stallion with my spurs. "He camped here to wait for me."

"Ah. I see, Sir Able. His Lordship felt it might not be wise for us to cook and sleep and—and to live, so to speak, Sir Able, in the area in which he had his vision."

Very softly and politely the servingman cleared his throat. "I myself was not privileged to witness it, Sir Able. From what His Lordship and Her Ladyship have said in my hearing, it was most impressive."

"It was," I agreed.

The servingman's voice fell. "His Lordship is eager to consult you concerning it, Sir Able. You may wish to prepare your mind."

Beel was seated on a stone, as I could see by then. He seemed to be deep in some discussion with Idnn, seated upon another, and with Garvaon, who stood behind her holding the reins of his horse.

A moment later Beel looked up, waved to me, and rose. "The horse I gave you was hurt in the fight last night. Sir Garvaon has told us. I wish I could give you another."

I dismounted. "I wish you could, too, My Lord. There are few horses and mules left, though, and a lot of those that are left are in worse condition than mine. He has a bruise and it's tender and sore, but I don't think the bone's broken."

"You beat them, though." Beel smiled.

"We didn't, My Lord. We fought them. That's the most that can be said. Our men—I mean Sir Garvaon's, and yours—are proud of that." I paused to let him talk, but he did not.

"It doesn't hurt them," I continued, "and may do good. But as for me, I don't think it's enough to have fought. I'd rather win."

Idnn said, "You killed four. That's what Sir Garvaon just told us."

Beel added, "An amazing feat."

"Two knights and twenty archers and men-at-arms—"

"Twenty-two," Garvaon put in.

"Thanks." I nodded. "So six of us for each we killed. We should have done much better than that."

"That's not fair!" Idnn exclaimed.

"Of course not, My Lady. This was a battle. Nothing was said about fair."

"I mean you're not being fair to Sir Garvaon and his men!" She looked angry.

Garvaon started to lay a hand on her shoulder, but did not. "Sir Able slew one single-handed."

"Then he's not even being fair to himself!"

Beel said, "Did you, Sir Able? If you did, you deserve much more than that stallion I gave you."

"It was dark, My Lord. I couldn't see how many of us were fighting him."

"Did you see any others?"

"That isn't the point, My Lord."

"Answer my question, Sir Able. Were you aware of anyone besides yourself engaging the Angrborn you slew?"

"No, My Lord."

"There isn't a knight in Thortower who wouldn't preen himself on such an exploit, Sir Able." Beel looked toward Idnn and Garvaon for confirmation, and got it. "Yes, by Holy Skai! And paint one of the Angrborn on his shield, too, with frost on his beard and a club in his hand."

"Then I'm glad I'm not a knight of Thortower, My Lord. As for my shield, Pouk has it. It's plain green, and it will stay like that 'til I do something better than I've done so far."

Idnn rose, her hands on her hips. "Listen to me."

"I have before now," I said, "and I'll hear you gladly again."

"Fine! You were both away when they came. The men-at-arms and archers had to fight without you, but they didn't run like the servants did, they fought as well as they could. How long did it take you to get down there from here? An hour, I swear!"

"Less than that, My Lady."

"An hour, and riding fit to break your necks, both of you. But you plunged in, horse and man, and you did all two men could do, fighting in the dark against giants as tall as that rock."

"Not quite." I sighed. "My Lady, I don't want to argue with you."

Beel chuckled. "But you will, Sir Able, just the same. Before you do, I have one question for you. I have asked it of Sir Garvaon already, and he has answered. Will you answer too, fully and fairly, this time without a bribe?"

"I didn't ask for a bribe, My Lord."

"Without setting conditions. Will you?"

"Yes, My Lord. If I can."

"Did you fight horsed, or on foot? Horsed, I'd think, since your horse was injured."

"On foot, mostly, Your Lordship. Mostly with my bow. May I ask why you want to know?"

Beel's smile faded. "The day may come, Sir Able, when I have to lead a hundred knights against the Angrborn. I hope it doesn't, and in fact I'm resolved to do everything in my power to ensure that it doesn't. And yet, it may. I'll try to lead them bravely, but it would be well to lead them wisely, too—if I can."

Idnn said, "You knights care little whether you live or die. We have to care more than you yourselves do. I said we, but I mean men like my father and my brother."

"You," Beel told her, "if ever you are a queen."

I saw Garvaon's jaw drop when he heard that. As quickly as I could, I said, "I rode into the fight, My Lord, but it seemed like the Angrborn I was after could see my horse, so I got off. That was when my horse was hurt. After that I shot arrows, trying to hit his eyes."

Beel nodded thoughtfully.

Idnn asked, "How many Angrborn were there? Does anyone know?"

"I don't, My Lady."

Garvaon said, "My men have told me there were a score or more. I'm not sure, myself, that there were so many. When I saw them in your father's bowl they seemed fewer, though more than ten."

"You saw them in my bowl?" Beel asked eagerly.

"Yes, Your Lordship. So did you, I'm sure."

"No—no, nothing of the sort. I've talked about this with Idnn, and it seems that each of us saw something quite different. Tell me exactly what you saw. Everything!"

"My wife's deathbed." Garvaon's voice was without expression. "She died in childbirth, Your Lordship."

Beel nodded. "I remember."

"Her bed, and me kneeling beside it. The midwives had taken my son. They were trying to revive him. I was praying for Volla when one came in to tell me he was dead, too." The slightest of tremors had entered Garvaon's voice; he paused to rid himself of it.

"At that point Sir Able said we were seeing the past."

"Yes, I recall that."

"What I was seeing in the bowl changed. I saw our camp instead, and Angrborn coming out of the hills to attack it. More than ten. But not a score. Thirteen or fourteen, they might have been."

Idnn said, "Sir Able must have seen them, too, because he told me there was fighting down there."

I shook my head. "I didn't. Sir Garvaon looked up and told us to listen, then ran for his horse. It wasn't hard to guess what he had heard."

"What did you see, Sir Able?"

CHAPTER 61

ALL OF YOU MUST FIGHT

"Nothing you would think important, My Lord. I saw myself receiving the accolade, then my servant and a woman I know beaten by one of the Angrborn. . . ."

"Yes?" Beel said eagerly. "What is it?"

"There was one thing then that may be worth telling you about, My Lord. A big building—a lot of thick towers with pointed roofs off in the distance. Maybe it matters, because the Angrborn who beat Pouk and Ulfa seemed to be going there. Do you know what it could have been?"

For a second it seemed Beel would not reply. Then he said, "Utgard, I believe. Utgard is King Gilling's castle. I have never seen it, or even spoken with anyone who has. But there are rumors. A mighty castle on a plain? A castle without a wall, guarded by a wide moat?"

"I didn't see the moat, My Lord. It was too far away for that."

"His Majesty has a plate with a picture painted on it. No doubt you've seen such plates?"

"With pictures? Sure."

"It is supposed to have been painted by an artist who had spoken with a woman who had escaped from it." Beel looked thoughtful. "I came here to make peace with the Angrborn, Sir Able. No doubt I have told you that before."

"You mentioned it, My Lord."

"Did I say that it was a last, desperate effort? No? Well, it was. We've tried to talk with them before. All those talks failed, perhaps only because we could not speak with anyone in authority. That was His Majesty's thought, Sir Able, and I concurred. My daughter and Sir Garvaon have heard all this before. They will have to excuse me."

Garvaon said, "Gladly, Your Lordship."

"Because I wish to say it one more time, now that I've failed. We hoped that coming in peace and bearing rich gifts for King Gilling, we might make contact with his Borderers and be given an escort to Utgard. Now those gifts are gone."

Idnn glanced at me, then looked away.

"Gone, from what Sir Garvaon has told me, and the mules that carried them as well. We have failed."

Garvaon said, “It wasn’t your fault, Your Lordship. Yo did as much as any man could.”

“I wasn’t even there. I never drew my sword, and I mu tell His Majesty so.”

“I know I am to blame for your absence.” I stood a straight as I had before Master Agr. “You don’t have to sa it. But if you want to, you can.”

“May,” Garvaon muttered.

“Make it as long as you like. So may your daughter. Or Si Garvaon. Nothing any of you say will be worse than th things I’ve said to myself.”

Beel raised his shoulders and let them fall. “Idnn, Si Able wished to find his servant, his horses, and hi weapons—his shield and helm, I suppose, and his lance an so forth and so on. If you want to play the fishwife agai this is the time for it.”

She shook her head.

“Go on. Tell him his mismanagement has resulted in ou disaster.”

“No, Father.”

“I thought not. I would invite Sir Garvaon to abuse a fel low knight who fought shoulder-to-shoulder with him, if didn’t know him too well to imagine that he would accep my invitation. Swert? Come over here.”

The mousy-looking servingman hurried over. “Yes, You Lordship?”

“You’re a servant, Swert. My servant.”

“Yes, Your Lordship.”

“I wish to consult you because Sir Able here also has servant. Another servant, in addition to the beggar.”

“Yes, Your Lordship. Pouk, Your Lordship. Sir Able tol me, Your Lordship.”

"This Pouk has been captured and enslaved by the Angrborn."

"Yes, Your Lordship."

"Sir Able sought to rescue him, and sought my help in his attempt. I gave it, and thus I have been ruined, and the errand I undertook for His Majesty has ended in failure. Sir Able is to be reviled on that account, and I feel you're the person to do it. Coming from you, the abuse should be doubly painful. You need not fear that Sir Able will strike or stab you. Sir Garvaon and I are here to protect you, though I feel sure nothing of the kind will be needed. Proceed."

"To—to . . . ?" The servingman looked helplessly from Beel to me and back again.

"To revile him," Beel explained patiently. "I have no doubt you command a hundredweight of filthy names. Employ them."

"Father . . ." Idnn's eyes were full of tears.

"To—to Sir Able, Your Lordship?"

"Exactly." Beel was adamant. "Begin, Swert."

"Sir Able, you—you . . ."

"Go on."

The servingman gulped. "I'm sorry, Sir Able, for what's happened, whatever it was. And—and . . ."

Idnn drew herself up. "Proceed, Swert. You know what my father wants. Do it."

"And if you're to blame, Sir Able, you're a very bad man. But . . . But so am I. Whatever anyone calls you, they can call me that too."

"There," Beel said. "Your disgrace is complete, Sir Able. You have been abused by my valet. Now cease this juvenile posturing and listen to me."

"I will, Your Lordship."

"I am His Majesty's ambassador to Jotunland. Had my embassy succeeded, the credit would have been mine and mine alone. It has failed, and the blame is mine. I accept it, and I am ready to stand before King Arnthor, to report that I have lost his gifts, and to welcome whatever punishment he may decree."

I glanced at Idnn, but she did not speak. If she felt joy at the prospect of returning to Kingsdoom, nothing in her face showed it. Garvaon looked grim and unhappy.

At last I said, "You're going back, Your Lordship?"

"Yes. I had thought of remaining here with Idnn until Sir Garvaon and Master Crol joined us with what remains of our party, but we must bury our dead. A good many of them, from what Sir Garvaon tells me. And no doubt there are other tasks too. We will return with you, and spend the night in whatever is left of our camp. I hope to inter our dead by sunset, and set out tomorrow morning. We'll see."

"Set out for the south?"

"Yes. I've told you so."

From his place in Idnn's lap, Mani raised an eyebrow.

I said, "You don't expect me to come with you, I hope, Your Lordship?"

The mousy-looking servingman smiled. That smile was suppressed almost at once, but not before I had seen it.

"I really hadn't thought about that," Beel said, "but you're not one of my retainers. You may do as you choose, though you would be very welcome if you chose to come with us. The horse I gave you is yours, of course. As is that helmet. What will you do?"

Uns arrived, panting and sweating. After glancing at him, I said, "I'll try to find a mount for my servant there, My Lord."

"We've none to spare now, Sir Able. So Sir Garvaon informs me. We will not have horses and mules enough, even, for our own needs."

Garvaon nodded.

"I know that as well as he does," I told Beel, "but the Angrborn will have plenty. I'll get one of those for Uns, if I can."

"You're going after them alone?"

"Yes, My Lord."

Uns, bowed already by his deformity, bowed lower still. "Not 'zacly aw 'lone, Ya Lordship, sar. I'll be holdin' Sar Able's stirrup, sar."

"Alone except for this—this hunchback?"

Mani sprang to my shoulder, an astonishing leap.

"I'll have my cat too, I think, My Lord, and the charger you gave me. My dog's still looking for Pouk, but he might come back. I hope so, and the Angrborn will find him harder to handle next time. The friends I described to you last night will be with me too, at least some of the time."

Idnn rose and hugged me. She was crying, and did not say anything that I can remember.

Beel drew a deep breath. "If my daughter's arms weren't around you, Sir Able, my own would be. No doubt you prefer hers, but do you really believe we stand a chance?"

" 'We,' My Lord?"

"I am a baron of the realm, entitled to a seat at the king's high table. They may say in Thortower that I failed, but they shall not say that I was bested in courage by a cripple."

"Then I do, My Lord. I listened to you. Will you listen to me, if I stop the juvenile posturing?"

Beel nodded.

"We talk about the Angrborn as if they were as big as a tower, or as tall as a ship's mainmast. I was told once by a good friend that I'd be shocked anytime I saw one."

I had decided to lie, and not to lie by halves, either. "All right, I was. But I was shocked at how small they were. They're no bigger, compared to Sir Garvaon and me, than we would be to boys. We call them giants and Frost Giants, and we say they're the Sons of Angr. But they're just big, ugly men."

"Brave words."

"When it's brave deeds we need. I understand." I took Mani off my shoulder, petted him, and set him down. "I need a number for them, so I'm taking thirteen. It may be off, but I won't argue now. We were taken by surprise last night by thirteen big men. Even so, we fought, and we killed about a third."

Beel nodded again.

"Sir Garvaon and I weren't there for the first part of that fight, and I'd like to think it would have made a big difference if we had been."

Garvaon said, "I'm as eager for this as you are, but let's not forget we've lost some men ourselves."

"I know it. I'll get to that in a minute. First I want to ask what would happen if things were turned around. What if we were to catch those nine big men off guard?"

No one spoke.

"I'm asking you, My Lord, but everybody else, too. I'm asking Lady Idnn and Sir Garvaon. And Swert and Uns."

At last Uns said, "I fit Org, sar. Wid me bare hands I done it."

"And alone. I know. I know what happened to you, too. Would you fight again?"

"If ya do, Sar Able, sar."

"That's all I can ask." I stopped to think things over. "When I came, Lady Idnn, you said the archers and men-at-arms hadn't run like your servants. Did you expect your servants to fight?"

"My maids? Certainly not."

"What about Master Crol? The muleteers? Swert there?"

Beel said, "Master Crol may well have fought. It would not surprise me if he had."

Garvaon said, "He did."

I nodded. "What about the others, My Lady?"

"I don't think so."

"None of them? What about you, Swert? Would you have fought, if you'd been there?"

"I hope so, Sir Able. If I'd had something to fight with."

That evening I talked to all the servants, and to the archers and men-at-arms.

"I've only got three things to say to you," I told them. "I'll talk a lot about those three things, because I think you'll want me to. I'll answer your questions as well as I can. But everything I've got to say will come down to those three things, so I'd like to get them out of the way before we do the rest." I studied them, hoping my silence would lend weight to my words.

"I'm asking you to fight. All of you. Everyone here. Lord Beel has ordered you to, but he can't make you do it any more than I can. All he can do is punish you if you don't. Whether you fight or not is up to you—that's the first thing I've got to say.

"You won't be fighting alone. Each man-at-arms and each archer is going to take charge of two or three or four of you, depending on how the numbers work out, teach you what you'll need to know, and lead you when we go to get our goods back from the Angrborn. Lord Beel himself will be leading the men-at-arms and the archers, and so will Sir Garvaon and I. That's the second thing."

They were looking at each other by that time, and I let them do it for more than a minute.

"Most of you have heard I killed one of the Angrborn last night. Sir Garvaon killed one too, but he had two archers and a man-at-arms fighting beside him. He likes to pretend that it makes what he did less than what I did. But what he did, and what I did, don't matter much. What matters is that our men-at-arms and our archers killed two before Sir Garvaon and I came down from the pass. It doesn't take a knight. A few brave men were able to do it without a knight to lead them. That's the third thing I have to say, and the most important." I stopped again.

"Some of you will have questions for me, or for Lord Beel, or for Sir Garvaon. Some may even have questions for Lady Idnn. Stand, and speak loudly. I've had questions for Lord Beel myself, and he's had questions for me. No one will be punished for asking a question."

A middle-aged servingman rose. "Is anyone not going to fight?"

"I don't know," I said. "We'll have to see."

The servingman sat down quickly.

"Lord Beel is going to fight. Lady Idnn is going to fight. Sir Garvaon is going to fight. The archers and men-at-arms are going to fight, and I am going to fight."

Master Crol called, "So am I!"

"And Master Crol is going to fight, of course. I took that so much for granted that I forgot to mention it. But none of us know about the rest of you. That's one of the things we're going to find out."

One of Idnn's maids got hesitantly to her feet. "We're supposed to fight, too?"

"Didn't Lady Idnn tell you?"

The maid's nod was timid.

"Then you know the answer. Let me explain. Ordinarily, women don't fight because they're not as strong as men. But what's my strength or Sir Garvaon's compared to the strength of the giants? You can fight them as well as we do, if you choose to do it. Lady Idnn's going to lead you and teach you. She and her bow have accounted for a lot of deer, but she's after bigger game now, and it's your duty to help her."

A cook sitting near the maid said, "Do we get to choose the man-at-arms we want?"

"Stand up." I gestured. "The rest can't hear you."

The cook rose, somewhat embarrassed. "You said that each two or three of us would have a man-at-arms to teach us. Do we get to pick which one?"

"Or an archer. No. They get to choose you."

The servingman who had stood up first stood up again. "I just want to say I'll fight, if you'll give me weapons."

I said, "When Lord Beel heard I'd killed an Angrborn, he asked how I did it. I told him with arrows, and he wondered how I could see to shoot, since we'd fought them at night. I explained that they're so big that they could always be seen against the night sky—so big I'd have found it hard to miss."

I held up my bow. "I made this. I didn't make all my arrows, but I made the best ones. There are trees here, trees tough enough to bend under the mountain winds and stand up again when the wind dies. The Angrborn took a lot of the treasure we had, but they left us a lot in the way of iron grates and pots and bronze fittings for the pavilions. The man who shoes our horses and mules can shape those things into arrowheads, and you're sitting on more rough stones to sharpen them with than you'll ever need."

I shut up to let them think about that. The sun had nearly

set, and the grave markers on the hilltop cast long shadows that seemed to reach toward us like so many fingers.

"Some of you may be helped by the Fire Aelf," I said. "I hope so. If you are, listen carefully to everything they tell you. They're good metal workers."

CHAPTER 62

AFTER THE RAIDERS

The mountains had dwindled to hills before I camped, high brown-and-yellow hills whose sand-colored stones were masked by dead grass. I had ridden—and walked while I led the limping stallion—until the sun was down, hoping for water and wood. The water hole I finally found held water nearly as thick as mud, but the stallion drank it thirstily.

I tied him to his own saddle, spread his saddle blanket on the ground, and laid another blanket over it. A fire would have been nice, but a fire might have caught the dry grass and burned half the world. That was how it seemed, anyway: a barren land that went on and on like the sea.

Besides, there was no wood.

After that, for what felt like hours, I lay shivering, wrapped in my cloak and the other blanket, looking up at the stars and hearing only the slow steps of the grazing stallion and the soft moaning of the wind.

It was late summer. Late summer and warm weather at Duke Marder's lofty gray castle. Warm weather in the Bay of Forcetti. There would be no ice in that bay for months.

Sweltering late summer in the forest where I had lived

with Bold Berthold. The bucks would have begun to grow antlers for the mating season; but those antlers would have a lot of growing to do still, weapons of gallant combat still sheathed in velvet. Knowing that summer lingered along the Griffin had brought me little comfort, and my mail even less. I was on the northern side of the Mountains of the Mice now, far north of the downs, and I believe at an elevation a good deal higher than that of the smiling southern lands.

Waves crashed against a cliff, and I leaped and sported in them, together with the maidens of the Sea Aelf, maidens who save for their eyes were as blue everywhere as the blue eyes of the loveliest maids of Mythgarthr, fair young women who sparkled and laughed as they leaped from the surging sea into the storm that lit and shook the heavens.

That lit and shook Mythgarthr. Why had I not thought of that? I rolled over, seeking to close blanket and cloak more tightly about me.

Garsecg and Garvaon waited on the cliff, Garvaon with drawn sword and Garsecg a dragon of steel-blue fire. The Kelpies raised graceful arms and lovely faces in adoration, shrieking prayers to Setr; they cheered as a gout of scarlet flame forced Garvaon over the edge.

He fell, striking rock after rock after rock. His helmet was lost, his sword rattled down the rocks with him, and his bones broke until a shapeless mass of armor and bleeding flesh tumbled into the sea.

I woke shuddering. My sea was this rolling expanse of dust-dry grass, lit by a fading moon lost among racing cloud. The cliff from which Garvaon had fallen was the Northern

Mountains now, mountains my stallion's hooves had somehow transformed into southern mountains; and the Kelpies were nothing more than a shrieking wind.

Shivering worse than ever, I tried to sleep again.

The Armies of Winter and Old Night advanced across the sky, monstrous bodies lit from within by lightnings. A flying castle, a thing no larger than a toy, barred their way—and barred their way alone. From its walls a thousand voices pleaded: *Able! Able! Able . . .*

But I slept upon the downs while these greater Angrborn brandished spears of chaos and bellowed hate.

I woke, and found my face wet with rain. Thunder shook the sky, and white fire tore the night. A wave of driving rain wet me like a wave of the sea, and another, and another.

There was no place to get away from the rain, no shelter anywhere. I tightened the studded chin-strap of my helmet and covered my head with the hood of my cloak, blessing its tightly woven wool.

I could not see. It might be night, it could be day—I had no way of knowing. The chain around my neck was held by a staple driven into a crevice in the wall. Once I had tried to pull it out, but I did not do that any more.

Once I had shivered. I did not do that any more either.

Once I had hoped some friend would bring me a blanket or a bundle of rags. That the seeing woman who had been my wife once would bring me a crust or a cup of broth. Those things had not happened, and would never happen.

Once I had shivered in the wind, but I had disobeyed, and would shiver no more. I was sleepy now, and though the snow brushed my face and crept up around my feet, I was not uncomfortable. There was no more pain.

Something rough, warm, and wet scrubbed my cheek; I woke to see a hairy, familiar face as broad and as brown as my saddle peering into mine. I blinked—and Gylf licked my nose. "Time to get up. Look at the sun."

It had climbed halfway up a cloudy sky.

"Found him." Gylf wagged his tail with vigor. "I can show you. Want to go?"

"Yes." I threw off my blanket; I was dripping wet but only moderately chilled. "But I can't, not now. I have to delay the Angrborn—and clean my armor and talk to you."

"All right." Gylf lay down. "Sore paws anyhow."

"But first of all, I have to find my horse. He seems to have strayed during the night." I got up and looked around, my hand shielding my eyes from the sun.

"Upwind. I smell him."

After half a mile, the track of the dragged saddle was so plain that even I could follow it. Snarling and snapping, Gylf held the stallion until I could grab its tether.

Back at the water hole, I pulled off helmet and hauberk and got rags and a flask of oil from a saddlebag. "I didn't have these when you and I were lost in the forest," I told Gylf, "but I've learned since. Being a knight's like being a sailor. You pay for the glory and freedom by oiling and scrubbing and patching and polishing. Or you don't get to keep them."

"Those were the days." Gylf rolled in the wet grass, rose, and shook himself.

"You liked it on the ship?"

"In the woods. I liked that. Just you and me. Good smells. Hunting. Fires at night."

I smiled. "It was kind of nice."

"Bad place." Gylf sneezed.

"The forest? I thought you liked it." My mail, well oiled when I left Beel's company, had not yet begun to rust. I shook it, dislodging a shower, then dried it with a clean, soft rag, working corners of the rag between the close-packed steel rings wherever I suspected a hidden drop.

"Here," Gylf explained.

I considered that. "Yes and no. I understand what you mean. It's too bare to have much game, and there isn't much water, though you couldn't say that last night. Then too, there's the Angrborn. This is their homeland, Jotunland, and they're terrible enemies. But Lord Beel talked about leading hundreds of knights against them, and this would be wonderful country for it. Give Lord Beel or Duke Marder five hundred knights and two thousand archers, and you might get a battle people would sing about 'til the sky fell."

Gylf grunted.

"Brave knights well mounted, with long, strong lances. Archers with long bows and a hundred arrows apiece. This is lovely country for charging horses, and lovely country for bowmen, too." Just thinking of it made me want to be there. "A year from that day, the Angrborn might be as rare as ogres are now. A hundred years from that day, half the people in Forcetti would think they were just stories."

Gylf brought me back to solid ground. "You're hunting them. You said so."

"Yes, I am. They jumped Lord Beel's company while Sir

Garvaon and I were gone, and Lord Beel and his daughter, too. We killed four, but the rest got away with the gifts we were bringing their king."

"Get 'em anyhow," Gylf remarked.

"Perhaps he may, or some of them. But it won't be the same as Lord Beel giving them on behalf of King Arnthor. So we're looking for those Angrborn. I rode on ahead, and the rest are following as quick as they can, although that isn't very quick since a lot are on foot now."

"I could find 'em. Want me to?"

"You have sore paws."

Gylf licked a front paw as if testing it. "Not bad."

"I want you to stay with me," I decided. "You were gone a long time looking for Pouk, and I didn't like it. Besides, you could use a few good meals."

"Sure!" Gylf wagged his tail.

"I've got some dried meat here." I took it from his saddlebag and gave Gylf a piece. "It's kind of salty. Can you drink the water in that hole? It's not so bad now, after the rain."

Busy chewing, Gylf nodded vigorously.

"You're probably wondering what happened to Mani."

Gylf shook his head.

"He's back with Lady Idnn."

Gylf swallowed. "Bad cat! Bad!"

"Not really. We talked it over. He wouldn't have been much use while I was out giant hunting, but he can keep an eye on things in Lord Beel's company for me. It might not be necessary, and I hope it isn't. But it's always better to be safe when you can."

A cloud veiled the sun, and Gylf muttered, "Aelf."

"You mean Uri and Baki?"

Starting on his second strip of dried meat, Gylf nodded again.

"They're out looking for the Angrborn who robbed us."

"Nope."

"You mean they found you and freed you. I had them do that first. Now they're looking for those Angrborn."

"Smell 'em," Gylf muttered.

There were giggles behind me, and I turned.

"Here we are," Uri announced.

Baki said, "If we had been Angrborn, we could have stepped on you."

"You Aelf can sneak up on anybody."

Baki shook her head. "Only on you stupid ones."

Uri added, "The rest always know when we are around."

I asked whether the Angrborn knew.

"No, Lord."

The sun, which had slipped behind a cloud, showed its face again for a few seconds, rendering Baki (as well as Uri) transparent as she said, "They are stupid, too."

"In that case you must've found them."

"We did. But, Lord . . ."

"What is it?"

"They are traveling fast. They can walk very fast, and they keep the mules trotting most of the time."

Baki said, "These hills level out up north, and there is the plain of Jotunland after that."

I nodded. "I understand."

"That is where their king's castle is. It is a very big building they call Utgard. The town is called Utgard, too."

I nodded again.

"We have been in there," Uri said somberly. "It is very, very big. Did you think the Tower of Glas was big?"

"Yes. Huge."

"You should see this. This is no joke, Lord, what you are doing."

Baki said, "It is a terrible place, and we want you to stop."

"Because you think I'll be killed?"

Both nodded.

"Then I'll be killed."

Gylf growled deep in his throat.

"Lord, this is foolish. You—"

I raised my hand, and finding the rag still in it began to clean my hauberk again. "What's foolish is spending your whole life being scared of death."

"You believe that because some knight told you."

"Sir Ravd, you mean. No, he didn't tell me that. Only that a knight was to do what his honor demanded, and never count his foes. But you're right just the same, a knight told me. That knight was me. People who fear death—Lord Beel does, I guess—live no longer than those who don't, and live scared. I'd rather be the kind of knight I am—a knight who has nothing—than live like he does, with power and money that can never be enough."

I got up and pulled on my hauberk. "You're afraid the Angrborn will get to Utgard before I catch them. Isn't that what you were going to tell me?"

Uri shook her head. "No, Lord. They are not far. You can overtake them today, if you wish."

"But you would be alone," Baki added, "and you would surely die. Those others, this Lord Beel you talk about and the other old gods who march with him, will never overtake the giants."

"Not if Utgard were a thousand times farther than it is," Uri confirmed.

"Then we've got to slow them down." I rolled up my own blankets and picked up the saddle blanket. "I told Lord Beel I would, and I wish that was all I had to worry about."

"Pouk," Gylf explained to Uri and Baki.

"Exactly. We've got to set Pouk and Ulfa free. They'll be slaves here 'til they die if these Angrborn kill me. You found them, Gylf?"

He nodded.

When I had saddled the stallion, I put on my helmet and buckled on Sword Breaker. "All right, where are they?"

"Utgard."

CHAPTER 63

THE PLAIN OF JOTUNLAND

Night had fallen before we reached the Angrborn's camp, but it lay upon the bank of a wooded stream, and the fire they had built there—a fire of whole trees, some so thick through the trunk that a man with an ax would not have felled them after an hour's hard work—lit all the countryside. Two mules turned on spits above that fire.

I had taken off helmet and hauberk and crept far into the firelight to see the Angrborn for myself. When I got back to the woods where Uri, Baki, and Gylf were waiting, I had already formed a plan.

"There are only seven." I seated myself upon a log I could only just see. "We argued about their number, and everybody thought there were more."

"In that case you will not need our help," Uri declared. "A mere seven giants? Why, you and your dog will have put an end to them before breakfast."

"Won't you fight them?"

Uri shook her head.

"You and Baki fought the Mountain Men."

"We distracted them, mostly, so that you could fight them."

"We are really not very good at fighting on this level, Lord." Baki would not meet my eyes.

"Because they used to be your gods?"

Baki sighed, a ghostly whisper in the darkness beneath the trees. "You were our gods, Lord. They never were."

"We could appear in their fire," Uri suggested, "if you think it would do any good."

"But the giants are not afraid of us," Baki added. "They would order us out, and we would have to go."

"If they did nothing worse, Lord."

Gylf growled.

"Then you're not willing to help us? If that's how matters stand, you might as well go back to Aelfrice."

"We will if you order it, Lord," Uri told me, "but we would rather not."

I was disgusted. "Tell me why I ought to keep you."

"Be reasonable, Lord." Uri edged toward me until her hip pressed mine; her hip was as warm and as soft as that of any human woman. "You yourself did not wish to fight them until you had rescued your servant—"

"Mate, too," Gylf added.

"From Utgard. Suppose we fought, all four of us. Baki and I, who can achieve next to nothing, and you and your dog. What would be the upshot? We would be killed, or more likely you and your dog would be, while Baki and I would have to flee to Aelfrice or die."

She stopped, inviting me to speak; I did not.

"What would be the good of that? A dead giant? Two? None, if you trust my judgment. A knight and a dog to feed the crows. Let us delay them, instead. Is that not what we set out to do?"

Ten minutes later, crawling through high grass toward a group of tethered mules, I found myself thinking that what I was doing was probably more dangerous than fighting. Every move I made rustled the grass; and if the Angrborn had not heard me, the mules tied to the gnarled birch I was creeping up on certainly had. They were pretty easy to see because of the firelight; their ears were up and forward, and their heads high. Their nervous stamping sounded louder than the purling of the stream. It seemed that the Angrborn must certainly hear it, and it struck me when I was very close that mules could kick and bite as well as or better than horses. They thought something was about to attack them, and they were by no means defenseless.

"Those Frost Giants are cooking a couple of you this very minute," I whispered.

Mani had said once that a few animals could speak; I had not believed him then and did not believe him now, but it was at least possible that he had been truthful.

"You're supposed to be sensible animals. Don't you want to get away from here?"

I had continued to crawl while I talked; now a rope touched my cheek. I drew my dagger and cut it and heard a little snort of satisfaction from the mule whose tether it had been.

Then I was at the tree and dared stand up, keeping the trunk between me and the fire. My dagger was good and sharp, but the tethers were tough; I was still sawing at them when a loose mule wandered by. With a sort of overwrought absentmindedness, I wondered whether it was one I had freed or one freed by Uri or Baki.

The tether I had been cutting parted, and I found the next one.

There was a rumble of angry voices, deep and loud, from the direction of the fire. One of the Angrborn stood up, another shouted, and a third snarled. I slashed at the tough tethers frantically.

Half a bowshot off, a mule crossed a patch of moonlight, galloping clumsily but fast, urged on by an Aelfmaiden lying like a red shadow on its back.

Another tether parted. Nearly dropping my dagger, I searched the trunk for more, but every one I found hung limp. Three Angrborn had left the fire and were walking toward me by that time, two shoulder-to-shoulder, the third lagging behind.

"Gylf!" I shouted. "Gylf!"

The bay of a hound on the scent answered me; in a moment that seemed long, it became the excited yelp of a hound with its prey in view. Somewhere a mule screamed, a stark cry of animal terror, and a dozen scattered in every direction. One of the giants dove for one as a man my size might have dived at a runaway goat, but it slipped through his hands. For a moment he held its tail; it kicked at his arm and vanished into the darkness.

The black beast that had killed so many Mice sprang at the throat of another Angrborn. Arms thicker than any man's body closed around it.

"*Disiri!*" I ran to the fight. The third Angrborn was lumbering toward me when a mule with a crimson shadow on its back dashed in front of him, and he tripped and fell.

An Angrborn rolled toward me, wrestling a creature that was neither hound nor wolf, an animal far larger than a lion.

Like a boulder tossed by a wave, Sword Breaker's hard-edged, diamond-shaped blade struck and struck again. Without time or preparation that I could recall afterward, I found myself astride the ravening beast I had fought to save, and racing like the wind across the hills.

I felt I rode a storm.

Before the sun rose, Gylf had dwindled to his ordinary size; and not too long afterward, he and I found the white stallion where I had tied it the night before. Instead of mounting, I untied it and took off its saddle.

"You're tired," Gylf commented. "You want to sleep. I'll watch."

"I am tired," I conceded, "but I don't want to sleep and don't intend to. I want to talk."

"I'll go."

"I don't want you to go. You're mine, assuming that the Bodachan had a valid claim on you, and I like you very, very much and want to keep you. But there are things I've got to know."

"I scare you."

"You'd scare anybody." Finding no log or stone to sit on, I sat in fern not far from the edge of the water.

"I'll go."

"I said I don't want you to. I don't even want you to hunt up a rabbit for us. We're still too near those Frost Giants for that. I want you to tell me what you are."

"Dog." Gylf sat too.

"No ordinary dog can do what you do. No ordinary dog can talk, for that matter."

"Good dog."

I groped for some way to frame a question that might get

a useful answer but had to settle for, "Why is it you get big when you fight something at night?"

" 'Cause I can."

"When we got Mani, I wanted to think you were like him."

Gylf growled.

"Okay, maybe I should've said I wanted to think he was like you, only a cat. That's how it seemed lots of times, but I'm pretty sure it's wrong."

Gylf lay down and offered no comment.

"Mani knows a lot about magic from watching the witch who used to own him. You don't know anything about magic, so what you do isn't. I don't know what it is but I know I need to think about it. Unless you tell me."

"Can't."

"Then maybe Uri can. Or Baki." I called for them, but neither appeared.

"That's not good," I said. "We've got to go to Utgard to get Pouk and Ulfa, and get back before Lord Beel's bunch gets here. We're going to need Uri and Baki but we may not have them."

Gylf raised his head. "Think they know? Might know?"

"They might," I said, "and they might even tell us. The Aelf can change shape." I paused to think. "Only not in the sunshine. But in Aelfrice, Setr changed into a man called Garsecg, and Uri and Baki had been turned into Khimairas. Or maybe turned themselves into Khimairas. I don't know which."

Seeing Gylf's look of incomprehension, I added, "Flying monsters. Only there's something wrong about all this. I can't put my finger on it, but I know there is."

"Sleep," Gylf suggested.

I shrugged. "You're right. I need sleep, and if I sleep I might think of it. Only just 'til dark, all right? Wake me when it starts to get dark, if you're awake."

It was dangerous, I thought as I stretched myself on the cool fern. We were within a few miles of the Angrborn camp; if they searched the woods for the mules, they might find us. More likely, the white stallion might be seen and caught and used for a pack horse. But pushing myself, and the stallion, and even Gylf to the point of exhaustion would be worse yet; and the lands nearer Utgard, from what I had been told, would have a lot more giants living in them than this dry hill country did.

As sleep came nearer and nearer, I tried to imagine one of the Angrborn plowing with oxen the way one of our farmers would with a toy tractor. Try as I might, I could not do it.

Water surged about me, carrying me with it. A school of fish like scarlet jewels passed, and met a second school of iridescent silver. They intermeshed, passed. The iridescent fish surrounded me, and were gone.

The girl-face of Kulili lay below me as an island must lie below a bird. Her vast lips moved, but the only sound was in my mind. *I made them. I shaped them as a woman molds dough, taking something from the trees, something from the beasts that felled the trees, and something from myself.*

I saw her hands then, hands knit of a million millions of thread-worms, and Disiri taking shape as they labored.

That dream was lost among other many others, dreams of death, long before my eyelids fluttered.

But not lost completely.

I woke at sunset, and in less than an hour I was riding north, with Gylf trotting beside the stallion. About the time the moon came up, I said, "I think I've got it. Not everything, but a lot of the things that were bothering me."

Gylf glanced up. "About me?"

"Other stuff, too. I was thinking you only changed at night."

"Mostly."

"Yeah, mostly. But not always. Not when you and me and old man Toug fought the outlaws, for instance."

We went on in silence, the stallion picking his way through the darkness as the moon through the cold sky.

"Do you remember your mother, Gylf? Do you recall her at all?"

"How she smelled."

"You got separated from her, somehow. Do you remember anything about that?"

"Wasn't to go." Gylf's deep voice sounded thoughtful. "Went anyhow."

I thought of little kids at home. "You wandered off?"

"Couldn't keep up. Brown people found me."

"The Bodachan."

He grunted assent.

"They bowed to me when they gave you to me. Remember? They tried to hide their faces."

"Yep."

"I think somebody in Aelfrice educated me, Gylf. I feel like I was taught a lot there. But I don't know why, or what I learned."

"Huh!"

"I don't even know if I really learned it. Only I think the Bodachan educated you. Trained you, or whatever you're supposed to say about that. Taught you to talk, maybe. And I think probably they told you about changing shape, how to do it, and you shouldn't do it in the sunshine, not here in Mythgarthr."

"Pigs."

I reined up. "What did you say?"

"Pigs. Smell 'em?"

"Do you think they're close?" I strained to look about me in the darkness, and sensed rather than saw that Gylf had lifted his head to sniff the wind.

"Nope."

"We might as well go on," I decided after a minute or two. "If we can't ride through this country at night, we sure can't ride through it in the daytime."

When we had topped the next hill, Gylf remarked, "Like 'em."

"The pigs?" I had been lost in my own thoughts.

"Aelf."

"They were good to you then. I'm glad."

"You, too."

"You've had a rough time of it with me."

"Just once."

"In the boat?"

"In the cave."

I rode in silence after that. There was a nightingale singing in the trees beside the river, and I found myself wondering why a bird that would be welcomed wherever it went would choose to live in Jotunland. It made me remember how I had stayed at the cabin so I would not get in your way. I had not minded it, and in fact I had liked it a lot; and that made me realize that I liked being by myself out there in Jotunland, too. People are all right, and in fact some are truly good; but you do not see the Valfather's castle when you are with them.

Besides, it was good to be alone with Gylf again. He had been right about the forest, and I had not thought nearly enough about that while it was happening. I thought a lot then about how he had gotten bigger, and about riding on his back instead of the stallion's. He was a big, big dog even when he was small, because it was the smallest he could make himself. If he could have, he would have been puppy-sized, like Mrs. Cohn's Ming Toy. It seemed to me a dog—a big dog like Gylf—was the best company anybody could have.

I tried to think about who I would rather have with me than Gylf. Disiri, if she would love me. But what if she wouldn't? Disiri was wonderful, sure, but she was hard and dangerous, too. She would not be with me again until I found Eterne, and maybe not then. I thought that if she felt about me the way I felt about her, she would stick with me every second.

Garsecg would have been all right, but no Garsecg was better, because he was really Setr. Idnn would have been a terrible worry. Pouk would not have been bad. He would have wanted to talk, and I would have had to shut him up—but I knew how to do that.

Finally I hit on Bold Berthold. He would have been perfect, and as soon as I thought of him, I missed him a lot. He had never been right the whole time I had known him, because of the way one side of his head was pushed in. He forgot things he should have remembered, and most of the time he walked like he was drunk. But when you were around him a lot you could see the person he had been, the man who had wrestled bulls, and there was an awful lot of that left. There had been no school where he grew up, but his mother had taught him. He knew a lot about farming and woodcraft, and about the Aelf, too. I had never asked him what I was supposed to say when I spoke for them, and now it was too late. But I felt like he might have known. Bold Berthold would have been perfect.

Ravd would have been wonderful too. Why did the best people I met have to die? That got me thinking about his broken sword—how I had picked it up and put it down again, and cried, and I thought that cave, where we had found Ravd's broken sword, must have been the one Gylf meant. At last I said,

"We've never been in a cave, except for the cave where the outlaws hid their loot, and we weren't in there long. Were you thinking of the cable tier? That was pretty bad for both of us."

"Just me," Gylf explained. "You weren't there."

"Garsecg's cave? I heard something about that. You were chained up in there?"

"Yep."

So Garsecg had chained Gylf up like the Angrborn had, and for a while I wondered why Gylf had let either one of them do it. Finally I saw that he did not like to change into what he really was. He did it when he had to fight, but he would rather let somebody chain him up than change.

"Garsecg's cave brings us back to shapechanging," I said, "and your shape does change, but mostly you get bigger. Garsecg told me once that though the Aelf could change their shapes, they were always the same size."

"No good."

"Oh, I'm sure it can be nice. Uri and Baki can take flying shapes, and I'd love to be able to do that. But if it's true, it isn't what you do. We're looking at different things that only seem to be about the same."

I searched for an analogy. "When I first left the ship with Garsecg, there were these Kelpies, Sea Aelf, all around me. I was afraid I'd drown, and they said not to be afraid, that I couldn't drown as long as I was with them."

Gylf raised his head again, sniffing the wind.

"Later it was just Garsecg and me, but I still didn't drown. After that, I dove into a pool on Glas. It went down into the sea, the sea of Aelfrice, and I was alone under the water until I found Kulili, but I still didn't drown."

"See the hedgerow?" Gylf inquired.

"I see a long, dark line," I said. "I've been wondering if it was a wall."

"Somebody's in it."

I loosened Sword Breaker in her scabbard. "I think the best thing might be to pretend we don't know he's there for a while yet. When we're closer, you might have a look at him."

"Right."

"What I was trying to say is that the Kelpies probably could protect people who were with them, but that wasn't what was protecting me. What was protecting me was something I'd picked up when I was first in Aelfrice, something that looked the same 'til you looked close."

"Huh!"

"So you don't change like the Aelf change. Disiri's tall and slim, but when we were alone—it was in a cave, but you weren't with me then at all—she made herself, you know, rounder." My cheeks burned, thinking about it. "And that was nice. Only she had to be shorter, too, to do it. Is there just one person in the hedge?"

"Badger, too."

"But just one human?"

Gylf sniffed again. "Think so."

"I told Garsecg about Disiri, how she had to be shorter to be rounder. But I should have thought about him. He turned himself into a dragon, and the dragon was a lot bigger than he was. He made himself look like me, too, although I'm bigger than he was. Could you make yourself look like me?"

"Nope."

"Could you be that really big thing you are sometimes? Right now?"

Gylf grew. His eyes blazed like coals, and fangs two feet long pushed his lips apart. A moan of fear, faint but not too faint to hear, came from the hedgerow, and he bounded away. I urged my stallion after him.

CHAPTER 64

A BLIND MAN WITH A WHITE BEARD

By the time I reached Gylf, he was his everyday self again, having decided that one large ordinary dog was more than enough to pin and hold an old woman. He backed away from her when I told him to, leaving her weeping and gasping, curled up like a prawn on the dry leaves under the hedge.

"Now, now." Dismounting, I knelt beside her and laid a hand on her shoulder. "Cheer up, mother. Gylf won't hurt you, and neither will I."

The old woman only wept. Something dark connected the hands that covered her face, and examining it more by touch than by sight, I discovered that it was a chain of rough iron a bit longer than my forearm. "I wish I had a lamp," I said.

"Oh, no, sir! Don't wish for that!" The old woman peeped between her fingers. "Master'd see us sure, sir, if you was to light a lamp. You won't, will you?"

"No. For one thing, I don't have one. Did your master put that chain on you? Who is he?"

"Yes, sir. He done, sir. You're one a' them knights, sir, ain't you? Like down south?"

"That's right."

"When I was a girl, sir, I seen some that come to the village. Big men like you they was, on big horses. An' iron clothes. Has you got iron clothes, sir?" One hand left her face to stroke my arm. "Well, I never."

"Are you a slave?" An eerie wail filled my mind as I spoke; I shivered, but it soon dwindled to nothing. "I asked your master's name. Whose slave are you?"

"Oh, him, sir. He's not a good one, sir, not like his pa, but I've seen worse, sir. Hard though, sir. Hard." The old woman tittered. "He'd like me better if I was younger, sir. You know how that is. His father did, sir, Hymir that was, sir. I didn't like him, sir, for he was bigger'n your horse twice, sir, only he was kindish to me because a' it, only I didn't know it was kindish then, sir, only he wisht I was bigger, sir, you know, an' I found out after, for I'm too old now, sir, so Hyndle leaves me be. It's the warm work for women, sir, is what they say, or else cold an' starve. Only I don't know which is worse."

"Hyndle is your master?"

The old woman sat up, nodding. "Yes, sir."

"Hyndle is Angrborn, from what you've said about him."

"Is that the giants, sir? Yes, sir. They do claim her for their ma, sir."

"If you're running away from him—"

"Oh, no, sir!" The old woman sounded shocked. "Why, I wouldn't do that. Why, I'd starve, sir, an' never get back to where the regular people live. An' if I did, I'd starve *there*, sir. Who'd feed a old woman like me?"

"I would if I could," I told her. "But you're right, I couldn't. Not now, at least. Why are you out here at night, instead of home in bed?"

She tittered.

"Are you an Aelf? Have you taken this shape to have fun with me?"

"Oh, no, sir!"

"Then why are you out?"

"You wouldn't believe, sir."

Gylf whined and I stroked his head, telling him we would leave in a minute or two.

"It's a man, sir. It is, and I shouldn't have laughed. Only it's a sore long way, sir, an' I'm a-weary with working all day. If—if you could ride me on for but a little a' it, sir, I'll bless you 'til the day I die, sir."

I nodded, thinking. "I was about to say that if you were running away I wished you all speed but I couldn't give you much help. I have to go to Utgard as quick as I can. I hate to put any more weight on this horse, because he's lame already. You can't weigh half what I do though, and my armor weighs half as much as I do." I stood and helped her rise, noticing just how thin and worn she looked in the moonlight. "So we'll just sit you up here."

She gave a little squeal as I lifted her onto the white stallion's war saddle.

"That's it. You don't have sit astride, and I doubt that you could in those skirts. Leave your feet where they are and hold on to the cantle and pommel. I'll lead him, and he won't be going any faster than I can walk. Where are we going?"

She pointed down the hedgerow. "It's a long, long way, sir."

"It can't be." I was watching where I stepped, and did not bother to look over my shoulder at her. "Not if you were planning to walk it tonight. You would have gone home after, too? And gone to bed?"

"Yes, sir."

"Then it can't be far." I started jogging, something I hadn't done for a while.

"Ain't you a-feared you'll lose your dog, sir?"

I strained to see him, but Gylf's seal-brown rump and long tail had disappeared in the moon-shadow of the hedge. "I'm not, mother. He's run ahead to scout out trouble, which is what I would've told him to do if I'd thought of it."

"Rabbits, too, sir. An' got a deep mouth from the look a' him."

"He does, but he won't be running rabbits this night." I jogged a hundred strides or so in silence, then slowed to a walk. "Did you ever tell me what your errand is, mother? A man, you said."

"Yes, sir." She sounded terribly sad. "You'll think I'm cracked, running after a man at my age."

"There's only one girl for me," I told her, "and people think me cracked because of it. So you're a crazy woman on the charger of a crazy knight. We freaks have got to stick together and help each other, or we'll be left to howl in the swamp."

"Will you tell me about her, sir?"

"For a year. But she isn't around, and your man is. Or he will be soon, we hope. Is he a good man, and does he know you're coming?"

"Yes, sir." She sighed. "He is. An' he do, sir. Can I tell you how it is with him an' me, sir? 'Twould ease my mind, an' you can laugh if you want to."

"May," I muttered, jogging again. "Yes, I may. But I don't think I will."

"Years an' years ago it were, sir. Him and me lived in a little bit a' a place down south. Every girl there had a eye for him, sir, but him, he had a eye for me. An' nobody else'd do. That's what he said, sir, an' the way it was, too."

"I know how that is, mother."

"May every Overcyn there be bless you for it, an' her too." The old woman was quiet awhile, lost in reminiscence.

"I got took, sir. The giants come looking for us, the way they does, sir, when the leaves turn an' they don't mind moving around. An' they found me. Hymir did, sir, my master what was. So I had to—had to do what I could for him, an' get it all over me often as not, an'—an' Heimir got born, sir. My son that was. Only Master Hyndle's run him off now, or he'd help me, I know." She paused.

"He's not what you'd call a good-looking boy, sir, an' it's me, his mother, what says it. Nor foxy neither, and didn't talk 'til after he was bigger'n me. But his heart . . . You're a good-hearted man, sir. As good as ever I seen. But your heart's no bigger'n my Heimir's, sir. No woman's never had no better son."

"That's good to know."

"For me it is, sir. Ain't you getting tired, sir? I could walk a ways, an' you ride."

"I'm fine." The truth was that it felt good to stretch my legs, and I knew I owed the stallion a little rest.

"You've run quite a ways, an' it's a good ways more."

"I close my mind." I wanted to tell her, but it was not easy. "And I think about the sea, about the waves coming to a beach, wave after wave after wave, never stopping. Those waves turn into my steps."

"I think I see, sir." The old woman sounded like she did not

"I float on them. It's something somebody taught me, or maybe just told me about and let the sea teach me, no magic. The sea is in everybody. Most people never feel it." Saying those things made me think of Garsecg, and I wondered all over again why Garsecg did not come to see me in Mythgarthr.

"It opened me up, it did, having my Heimir. So then we

ould if you take my meaning. Like a real wife should, sir, he regular way."

"You and the Angrborn who had taken you, mother? This Iymir?"

"Yes, sir. Not that I wanted it, sir. Hurt dreadful every ime. But he wanted it an' what he said went in them days. So then I had my Hela, only she's run off. Master shouldn't ouch her, her being his half-sister, only she's . . . Well, sir. You wouldn't say it, sir. She's got that big jaw they all ave, sir. An' the big eyes, you know. An' cheeks like the orns on a calf, sir, if you take my meaning. Only good kin, sir, an' yellow hair like I used to, too. That yellow air's why my master that was, that was her father, took ne, sir. He told me that one time, so it was bad luck to me. Only if it'd been black or brown like most, probably he'd a' ilt me."

The hedgerow had ended, though the path had not, weav-ng its way among trees and underbrush bordering the river.

"There was times," the old woman muttered, "when I visht he had."

"Is it your son Heimir we're going to meet?"

"Oh, no, sir. I don't know where he's at, sir. It's the man I old you about, him I was going to marry all that time ago. Ie's got took now, sir, if you can believe it. Got took for ighting them like he did, with a white beard, if you can be-ieve it. An'—an' I hope your horse don't fright him, sir. The oise a' it, I mean."

I smiled. "He clops along no louder than other horses, I ope, and somebody with guts enough to fight the Angrborn sn't likely to be afraid of any horse. Besides, he'll see you n his back, unless the moon—"

"Oh, no! He won't, sir. He can't, sir. It's—it's what makes im think, sir, deep down, you know . . ."

The old woman sounded as if she were choking, and glanced back at her. "Makes him think what?"

"That I'm like I was back then, sir. You—you're youn yet, sir."

"I know, mother. Younger than you can guess."

"An' just to have him think like he does, deep down . . Oh, I've told him, sir. I couldn't lie about nothing like tha Only when he sees me inside a' himself—an' that's the onl way he can, sir. . . ."

"You're young again. For him."

"Yes, sir."

"Sometimes I'd like to be young again myself, mothe Young outside as well as inside. I take it he's blind?"

"Yes, sir. They blinds 'em, sir, mostly. The men I mean. Bi as they are, they're a-feared a' our men." The old woman' pride kindled new warmth in her voice. "So they blinds 'en an' they blinded him, old as he was. He sees me, sir—"

Whining, Gylf had trotted out of the night.

I dropped the reins and laid a hand on Gylf's warm, dam head. "You found someone."

Although I could scarcely see Gylf's nod, I felt it.

"Dangerous?"

A shake of the head.

"A blind man with a white beard?"

Gylf nodded again.

From the white stallion's back, the old woman said, "U there's where we meet, sir. See that big tree up against th sky? It's on top a' a little hill, only we got to go through th ford, first."

"We will," I told her.

CHAPTER 65

I'LL FREE YOU

The ford proved shallow when we reached it, its gentle, quiet water scarcely knee deep. On the other bank, I dried my feet and legs as well as I could with a rag from my saddlebag, and pulled my stockings and boots back on.

"It's deeper in the spring," the old woman explained. "It's the only place where you can cross, then. Will you help me down, sir?"

I rose. "On the War Way I saw a ford so deep we didn't dare ride across it for fear we'd be swept away." I took the old woman by the waist and lifted her down. "We had to hold each other's stirrup straps and lead our horses, while the water boiled around us."

"You couldn't have got across, sir, in spring. Only the giants."

I nodded.

"From here I'd better go ahead, sir. I'll walk fast as I can, if you'll follow me. You won't leave me, will you? I want you to see him, sir, an'—an' you an' him talk."

"I won't," I promised. "I need to speak to both of you about the road to Utgard."

"You an' your horse'll have to go pretty slow or else get to where he is afore I do."

I nodded as I watched her vanish into the night. Under my breath I said, "We'd better wait here for a minute or two, Gylf."

"Yep."

"Was there just the one old man?"

"Yep. Good man." Gylf seemed to hesitate. "Let him pet me."

"Was he strong?"

Gylf considered. "Not like you."

Some distance off, a hoarse voice called. *"Gerda? Gerda?"*

"Close now," Gylf muttered.

"Close enough for him to hear her footsteps, anyway. And for us to hear him." I picked up the lame stallion's reins.

"Hungry."

"So am I," I conceded. "Do you think they might find a little food for us? There ought to be tons in the house of one of the giants."

"Yep."

"Where is the house, anyway? Did you see it?"

"Other side of the hill."

I tossed the reins onto the stallion's neck and mounted. "There should be sheep and pigs and so forth, too. If worst comes to worst, we can steal one." I touched the stallion's sides with my spurs, and he set off at a limping trot.

"Got your bow?"

Bow and quiver were slung on the left side of my saddle; I held them up. "Why do you want to know?"

"They blind them," Gylf said, and trotted ahead.

The hill was low and not at all steep. I stopped near the top to take a good look at the black bulk of a farmhouse a good way off that seemed, in the moonlight, too big and too plain.

"Over here, sir," the old woman called. "Under the tree."

"I know." I dismounted and led the stallion over.

"Dog's here already." It was a man's hoarse voice. "Nice dog."

"Yes, he is." Wishing I had a lantern, I joined them, leaving the stallion to get whatever supper he could from the dry grass. "I'm a knight of Sheerwall Castle, father. Sir Able of the High Heart is my name."

"Able," the old man said. "I'd a brother a' that name."

I nodded. "It's a good one, I think."

"His name's Berthold, sir," Gerda said. "Bold Berthold, they called him when we was young."

In a little spot of moonlight, I could see Bold Berthold's hand grope for hers, and find it.

CHAPTER 66

WHICH AM I?

Of course I knew who he was then, and I wanted to hug him and cry; but I knew, too, that he would never believe who I was. And if he did, he would believe all over again that I was the brother he had lost. I could not have handled it, and I knew it. I made my voice as hard as I could, and I said, "I've brought Gerda safely to you, and that's what I promised her I'd do. You two have got a lot to talk about, and I've got urgent business in Utgard. How do I get there?"

"North," Bold Berthold muttered. "Follow the star. That's all I heard."

"You've never been there yourself?"

"No, sir."

"I haven't neither," Gerda said.

"You must have heard reports."

"It's a bad place, even for them, sir. I hate to see a young man like you goin' there."

Bold Berthold was groping for me. "Can I feel of you? You sound like my brother."

I touched Bold Berthold's hand.

"Bigger'n mine." His hand had clasped mine. "He ain't but a slip of a lad, my brother ain't."

Gerda said, "I recollect Able now. He was little when you was big, that's right, but he must be as old as us, or near it."

"Able was took. Gone years and years. When he come back he wasn't no older than before. 'Twasn't last year. Year 'fore that, maybe." Bold Berthold fell silent, and from the twitching of his white beard I knew his mouth was working. "Thought he'd come get me. Maybe he's tryin'. Wasn't but a slip of a boy. Only he growed."

"There's a Able here now," Gerda reminded him; Gylf wagged his tail, a faint rustling among the fallen pine needles.

"I been tryin' to get her to run with me, sir," Bold Berthold explained, "only she won't, and I won't without she does. So we don't, neither one."

I nodded, although Bold Berthold could not see it and it is doubtful that Gerda could. "That's right, she told me she didn't want to escape."

"I only said it 'cause I wasn't sure I could trust you, sir. Not then I wasn't. I'd like to, if we could an' not get caught." She spoke to Bold Berthold. "That's why I brought him. He's a knight, a real knight an' not feard a' anything. He'll help us."

"They don't care 'bout common folk," Bold Berthold mumbled.

"I'll help you if I can," I told him, "only there's no point in either of you going to Utgard with me, and I have to go there to free my servant." I sighed, wondering whether I could really pull it all off. "Also a woman called Ulfa who helped me one time. Pouk's blind now, I suppose; but I have to free him just the same. No—more than ever." I had not meant to add, "Just as I've got to free you and Gerda," but it slipped out.

"Thank you! Oh, thank you, sir!"

"After that, I have to help a certain baron take back the treasure he was bringing King Gilling. Then maybe I can find Svon and Org. Svon's my squire. Org is . . . I don't think you'd understand. But I wish he were here, and Svon, too."

At my elbow, a new voice said, "I will find them for you if you want me to, Lord."

Gerda gave a small shriek.

"Not yet," I told Uri. "I've been wondering where you two were."

"Scattering the mules, of course. The Angrborn would have them all back by this time if it were not for us."

"Are you all over black?" Gerda asked Uri. "I can't hardly see you, even. It's like I was blind myself, or as bad as."

"I am a woman of the Fire Aelf," Uri explained, and brightened until she glowed like a red-hot poker.

"Comin' to torment me?" Bold Berthold rumbled. "Well, do your worst, all of you."

"I am on my lord's business," Uri told him. "If you desire to be tormented, I will try to find someone to do it when I have more time."

Bold Berthold's right hand darted out, catching her by the neck. "There. I got her, Sir Able."

"Please let her go. She's no enemy of yours or mine."

Bold Berthold's left hand found Uri's arm, and he released his hold upon her neck. "Don't feel solid, like. They never does."

"They seem less real here than we do, just as we seem

more real in Aelfrice than we do here." Inwardly I was full of doubt, but I kept going. "Uri and Baki—Baki's another Aelfmaiden—fade and get weak under our sun."

Uri said, "Will you not make him release me, Lord? What have I done to you or to him that was less than good?"

Gerda muttered, "Let her go, Bert," and tapped his hand; but Bold Berthold did not.

"Well, you picked me up and flew away with me one time," I told Uri, "you and Baki and some more of your friends." I paused, considering. "I don't think you should have asked me that question."

"Then we will say I did not ask it."

"It's a little late for that." I rubbed my chin. "Was I more real than you and Baki in Aelfrice, Uri? Garsecg told me I was."

Gerda tittered nervously.

"These are questions for philosophers, Lord."

"You and Baki have visited me here many times. Why doesn't Garsecg come to me here, the way you do?"

"These's bad 'uns, Sir Able," Bold Berthold declared. "Don't you trust 'em!"

"I have already." I sighed again. "Often. Why doesn't Garsecg come, Uri?"

"You have asked previously, Lord. Inquire of Garsecg himself."

"I don't have to, because I know the answer. So do you. Why don't you say it?" I tried to sound like I had not just thought of it.

Uri did not speak. Her fire died, so that for a moment it seemed Bold Berthold held empty darkness.

"Okay, let's go on to another question, one you won't be able to say I've asked already. Since you Aelf can fight any time in Aelfrice, and there are thousands and thousands of you there—"

"We cannot fight like you, Lord."

"Why does Garsecg want me to fight Kulili for him? A whole host of you Aelf couldn't kill her. Yet Garsecg, who's afraid to come here and talk to me, wanted me to fight her for him. Doesn't that seem peculiar?"

"May I speak freely, Lord?"

"Sure," I said.

"These are high matters. It is not well to speak of them before persons of no distinction."

"Before Gerda and her friend, you mean."

"Yes, Lord."

"I don't agree that they're without distinction, Uri. But to spare your feelings, I'll just say one thing, then we can talk about something else. The one thing is that Garsecg did come here to Mythgarthr. He came when I was wounded, and we talked a little on the *Western Trader.* He came again when we were on the Tower of Glas. Did I promise I'd say one more thing? Only one?"

"Yes, Lord."

" 'Twasn't no promise," Gerda put in.

"If it was a promise, I'm going to break it," I told her, "because I want to tell Uri that Garsecg looked unreal in both places. He looked like thin blue glass, even when I saw him by starlight. Is that enough, Uri?"

"More than enough, Lord."

"Do you understand that I know the answers to all the questions I asked you?"

"Yes, Lord. I am your slave, Lord. Your most humble worshipper."

"You'll tell Garsecg when you return to Aelfrice. Don't you and Baki meet with him there, to report on me?"

"Lord, I have no choice!"

I shrugged. "Where's Baki?"

"Still scattering the mules, Lord." Uri sounded very, very relieved. "There remain a few the Angrborn have not yet caught. She affrights them in various ways, as I did where they were more. We also took the forms of donkeys and other things to lead the Angrborn astray."

"What will she do when the last is caught?"

"Come here, Lord, to tell us so."

"Good. Bold Berthold, is that the house of your owner to the north?"

"Must be. No others 'round here."

Gerda added, "Yes, sir. Bymir's his name, a harder master no one never found."

"Has this Bymir no cattle? I saw no barn."

Bold Berthold chuckled. "Eyes don't know ever'thing, sir knight. Cow shed and barn's on the other side of the house. House's big, but the cows ain't."

"I understand. Who milks them?"

"I do, sir."

"That's good. Gylf and I are tired and hungry. So is my horse. We're going to sleep in that barn. Don't tell your master."

"No, sir."

"We'll go now, and take Uri with us. When you get home, I want you to find some food for us. Can you do it?"

"Yes, sir. An' I will."

"Thanks. We'll leave in the morning, and we won't take anything else or do any harm while we're there."

Gerda said, "What about us, sir?"

"I have to go to Utgard for Pouk and Ulfa. I told you about that. When I've got them, we'll come back this way and take you south with us."

"You're a good man! I knew it soon as I saw the old lady with you, sir."

"Can't pay," Bold Berthold muttered. "Wish I could."

"You'll pay with the food from your master's kitchen." I had not understood Gerda and decided to ignore it. "Let go of Uri now."

Bold Berthold did, and Uri skipped from the shadow of the pine into the moonlight. "Thank you, Lord!"

"You're welcome. Go and have a look at that farm for us. Then come back and tell me about it."

The lame stallion had strayed quite a way down the hillside while we talked, but Gylf caught it without much trouble. When we were some distance from the hilltop (and about half a mile from Bymir's hulking farmhouse) he said, "Which one's really me?"

I asked what he was talking about.

"You said about Garsecg. He isn't real here."

"That wasn't quite it." I considered what I ought to say. "Do you remember the man with wings?"

"Sure!"

"You liked him."

"A lot!"

"Then maybe you noticed that the log he sat on didn't seem as real as he did. Neither did the pool, or the woods. It wasn't that they weren't real, and it wasn't that they had changed, either. Mythgarthr hadn't changed, but he was more real than Mythgarthr, or anything in it. When Uri and Baki come here from Aelfrice, they seem like they're as real as we are. But they're not, and when the sun hits them, you see it. When Garsecg came here, you could see it even at night."

Gylf trotted on in silence for a minute or two; then he asked, "Is it the way I am now? Or is it the way I am when we fight?"

"I don't know. I understand a lot more of this than I used to, but I don't understand it all. Maybe I never will."

"Do I seem realer like this? Or the other way?"

"Maybe you're real both ways. I know you want to talk about you, but I'm going to talk about Garsecg some more, because I don't understand you and I never have. But I think I'm beginning to understand him better than I did at first. You got him to heal me. Did you like him?"

"Nope. Not much. But they said he could do it."

"He said he didn't. He said the sea healed me. But later on, when I was hurt in Sheerwall, Baki did it. You weren't there then."

"Nope."

"I bit her and drank her blood. It sounds horrible when I say it like that."

"Not to me," Gylf declared.

"Well, it does to me. Only when we did it, it wasn't really horrible at all. It was nice, and I understood the Aelf better afterward. Maybe Garsecg couldn't have come up here at all if his father hadn't been human. Was it the Kelpies who told you to find Garsecg? It must have been."

"Yep."

"Maybe they bit him, when they were hurt. Did I ever tell you about the dragon? I mean, about Garsecg's turning into one?"

Gylf looked up in surprise. "Wow!"

"Yes, it jolted me, too. But when I had time to think about it more, which wasn't 'til we separated, it surprised me a lot more. We were on a really narrow staircase, and the Khimairas were diving down at us to knock us off, Uri and Baki and a bunch of others."

Gylf grunted to show he appreciated the seriousness of that situation.

"Dragons can fly. There were pictures in Sheerwall, one on one of those embroidered wall hangings they had and one on a big flagon that Duke Marder drank out of at dinner. They had wings, both of them."

"Uh-huh."

"Besides, I *know* Setr can. I've seen him do it. So if Garsecg could turn into a dragon, which he did, why not a big dragon with wings? He could have chased the Khimairas. You can't change yourself like that, can you? Besides getting a lot bigger and fiercer the way I've seen?"

"Nope." Gylf stopped, one forefoot up, to point with his nose at the enormous steeple-roofed house of rough boards we were headed for. "Maybe we should go 'round."

I thought, then shook my head.

CHAPTER 67

YOU LOSE TRACK

The interior of the barn was as black as pitch, but Gylf's nose found corn for the white stallion, and the stallion, almost as quickly, found a water trough for himself; I removed his saddlebags, saddle, and bridle. And while I was searching for a place to put them, by sheer good luck I bumped into the ladder to the hayloft. Moonlight crept in there, so that after the blind dark below it seemed bright enough to read in. I forked down half a cartload of hay for Gylf and the stallion, took off my boots, and fell asleep as soon as I lay down.

Thunder woke me up—thunder, lightning, and driving rain that came through every crack in the roof of the barn. I sat up, afraid and not knowing what had happened, and the next time the lightning flashed I was looking squarely into the ugly face of the Frost Giant I had seen years ago beside the Griffin—the giant whose face and towering stature had sent me running back to Bold Berthold's to warn him.

"Thought I wouldn't see your horse's tracks."

The giant's voice was deep and rough, and would have been terrifying if heard thus suddenly on a sunny summer day. It suffered now in comparison to the thunder. "Thought the rain'd wash 'em out, didn't you?"

I shook my head, yawned, and stretched. He wanted to talk before he fought, and that was fine with me. "I didn't know it was going to rain, and didn't care whether you saw my horse's hoofprints or not. Why should I?"

"Sneaking. Hiding."

"Not me." I rose and dusted off the hay in which I had slept, wondering all the while where Gylf was. "Traveling late is what you mean. I've got urgent business with King Gilling, and I rode 'til my horse was fit to drop. If you had been awake, I'd have begged food and accommodation from you, but your lights were out. I came in here and did what I could. Can you spare a bite of breakfast?"

The lightning flashed again, and I realized with a sort of sick relief that his head was not severed and standing on the floor before me, but thrust up the hatch in the floor.

"Knight, ain't you?"

"That's right. I'm Sir Able of the High Heart, and your hospitality has earned my gratitude."

Another lightning flash showed a hand coming at me. I drew Sword Breaker and struck at the darkness where that hand had been; the sickening crack of breaking bone was followed by a bellow of pain from the giant.

The whole barn shook when he crashed into some part of

it. For a second I could hear the thudding of his footsteps through the rattle of the rain. A distant door slammed.

He would doctor his hand, I decided, and perhaps fetch some weapon; the question was whether he had barred his door as well as slamming it.

No, I decided as I climbed down the ladder, there were really two questions. The other one was could I beat him?

Bold Berthold was outside, between the house and the barn, feeling his way through the driving rain with a stick and hugging something wrapped in rags to his chest.

"Here I am," I called, and trotted over to him, wet to the skin and nearly blown off my feet the minute I left the barn.

The stick found me, and he tried to give me his bundle. "Come lookin' for you last night, but you wasn't there. In the barn, you said, and I poked everywhere and called your name, only I never could find you."

"I was in the hayloft, asleep." I felt a sudden shame. "I should have thought about you. I'm sorry."

He took me by the arm. "You hurt my master?"

"I tried to. I think I broke a bone in his hand."

"Then you got to get away!" A flash of lightning showed Bold Berthold's contorted face and the empty sockets that had held kind brown eyes.

"Was he the one who blinded you?"

"Don't matter. He'll kill you!"

"It does matter. Was it?"

"They all do it." His voice shook with urgency. "You got to run. Now!"

"No. You've got to get me into the house. Into the kitchen would be best."

There were half a dozen knives in there, but they were of a size for the trembling women who served Bymir and not for Bymir himself, knives hardly bigger than my dagger.

"He's coming," one of the women called as I rummaged through a clattering drawer; and in desperation I snatched a spit long enough for oxen from a vast fireplace. One end was offset to make a crank, the other sharp so it could be run through the carcasses. I put that end into the glowing coals, feeling the sea of battle pounding in my veins, and waiting for the storm.

When Bymir lumbered through the doorway at last, his groin was level with my eyes; I rammed the sharp end of the spit into it.

When he bent double, into his throat.

He would have fallen on me, if I had not jumped to one side. When I got the spit out, I saw that he had bent it a little in falling. I straightened it over my knee.

"Was that him?" Bold Berthold gasped. "That what fell?"

The women (there were three, all slatternly and thin) assured him it had been.

I had taken hold of Bymir's left boot and pulled the leg straight. "He doesn't seem so big now that he's lying here."

"Lookit the blood," one of the women whispered. "Don't slip in it, sir."

"I'll try not to." I had been avoiding the seething mess anyway for the sake of my boots, although I was tempted to stamp on the ugly little creatures that swam in it. "Four and a half steps. I'm going to say a yard for each step, so he was thirteen and a half feet tall, or about that. It's good to know."

I turned to face Bold Berthold, laying my hand on his shoulder. "I have to go to Utgard, as I told you last night, but I'll come back as quick as I can. In the meantime, I want you and these women to cut up this body and get rid of it in any way that works. If other Angrborn ask . . ."

"Yes, lad. What is it?"

"The wind. The wind is in the chimney."

A wild north wind moaned there as I spoke, as though it had heard me.

"In a storm like this'n? 'Tis a big chimney, sir, an' the wind always gets in there."

"I've got to go. Gylf's gone already, it seems. After the Valfather's pack, though I didn't hear them tonight. Is my horse still in the barn?"

"'Spose so, sir. Found it there when I was lookin' for you. Your saddle's there, too."

"I'll come back as soon—as soon as I do." I snatched the rag-wrapped bundle Bold Berthold been holding, clamped it under my arm, and dashed out into the storm again.

The nearest wood, I felt sure, had been the one where Gerda and Bold Berthold had met; I recalled that it had been on the side of the house opposite the barn. Keeping the wind to my left as well as I could, I spurred the stallion until water and mud exploded from under his hooves.

Lightning showed me moss-grown trunks, and I shouted for Disiri. There was no reply, but the rain stopped.

Not slacked, but stopped altogether. No lightning flashed, no thunder boomed, and no icy drops fell from the leaves above my head even when I stirred them with my hand. The darkness remained; but it was darkness less black than green. From the slope of some far mountain, a wolf howled.

I rode on, and crossed a purling silver stream that was never the small river of Jotunland. No sun rose, and no stars shone; yet the green dark seemed to fade. Although the air around me hung motionless save where my breath disturbed it, a wind soughed among the treetops, chanting a thousand names.

Among them, both of mine.

I reined up to listen, and rose in the stirrups to be nearer the sound.

"Walewein, Wace, Vortigern, Kyot . . ."

The names that I had heard, my own, were not repeated.

"Yvain, Gottfried, Eilhart, Palamedes, Duach, Tristan, Albrecht, Caradoc . . ."

Someone was running toward me—running, stumbling, and running again. I heard the runner's gasps and sobs before the leaves parted and a teenager with staring eyes and torn clothes stumbled through to cling to my boot.

"Who are you?" I asked.

His mouth opened and closed, but only sobs came out.

"You're dirty enough, and scared almost to death, it seems like. Is somebody chasing you?"

Still sobbing, he shook his head.

"This is Aelfrice, isn't it?" I paused to look around. "It's got to be, but if that's your natural shape, you're no Aelf. Why were you running?"

Pointing to his mouth, he shook his head again.

"Hungry?"

He nodded, and it seemed to me that a glimmer of hope came into his eyes.

"I don't . . . Wait a minute."

Bold Berthold's bundle was a good-sized loaf of coarse bread and a lump of cheese. I tore the loaf in two, broke the cheese, and gave the smaller halves of each to him. It was fresh bread and good cheese.

"It's polite to talk at table," I told him when I had swallowed the first bite. "When I was little, my brother and I just dug right in, but that's not the way they eat at Duke Marder's castle. You're supposed to talk about the weather, or hunting or somebody's new horse."

Pointing to his mouth as he had before, he shook his head

"You can't talk?"

He nodded.

I dismounted. "Swallow that cheese and open your mouth. I want to have a look."

He did as he was told.

"Still got your tongue. I thought maybe somebody'd cut it out."

He shook his head.

"Lord Beel told me once that if you hit somebody's face with witch hazel, you see the true shape. Maybe that would work on you, but I don't see any around here. Is that your true shape?"

He nodded.

"Maybe you were born like this?"

He shook his head.

"You know, you look familiar." He did, too; I tried to recall the boy Modguda had sent for Pouk. "How'd you get to Aelfrice?"

He pointed to me.

"I brought you?"

He nodded, still crying.

"Just now?" Taking a bite from what remained of the cheese, I thought about that. "You followed me from Bymir's farm?"

The boy shook his head.

"But I brought you?"

Another nod.

I snapped my fingers. "Toug!"

A round dozen joyful nods.

"I was here with you—it's been years ago. It doesn't seem like it, but I guess it has been. How long have you been here?"

He shrugged.

"It seems like that's the way it always is. You lose track

here. Maybe there really isn't any time. Let's see. Queen Disiri took you?"

Looking frightened, Toug nodded.

"She said she had something to tell you, or to ask you. The two of you went off together, and you never came back."

Toug shook his head.

"You did? When?"

Toug pointed to the ground at his feet.

"Now?"

Toug nodded.

"You just left her?"

He nodded again.

"Can you take me to the place?"

Another nod.

"Then let's go!"

He pointed to the stallion, his eyes questioning.

"You're right." We can ride faster than we can walk, even through these trees."

I let him climb into the saddle and got up behind him. "Hold on to the pommel and point. Which way? I won't let him trot much."

Crying again, he pointed; I clapped my borrowed spurs to the stallion's sides.

CHAPTER 68

IN THE GROTTO OF THE GRIFFIN

Twilight found us among mountains, camped beside a rushing stream.

"This isn't Aelfrice." It was something I had said before; Toug nodded miserably, as he had the other time.

"It was in this gorge that things changed, I think. One end is in Aelfrice and the other here. For us. For today. That's how it seems to me, anyway. I've been in mountains like these before, and it wouldn't surprise me if these are the same ones, though I haven't seen the War Way. Was it near here you parted from Disiri?"

Toug rose and began to walk, pointed, then indicated by a gesture that I was to follow. With a worried glance back at the tethered stallion, I did.

By the time we reached the carved stone from which the stream issued, the light had failed. The place where water came out was a big cave, I thought at first, a cave with an overhanging, downward-curved roof, so that the long smooth expanse of stone over which the water flowed seemed almost a portico. It was not until I returned to our fire and came back with two burning sticks that I saw the eagle eyes and the pointed ears. I would have gone in then, as Toug urged by eager smiles and gestures.

"There is danger within!"

I turned, but the location and identity of the speaker were lost in darkness.

"It was my home once."

The voice was deep and slow and lisping; I felt sure it came from no human lips. I raised my burning sticks, moving them to fan the flame. Something huge clung to the cliff face, something ghostly white and assuredly not human.

"Strength will not avail against Grengarm," the great voice announced, *"until you grasp Eterne. As you will. Nor will cunning, once you have her."*

Wings sprouted from the white form on the cliff face, each wing larger than Beel's pavilion. It sprang into the air. Lightnings played about its wings; the wind those wings raised blew out my sticks and knocked Toug off his feet and nearly into the rushing water. For seconds that seemed whole minutes, that ghostly shape eclipsed the moon; then it was gone.

I helped Toug stand up and grabbed him by the shoulders. "Disiri isn't here, is she?"

He could not speak, and if he nodded or shook his head, it was too dark for me to catch it.

"Listen now," I told him, "and listen good. I told you to take me to Disiri, not here. She talked about this sword—getting it for me. I wouldn't wear a sword because of it. I didn't want a substitute. I didn't want a compromise. I wanted Eterne, the sword she'd promised me. But that's not what I want now. I want her."

Toug had begun to sob, and realizing that I had been shaking him hard, I dropped him.

"Only her." I poked Toug with the toe of my boot to make sure he had understood. "You can wait here if you want to. I'm going back to the fire."

He clung to me all the way back, and when we got there and I had thrown all the wood we had collected onto it, I said, "You're afraid of that thing that talked to us. So am I. What was it?"

He just stared.

"A griffin?"

He nodded.

"You saw it before, I suppose, when you were here with Disiri. There aren't suppose to be any, not really. Not anymore, and most people would say not ever. Sensible people never believe in things like that." Half to myself I added, "Of course there aren't supposed to be ogres, either, but Org's real enough. Probably you're afraid the griffin's going to eat you."

Toug nodded again.

"Or the dragon will, because there's a dragon in there. That's what the griffin said. Grengarm—he's a dragon, the one who has my sword. Did you see him, too?"

Toug shook his head.

"Well, you're not going to. We're going to Utgard. Your sister's there, for one thing, and you and I are going to get her out. You don't have a blanket."

He nodded, looking hopeless.

"You can use the saddle blanket, but you'd better get more wood for the fire before you even try to sleep."

While he was collecting fallen branches from the sparse growth near the water, I got my bedding out of my saddlebag and lay down. "If you decide to head back to Glennidam on your own," I said, "bon voyage and I hope you have a fun trip. But if you take anything of mine, I'll come after you. If the Mountain Men don't get you, I will. Remember that."

In dream I was a boy I had never been, running over the downs with other boys. We caught a rabbit in a snare, and I wept at his death and for some vast sorrow approaching that

I sensed but could not see. We skinned and cleaned the rabbit, and roasted it over a little fire of twigs. I choked on it, fell unconscious into the fire, and so perished. I had wanted to save the bones for my dog, but I was dead and my dog had followed the Wild Hunt, and the rabbit's steaming flesh was burning in my throat.

It was still dark when I woke, but no longer quite so dark as night should have been once the moon had set. Toug crouched weeping on the other side of the fire, a small fire now, although there were a score of charred stubs around it.

Rising, I gathered them up and tossed them into the flames. "What are you afraid of?" I asked; and when he made no gesture in reply, I sat down beside him and put my arm over his shoulders. "What's the matter?"

He pointed to his mouth.

"You can't talk. Do you know why you can't?"

Sobbing, he nodded and pointed to my side.

"Did Disiri do this to you?"

He nodded again; and after that, I sat up with him until the renewed fire had very nearly burned itself out; and since he could not talk, I talked a good deal, all about Disiri and my most recent adventures. At last I said, "You wanted me to go into the mountain where the dragon is. Was that because Disiri told you you'd be able to speak again if I did?"

He picked up a scrap of charred wood and smeared a long mark on a flat stone, with a smaller one across it.

"The sword?"

He nodded.

"You'll be able to talk again if I can get Eterne?"

Nodding vigorously, he smiled through his tears. His eyes shone.

I rose. "You stay here. You'll have to look after my horse, but you can use my blankets. Don't touch my bow or my quiver. You grew up in the forest, didn't you? Of course you did. You ought to know how to set snares. You must be hungry, and now that the bread and cheese are gone we don't have anything here." I stopped for a minute to think things over, then added, "I wouldn't try to get back to Aelfrice, if I were you."

The carved griffin's face (when I reached it and could inspect it by daylight) was even larger than I had imagined, huge, ancient, and weatherworn. That great beak might have crushed a bus, and its bulging, staring, frightful eyes were a good half bowshot up the cliff face. Something about those eyes troubled me, so that I studied them for quite a while before shrugging and seating myself on a stone to pull off my boots and stockings. Those eyes had been trying to tell me something, but I was pretty sure I would never understand it.

The Griffin raced out of the griffin's mouth, icy cold and foaming. Even though the water seldom reached my knees, I was forced to tuck my boots into my belt and cling to every little handhold I could find on the side so that I could work my way up the slope against the current. When it seemed that I had gone a long way into the mountain, I stopped and looked back. The circle of daylight that was the carved griffin's mouth seemed as distant and as precious as the America I still thought of now and then, a lost paradise that faded with each struggling step I managed.

"A knight," I told myself, "doesn't bother to count the enemy." Another step, and another. "But I wish I'd found Disiri—that I could see her once more before I go."

Ben, I cannot tell you how I knew then that I was going to lose even the memory of her. But I did.

Later, when the daylit opening seemed no bigger than a star, I said, "I wish Gylf were here."

There was light ahead. I hurried forward, fighting a stream that was deeper but less swift—and plunged into dark water, stepping into a well that I had failed to see and sinking at once under the weight of my mail. Fighting it like a maniac, I pulled it through my sword belt and over my head and sent it plunging to the bottom before I realized I was in no danger of drowning. I could not breathe under the water, but I had no need to. I swam back to the surface (it seemed very remote) and pulled myself out, spitting water and shivering.

When I got my breath, I found that the wide chamber in which I huddled was not entirely dark. Two apertures high in its wall—the griffin's eyes—admitted faint beams of daylight, and those beams focused on an altar, small and very plain, some distance from it.

Finding that I was still alive and in urgent need of exercise to warm myself, I got up and went over to look at it. The side facing me was featureless smooth stone, the top equally plain, and dampened by slow drops that fell like rain from the ceiling. The other side had been carved, however; and though the thin daylight from the griffin's eyes did not find its incised curls and flourishes, I traced them with my fingers: Kantel, Ahlaw, Llo . . . *Call and I will come.*

"I can't read," I told myself, "not the way they talk here or the way they write what they say. So how come I can read this?" And then, "These are Aelf letters!"

I stood up, half stunned. A thousand memories washed over me like the warm blue waves of that crystal sea—the laughing Kelpies who had carried me to Garsecg's cave, the drowning island, the long, swift swim that brought us to the Tower of Glas.

Call and I will come.

"Then call I do," I said. It sounded louder than I had intended it to, and echoed and reechoed through the chamber. "I call upon the griffin, or on whoever's altar this may be."

My words died away to a murmur.

And nothing happened.

I went back to the well from which the little river we called the Griffin rose. There was no sword, no griffin, and no dragon in the grotto in which I stood; but my boots were in there, somewhere down in that well, with my stockings still stuffed down in them. They were floating between the surface and the bottom, very likely. My mail was in there too—on the bottom, beyond doubt.

I took off my sword belt, wiped Sword Breaker and my dagger as well as I could, and stripped. Trying to remember the swing of the sea, I dove in.

The water was bitterly cold but as clear as crystal, so clear that I could see a little bit by the dim light from the grotto. Way down where the light had just about faded away, something dark floated past my face. I grabbed at it, and it was a boot. I relaxed and let the current carry me up.

With a triumphant roar I broke the surface. I threw my boot out of the well, pulled myself up, and sat shaking on its edge. If I had found one boot, I might be able to find the other. If I found them both, it might be possible to get back my mail.

I got up and emptied the water from the boot I had rescued. My stocking was still in it. I wrung it out and carried it and all my clothes to the driest place I could find, a point some distance behind the altar where the grotto narrowed and slanted down into the earth. After spreading my shirt and trousers there, I dove into the well once more.

This time I was not so lucky, and came back to the surface empty-handed. Pulling myself up, weary and freezing, I decided to make a thorough examination of the grotto before diving again. It would give me time to catch my breath and to warm myself somewhat.

The dark passage behind the altar descended steeply for the twenty or thirty steps I followed it, and was soon darker than the wildest night. A dozen other murky openings in the walls of the grotto led into small caves, all of them more or less damp. Grengarm, I decided, probably had a den in the roots of the mountain, down the long passage. Grengarm would not be able to see me, and that was surely good. I, on the other hand, would not be able to see Grengarm either.

Shuddering at the recollection of Setr, I dove again, swimming down until I thought my lungs would burst and at last catching hold of something that seemed likely to be a stick of sodden driftwood.

At the surface, it turned out to be my other boot. I felt like a kid at Christmas. I was so cold and weak that I was afraid for a minute that I would not be able to pull myself out of the well, but I danced on the damp stone floor of the grotto and even tried a few cartwheels before wringing out this stocking and laying it beside the first one.

Those stockings were in the entrance to the passage behind the altar, as I said; looking down it, I found it was not quite so dark as I had imagined. Thinking things over, I decided that I had remembered the utter blackness fifteen or twenty yards farther, and had transferred it to the entrance.

Your mind plays strange tricks on you—that is what I told myself. I could read Aelf writing, though I had just about forgotten I could write it. Now that I knew I could, I could see that it must have been one of the things I learned in Aelfrice before I came out in Parka's cave. The Aelf had wiped a lot of things out of my memory—who knows why? All my memories of that time had been erased. But they had not wiped out what I was supposed to say to somebody about their troubles and the injustices they had suffered. I could not remember any of the details, but they had to be there just like the shapes of the Aelf letters. "They sent you with the tale of their wrongs and their worship," Parka had told me. When they had left their message, they must have left what I had learned about their writing, too. Maybe they had to.

By the time I had thought all that, I was back at the well. I knew I would have to reach bottom this time if I wanted my mail back. I would have to give it everything I had—every last ounce. A good dive to start with, jumping as high as I could and breaking the water like an arrow to get as deep as possible.

I made a good dive and swam down until my ears ached, but there was nothing but water ahead when I had to come up.

After sight-seeing around the grotto a while to warm up and catch my breath, I picked out a nice smooth stone almost too heavy to carry and jumped into the well holding it. Down and down it carried me until the light vanished. Here there was (it seemed to me) a new quality to the water—it was still cold, and still very different from even the coldest, wettest air. But it was not suffocating anymore. It was water that had stopped trying to drown me.

I was so surprised, and so scared, that I let go of the stone, drifting up at first, then swimming upward with all my might when the tiny circle of blue light that was the top of the well showed again.

This time I shot out of the water, chilly and tired but not exactly breathless. That was Aelfrice down there, I told my-self. The water in Aelfrice knows who I am.

The pool I had dived into on the Isle of Glas had its bottom in Aelfrice, I remembered. So had the sea, or that was how it seemed when the Kelpies had dived into it with me. So had the pool into which the winged man had sunk, for that matter. There was no reason this well should not take me to Aelfrice too, although I suspected it would not take everyone there.

"But I'm not everyone, after all." This time I chose two smaller stones, nicely rounded.

Something moved in the chill, blind depths. I could not feel it, but I felt the little currents it made. And then, with the outstretched hands that held my ballast stones, I felt something new. Rough and hard. Flexible. Letting go of one stone, I grabbed it, then dropped the other.

My return to the surface hurt like the devil. Again and again I just about let go of the slimy, shapeless thing that held me back. From its weight and feel, I was sure it was the hauberk of double mail I had taken from Nytir, although there seemed to be something else caught in it—something long, awkward, stiff, and bumpy.

At the surface at last, and grasping the well's edge with one hand, I heaved the whole mess up and out onto the rough floor of the grotto, foundering in the process but bobbing up once my arm was free. About ready to drop, I climbed out of the well, carried up by a sudden surge of rising water, an uprush that seemed to have become a lot stronger since the last time I paid attention to it.

When I climbed out of that well and shook myself as dry as I could, combing water from my hair with my fingers, the ringing in my ears made me deaf to the music echoing faintly through the grotto. I shivered and gaped and spat, shaking my head.

Then I heard it.

Eerie and splotched with sour chords, sinking and rising again, foreign and familiar all at once, it snapped like a flame, then sang the way a swan sings when a hunter's arrow takes her life. It scared me half to death—but it made me homesick for someplace I could not remember.

I ran around the altar to the passage where I had left my

clothes. Lights no bigger than lightning bugs danced a long, long way down.

As quickly as I could, I dressed myself again, forcing my feet into my wet boots, although it felt as if I might break every bone in them.

The hauberk I had brought up from the bottom of the well was tangled with water-weeds and filthy with mud. I rinsed it in the cold, clear water that would become the Griffin. A sword belt of fine metal mesh was linked to it; and a gem-encrusted scabbard hung from the belt. I drew the blade halfway to look at it. It was black, but mottled with silver in a way that made me think of a knife I saw in Forcetti.

I turned it over. Was it really mottled? Or marked? Or just darkened by years underwater? Sometimes I seemed to see writing there, other times, none. The hilt might have been gold or bronze, a little green now with corrosion.

A thousand clear voices had joined the music—a chant like the chants in church. As quickly as I could, I pulled on the hauberk, finding it lighter than I remembered.

I had left my own sword belt behind. I was running to get it when the well erupted. Water swamped the floor, and spray rose to the lofty ceiling. From that eruption a snout like the bottom of a wreck emerged; and seeing it I hid in one of the smaller openings, a little cave in which I knelt behind a rock and wrapped the mesh sword belt around me, unriddling the jeweled catch a lot faster than I had any right to expect.

When I looked up again, the dragon's head was above water. Its scales seemed black in the dim light; its eyes were of a blackness to turn all ordinary black to gray, the kind of black that drinks up every spark of light.

Coil by coil it rose, and I believe it would have spread its wings if it could; but wide and lofty as the grotto was, it was not big enough for that. Half open, the wings filled it, so that it seemed for a minute or more to have been hung with curtains of thin black leather—curtains hanging from cruel, curved claws as black as ebony.

Sea-green, many-colored, and fiery were the marching, singing Aelf who poured from the passage to hail Grengarm; but black was the robe of the bound woman they laid on his altar: long and curling black hair that did not quite veil her nakedness. Under it, her skin was as white as milk.

I stared, dazzled by her beauty but by no means sure she was human.

One of the Aelf, robed and bearded, indicated her by a gesture, made some speech to Grengarm that was lost in the music and the singing, and fell to his knees, bowing his head to the rocky floor.

Grengarm's mouth gaped, and a voice like a hundred deep drums filled the whole grotto. "You come with spears. With swords." The curved fangs his open mouth showed plainly were longer than those swords, and as sharp as any spear. "What if Grengarm finds your sacrifice unworthy?"

The singers fell silent. The harps and horns and flutes no longer played. From far away came the thud of mridangas, the chiming of gold thumb cymbals, and the jingle of sistra. My heart pounded, and I knew then that I had danced once like the dancers that were coming.

These were Aelfmaidens, twenty or more, naked as the woman on the altar but crowned with floating hair, leaping and turning, dancing each to her own music, or perhaps all dancing to a music beyond music, to a rhythm of sistrum, cymbal, and mridanga too complex for me to understand. They twirled and dipped, stepped and capered as they played; and I saw Uri among them.

Folding his wings, Grengarm moved the way a big snake moves, advancing toward the altar. The dancers scattered, and I, almost unconsciously, drew the sword I had just found.

A phantom knight stood before Grengarm as soon as my blade cleared the scabbard, a knight holding his sword above his head and shouting, "Cease! Cease, worm! Or perish."

CHAPTER 69

GRENGARM

The dragon reared as a cobra rears, and wings smaller than the great wings on its back stood out upon its neck. "Who has overturned your stone, shade, that you should rise to oppose Grengarm?"

"What stone was overturned," the phantom knight replied, "that you have seeped from beneath it, shadow?"

Still on his knees, the robed and bearded Aelf called, "This is none of our doing, Lord. I see the hand of Setr in it."

"Setr's hand is stronger." Grengarm might have been amused. "Shade, wraith knight, what will you do if I burn hyssop? Or call the gods of your dead? Would not a puff of my breath disperse you?"

I knew what sword I held, as sword in hand I rose from my hiding place. "He'd call on his brother knight!"

Grengarm moved more quickly than I would have believed possible, his strike preceded by a sheet of fire the way the bray of a trumpet precedes the charge. I thrust, both hands on the hilt—and half blind with fire and smoke heard my blade rattle among his fangs—slashed and slashed, and slashed again, the dark two-edged brand slicing flesh and splitting scale and bone with every stroke.

Knights fought shoulder-to-shoulder with me who were almost real, staunch men whose eyes looked full upon the face of Hel; but behind Grengarm, and at his flanks, the Aelf fought for him with spear, shield, and slender Aelfsword, and fell bleeding and dying just as men in battle die.

Grengarm gave way, and would have dived into the well, but I and a score of knights barred his path. Like lightning he turned aside—

And vanished. Blood ran from the mouth of a piteous dwarf who scuttled toward the rushing water. I sprang after him. Fire checked me. He plunged into the Griffin and was gone.

The Aelf fought on, but the phantom knights closed about them with war cries the eldest trees were too young to have heard. From the depths of time rose the thunder of hooves.

Eterne shattered Aelfswords and split heads until the last Aelf alive fled down the dark passage; panting, I turned to the woman on the altar.

An Aelf as gray as ash sawed at her bonds with a broken sword. His head had been nearly severed, and blood dribbled from his fingers to redden her milky skin and raven hair; yet he worked away, turning this way and that to bring the cords in view.

She called, "Sheath your sword and lay these specters before they harm us. And please—I beg this—free me."

I spoke to one of the phantom knights. (He had removed his helm, and there was sorrow in his face, Ben, to tear your heart.) "Who are you?" I asked. "Should I do as this woman advises? On my honor, I won't send you away without thanking you."

They gathered around me, muttering that they had done no more than their own had required. Their voices were dry and hollow, as though a clever showman pulled a string through a gourd to make it talk.

"We are those knights," the knight I had spoken to said, "who bore Eterne unworthily."

"You would be wise," another told me, "to do what she wishes. But unwise to trust her."

From the altar, the woman called, "Cut me free and give me a drink. Have you wine?"

The phantom knights and I spoke further; I will not tell you what we said now. Then one brought a skin like a wineskin that the Aelf had dropped. He pulled the stopper and poured some into the little cup that was the other end of the stopper. That is how those things are made in Aelfrice. It was strong brandy, as its fumes told me; I had no need to taste it.

I wiped Eterne clean with the hair of a dead Aelf and returned her to her scabbard, thinking to take the wineskin—and the knights vanished. Picture a hall lit by many candles. A wind sweeps it, and at once the flame of every candle is put out. That was how it was with them.

The skin fell to the stony floor of the grotto and most of the brandy was wasted, though by snatching it up I managed to save a little. That little I carried to the woman on the altar, and when I had fetched my old sword belt and cut her free with my dagger, I poured it into the cup and gave it to her.

She thanked me and thrust her finger into it. At once it burned blue, and she downed it fire and all.

"Good lord!"

That made her smile. "Say, 'good knight.' " She stroked my cheek. "I am no lord, Sir Knight. No lady, either. Are you a subject of my brother's?"

I said I was a knight of Sheerwall.

"You are, and when we meet again you will bow to me while I smile oh, so coldly!" Her breath was heavy with brandy. "But we are not at court—what are you doing?"

I was taking off my cloak to give to her. "It's still wet," I warned her.

"I will dry it." She left the altar then, slender and swaying like a willow in a storm, and let me put it about her shoulders. I am accounted tall, but the cloak that fell to my ankles failed to cover her knees.

"We will both be wetter than that cloak, Your Highness, before we are out of this place."

She held up the empty skin. "They brought this for me." She laughed as she tossed it aside, and her laughter was lovely and inhuman. "Ah, the tenderness of my old guardians! 'Let her be stupefied, and happy, until Gren-garm's jaws close upon her.' I wish we had more arrack."

I searched for another skin, but she stopped me. "There is no more, more's the pity—it would have dried you. As for me, I will not be wet, and before I go I will confide to you, my kind knight, a great secret." She leaned toward me, and whispered, "Had he who turned that altar devoured me, he would have been as real here as in Muspel."

At the final word my cloak slumped, empty, to the stone floor, and the dead Aelf with it.

Outside, the sunlit gorge held no one save myself. I climbed out of the stream slowly, choosing every hand- and foothold, conscious only that I did not want to fall back into the water—no matter what else might happen, I did not want to fall back into the water. The thing I remember best about that time (almost the only thing I remember at all) is how tired I was.

At our camp, where we had built our fire and tied the lame white stallion Lord Beel had given me, I had rags and a flask of oil. I wanted to get them and oil the strange mail I had pulled out of the well. I remember looking at it in the sunlight and noticing that every fifth ring was gold. I wanted to oil my dagger, too, and Sword Breaker, which I had carried with me; most of all, I wanted to care for Eterne. I would have to draw her to clean and oil her blade, and the phantom knights would come. I knew that, and tried to think of some way to prevent it, but could not. I was worried about the scabbard, too. It was of gold set with precious stones; but I knew there would have been a lining of some kind, probably wood, and I was afraid it had rotted away.

Behind me, the great, deep, lisping voice of the griffin rumbled, "Would you see him? Look west."

I looked at the griffin instead. Stared, in fact. He was all white save for his beak, his claws, and his wonderful golden eyes. "Look west," he said again.

At last I did. There was a storm gathering in the west, thunderheads plucking at the sun; against the darkness of the storm, something flew that seemed darker still.

"Yes. Will you spare him?" From his roost upon the cliff, the griffin dropped into the ravine, and his weight shook the earth. "Or will you destroy him?"

"I can't," I said. "I would kill him if I could."

"I fly as swift as he, and swifter. Will you go?" The eagle face loomed over me, and the claws gripping the rocks of the gorge might have held me as a child holds a doll.

Ravd had not been among the phantom knights who had fought beside me, but it seemed to me that Ravd's phantom stood behind me as I said, "I will."

The griffin nodded, one solemn bowing of his great, grim head. I waited, wanting to rest and knowing that I was going into the fight of my life instead; and he did something that surprised me as much as anything that happened in the grotto. Turning to look down the gorge, he called, *"Toug!"*

Toug appeared so quickly that I knew he must have been watching us from some hiding place. "Here's your bow, Sir Able," Toug said, "and your arrows are in here, and here's your helmet. You left that, too."

I took them, and gave him Sword Breaker and my old sword belt. "You can speak again."

"Yes, Sir Able, because you got it. Got the sword. I've been waiting, he'd already talked to me—"

I turned again to stare at the griffin.

"Yes, him, and he said I could go if it was all right with you because he saw I wanted to so much only I couldn't answer, and then I *could,* and we knew you'd gotten it then and it was going to be all right. So can I, Sir Able? Can I go with you?"

"May I," I said, and felt Ravd's hand upon my shoulder, though not even I could see him.

We rode the griffin's neck, both of us, half buried in his white feathers to keep out the cold, me before and Toug behind. "You will be a knight if you live," I told him over the roar of the beating wings, "after this, no other life is possible for you."

"I know," Toug said. His arms were about my waist, and he clung as tightly as a limpet.

I felt the spirit of prophecy come upon me, the spirit that comes to those about to die. "You will be a knight," I repeated, knowing that in his heart Toug—a boy now verging on manhood—was a knight already. "But nothing you do as a knight will be as great as this. You begged a boon, which I granted. Now I in my turn beg a boon of you."

"Yes, Sir Able." His teeth chattered. "Anything."

"Say, 'granted, whatever it may be.' "

"Granted, whatever it may be," he repeated. "Just don't ask me to jump." He was looking down at the slate-green sea so far below.

"I want you to have this griffin painted on your shield. Will you do that?"

"You—you should have it, Sir Able."

"No. Will you not grant my boon?"

"Yes, Sir Able. I—I will."

The griffin looked back at us, then down; and following the direction of his gaze I saw Grengarm in the sea.

Like a thunderbolt, the griffin dove with outstretched claws; and Grengarm dove too, diving as the whale dives, but not before my arrow found him.

We skimmed the waves; and I, seeing them and feeling their warm salt breath upon my face, loved them as a man loves a woman.

"He must rise to breathe," the griffin told us. His words were timed to the beating of his wings, each syllable the thunderous downstroke that kept us up. "But the time may be long, and when he rises he will be far away."

We rose too, slowly and by wide circlings, and the air about us grew cool again. "If he rises by night," I said, "we won't see him."

"I will see him," the griffin promised us.

The sun was low and dim when the griffin dove again and my arrow caught Grengarm behind the head.

The third time he surfaced, at an hour when the sun was hidden behind the western isles, he did not dive but beat his vast black wings against the tossing waves and rose into the air as a pheasant rises before dogs. Long we pursued him and high we rose, and saw a million stars under us like diamonds cast on a blanket of cloud.

Between the moon and the Valfather's castle we overtook our prey. Griffin and dragon met in a battle only one could survive, at a height so great that the castle (whose shining towers rise from all six sides so that to the undiscerning it appears a spiky star) looked far larger than dark Mythgarthr. Its battlements were lined with men who watched and cheered; and every window of every tower displayed a fair face.

As Grengarm's fangs closed on the griffin's throat, I scrambled from griffin to dragon with the wind of their wings singing in my ears, the sword Eterne in my hand, and a score of phantom knights blown like brown leaves around me. And I drove that famous blade to the hilt where my arrow had shown the way, and felt Grengarm die beneath me. His thundering wings grew flaccid, and the griffin, unable to bear him up, released his grip. As we fell, I pulled Eterne from the grievous wound that she had made and washed her in the wind, scattering drops of the dragon's blood across the sky.

And I sheathed her, thinking that though I perished the sword and scabbard should remain together.

It was at that moment, when the phantoms had vanished, that Grengarm turned his terrible head toward me, craning it upon a neck a thousand times mightier than any crane's, and opened his maw wide. And I, staring into it as into the face of death, understood certain things that had been hidden.

A galloping horse dove for me as I stared, its silver-shod hooves driving it earthward more swiftly than even the griffin's wings. The maiden who rode that horse snatched at me and missed her grip; but a second rode hard behind her, and a third hard behind the second, shouting for joy as she galloped down the starry sky and lashing her steed with its reins; and this third maiden caught me up, one strong arm across my back and beneath my own right arm, and set me on the saddle before her as I myself had set Toug, when Toug could not speak. I looked back at her; and I saw that though

I might be counted a fighting man to match the best, my head was no higher than her chin.

"Alvit am I!" the maiden shouted. "Your name you need not tell! We know it!"

So low had we come that the clouds were above us, and up a lofty mountain of cloud Alvit's white steed cantered, never stumbling and never tiring. From the summit of that cloudy mountain it launched itself again on hooves that drummed a road of air.

"This is the finest thing in the world," I said, and thought that I spoke solely to myself, words to be lost in the swift wind of the white steed's passing.

But Alvit said, "It is not, but a thing outside the world. Love you a good fight, Sir Able?"

"No," I said, and looked squarely into my own soul. "I fight when honor says I must, and with everything I've got. And I win whatever way I can."

She laughed and held me tighter, and her laughter was that strange and thrilling sky-sound men hear sometimes and puzzle their heads over afterward. "That is enough for us, and you are a man after my heart. Will you defend us from the Giants of Winter and Old Night? Will you, if we lead you in battle?"

"I will defend you against anything," I told her, "and you don't have to lead me. Nobody does. I'll lead myself, and fight on, when any leader you may give me falls."

Bending over me, she kissed me as the last syllable left my lips; and it was such a kiss as I had never known, and will never feel again, a kiss that turned all my limbs to iron and lit a fire behind my ribs.

Soon after, her steed rolled over as it ran in a most peculiar way, and it could be seen that the Valfather's castle, which had seemed to be above it, was in fact beneath it; and in a moment more its silver shoes rang on the crystal cobbles of a courtyard.